THE LADY AND

Alina stood staring at the roo
The primitive cabin was not
dishes in the sink, a shirt was
faded sofa, and the floor needed a good sweep. There were no curtains at the windows, no rugs on the floors, no pictures on the walls, nothing to make the atmosphere homelike. Cordelia would laugh to see Alina's tiny new home. She sank onto her chair and stared at the fire through tear-filled eyes.

"Oh, Papa," she whispered. "I didn't plan this too well. I don't know how long I can last here." She wrapped her arms around herself. The cabin was so small! It would be difficult to avoid Beau Parker in this place, yet avoid him she must, as much as possible. He posed a danger to her.

Alina was startled by the thought. Danger? How? She straightened her shoulders and dropped her hands to her lap, then closed her eyes. She searched her heart for a warning about the cowboy. None came.

Her eyes few open and focused again on the flames as the realization struck her: the danger was in the way he looked at her, in his voice, in the warmth that surged through her at his touch. The danger was in her unwanted and growing fascination with the man. The true danger was within her. *Like the moth to the flame,* she thought bitterly. *And here I am, trapped in this tiny cabin with him.*

THE IRISH ROSE

JESSICA WULF

ZEBRA BOOKS
KENSINGTON PUBLISHING CORP.

ZEBRA Books are published by

Kensington Publishing Corp.
475 Park Avenue South
New York, NY 10016

First Printing: January, 1994

Printed in the United States of America

Acknowledgments

This book is literally my life's dream-come-true. Because it is my first book, there are many people to whom I owe a debt of gratitude, and I would like to mention them here:

Ann LaFarge, who "discovered" me and made it all happen.

Meredith Bernstein, my agent, who has taken such good care of me.

Beth Lieberman, my editor, whose help and advice made this a better novel.

My family: you always believed in me. My mother, Sharlene; my father and stepmother, Neil and Lan; my stepfather, Ron; my sisters, brothers, and beloved in-laws: Barb and Bill, Christopher and Selina, Laurie, John, Steve and Paula, Fred, Kevin, Kim and Tien, Tony, and Andy; and, of course, the kids: Matthew, Nina, Amy, David, Molly, and Emily.

Sundance and Jesse, who have always loved me just as I am.

My sister-friends: Nancy, Cynthia, Leslie, Kathleen, Diane, Judith, Kay, Judy, and Rayann. Over the years, you bore with me through my shaky beginnings when my writing career was just a dream, and you read my early drafts without complaint.

My writing buddies: Barbara K., Margaret, Denée, Lee, Pat W., Pat M., Joyce, and Carol. You kept me going when the going got tough.

Jean J.: Thank you. You knew I could do it before I did. You made a difference in my life.

Bonnie, Ray, Lillian, and Ruth, in Laramie: your kindness, hospitality, and assistance was of immeasurable value.

My special friends, both near and far, who always encouraged me and believed in me: Trisha and Patrick, Emily, Marge, Kathy, Ann, Susan, Jean S., Buff, and Rose.

Ewald (with special love), Dave, Barbara S., and Don: I wish you were here.

Dr. Vandenbusche, Dr. Bramble, and Dr. Edmondson: I'm finally using my history degree.

Professor John Cope: You were the first person to see promise in my writing, so long ago. You gave me hope.

Thanks to Maggie: your early guidance and suggestions had a valuable impact on this book and my career.

A very special thank-you to Sandie: your editorial advice, your hard work above and beyond the call of friendship, and your undying support and encouragement helped this book become a reality.

But most of all, I want to acknowledge my husband, Drew, the hero in my own life: your love and acceptance gave me the courage and freedom to find my path. It is to you that I dedicate this book, with love.

J. W.

Prologue

August, 1871

The tall man rode easily in the saddle, his eyes intent upon the ground. His bay gelding danced with impatience, eager to run again, but the man controlled the horse with absent-minded expertise. The trail he followed was several days old; from time to time he stopped to study a hoofprint or a chipped stone or a broken branch. He found a red ribbon tied around the trunk of a towering pine and angrily ripped it away; several times he found the imprint of a surveyor's tripod in the soft dirt. Someone had been exploring his land.

He came to a large outcropping of rock and pulled his restless mount to a halt. The horse stomped and tossed its head, a low nicker coming from its throat. The man leaned forward to pat the animal's damp neck.

"I know, boy. Something doesn't feel right to me, either." He spoke softly, and as he straightened, he slipped his rifle from the gun case. They skirted the rock formation; once around it, the path wound down a small hill and disappeared in a stand of rustling aspen. He paused before entering the cool shadows of the trees and twisted to study the tumbled rocks. He found nothing unusual, and reluctantly nudged the gelding forward.

At that instant, something slammed into the man's back, almost knocking him from the saddle. As the sound of a gunshot assailed his ears, a second bullet tore into him not far from the first. The reins and his rifle dropped from suddenly nerveless fingers, and he fell to the ground. The horse reared and sidled toward the trees, then returned to nuzzle the motionless man. The bay waited patiently, tail swishing, the reins hanging.

The man stirred, fighting to remain conscious. Oddly, he felt no pain, but his arms and legs were numb and heavy. It was difficult to breathe, and he tasted blood. He managed a weak smile when the gelding nudged him again. He heard footsteps and other horses ominously close by, and willed himself to reach for the rifle that lay not far from his right hand, but he could do no more than move his fingers. Rough hands grabbed his shoulders and dragged his limp body to a sitting position against a thick-trunked aspen. Then the pain came, in crashing waves, and a low groan escaped his bloody lips. He leaned his head back and forced his eyes open, blinking against dappled sunlight that seemed unnaturally bright. He noticed a cowhand a short distance away, holding the reins of two horses. The wounded man blinked again and his gaze focused on an attractive young woman dressed in a stylish riding outfit, a rifle in her hands, a cruel triumph shining in her eyes. He struggled to clear his throat.

"I'm not surprised . . . it's you," he rasped. A trickle of blood ran down his chin.

She stood at his feet and slowly shook her head in mock regret. "This violence," she said with a dainty shiver as she pointed with the rifle to the ugly exit wound on his chest, "would not have been necessary had you only cooperated."

"You would've had to kill me . . . sooner or later." He coughed, causing a fresh stream of blood to flow from his mouth. His breathing was very shallow. "I survived all four years . . . of that damned war . . ." His voice had fallen to a whisper. He coughed again as a shudder ran through his body. A wry smile twisted his lips. "And in the end I am murdered . . . by a woman . . . scorned." He paused, striving to breathe. "You have killed me . . . but in the end, it won't matter." He was so tired! His eyes fluttered as he looked up at the woman. His calm and fearless acceptance of his own death surprised him and irritated her.

"Why won't it matter?" She leaned toward him, her eyes narrow with suspicion.

"I figured out . . . what you're up to; others will, too. You can't kill them all." He coughed. "And there is . . . my family." His mind touched wistfully on his mother and his brothers.

The woman whirled away. She hadn't thought of others, or of a vengeful family. Was it possible she had acted hastily? She glanced back at the dying man with no compassion. It was strange to remember that he had once been her lover, and a good one. She had welcomed him into her body and had greatly enjoyed the times in his arms. Now she had taken life from him, with the idea that it was an easy solution to her problems. Instead, perhaps she had created more serious trouble. She stomped over to slam the rifle into its sheath and motioned to the cowboy to help her up into the sidesaddle. She looked with distaste at the still man on the ground, her lips pressed in a thin, angry line. Damn him! Even in death he bested her, upset her, threw doubt on her plans. And for that, she raged, she would never forgive him!

"Tie him in the saddle and let his horse take him home," she commanded as she jerked her nervous mount's head around with cruel force. "And cover these tracks." She lashed at her horse with a quirt, then was almost unseated when the mare bucked against the stinging leather. She swore at the confused animal, but did not hit it again. The horse took a few tentative steps, and when its mistress offered no resistance, continued on around the rock formation. The woman did not look back.

The cowboy watched the woman's departure, his features expressionless. He glanced at the wounded man, then led his horse off a short distance. He would wait; the man deserved to die in peace.

A soft breeze rustled the leaves of the aspen trees, and the diffused sunlight touched the dying man's face with gentle warmth. The bay leaned forward to nuzzle him again, and he wearily rubbed his head against the animal's soft nose. *Funny,* he reflected. *I thought I'd fight it more, but I guess it's just time to go. I'll miss ol' Bay, though. He's been a good horse.*

" 'Bye, Bay," he whispered, and closed his eyes. His labored breathing slowed, then stopped, and his lean body relaxed in final surrender.

Chapter One

Chicago, Illinois, December 4, 1871

"The nerve of that woman!"

The door bounced off the wall behind it as an indignant young woman in a black cape stormed into the office. She was followed by a thin, balding man in a greatcoat who shook the water from his hat as he closed the door. He hurried across the chilled room and placed the hat on one of a series of hooks protruding from the wall next to a cold potbellied stove. The woman jerked the hood of her damp cape back, pulling soft strands of dark hair loose, and struggled to untie the stubborn knot at her throat. Although this was her first visit to the office since it had been rebuilt following the Great Fire two months ago, she did not notice the pleasant smell of fresh lumber, nor the hundreds of leatherbound books lining one wall. She was oblivious to the tall potted palm that stood in the corner next to the new oak desk in front of her, and she was not aware that as yet, no curtains decorated the two windows.

"I cannot believe our legal system could fail me so dismally!" Alina Elizabeth Gallagher raged as she at last succeeded in freeing herself from the heavy woolen cape. She marched over and hung it on a hook while the man set a leather folder on the desk. After hanging his coat next to

Alina's cape, he turned to the stove and concentrated on building a fire.

"How *dare* she have my father declared dead?" Alina demanded of no one in particular. She paced the luxuriant Oriental rug in the center of the room. "And how could that judge go along with her? It is as if he didn't hear a word you said, Mr. Percival, and of course, my testimony was of no import, even though it is my life he so casually decided!"

Seamus Percival straightened and closed the grate on the now warm stove. He rubbed his hands together as he made his way around the desk.

"The court has declared your father missing and *presumed* dead," Percival corrected her. His tight jaw belied the calm tone of his words. "That is not the same as having him legally declared dead, but it is the first step. Neil Gallagher must be missing for seven years in order for the process to be complete."

Alina strode forward between the two wing-backed chairs that faced the desk, her eyes boring into Percival's. "It wasn't her place to begin these proceedings, any more than it is her place to be my guardian. My *guardian!*" She turned to walk the rug once more, twisting her hands. "Please tell me again what rights she has over me. I must understand this."

Percival pushed the wooden desk chair back and sank into it, reaching for the wire-rimmed spectacles in his vest pocket. He adjusted the wires around his ears and cleared his throat as he opened the leather folder.

"Judge Warren has named Cordelia Randall your legal guardian until your twenty-first birthday. She is now also the trustee of your father's domestic estate until you reach your twenty-fifth year, you marry with her approval, or your father returns, whichever is first. Until any of these occurs, I'm afraid she has almost total control of your finances, Miss Alina." He looked at her over the rim of his spectacles. "In all fairness, it is true that someone should see to your financial affairs. You are only twenty years of age and all alone."

"I will be twenty-one in May, Mr. Percival, and you and

I have done well enough with my financial affairs," Alina snapped as she turned to face him, her hands on her hips. "That woman has no concern for my welfare. Control of my father's money and the continuation of her increasingly extravagant life-style are her motivations. You must be aware that she is constantly exceeding her allowance limits. And it was a very generous allowance my father arranged for her, I might add!"

Percival nodded tiredly. He noticed how Alina resembled her long-dead mother in that moment. Her hands on her hips emphasized the narrowness of her trim waist, set off by her snug-fitting dark blue day outfit. Her raven-black hair was pulled up to the back of her head and arranged in a display of natural curls, secured with pins and a ribbon. Moisture in the air had caused the fine tendrils framing her lovely face to curl more than usual. The rosy bloom on her cheeks was also natural, perhaps encouraged, he mused, by either the cold weather or the force of her emotions. The color of her dress only highlighted the already startling blue of her eyes, ringed with lush black lashes. Those remarkable eyes now flashed with indignation and frustration.

"Her scheming is all for naught, though, as my father is *not* dead!"

"Miss Alina, there has been no sign or word of your father since the *Brianna* foundered in that typhoon in September." Percival's voice was patient, as if he were explaining a lesson to a distracted child. He watched the emotions flicker across Alina's pale features, his own face full of genuine sympathy. "Even now, the ship is making her way home, but you must face the fact that your father will not be on board when she docks."

"That does not mean he is dead," Alina said stubbornly. She walked over to the window and looked out on the nearly deserted shipyard. The blowing rain pelted the glass, running down like the tears Alina felt in her heart and struggled to control.

"My dear," the man sighed. He removed his spectacles

and rubbed his eyes. "There are ways of sending communications, even from China. The first mate had no trouble notifying us of the damage to the ship. He saw your father washed overboard, in very rough seas. Surely, if he were alive, Captain Gallagher would have found some way to let you know. You must be realistic," he finished, his voice kind.

Alina took a deep breath and whirled to look at him. "Mr. Percival." Her heavy skirts settled around her feet as she waited for him to meet her direct gaze. Her voice was eerily calm, yet filled with conviction when she continued. "I would *know* if my father were dead, just as I *knew* Sean was dead long before his wrecked boat and drowned body were found, just as my mother *knew* the moment Joseph was killed at Gettysburg."

Percival stared at her with something akin to horror as he hurriedly crossed himself. He jumped up and rushed around the desk to escort Alina to a chair. "Now, don't be saying things like that. Such knowings are of the devil himself." A memory flashed into his mind. The previous spring, while she was attending school in England, Miss Alina had supposedly sent a frantic cable to her beloved brother, Sean, warning him to be careful of his life, to beware of the lake. According to the rumors, the unread message was found on a table in the entryway, having been delivered not long after Sean had taken the ketch out for an early morning sail on Lake Michigan, an excursion that had ended in tragedy.

Alina rolled her eyes at the older man's superstitions as she sat down, but she cautioned herself to choose her words with greater care. Percival could very well be her only ally in this matter, and she could not afford to frighten or antagonize him. She waited quietly while he made his way to the side table next to the door and a minute later murmured her thanks when he handed her a crystal tumbler filled with cool water. He walked back around his desk and settled into the swivel chair. Alina meekly sipped the water, then set the glass on the edge of the desk.

"My Great-aunt Elizabeth should be named my guardian, if indeed I need one. Cordelia's long-ago marriage to my uncle does not give her familial rights over me. Uncle Bruce died almost thirty years ago, for heaven's sake!" Alina gripped the arms of the chair. "Father took her and that son of hers in after the death of her second husband, and although she has been with us for several years, she has no legitimate ties to my family. She continues to live under our roof only at my father's indulgence, and this is how she repays his kindness!"

"The judge decided against appointing your great-aunt as guardian because of her advanced years and the fact that she is in San Francisco for an undetermined length of time," Percival explained patiently.

Alina spoke through clenched teeth. "But I shall reach the age of emancipation in six months! Why did the judge bother to grant Cordelia guardianship for such a short time? And why did he name her trustee until my twenty-fifth year?"

Percival again cleared his throat. "She wanted to have guardianship of you until your twenty-fifth year as well, but the judge had no legal grounds to grant that. It is not unusual to have a guardian until the age of twenty-one, nor is it unusual to have a trustee until the age of twenty-five, or even thirty. The judge agreed to her request of that age because you are a female of tender years, with no living male relatives in evidence, and because of the size of your eventual inheritance." He reached for his spectacles. "Did you not hear the judge's statement?"

Alina rubbed the side of her neck. "I heard some of it, but I just could not believe he was deciding in her favor." She leaned back in the chair.

"Perhaps when your great-aunt returns, something can be done. In fact, if I know Elizabeth Hammond at all, something definitely *will* be done. Her feelings toward Mrs. Randall are no secret." Percival smiled, but no hint of humor touched his eyes. "Things would have turned out differently if Mrs. Hammond had been there today. Have you any idea whether her cousin is recovering?"

Alina shook her head. "I received a letter from her just last week. The doctors say there is not much hope, that it is only a matter of time. There is no way to know when Elizabeth will be home, and I can't ask her to leave her dying cousin in order to help me with this situation." She leaned forward. "What can we do, Mr. Percival? Help me fight this!"

"The court has ruled, and for now, there is nothing we can do." His elbows rested on the desk as he dangled his spectacles from his fingers. "I am your father's solicitor and business manager, but I have no power in the area of his personal affairs, and that includes you. Fortunately, your father was very clear in the contract he and I signed. I have unlimited authority in any matters pertaining to the Gallagher Trade and Shipping Company. She did not succeed in wresting that from you, or me." He looked at her pleadingly. "You must try to understand the difficulty of my position. I have an obligation to your father to take care of his company, and I will do everything in my power to do so. In addition, I have a large family to support, as you well know. Believe me, Miss Alina, I don't care for Mrs. Randall any more than you do, but she is conniving and ruthless when it comes to getting what she wants. For the sake of your father's company, and that of my family, I dare not antagonize her. I am sorry, lass, truly I am." He leaned back in the chair.

Alina stood and turned away in disappointment, her mind racing as she again paced the rug. For several minutes the only sounds in the room were the ticking of the mantel clock that rested on a bookshelf and the wind blowing against the windows.

"Perhaps I can petition the court on my own behalf, prove to the judge that you and I are handling my affairs quite successfully," Alina suggested, worrying her bottom lip with the knuckle of her right thumb.

"As she is now your guardian, Mrs. Randall could probably stop any such action on your part before you got to court, at least until May. Besides, you must remember that Judge Warren is a . . . special . . . friend to Mrs. Randall."

Alina turned to look at him in amazement. "What do you mean, 'a special friend'?"

"Please, Miss Alina, don't ask me to elaborate. 'Tis not a fitting subject to be discussing with respectable young ladies." Percival's face was a dull red as he fumbled with some papers with one hand and struggled to don his spectacles with the other. He adjusted the lenses and watched Alina move closer to the desk.

"How do you know this, Mr. Percival?"

"The justice system in this city is made up of a small and tightly knit group; we know a great deal about each other. I asked that the case be assigned to a different judge when I first received the papers, but Judge Warren refused to excuse himself."

Alina fell into her chair. "Well, that explains many things. Cordelia was *sure* the judge would decide in her favor. We never had a chance for a fair decision, did we?"

Percival shook his head. "I'm afraid not, lass."

For the first time, Alina acknowledged the seed of genuine fear growing in the pit of her stomach. The room was silent until Percival coughed.

"This is none of my business, Miss Alina, but I must ask you about something I heard today, something that disturbs me a great deal." He shifted uncomfortably in his chair, but his gaze remained steady.

Alina raised her eyebrows in curiosity. "By all means, Mr. Percival, please ask me anything you wish."

The solicitor took a deep breath. "What exactly are your feelings toward young Mr. Randall?"

"That obnoxious cad? He introduces himself as my cousin, although he was born of Cordelia's second marriage. Since his expulsion from Harvard, he has become quite insufferable. He is growing more conceited and overbearing with each passing day. I have no doubt he helped Cordelia hatch this scheme!" Alina stopped for a moment, aware that her voice had risen. "Why do you ask?"

Worry was etched into Percival's face. "If that is how you feel about him, why are you going to marry him?"

Alina sat upright. "Marry Donovan? I cannot *abide* the man! Where did you ever get such an idea?"

"After you left the courtroom, Mrs. Randall and her son approached the bench. They spoke in low tones, but I heard most of what they said. The judge distinctly congratulated Donovan on his engagement."

"Well, he's not betrothed to me!"

"But they were talking about you. The judge even commented that Donovan would have his hands full, that you did not seem the type to submit meekly to a husband. Donovan assured him that he could handle you, and Mrs. Randall asked the judge to keep the secret, as announcement of the betrothal would not be made until the holiday party in two weeks."

Alina's face drained of all color. She felt the trap closing on her spirit, on her very life. "My God," she breathed. "Donovan has been annoyingly persistent in his flirtations of late, but I never took him seriously. Oh, Mr. Percival, I've badly underestimated Cordelia!" She rose from the chair, twisting her hands. "Does she honestly think she can force me to marry him?" Anger grew in her, chasing away the fear.

"Perhaps they thought to catch you off guard. If they make the announcement unexpectedly, to a large group of your father's friends—indeed, some of the most influential and powerful people in Chicago—maybe they hope you will go along with it, to avoid a scandal," Percival mused, watching her over the rim of his spectacles.

"Then they don't know me very well, do they?" Her eyes flashed fire. "I won't hesitate to make a scene. The people coming to the holiday gathering are *my* family friends, like yourself. *She* is the intruder here!"

"Miss Alina, I must caution you . . . Mrs. Randall has

been accepted by society, mostly by her own endeavors, but your father's influence, and the fact that he took her into his home when her husband died, helped establish her. I'm certain that more than one self-righteous dowager will applaud Cordelia's guardianship of you. It is unusual for a young woman to enjoy as much freedom as you have since you returned home, with no guardian and no chaperon; in their eyes, it is probably less than respectable. You must be very careful, my dear."

Alina sank back into the chair, the fear returning. "I walked right into the snare, didn't I? She must have been planning this for months. When Elizabeth left for the West Coast, she made her move." A puzzled frown wrinkled her forehead. "She arranged the trusteeship and the betrothal at the same time. Why both?"

Percival made a tent of his fingers as he contemplated her question. "Her tenure as trustee will end with the return of your father, an event Mrs. Randall does not anticipate, for she is certain he is dead. It will end upon your twenty-fifth birthday, which gives her four years to make her arrangements. And it will end upon your marriage to an approved mate."

"What if I marry without her approval?"

The solicitor's eyes narrowed in concentration. "Legally, she cannot stop you from marrying, but she certainly can, and, I have no doubt, would, cut you off financially until you turn twenty-five." He looked at her with interest. "Did you have someone in mind?"

Alina sighed. "No."

Percival thought for a moment. "You may have something there, lass. Perhaps she intends to discourage other suitors by announcing this betrothal. I would not be surprised if she insists on a long engagement, however, for if you marry her son, the control of your father's estate transfers to him. My guess is that she will keep you under her hand as long as she can, then marry you to Donovan. That way, she can at least keep the money in her family."

Alina slowly nodded. "I agree, Mr. Percival, with all you have said. I haven't seen what has been going on around me since I returned from England. It is so hard, with Sean dead, and Papa lost, and Elizabeth gone. I've been lonely, feeling like a stranger in my own home because of those two. And now this." After a moment of silence her eyes met his, her gaze piercing and determined. "I cannot stay, you know. I'll not allow them to succeed. The trustee business alone I would have found a way to deal with, but not Donovan. I sense an underlying violence in him, and I fear he will become unbearable."

Percival nodded. "I'd not want him near one of my daughters, and I feel the same way about you, lass. There's something about him that bothers me, too." He sighed, a helpless look on his face. "But where will you go? She'll know to look for you in San Francisco."

Alina jumped up and wandered restlessly over to the window. "I have two dear friends from childhood. Jenny lives in Philadelphia, and Susannah in Charleston. Either would help me, but Cordelia knows of them, as well." She turned with a sad smile. "I wish we had news of my cousin Conor. I would go to him if we knew where he was."

Percival's face lit up. "In all the excitement of this hearing, I forgot to tell you . . . Late yesterday I received an answer to one of my inquiries." He thumbed through a stack of documents on the corner of his desk.

Alina felt a rush of hope as she hurried to the desk. "You have found him?"

"Unfortunately, no, but someone in Lynchburg remembers him." Percival perused the sheet of paper he held. He began to read. " 'If the man you seek is approximately twenty-eight years of age, son of the late Gerald O'Rourke, and veteran of the glorious Army of the Confederacy, I may have an indication of his direction.' " Percival looked up over the rim of his spectacles. At Alina's excited nod, he continued. " 'It is believed that young Mr. O'Rourke left for the wilds of Texas several months ago. He had mentioned

Austin.'" Percival pulled a clean sheet of paper from a drawer and took the lid from the inkwell. "I will send a wire to the law officials in Austin today."

Alina turned back to pace the rug. "Texas. Why would he go to Texas? We've no kin there that I know of." She sighed. "Conor just hasn't been the same since the war, Mr. Percival. My mother's sister died within a few weeks of her husband some years back, and he was their only child. He refused my father's invitation to come and live with us. Long ago Papa told me he'd heard rumors about Conor, that he was building a reputation with a gun, and that he didn't stay in one place much anymore. But Texas?" Alina returned to the window. "We surely can't find him in the next two weeks."

"Perhaps not, but don't lose hope." Percival's pen scratched across the paper. "You must go away, someplace where you can hide until we locate Conor. I will get you the necessary funds." He squinted up at her. "Actually, we have a little more than two weeks to plan, Miss Alina. The holiday celebration is planned for Friday, the twenty-second."

Alina could not resist the man's excitement. "You are right again, Mr. Percival. For all we know, Conor settled in Austin." Her eyes regained their customary sparkle. "We shall meet again in a few days and decide the best course of action."

The solicitor nodded his agreement, then stood. "Now you must be on your way, young lady. We don't want to arouse suspicions." He pulled Alina's cloak from the hook and settled the soft wool around her shoulders.

"I will wire Elizabeth at once." Alina tied the strings of the cape at her throat. "I cannot thank you enough for all you have done," she said sincerely. She laid a hand on his arm and placed a soft kiss on his cheek. Percival patted her hand.

"There, now, Miss, 'tis no more than your father would do for one of my dear daughters, were they in such trouble, and well you know it. You just watch yourself, and that impulsive temper of yours," he admonished. "I've known you since you were a little thing, always pestering your brothers, and I've seen your anger get you in plenty of hot water. You must be very careful, my dear, and wise. Control your anger and allow it to empower you. And neither of us will underestimate Mrs. Randall again." He winked at her, a fatherly gesture that touched her heart.

Alina smiled as she pulled the hood over her head. "I will heed your words," she promised. She stepped toward the door, then paused and looked around the room. "For heaven's sake, Mr. Percival. I didn't even notice the office." She waved at the rows of books. "I am so thankful you were able to save your library that terrible night." She turned in a full circle. "It is very nice."

Percival accompanied her down the stairs and handed her up into her waiting coach. Alina's groom moved from his dry spot on the porch to clamber up onto his seat, pulling his hat more tightly around his ears.

The solicitor squinted up at the dark clouds. "My guess is this will turn to snow before the light is gone," he predicted.

Alina leaned forward on the seat and held out her hand. "Thank you, Mr. Percival," she said softly, affection and gratitude shining in her eyes. "I would have been lost without you this day."

Percival nodded, taking her offered hand in both of his. "As I explained earlier, I must be careful myself, but I will do what I can, lass. All will be well," he said in a reassuring tone. He patted her hand, then stepped back.

"Malone, I should like to visit the point on the North Shore before we return home, if you please," Alina called to the groom.

Malone was not pleased, but he curtly acknowledged Alina's request and took the reins in hand. She settled back against the cushions as Percival closed the carriage door and raised his hand in a sign of farewell. He stared after the departing coach, his heart heavy, then with a sigh, turned to the door and let himself in out of the weather.

* * *

The ash-colored waters of Lake Michigan boiled and rolled as the worsening storm sent whitecaps dancing across the tops of the waves. The rain had stopped, but the powerful wind buffeted the slender woman who stood alone on the rocky point. Alina's black cape billowed out behind her, like a dark sail on one of the many ships that were hurriedly tacking their way to the safety of the docks. The gusts tore at her head with devious fingers until the pins and the ribbon that held her raven tresses were blown away, leaving her long, heavy curls to whip and fly around her face. Her blue eyes were turned to the angry heavens; the tortured clouds reflected the anguish in her heart.

"Oh, Papa!" Alina cried. "I need you!"

She held her hands out as if in supplication and closed her eyes. She concentrated on her breathing, which was now calm and deep. In her mind's eye, she flew over the waters of the huge lake, over the land, across the far seas, searching.

"Where are you, Papa?" she whispered, her brow wrinkled with the tremendous effort she was making. She stood steadfast against the storm, and waited. At last, her patience was rewarded. A softly colored picture filled her mind, of a bearded man lying on a pallet. She saw him toss his head and grimace as if in pain, while a pair of small hands moved to put a bowl to his lips. Then the scene faded. It had lasted only a moment, but it was long enough. Alina dropped her arms; her head and shoulders slumped with fatigue. *Thank God. He lives.* Peace filled her heart; she knew her message was true, although she could not share it with anyone, or prove it, for that matter.

The rain began again; freezing drops pelted her. She turned from the turbulent waters, pulling her wayward cloak around her chilled body, struggling to push her wild hair under the hood. She made her way across the rain-slick rocks to the carriage that waited on the road, ignoring Malone's impatient look. The surly groom helped her into the coach.

"Would my lady care to return home now?" he asked with heavy sarcasm. At her tired nod, he closed the door, shaking his head in frustration. "The stupid chit," he muttered as he pulled himself onto his high and now very wet seat. He was soaked to the skin and hungry besides, and he had no patience with his eccentric young mistress on such a dreadful day. Why, 'twas a day for the devil himself, with this terrible storm upon them! Lordy, but the girl was so strange! Malone crossed himself, then took up the reins and clucked at the pair of horses that ducked their heads against the continual onslaught of wind and rain.

"Let's get on home, there, lads!" he cried, and turned the coach sharply. He was mindless of the rough road and how it threw his passenger about the interior of the vehicle, mindless of everything save getting his beloved horses to the warmth of their stalls and getting himself a well-deserved whiskey.

Alina let herself in the ornate side door, where Malone had stopped the drenched team under the portico long enough to hand her down from the carriage. A chill raced through her exhausted body. A hot bath and a cup of tea would be most welcome while she tried to think of a workable plan. She made her way toward the gracefully curved staircase, untying her cape with numb fingers, unaware of the damp trail her skirts left on the polished floor of the grand entry hall.

As she passed the open door of her father's study, her weary gaze fell upon Chambers, the family's longtime butler. The old gentleman was in his shirtsleeves, his bushy white hair in disarray, his full mustache unable to hide the grim set of his lips. He carefully wrapped a small figurine of an elephant carved from ivory in a soft cloth, then bent and placed it in a large trunk that lay open on the floor in front of the massive oak desk. Alina slipped the wet cloak from her shoulders and draped it over her arm as she entered the study. Loneliness for her father filled her and she closed her eyes against the pain. Whenever she was overwhelmed by a need to be with him, she would retreat to this room, his room, and sit in one of the two tufted leather chairs that faced the fireplace. She would imagine her father in the other chair, as he had been in happier times, reading to her, playing chess with her, or just talking to her. She became aware that Chambers was muttering under his breath and opened her eyes. The butler took an intricate porcelain dove gently into his gnarled hands, and with reverence, wrapped it, then turned to the trunk. His thick eyebrows raised when he saw her.

"Good afternoon, Miss," he said gruffly as he placed the protected dove next to the elephant with great care.

"Chambers, whatever are you doing?" Bewilderment covered Alina's face as she came further into the room and realized that many of the furnishings were gone.

"Following *her* instructions," Chambers answered, his old voice trembling with rage. "She threatened me with dismissal, she did, informed me that *she* was running things around here now, she and that whiny little housekeeper, Mrs. Barnett. As you were not here, Miss Alina, I felt I had no choice except to obey her, but I would be delighted to put this room to rights, if you'll just say the word."

"What can she be plotting?" Alina wondered; her troubled gaze inspected the room. The sense of dread that had nagged her since the meeting with Percival grew stronger.

"Ah, there you are." Cordelia Randall's polished voice came from the open door. Alina turned to the older woman and recognized a triumphant gleam in those glittering dark eyes. An intense rage jumped to life in Alina's heart and she took a deep, calming breath. *Don't act so victorious yet, Cordelia Randall.* With a defiant shake of her head, Alina tossed her wet hair back over her shoulders as she took in the other woman's stylish dress and confident demeanor. Strands of gray showed in Cordelia's perfectly coiffed brown hair, and the beauty of her youth had dimmed, but, in spite of the coldness of her heart, she was still an attractive woman. *You may have the upper hand now, but I am the daughter of Neil Gallagher, and you will soon know that his blood does indeed run in my veins. The battle lines have been drawn.* Alina straightened her shoulders and composed her features, all sense of fatigue gone.

To the silent Chambers, Alina matched Cordelia's regal presence with ease, although the younger woman was almost bedraggled. She stood straight and tall, her slim body held with a dignity her sodden dress could not hide. Her damp hair hung in long curls down her back. Soft tendrils framed her calm face, a face that was deathly pale with the exception of two bright red spots on her cheeks. With no hint of fear in her clear blue eyes, she stared at Mrs. Randall, and Chambers was filled with pride for his young mistress.

"It would appear that you have designs on my father's house." Alina waved one hand to indicate the half-empty room.

Cordelia moved into the study and looked around thoughtfully. "Yes, I have a need for it, and for now, your father doesn't. Perhaps he never will again." Her cold eyes settled once more on Alina's pale features. "I'm sure he wouldn't mind."

A small choking sound came from Chambers as he struggled to control his tongue, his lined face red with outrage. Alina sent a warning glance in the direction of the old butler.

"Your plan went very well, Cordelia." Alina's tone was cool.

"I hope that simpering little fool of a solicitor filled you in on all the details of the court order. If not, I would be happy to answer any questions you may have." Cordelia walked around the room, envisioning the changes she would make. "These curtains are wretched," she said, fingering the tasteful, heavy golden velvet. "They simply must go."

"Yes, Mr. Percival explained the terms of your guardianship, as well as those making you trustee," Alina said heatedly. "And he is not a simpering fool. He honors his word and is loyal to his friends, concepts with which I am certain you are not familiar."

Cordelia turned once more to Alina; a condescending smile played about her thin lips. "Your ill-considered defense of those weaker than yourself will be your undoing one day, my dear. Your righteous anger clouds your judgment." The empty smile fled her face and her voice became harsh. "Percival's loyalties lie with the wrong camp. It's only a matter of time; he will be replaced with someone more sympathetic to my cause."

Alina dropped her eyes and fought to keep a rein on her temper. *Patience,* she counseled herself.

Cordelia eyed Alina's disheveled state with distaste. "I see you have been to the North Shore again, and in this weather. Really, Alina, you look like a common ragamuffin. You'll not be allowed to join Donovan and me for the afternoon meal." She turned toward the door and spoke over her shoulder. "You have been given too much freedom in the past; as your guardian, it is now my responsibility to see that you behave in a decorous manner at all times. That will preclude your visits to the shore. Watching for your father will not bring him home." The expensive silk of her dress rustled with a soft sighing sound as she sailed imperiously across the entry hall.

Alina clenched her fists in humiliation and rage at the rude dismissal, then turned to face the shocked old butler. She was touched by the mixture of astonishment and fear on his weathered features, and she placed a gentle hand on his arm.

"It is true, Chambers. She is my guardian, for a few short months, and unfortunately, trustee of my father's domestic affairs for much longer."

"Miss, how could such a travesty occur? I don't understand."

"I do not understand all of it myself, but she laid a very clever trap. And she is not finished with her wiles."

"What do you mean?" His concern was comforting, as was the hand he placed over her cold fingers.

"Do not worry yourself." Alina smiled up into Chambers' kindly eyes. "She will not defeat me. I am my father's daughter."

"You are that," he agreed.

Alina surveyed the room with sadness. "We must go along with her for now, although God knows it sickens me. Do as she tells you and protect yourself from her wrath. Tell your dear wife the same. For the next few days, at least, you both must trust me and do as I ask, as difficult as it may be at times."

"As you wish, Miss," Chambers answered with resignation.

Alina gave him an encouraging smile. How she looked like her dear, departed mother in that moment, the old man thought. He recognized in her the fire and spirit of Brianna Gallagher, as well as the strength and determination of Neil Gallagher, and for the first time since this long, discouraging day had begun, he felt a sense of relief. Cordelia Randall had underestimated the young miss.

"Please have a bath prepared for me, and send up a light meal with a pot of strong tea." Alina's eyes again traveled around the study. "I swear that someday we *will* put this room to rights," she said fiercely. She headed for the door. "Do as she says, Chambers. Pack everything and make arrangements to send it to Aunt Elizabeth's house for storage. At least there, Papa's things will be out of her reach."

She stopped at the trunk, handed Chambers her soggy cape, and reached for the wrapped dove. Her mother had given the piece to her father on a long-ago anniversary, and had told him that it symbolized the beauty of the love she felt for him. Brianna's gift seemed out of place in the masculine study, but Neil had always treasured it.

"I will take care of this," she said, her eyes misty. Chambers nodded. "And the chess set." She looked up to see the set still in its proper place on the small table next to her father's chair. "I must have that, also."

"Of course, Miss. I will wrap it for you."

"Please see to my cloak, Chambers, and try not to worry."

Chambers followed Alina to the door and watched as she climbed the stairs. When she reached the top and disappeared, Chambers sighed and headed toward the kitchen. He felt old beyond his years, and helpless. That was the worst, he decided. The young miss needed protection and he could not provide it. He dreaded telling the distressing news to his fiery little wife. Effie would want to take a butcher knife to that Randall witch, and, God forgive him, he would want to help her. He sighed again. Miss Alina was right, though. It was best to bide their time. He and Effie would not let their mistress down.

Alina clutched the dove to her breast as she moved down the hall toward her room. The determined confidence she had shown to Chambers dissipated as soon as she was out of his sight. There were others to think of besides herself, she realized. No matter what she decided to do, she could not leave Chambers and Effie to deal with Cordelia alone, and there were probably other servants needing her protection as well. She sighed and rubbed her aching head with one cold hand. The situation was worsening by the minute.

She became aware of sounds ahead of her and looked up to see two figures at a distance. In the gloomy light of the long hall it was impossible to see who they were until she was upon them. She saw that Donovan had backed a young housemaid against the wall. He held her chin in a cruel grip with one large hand as he savagely kissed her, while his other hand fondled her breast. The whimpering girl struggled to escape.

Rage again replaced fatigue when Alina saw Maggie's pleading, tear-filled eyes. "Let her go, Donovan!" Alina snapped. Donovan released the girl and nonchalantly straightened his cravat. There was no trace of embarrassment or shame on his flushed face. Maggie sagged against the wall and pulled her bodice together as silent tears coursed down her cheeks.

"Maggie, take this to my room and wait for me there." Alina's voice was firm but kind as she put the wrapped dove into Maggie's trembling hands. With a reassuring nod, she pointed the girl down the hall, then turned to face Donovan.

He was of average height and stocky build. Thanks to the generous allowance her father had provided for Cordelia, he was dressed in the height of fashion. Although some would think the twenty-five-year-old man handsome, Alina found nothing about him attractive.

"How dare you?" she demanded, her voice shaking with anger. "You are a guest in this house!"

"Don't tell me you're jealous, dear Alina." He ran one hand through his thick, sandy hair as he leered at her. "And who, indeed, is the guest now that my beloved Mama is in charge?"

"Her guardianship of me does not give you license to force yourself on my servants! Nor will I tolerate such behavior!"

Donovan advanced on her, his brown eyes narrowed. "*You* will not tolerate my behavior?"

Alina backed against the wall. Never had Donovan treated her with such rudeness. She feared his new attitude was more in keeping with his true character. He was very close; she could feel his hot breath on her face.

"I will not tolerate it," she repeated, meeting his furious gaze unflinchingly.

Donovan placed his hands flat on the wall above her shoulders. "You will have nothing to say about my behavior, Miss Gallagher. Things are going to change, and you'll not act so superior, not to me. The day is coming when you will do exactly as I say, when I say." He moved one hand to the cool skin of her cheek, then with his forefinger slowly traced a line down the side of her throat to her damp bodice. His finger stopped on the beginning swell of her breast. "And that will include," he continued in a lewd whisper, "lifting your skirts and spreading your legs anytime I wish to take my pleasure of you, even if it is just before the afternoon mea

The hot fury that roared through her at his words overcame any sense of shock she felt. "I think *not,* Mr. Randall!" Alina knocked his hand from her breast and pushed him away. "Gloat while you may, you and your 'beloved Mama,' but I swear, you both will live to regret this day."

Donovan lifted a drying strand of hair from her shoulder. "Are you still looking for your father to come home and rescue you?" he asked with a derisive laugh.

Again, Alina slapped his hand away. "He *lives,* Donovan, and in time you will know it." Her blue eyes flashed fire in the dim hallway, and it was Donovan who uneasily stepped back.

"There you are, Mr. Donovan." Chambers walked toward them, carrying a china teapot and cup on a tray. "Mrs. Randall awaits you in the dining room."

Donovan glanced over his shoulder, then turned to go.

"Donovan." Alina's quiet voice stopped him. "Do not *ever* presume to touch me again."

He clenched his fists in impotent frustration, then elbowed past Chambers, nearly upsetting the tray. He stomped down the stairs.

Chambers glared after Donovan. "Is anything wrong, Miss Alina?"

Alina pushed away from the wall. "No, nothing I cannot handle. Donovan is just acting his usual boorish self."

They walked the remaining distance to Alina's room in silence. At the door, Alina reached for the tray. "I will take this. Please bring another cup when you return with my meal."

Chambers raised his eyebrows, but said nothing. He retraced his steps as Alina let herself into the room. She set the tray on a small tea table near the fireplace. Maggie was crumpled in a miserable heap on the hearth rug, her thin shoulders shaking with sobs.

"There, there," Alina murmured as she dropped to the

herself and put a comforting arm around the girl. "It's over now. He's gone."

Maggie raised despairing eyes to Alina. "He'll find me again," she whispered. "He's been after me for weeks. He ordered me to bring his brandy to his room last night, and if Mrs. Barnett hadn't passed in the hall, he'd have taken me then. He's sworn to have me, Miss Alina." Her voice had risen to a cry. "I'm a good girl, Miss, truly I am! I've not led him on. I stay as far from him as I can. I hate him, God forgive me!" She buried her face in her hands as fresh sobs overcame her.

Alina's jaw tightened. She silently berated herself for not noticing the situation earlier, then made soothing noises and helped the girl to her feet. "Listen to me, Maggie." Alina raised the maid's chin with one hand, careful to avoid the bruises Donovan had left on tender skin. "If he tries to touch you again, you scream, you fight, you do whatever it takes to get away from him. You will not have to tolerate such treatment in my house. I will set him straight on that. Do you understand?"

Maggie nodded; hope flickered in her tear-filled eyes.

"Why did you not tell me earlier?" Alina asked gently.

Maggie stared at the floor and twisted her hands. "I need to work, Miss. I was afraid I'd be turned out."

Alina guided the girl to an overstuffed chair that faced the fire. "Not while I am here, you won't be," she promised. She turned to the table and poured hot, fragrant tea into a delicate china cup. "Drink this," she instructed, as she placed the cup in Maggie's trembling hands. "You'll feel better."

Maggie obediently took the cup, then started when she realized that her mistress was waiting on her. "Oh, no, Miss, it's not proper!" she cried, and began to rise.

"Stay." Alina pulled a Chippendale chair from her writing desk and set it next to Maggie's chair. "For now, we are not mistress and maid. We are two women sharing a pot of tea."

"But you've no cup," Maggie protested.

"I do now," Alina said, as she answered the knock at the door. She took the luncheon tray from Chambers and closed the door, then set the tray on the writing desk. After filling her cup, she returned to the Chippendale chair. A shiver ran through her as she sipped the hot beverage. She needed to get out of her damp clothes, but she sensed that something else was troubling Maggie. The girl did not drink, nor take her eyes from the fire.

After a few minutes, Alina spoke. "Do you not care for tea?"

Maggie jumped guiltily at the quiet question. "Oh, no, Miss. I mean, I like it well. This just feels strange."

Alina nodded in understanding. Maggie took a hesitant sip of the brew, then closed her eyes in misery.

"I cannot keep still, Miss. I must speak."

Alina set her cup on the tea table and folded her hands in her lap. "Please do, Maggie."

"Perhaps you care for Mr. Donovan, Miss, but don't marry him," the girl pleaded. "He has ill intentions towards you!" Her cup shook in her hand, threatening to spill its contents.

Alina's eyes widened. "How do you know of that?"

Maggie set her cup next to Alina's and came out of her chair to kneel at Alina's feet. She grasped her mistress's cold hands. "I know I'm speaking out of place, Miss, and you may turn me out after I've had my say, but you must know what he said of you."

"I will not turn you out, Maggie. I gave my word. Now, tell me what troubles you."

"It was early this morning, Miss, before they left for the court. I was clearing the morning table. They were in the sunroom. Mr. Donovan and Mrs. Randall, I mean. They were talking of the betrothal. Of course, it was the first I knew of it. I could not believe it, Miss!" Maggie's hold on Alina's hands tightened.

"Go on," Alina encouraged her.

"He said things about you, Miss, how he would do terrible things to you if you did not agree."

"What terrible things, Maggie?"

Maggie buried her face in Alina's lap. "Please don't make me say!"

Alina drew Maggie's face into her hands and looked into her teary eyes. "Maggie, you *must* tell me. It is of the utmost importance. I must be able to protect myself."

"He said he would force you, Miss, by whatever means necessary. He said he would m-make you w-with child if he had to! Please do not wed him! He is evil!"

Alina's hands fell to her lap as her thoughts raced in horrified circles. Maggie sat back on her heels and dropped her eyes, but after a moment raised her scared young face to Alina.

"What will you do, Miss?"

"I do not know yet, but you have done me a great service." She took the girl's hands and squeezed them in gratitude. "Now, we have work to do, my girl." Alina stood and helped Maggie up. "Get Chambers for me this instant, but discreetly." She tucked strands of soft brown hair back under Maggie's white cap. "Do not alert them. Tell him something is amiss with my meal. Now, go!" She shooed Maggie to the door. "And wipe your eyes!"

Maggie brushed her hand across her face. "Yes, Miss!" she answered with a brave smile, then was gone.

Alina dragged her chair back to its proper place at the writing desk and impatiently moved the luncheon tray to the four-poster bed. She no longer felt hungry or cold. She yanked a sheet of her personal letterhead from its slot, then unscrewed the lid from the inkwell. Taking the pen, she wrote:

My dear Mr. Percival,

The situation is far more desperate than we have imagined. I have reason to fear for my physical safety and must be away immediately. Please have funds available by morning. I must remain hidden until I reach my majority or Conor can be located. I will communicate when I can safely do so. Watch your back, dear friend. They mean you harm.

A. E. G.

Chapter Two

Laramie City, Wyoming Territory, December 31, 1871

A cheery fire crackled and popped on the hearth of the marble-framed fireplace, seeming to carry on a lively conversation with itself. The warmth of the blaze radiated to the four corners of the luxurious office, the light showing off the rich furniture. The inviting room was a haven from the mournful wail of the winter wind that begged for entry at the red velvet-curtained windows. Comforting warmth and bone-chilling cold. Peaceful light and fearsome dark. Enemies kept apart by fragile glass and brick bound with mortar. Their furious battle was lost on the young woman seated at the mahogany desk. Alina Gallagher was slumped forward, overcome by fatigue and a gnawing depression. Her dark head rested on an open account ledger, her eyes and mind closed to the world as she dozed. The light of a coal-oil lamp, cleverly fashioned from a bronze statue of a naked woman, touched Alina's shining blue-black hair and fair skin. Her breathing was deep and even.

A gunshot brought Alina's head up, her eyes wide with fear. The shot was followed by another, and yet another, accompanied by riotous laughter and cheering. Her wild gaze focused on the imported clock on the mantel; it read midnight. She blinked and took a deep breath. Midnight on New Year's Eve! That explained all the noise. Alina leaned back in the tall chair and wearily passed a hand over her eyes. She tried to recapture some of the excitement and hope she had felt at the onset of previous years. Last year at this time she had been in England with her father.

The door was flung open and Katie Davenport burst in, laughing, a bottle of champagne in one hand, an empty glass in the other. Katie was not a small woman; indeed, there was nothing small about her in any way. That included the generosity of her heart toward those she loved, as well as her voice.

"Happy New Year, honey!" she boomed as she approached the desk. Katie was a tall, handsome woman in her late thirties. Her elegant yellow satin dress, trimmed with black ribbons and fringe, complemented her voluptuous figure and set off her russet hair and shining brown eyes.

Alina rose to greet her friend and was enveloped in an energetic hug that took her breath away.

"Get back out here, Kate!" a man called from the door, his voice barely audible above the noise from the saloon.

Katie laughed and waved him away, then turned back to Alina. She looked at the younger woman with affection and admiration as she set the bottle and glass on the edge of the desk and put her hands on her full hips.

"Alina, girl, ya just look lovely tonight," she sighed, taking in the dusky blue ballgown that graced Alina's slender form. The dress was off the shoulders, with a tight, low-cut bodice and a waistline that came to a vee in the front. The sides of the fringe-trimmed overskirt were swept back and up to a small bustle. Her raven locks were arranged in rolls and curls, with a blue ribbon woven throughout, and wispy curls played around her forehead. Dainty antique earrings made of silver filigree and small blue stones of topaz winked from her earlobes.

"Well, you have yourself to thank for that, and so do I." Alina fingered the rich material of the skirt. "It was a lovely Christmas gift, Katie."

Katie nodded with satisfaction. "I want all of my girls to

look good, and that includes my little bookkeeper, not that ya need any help in looking good. Ya're as pretty as a picture all by yourself, and that's a fact." She waved a hand at the ledger. "Are ya through with this mess yet, honey?"

"Almost," Alina answered with a twinge of guilt for the small lie.

"Well, hurry and come and join us." Katie reached out to push a glossy black curl behind Alina's ear. Alina responded with a quick hug.

"Go back to your party; I'll be out soon."

Katie nodded, then her gaze fell to the champagne bottle. "Oh, have a little of this." She grabbed the bottle and splashed some of the bubbly liquid into the glass on the desk. "It'll perk ya right up." She headed toward the door with the bottle. "Hurry," she urged.

Alina nodded with a smile and was relieved when the closing door shut out most of the noise from the outer room. She had long ago finished the work on the ledger, but she had no wish to join Katie's wild party. It had only been three weeks since Alina had started this job, and she was still not comfortable in the saloon. She picked up the stemmed glass and sank into an overstuffed chair in front of the fireplace. Her thoughts wandered over the past three weeks as she sipped the champagne.

The escape from Chicago had been surprisingly easy. How she would have loved to have seen Cordelia's face, and Donovan's, when they realized she was gone! Alina took comfort in knowing that Chambers, Effie, and Maggie were safely ensconced at Elizabeth's house, along with several trunks and boxes of her father's belongings. Her own trunk had been smuggled out with the rest, and had been waiting for her at the train station.

It had also been easy to decide that Laramie City was the place to hide until her birthday in May. The small, new town, only three years old, had been a railhead at one time, before the tracks had gone on to unite the country in Utah. Alina had never heard of Laramie City before the train was forced to stop there for a day when snowdrifts closed the tracks to the west. She had purchased a ticket to San Francisco; with any luck, Cordelia and Donovan would assume that she had gone to California. If trouble did develop, Aunt Elizabeth and San Francisco were only a train ride away. Alina closed her eyes and swirled the champagne in the glass.

It had not been as easy finding a job. Few people had been willing to hire an unmarried woman new to town, with no work experience, especially one who refused to answer any questions about her background. But Alina needed a job. She had enough money to meet her expenses until May, but only enough, and she did not yet dare contact Percival to request additional funds. There was nothing extra for an emergency, and she would go mad from boredom with nothing to occupy her time.

Katie had needed help with the bookkeeping, and the wage had included room and board, with no personal questions asked. Alina had been thrilled when Katie'd paid her for the first time; it had given her a sense of pride she had never known. She had doubted the respectability of employment in a saloon, even one as elegant as the Satin Slipper, but her options had been limited. Besides, Cordelia would never think to look for her in a saloon. A smile came to her face as she remembered her shock at the discovery that whiskey was not the only comfort offered to the patrons of the Satin Slipper.

Alina sighed and rose from the chair, wrinkling her nose at the now warm champagne. She set the glass on the mantel and gazed at the fine design etched in the thin crystal. She was reminded of the delicate set of crystal her mother had used on only the most special of occasions. That set was now in the hands of Cordelia Randall. A fierce determination hardened her features.

"I swear to you, Mama, I will put your house in order," she whispered as she stroked the stem of the fragile glass. She blinked impatiently at the tears that had formed; the time to cry would come later, when all was well again.

With a restless shake of her head, Alina turned from the mantel and the memories the glass evoked. She forced her thoughts to the present. 1872 . . . a new year. She fervently hoped it would be a better year than the previous one, then a cynical smile touched her lips. *What silly creatures we humans are. This is a day like any other, and yet we look upon it with such hope.*

Alina stopped at the desk and closed the ledger book. She was pleased that it had been a profitable year for the Satin Slipper. Katie had no head for numbers and accounting, and her language was not refined, but she had a gift with people, and that gift was responsible for the success of her establishment. If a man was relatively clean and minded his manners, he was made welcome at the Satin Slipper, be he rancher, cowboy, railroad hand, miner, or businessman. Katie treated her ladies with the same fairness. Each woman decided for herself how far she would service the customers; some were dance partners and drink servers, some shared the comforts of their bodies.

Alina wandered over to the window, shivering as she looked out over the snow-covered plains. A quarter moon tried in vain to show itself off through clouds pushed by the relentless wind. Because of the saloon's position on the eastern edge of town, Alina's tired eyes could see no sign of life, not even a tree.

She yawned and looked at the clock; it was almost one o'clock. The fire had died down, and the room had taken on a chill. The clamor from the saloon had not abated, and although she dreaded it, the only way to get to her room was through that door.

Alina put the ledger book in the desk drawer and blew out the flame of the lamp. She banked the coals in the fireplace, then stepped through the door and pulled it closed behind her.

She leaned back against the strength of the solid wood and looked around in amazement. Never had she seen the Satin

Slipper so crowded. The saloon was a teeming mass of humanity, with cowboys, railroaders, and businessmen wearing everything from worn denims and leather chaps to expensive suits and linen shirts. Interspersed among the men were Katie's ladies, dressed in beautiful and costly ballgowns of the latest fashion, standing out like bright, colorful birds in a dark and smoky forest.

The members of the small orchestra that usually performed quiet background music, or perhaps a waltz, were playing as loudly as they could in order to be heard over the roar of celebrating guests. A few couples were making drunken attempts to dance, while others cheered them on. Alina pulled her gown up higher on her shoulders, wishing it did not complement her as much as she knew it did. Katie saw her at that moment and called from behind the bar.

"Alina! Come on back here, honey!" Katie's cheeks were red, her warm brown eyes were shining with excitement, and stray wisps of burnished red hair framed her attractive face. She waved to Alina, motioning her to come.

With great reluctance, Alina moved the short distance to the end of the bar and guarded her skirts as she passed through the low gate. Katie gave her an exuberant hug, then pushed her toward the tap.

"Help me draw beer for a minute!" she shouted. "Jake had to step out back and I'm a little behind!"

Alina felt that everyone in the room was watching her, as indeed many were. A few appreciative whistles rang out, and when she read open lust on the faces of some of the patrons, she turned to the tap with a blush.

"Hey, Kate, ya got a new girl?"

"What's your name, sweet thing?"

"How much fer a tumble with 'er, Katie?"

Her face flaming, Alina kept her eyes on the tap and filled glasses as fast as she could.

"Forget it, boys!" Katie yelled, an uncustomary harshness to her voice as she lined the full glasses of beer on the bar. "This little one ain't for the likes of ya'll and I will personally de-man any fool that bothers her!" Katie's eyes searched the room and fell on a dark-haired woman in a bright red gown whose full lips were painted to match her dress. "Delilah, get on up here and sing one of your special songs for the boys!"

With an arrogant toss of her head and her hands on her swaying hips, Delilah sauntered to the bar. She stared malevolently at Alina for a moment before she turned and allowed a tall man in stained buckskins to lift her to a sitting position on the bar top. She looked around the room in a coquettish manner and waited until most of the noise quieted, then began to sing. As the song progressed, the lyrics and Delilah's clear, sweet voice became increasingly bawdy, and she inched her skirts up until they were bunched around her hips, exposing her legs from ankle to thigh. Alina's ears burned, but she was grateful the attention had been diverted from her.

Jake, the short, powerfully built bartender, returned to his post at last. Alina relinquished her duties at the tap in relief and turned to leave as Jake spoke to her.

"I know you want to get on outta here, honey, but would you do up a few of these glasses for me before you go? Please?"

Alina looked at him with dismay, but he had a pleading grin on his bearded face, and she relented with a sigh.

"Only because it's you that's asking, Jake," she retorted affectionately as she gathered several dirty glasses from the crowded bar top. Jake had always been kind and respectful toward her, which could not be said of all the employees of the Satin Slipper. Alina piled her collection of glasses into the bucket of warm, soapy water that sat next to a bucket of rinse water on a low shelf at the end of the bar. She found a clean towel that was large enough to tie around her waist, and as she washed, she tried to ignore the finale of Delilah's song and the riotous laughter and applause that followed.

Alina glanced up from her task and noticed an expensive hat resting on its top not far from the edge of the bar. She raised her head further to find a pair of dark eyes watching her.

"Is that your hat?" she asked the owner of those intense eyes.

"Yes, ma'am." The man's voice was calm and deep, with a distinctive baritone quality to it. "Is it in your way?"

"No, but I fear I may splash it." As Alina dried a glass with a corner of her makeshift apron, she looked fully at the man for the first time. He had dark, rather long hair and a full, neatly trimmed mustache. His frock coat was of black broadcloth, with a matching shoestring tie, and he wore a burgundy brocade vest over a clean white shirt. The tanned skin around his warm brown eyes crinkled when he smiled, as he did now. Alina blinked, struck by the illumination that smile brought to the man's handsome face. It seemed to her that the noise of the saloon faded away as their eyes met and locked for a long moment, then he pushed his hat against the wall.

"I appreciate your concern, ma'am."

Alina blinked again and shyly returned his smile, then directed her attention to the few remaining glasses. She fought the urge to shake her head in an attempt to free herself from the man's spell and stole a glance at him. His eyes had not left her face. Her cheeks warmed and she turned away. As she dried the last glass, she saw Katie toasting two men who were laughing with her. Jake was deep in conversation with a pretty blond dancer named Sophie, and Alina knew she would not be missed if she left. She watched Jake and Sophie with an understanding smile; she suspected they had romantic feelings for each other.

A powerful feeling of loneliness settled over Alina. It was New Year's Eve and she had no one to share it with: no close friends, no family, no special man. Her sad eyes wandered over the crowded saloon. No, she would not be missed by anyone here. More determined than ever to reach the peace of her room, she removed the towel from her waist and set it next to the rinse bucket. The man with the brown eyes spoke.

"Will you join me in a toast to the New Year, Miss?"

Alina looked up in surprise as he invitingly waved a hand at the half-empty bottle next to his glass. She blushed, mortified that he thought she would drink whiskey.

"No, thank you, sir." She raised her chin. "I do not partake of hard liquor."

"Forgive me," he said earnestly as he leaned forward. "I meant no offense. I would be honored to purchase the beverage of your choice, be it champagne or tea."

Alina's heart softened when she read the silent appeal in his eyes. She located a pitcher of water next to the tap and poured a small amount into one of the freshly washed glasses, then turned back to the waiting man.

His breath caught at the transformation of her young face as a dazzling smile displaced all traces of worry and fatigue. The color of her gown highlighted the brilliance of her luminous eyes, just as her shining black curls accented the delicate perfection of her creamy skin. He raised his glass in a silent toast to her beauty, while his lips paid service to the New Year.

"To a prosperous and happy year, Miss."

"And the same to you, sir," she responded with sincerity. Their glasses touched, then each drank. Alina watched him for a moment. He was a fine-looking man, well dressed and clean. She was impressed by his courtly manners and wondered about his background. She would have enjoyed talking to him, but she was not sure that meeting in a saloon was entirely proper, even in the relaxed social atmosphere of the West, and the hour was late. She rinsed and dried her glass, then returned it to the shelf.

"I must go," she said. The man's expression was sad as he lifted his glass to toast her again. She moved to give Katie a quick hug and wiggled her fingers at Jake and Sophie, then pushed through the gate.

The tall post of the stair rail was within Alina's reach when someone took hold of her left hand. She turned, a scathing demand of release on her lips, and saw that her hand was held in the grasp of the man from the bar. There was an engaging smile on his face. He pulled her closer in order to be heard.

"My apologies for accosting you in this manner, Miss, but where I come from, it is a longstanding tradition to welcome the New Year with a waltz. I don't want to invite a year of bad luck by neglecting something so important." His tone was solemn, but his eyes sparkled with mischief.

Alina raised her eyebrows in skepticism as she gently pulled her hand from his. "And where is this place that sets such great store by this time-honored tradition?" A smile played about her lips. He was taller than she had imagined, and she could see now that the proportions of his lean body were a fitting match for the handsomeness of his face. His black suit was simple, but it was well made and fit his broad shoulders, narrow waist, and long legs perfectly. His appearance was striking and elegant, even if his polished western boots were well used and he wore a gunbelt under the fine coat. He exuded a calm confidence that made her suspect he knew how to use that gun.

"Virginia," he answered in a serious tone as he tried to keep from smiling. Now she recognized his faint accent.

"Virginia, indeed," Alina retorted, then her voice slipped into a perfect Irish brogue. "I'd have guessed Ireland, for surely ye've been kissin' the Blarney Stone."

The man covered his heart with his hand. "And she is clever, too," he groaned, closing his eyes a moment. Then he looked at her, his mood suddenly serious. "Please dance with me."

His simple plea touched something deep inside her. Alina was aware of the loneliness behind his gentle bantering, for she felt it herself. She loved to dance and had not done so in months. She relented and held out her hand. "Very well, sir, but only one dance."

He rewarded her with a smile that threatened to take her

breath away, then seized her hand and forged a path through the crowd. He made his way to the orchestra leader and spoke to him. At that man's nod, Alina's partner turned to her and bowed. She executed a dainty curtsy as the soft strains of the waltz began.

His arm circled her waist and she placed a hand on his shoulder while their free hands joined. He felt good, and warm, and strong. Her breath caught when his fingers tightened on hers, and she would not look up at him.

At first, their movements were hampered by the crowd around them, but a space gradually cleared and widened as the other guests noticed them. The large room grew quiet except for the familiar and somehow comforting music as all eyes followed the handsome couple now freely whirling in the graceful dance. Alina's nervousness vanished as she gave herself up to the music and the command of his arms. He was an excellent dancer, and guided her around the floor with ease. The fears and tension of the past weeks fell away, as did the persistent loneliness of the night, and just for a while, she felt happy and at peace. As they moved in perfect harmony, she glanced up and caught his eye. Her face must have shown her joy, for he smiled and his fingers tightened on hers again.

Alina's gaze fell to their entwined hands and an unexpected thrill of excitement raced through her; his touch was warm, his fingers long, his nails trimmed and clean. She had a fleeting memory of her father saying that you could tell a lot about a man by how he kept his hands. She mentally shook herself. This man had an unsettling and unwanted effect on her. She forced her wandering mind to focus on the music. How she loved to dance! The waltz lasted a few minutes longer; then, as the final strains were played, he released her waist. She turned under his arm and gracefully sank into a deep curtsy. He bowed again over her hand, and it was finished.

After a moment of silence, the room erupted in wild applause as the man led her back to the stairs. The orchestra began to play once more, the dance floor filled, and the noise level rose. Alina climbed to the first step and faced her escort; her eyes were now level with his.

"Thank you, sir. That was lovely."

"It is I who should be thanking you. The pleasure was mine." He hesitated, then seemed about to speak again.

Alina spoke quickly. "Goodnight, and I hope the coming year is happy and lucky, now that tradition has been honored."

Disappointment flashed across his face. "Goodnight to you, Miss, and thank you again." He disappeared into the crowd. Alina frowned at his sudden departure; she felt a vague disappointment herself. At that moment, Moses Blackthorn passed in front of her, headed toward the kitchen with an empty coffeepot in one hand and a tray of dirty cups balanced on the other.

"Moses," Alina called, hanging on to the stout post at the bottom of the stairs.

"Yas, Missy." Moses' dark, gray-haired head nodded with excitement. "Ain't nevah seen nothin' like this!" His deep voice still carried heavy traces of his early life in Georgia.

Alina smiled at his enthusiasm. "I know you're busy, but is there any way you can bring me some water so I can wash?"

He broke into a wide grin. "For you, Missy, is no trouble. Yo' fire is already lit, so yo' room be nice and toasty."

On impulse, Alina hugged the old man, careful not to upset his tray. "You spoil me, Moses," she said happily. "Thank you." She planted a kiss on his leather-like cheek. "And Happy New Year!" The recipient of her affection glowed at the unexpected attention. Alina started up the crowded stairs. Suddenly she turned, remembering that Moses' wife was still working in the kitchen.

"Give Emerald a kiss for me, too!" she shouted, and at Moses' grinning nod, continued up the stairs. It was necessary to use the rail to pull herself through the mob. She brushed off grasping hands and closed her ears to the suggestions and offers made. She was compelled to kick one persistent young man in the shin, and ignored his yelp of pain. Finally she topped the stairs. Even the landing was full of people, singing and laughing, but up here some of the women were in various stages of undress, covered with expensive silk robes allowed to hang open in the front.

Alina felt a strange sense of aloneness and alienation as she looked over the crowd one last time; she did not belong here. May suddenly seemed a long way off.

The handsome stranger was no longer at the end of the bar. She caught Katie's eye and waved; Katie blew her a kiss. With a weary sigh, she pushed through the curtains guarding the long hall that led to her room and was gratified to find the dimly lit corridor empty. She tried to ignore the giggles and noises that came from the closed doors she passed. It was a relief to slip into her room and turn the key.

As Moses had promised, a fire burned in the small potbellied stove, sending waves of warmth to the corners of the room. The coal-oil lamp on the dressing table was also lit, and its light reflected in the beveled mirror on the wall above, revealing a cozy place, simple yet comfortable.

A double-sized bed with a brass headboard was pushed against the far wall in the corner, the pillows fluffed, the blankets folded back invitingly. Alina blessed Moses for his thoughtfulness at the sight of a lump under the covers at the foot of the bed, which indicated a wrapped, heated brick. An old rocking chair rested by the stove and a large basket of wood sat on the floor, patiently awaiting its fate. A commode by the single window held a washbasin, and a towel and a clean cloth hung on nails above it.

Alina moved to the dressing table and turned up the lamp. She removed her earrings and laid them next to a bottle of rose water, caressing one for a moment. Her gaze fell on the double-windowed frame that held the treasured pictures of her parents. The memory of her beautiful mother in a blue and silver dress, wearing the jewels Alina now touched, flashed to her mind. Fatigue and grief overwhelmed her. *This does you no good, girl,* she told herself as she rubbed her eyes.

Hopeful that Moses would soon arrive with the water, she stretched in weariness, then began to unfasten the maddening row of tiny hooks down her back. The dress fell to the floor with a soft rustle, and as she picked it up, her nose wrinkled in distaste. Even the short time she had spent behind the bar had been enough to permeate the lovely gown with the smell of tobacco smoke and splatter the front of the skirt with small spills of beer. She draped the soiled dress over the top of the trunk nestled at the foot of the bed and hoped it was not ruined.

Alina slipped out of her petticoats and untied the knot that held a crinoline bustle at her waist. She unlaced her high-topped shoes and kicked them off with a sigh of relief, then removed her stockings. She promised herself she would wash them out first thing in the morning as she tossed them on top of the discarded dress. Wearing only drawers and a camisole, she took her blue linen wrapper from a hook, pulled the garment on, and tied the belt. The wide, lace-trimmed cuffs fell to her elbows when she drew out the pins and ribbon that held her hair in its arrangement. She took her brush in hand, and leaning forward, began to work through her long, curly tresses.

Her thoughts turned to the memory of the waltz and the man who had so expertly danced with her. He had been so polite, and he was so handsome! She knew she would not forget his eyes for a long time. No man had ever looked at her as he had, nor had she ever reacted to a man as she had to him. With a faint and unfamiliar sense of longing, she wondered who he was, and if she would ever see him again.

A knock came at the door.

"Just a minute, Moses," she called, trying futilely to free the brush from a tangle. In exasperation, she moved to the door and felt for the key. Her hair still covered her face as she turned the key and stepped back.

"You can set it down anywhere. I cannot seem to free this brush." Her fingers picked at the offending instrument.

The door closed and she heard him set something on the dressing table. He gently pushed her hands away and with care, liberated the brush. Alina threw her hair back over her shoulders as she straightened and massaged her tender scalp.

"Oh, thank you, Moses. I'd have been all night working that out." She turned with a smile and froze as her eyes fell on her emancipator. It was not Moses at all, but rather the stranger with whom she had welcomed the New Year!

She stepped back in astonishment. "How did you get in here?"

With a slight bow, the tall man removed his hat. "Why, you yourself let me in." He smiled at her. "Surely you remember."

"Well, yes, I did, but I thought you were Moses." Her eyes narrowed with suspicion. "How did you find me?" she demanded, her hands on her hips.

"I must confess that I followed you. I hope you can forgive me, because I could not stop myself." He bowed again. "Beauregard Parker at your service, Miss." His warm smile reached his eyes as those brown orbs covered Alina from head to foot and returned to gaze at her face with obvious pleasure. She stepped back again, self-conscious in her state of undress.

"I am grateful for your timely assistance, Mr. Parker, but now, if you will excuse me, I wish to retire." Her voice was firm as she opened the door and waited with her hand on the knob.

The man stood silent, his hat in one hand, her brush in the other. He took in the blue robe that made her eyes even more striking, her creamy skin accented by the indignant flush on her cheeks, her magnificent hair that tumbled to her waist in a cascade of glossy black curls. "Who is Moses?" he asked, making no move to leave.

"Moses works here," Alina explained with some irritation. "He is bringing me some water. Now, if you please, sir." She nodded toward the open door.

Beauregard set her brush and his hat on the dressing table. "Are you expecting anyone else besides Moses tonight?"

"No, not that it is any of your business," she snapped.

He began to walk toward her.

"Once more, I thank you for coming to my rescue. I hope you do not ruin the favorable impression you first made by forcing me to insist that . . . you . . . leave." Her voice trailed off when he stopped in front of her, very close. No words came to her usually quick tongue as she tossed her hair again in an effort to disguise her growing discomfort at his strange behavior. She met his intense stare with defiance.

In one swift movement Beauregard pushed the door closed with his right hand while his left arm snaked around Alina's waist. She gasped in outrage and brought her hands up to his chest in an attempt to push him away, determined to ignore the irritating tremor of pleasure she felt at his touch.

"Mr. Parker, you forget yourself!"

He raised his right hand to her chin and lifted her head. "You are far lovelier than anything I expected to find here." His laughing eyes mocked her furious ones. "Please tell me your name," he implored.

"Then will you leave?" she demanded.

"No," came his whispered reply. He wrapped his hand in her hair and gently pulled her head back to an advantageous position. He caught the scent of roses when he lowered his mouth to hers. His kiss was soft and light, almost as if he were testing her reaction. He sighed and held her close as he buried his face in her fragrant hair; his mustache tickled her ear.

Alina stood still, her hands trapped between them, surprised by his gentleness and confused by her own reaction to his kiss. She had been drawn to him from the moment their eyes had first met; she had felt a connection to him when she had recognized his loneliness, for it matched her own. And so she found his soft kiss not only pleasant but oddly comforting. She slipped her hands from between their bodies to encircle his waist, her touch light. Her father and brothers were the only men who had ever embraced her, and it felt good to have strong arms around her again. She had been alone for so long! Her eyes closed and she briefly rested her head against his shoulder, savoring his closeness. She could feel the pounding of his heart. But she feared Beauregard misunderstood her position at the Satin Slipper, and she gently pushed him back.

"Please listen to me," she pleaded. "I don't work in the capacity you may assume. I am Katie's bookkeeper, nothing more."

His eyes narrowed. "A bookkeeper? Living here? Dressed in that?" He waved a hand at the crumpled dress on the trunk. "And working behind the bar at one o'clock in the morning? Don't play games with me, woman," he warned. "I'm tired and a little drunk, and I just want you to do your job, without any nonsense." He moved away from her and took off his coat, then hung it on a hook next to her night-dress. He reached for the bottle of whiskey he had set on the dressing table and took a quick swallow. As he set the bottle down, he saw in the mirror that Alina was reaching for the doorknob.

"I am going to get Katie. She will find someone to take care of your . . ." she paused and looked over her shoulder at him with disdain, "needs."

A memory of the early evening came to Beauregard's mind. He saw again the alluring, full figure, the flattering, costly gown, the elaborately styled golden hair and mocking brown eyes of Madeline Petrie. He felt her soft curves pressed wantonly against him, teasing and taunting him, promising what she had no intention of giving him. His hands clenched in rage as he thought of her in her father's fine house, surrounded by her fine friends, no doubt laughing at the idea that a mere cowboy would allow himself to want her, to perhaps love her.

He had come to the Satin Slipper to ease the frustration and emptiness he felt, and now this little chit was refusing him, too! It was her job to want him! In two long strides, Beauregard was at her side, his handsome face dark with fury. He knocked her hand away from the door and grabbed her shoulders, forcing her to face him. "I told you to stop it!" He glared at her. "Is it the money you're worried about? You'll be well paid if you do as I want."

Alina twisted from his grasp as her right hand shot out and connected solidly with his cheek. "How *dare* you!" Her eyes were spitting fire, her hands now on her hips, her breasts rising and falling beneath the robe in time with her agitated breathing. "Get out of here, Mr. Parker!"

He looked at her in amazement as he rubbed his stinging cheek, then chuckled, a strange, humorless sound. "I do like a woman with spirit." He pulled her to him again and grabbed her chin with one hand. He began to kiss her, with more force than before. Alina struggled against him, then relaxed as she realized that she could not defeat his superior strength. She had to think! Where was Moses?

Beauregard's kisses gentled when he felt her surrender. He turned and walked her toward the bed, one arm draped over her shoulders, the other bent so that he could touch her cheek. With reluctance, Alina moved her right arm to encircle his waist; her hand brushed against his pistol. An idea came to her. Beauregard lowered his head toward her lips. She forced herself to return his kiss as she twisted her hand to grip the gun handle. In one quick motion, from behind his back she yanked the weapon out of the holster, stepped in front of him, pressed the barrel against his ribs, and cocked the hammer, never taking her mouth from his. He froze, still breathing against her now motionless lips, then spoke in a calm tone.

"Are you going to kill me?"

Alina stayed close to him, pulling her head back to glare up at him. "I ought to, Mr. Parker." She pressed the barrel more firmly against his side. "But I won't, unless you fail to leave my room at once, and I assure you, sir, that I will hit what I aim for."

"It's hard to miss anything at this range." His voice was heavy with sarcasm as he took a cautious step backward, his arms falling to his sides.

Renewed anger at his remark caused Alina's lips to tighten. Without warning, she jerked the gun to the left and fired at the far wall, then returned the barrel to press against his stomach. Beauregard turned shocked eyes to the wall as he stepped back again.

"It is also difficult to miss the wall," he commented, but his tone was not so sharp.

"If you will examine the wall with more care, Mr. Parker," Alina said with feigned sweetness, "you will see that the center is gone from the knothole directly to the left of the window." He stared at her in disbelief, then strode to the window when she motioned with the gun. To his astonishment, he saw that she was right. The knothole was about two inches across and through the middle was a neat hole. He could feel a stream of icy wind blowing into the room as he ran his finger over it. He turned to Alina, now standing near the door, with new respect.

"I don't know what type of woman you are familiar with, Mr. Parker, but I do not lie." Her voice was cold with fury. He walked toward her, his hands held out in front of him.

"I'm going to get my coat." He passed her to take the garment from the hook. "I've made a mistake."

"I told you that," Alina snapped. "Not all women who work in saloons are whores. Why would you not listen to me?"

Beauregard's tired gaze fell on the bottle of whiskey that stood on the dresser. Shame washed over him. He reached for the bottle and his hat.

"Do you enjoy forcing a woman to be with you? I want some answers, Mr. Parker!"

He turned. "I do not usually have to force women to be with me," he answered stiffly as he looked into her angry eyes. His gun was still trained on him. "Neither do I usually behave in such a barbaric fashion. It was a combination of too much inferior whiskey and a bad day, although I know that is no excuse."

Beauregard crossed the room, tossing his hat on the seat of the rocker. He pushed the curtains back from the small window, forced it open, then threw the bottle as far as he could into the still night. After closing the window, he turned to the stove and added fuel from the basket on the floor. He straightened and looked at Alina. How beautiful she was! She stood there, so quietly defiant with his gun, the soft light from the lamp caressing her. Her magnificent eyes glared at him, her luxuriant hair tumbled around her shoulders and down her back. He felt a powerful pang of regret. This was an extraordinary woman, and he had behaved like a savage. He wondered if he would have gone as far as rape if she had not stopped him. He found it frightening that he had not been able to control his rage.

"Your display of thoughtfulness comes too late." There was a touch of sadness in her voice. She nodded at the now crackling stove.

"I know." He picked up his hat and faced her. "I offer my sincere apologies to you, ma'am." He hesitated, but she remained silent. "Will you give me my gun?"

"Take it and go," Alina said wearily, as she turned the pistol and handed it to him handle first. He slid the weapon into the worn holster. She opened the door and waited, her hand on the knob. She stared at him fearlessly.

Beauregard stopped in front of her and gently touched the red mark his fingers had made on her chin. She flinched and jerked her head away.

"I am so sorry," he whispered.

"Just go, Mr. Parker."

Beauregard turned into the hall and came face to face with a short, gray-haired black man who held a bucket of water. The older man stared at him with suspicion.

"Everthin' be all right, Miz Alina?" Moses asked as his eyes went from her white face to Beauregarde's sober one. "Ah swear Ah heard a gunshot."

"Everything is fine, Moses." Alina reached for the bucket he held out to her. "Please escort Mr. Parker back to the saloon." She paused. "Thank you for the water."

"Yo' welcome, Missy, and g'night now." The old man stared pointedly at the younger man as Alina closed the door on them. Beauregard heard the key grate in the lock, and he looked at the door for a long, miserable moment. The aching loneliness that had gripped him earlier in the evening returned with even greater force, and he wished with all his heart that he could take back the last half hour. He thought of the magical dance with sadness. He wondered if there was any way he could ever make it up to her, to perhaps recapture that magic. Moses had called her "Alina." A beautiful name for a beautiful woman. With a tortured sigh, he crammed his hat on his head and strode down the hall, followed by the protective Moses. Beauregard determined that it would be a long time before whiskey passed his lips again, and that Madeline Petrie could go straight to hell.

Chapter Three

Alina set the heavy bucket down and leaned against the locked door. The full realization of what had almost happened hit her. She began to tremble. Would she have shot the man if he had not stopped? *Yes, God help me, I would have.* Tears came to her eyes, and this time she let them fall.

"I don't know if I can last until May," she whispered as she paced the small room. It deeply troubled her that her romantic and exciting dance partner had thought her a whore. He had been so gentle and polite, at first anyway. Yet, was his deduction so surprising? What if someone else came to the same conclusion, someone not so gentle and polite? She shivered at the thought of some of the men she had seen in the saloon touching her.

Alina poured water into the cast-iron kettle on the stove, then moved to the window and pushed the curtains aside. She pressed her forehead against the pane and caught a glimpse of the frozen world outside, hauntingly lit by the eerie light of the fading moon, before her warm breath clouded the window. Her eyes closed and she rested there until the water began to boil.

She splashed hot water into the washbasin and added a small amount of cold water from the bucket, then opened the robe and let it fall to the floor. The camisole and drawers landed on top of the dress. Alina wet the washing cloth and slapped it against her skin. She gasped at the heat of the water but rubbed with fierce determination, for somehow she felt unclean. The tears started again as she remembered the waltz with Beauregard Parker. She felt a deep sadness and sense of loss; the beauty of the memory was now destroyed.

She retrieved the robe from the floor and hung it on a hook, then pulled her flannel nightdress over her head. As she wove her hair into a thick braid, she surveyed the room with a critical eye. There was no evidence that anything unusual had taken place, yet it was not the same. She no longer felt safe here.

Alina climbed into bed and drew the blankets up to her chin. She left the lamp on and stared at the ceiling for a long time, until her exhausted mind could handle her tortured thoughts no longer. Finally, mercifully, she slept.

Madeline Petrie stared intently into the ornate dressing table mirror, critically surveying her big brown eyes and blond hair. Her gaze touched upon her upturned nose, her flushed cheeks, and her full, pouting lips, then dropped to where her large breasts pressed against the confinement of her thin nightdress. She nodded in satisfaction and reached for the glass of wine that sat next to the glowing lamp.

The evening had gone well, she thought smugly. She knew she had sparkled as the hostess of her father's year-end party. She had taken particular delight in playing emotional cat-and-mouse with a certain maddeningly attractive cowboy. Her eyes narrowed with predatory glee as she recalled the seething anger and frustration etched on a handsome face.

"I've got you now, Beauregard Parker," she whispered to her reflection before sipping her wine. She closed her eyes and built a picture in her mind of a tall, lean man with long, dark hair curling to his shoulders, hot eyes burning with passion, a neatly trimmed mustache hiding a sensual mouth.

She trembled with delight at the memory of that educated

mouth on hers, on her neck, nibbling at her ear. She shakily set the wineglass on the edge of the dressing table and leaned back, her eyes again closed. Her hands moved to her breasts, retracing the paths his long fingers had followed earlier in the evening. She moaned with pleasure as her sensitized nipples hardened, remembering his whispered pleadings to let him take her upstairs. It had been so hard to turn him down! One hand continued its caresses while she reached for the glass with the other.

All things in their own good time, she thought as she gulped the wine. Even Beauregard Parker. At least she knew he would be worth the wait. She had found playing the virgin very tedious, but she was certain, after his actions tonight, that he would do as she wished. With a snort of derisive laughter, she remembered his barely controlled anger as he had stormed into the frozen night, warning her not to play with him. "Of course I will play with you, Mr. Parker," she assured her image in the mirror.

She would let him stew for a while, then arrange to meet him and express her willingness to be his lover. Her "capitulation," along with the proper combination of tears and feigned fear of her father, should neatly close the trap. No mere cowboy would stand up to Richard Petrie's rage over a compromised daughter.

Marriage to Beauregard Parker would solve many problems; it was an added spice that he was so attractive and independent. Just the thought of him in her bed was arousing.

Madeline ran her tongue over her lips. She slid lower in the chair, moving her legs apart as one hand searched feverishly for the hem of her nightdress. The now empty wineglass fell to the carpeted floor. A shudder ran through her at the secret touch of her fingers. She entertained the idea of sending for one of her father's ranchhands, as she had done many times before, but she decided against it. Beauregard Parker was within her reach. She returned her mind to the quiet cowboy and gave in completely to the pleasure of her private games.

Alina was awakened from a deep, drugged-like sleep by a persistent pounding on her door. She became aware of her name being called. She huddled under the blankets, hiding her nose from the biting air, trying to remember why she felt so distressed. The memory of the night before came back in full force.

"Oh, God!" she cried as she buried her face in the pillow.

"Alina! Girl, are ya all right?" Katie's worried voice was muffled through the door. "I'm coming in!"

Did I really shoot out a knothole? Alina lifted her head and peered at the wall next to the window; sure enough, there was a dark hole. She groaned and pulled the blanket over her head.

Katie's master key made short work of the lock. Emerald followed her in and promptly pulled back the curtains. Light filled the small room.

Alina peeked at the two women over the edge of the blanket. Emerald wore a cheerful plaid gown that made her look more rotund than she was, and a long, clean white apron was tied at her thick waist. Katie had covered her lacy nightdress with an expensive bronze silk dressing gown. Her hair lay about her shoulders in unbrushed disarray. She came to Alina's side, concern etched on her kindly features.

"Are ya sick, honey?"

"Hell, she's sick from drinkin' too much, just like the rest of us are," sneered a rough voice from the door. Katie whirled to see Delilah leaning against the frame, a loose wrapper barely covering her voluptuous nakedness.

"I am not sick," Alina denied hotly as she sat up in bed. Delilah ignored her.

"What is it with her, Katie? You don't check on any of us like you do her, and she ain't even makin' you any money, unless she's doin' it on the side and keepin' it all for herself."

Delilah sashayed into the room, glaring at Alina, her hands on her full hips. "What hold does this little bitch have on you?"

Alina gasped in outrage as she moved to jump off the bed, but Katie reacted first. Her hand struck Delilah's cheek with a resounding smack. She pushed the astonished woman into the hall. "Get yourself from my sight and mind your own damn business!" She slammed the door, then turned back to Alina. "I'm right sorry about that display, honey. If she wasn't so popular with the boys, I'da fired her a long time ago, and I'm still not sure she's worth all the trouble she causes." She came closer and pushed a strand of Alina's hair back from her face. "Are ya sure ya're all right? Did ya drink too much, girl? If that's the problem, Emerald here can fix something for ya that'll help."

Emerald looked up from her efforts to get the fire going with a sympathetic nod. "Not no one feels too good this mawnin'." She shook her dark, graying head. "Even my Moses be feelin' somewhat po'ly."

"Katie, you know I don't drink." Alina's tone was sharp with irritation.

"Oh, I saw ya toasting with that handsome Beau Parker last night, and I saw ya dancing with him, too." Katie smiled knowingly as she settled on the edge of the bed and patted Alina's hand. "He's a fine man, girl. Ya could do a lot worse."

Alina threw herself off the bed. "Will you stop it? He is not a fine man!"

Katie and Emerald looked at her in astonishment. "All right, girl," Katie said quietly. "What's bothering ya?"

"I need to wash my face and get my thoughts together. Can I meet you in your office in a few minutes?" Alina looked from one to the other. "Emerald, you come, too. Please?"

Emerald moved to Alina's side and laid a cool hand on her forehead. "Yo' head ain't feverish," she reported as she looked into Alina's pleading eyes. She turned to Katie. "Let's us go, Miz Kate. Give the girl time to prepare herself." She pushed Katie out of the room with a kind wink at Alina, then pulled the door closed. "Ah doan know what's troublin' the child, but she'll tell us soon enough. And yo' doan look too good yo' own self, 'cause yo' did drink too much, and Ah knows it." Emerald put her arm around Katie's waist and guided her down the hall.

A short time later, dressed in a simple black skirt and a white high-collared blouse, Alina stood at the top of the stairs and looked down on the empty saloon. A half-hearted attempt had been made to put the tables and chairs in some kind of order, and all of the dirty glasses had been moved to the bar, but a great deal of work remained to be done. As she descended the stairs, the air seemed to get heavier, laden with the smell of stale beer and smoke: tobacco smoke, coal-oil smoke, wood smoke. It was not a pleasant smell.

Alina paused and stared at the dais where the orchestra had played. Sadly she wondered if she would ever be able to hear a waltz again without it causing her pain. She refused to acknowledge the unwelcome memory of Beauregard Parker's smiling eyes and gentle kiss. With a frustrated shake of her head, she entered Katie's office and closed the door. Emerald sat in one of two chairs that faced the desk where Katie was seated, tenderly nursing a steaming cup.

"Have some coffee. It's damn good." Katie waved at the china pot resting on a tray on the edge of the desk. Alina filled a cup and sat down. She did not bother with a saucer, and there was no milk or sugar. She took a tiny sip, knowing it was too hot, but she seemed to need its strength.

"Out with it, girl," Katie ordered, more harshly than she'd intended.

Alina looked up in surprise.

"Something's bothering ya, and I hope ya see fit to share it with us." Katie smiled in what she hoped was an encouraging manner, though it hurt her head even to move her lips. She adjusted the belt on her elegant dressing gown and waited.

Alina set her cup on the desk and jumped to her feet. She paced the rug that lay in front of the fireplace and worried her lip with her knuckle. Her hair was pulled back, tied in a black ribbon at her neck, and her free-falling curls danced back and forth with the nervous movement of her slender body. "A man followed me to my room last night, thinking I was one of the, uh, working ladies. He wouldn't believe I was only a bookkeeper."

Katie's face blanched and her hands tightened into fists. "Alina, were ya assaulted?" she asked fearfully. Emerald set her cup down and watched the pacing young woman with concern.

"No, no." Alina hastened to reassure them. "I was not hurt. But I don't know if he would have stopped if I had not taken his gun from him."

Katie was incredulous. "Ya took his gun from him?"

At Alina's absentminded nod, Katie glanced at Emerald, who rolled her expressive brown eyes.

"Then what'd ya do?" Katie prompted.

"I threatened him, but he didn't believe I knew how to use the gun, so I shot the center out of a knothole in the wall." She turned to Katie, her apology written on her lovely face.

"Ya shot the center out of a knothole?" Katie repeated, her mouth sagging in amazement.

"I'm sorry about the wall, Katie." Alina twisted her hands. "I'll pay to have the board replaced."

"Never mind the goddamned wall, girl! Tell us what happened!" Katie rose from her chair and leaned forward, her weight resting on her braced hands.

"Well, then he left."

Katie sat down again as if her legs had failed her. "He just left?" she croaked.

"Yes. But Katie, I'm afraid someone else may make the same mistake, someone I may not be able to stop, and I cannot risk that." Her eyes begged Katie to understand. "I never thought about the potential danger I face here," she finished lamely.

"So are ya telling me ya wanna quit? Is that the point of all this?"

"Oh, no." Alina moved forward to grasp the back of her chair. "I need this job, Katie, if you still want me. I just can't work behind the bar again. I'll help all I can in the kitchen, and any other way you want me to, but not in the saloon. I don't want this to happen again." She waited anxiously for Katie's reaction.

Katie leaned back with a sigh of relief. "I don't want to lose ya, honey. I don't know how I got along without ya before. We'll keep ya out of the saloon." She looked up at Alina, guilt and regret evident on her face. "I'm damn sorry about this whole thing. It was my fault, really. I called ya behind the bar." Her eyes narrowed in thought. "I also told them to stay away from ya. Do ya know who this man was?"

Alina gripped the chair more tightly. "It was your 'fine' Beauregard Parker."

"Beau?" Katie roared. "I'da never thought it of him! Wait 'til I get my hands on his handsome hide!"

"I never want to see him again." Alina's voice was hard.

A knock sounded at the door. At Katie's short "Come in!" the door opened and revealed the very same Beauregard Parker. He surveyed the suddenly silent, accusing group of women.

"Good morning, ladies," he said politely. He twisted his hat in his hands.

Katie stood. "Get in here and close that door, Beau Parker," she thundered.

Beau did as he was instructed. His long legs were covered with clean, faded denim and he wore the same boots from the night before. A blue workshirt showed between the lapels of his long duster, as did a knotted neckerchief. His hair and mustache were neatly combed, and his expression was somber as he waited, tall and silent.

Katie moved around her desk and crossed her arms over her ample bosom. Emerald rose from her chair and glared at him, the recrimination in her angry eyes easy to read. Alina turned away and stared into the fire.

"I'd say ya have some explaining to do." Katie's tone was harsh.

"There is no satisfactory explanation, Miss Davenport."

Alina closed her eyes at the sound of his deep, masculine voice. He continued. "My behavior last night was inexcusable, and I've come to again offer my apologies to Miss Alina."

Alina started and looked at him. How did he know her name? He took a few steps toward her, then stopped when she drew back.

"I can't tell you how sorry I am, Miss. I will do anything to make up for my actions."

Alina steeled herself against the genuine remorse she found on his face. "There is nothing you can do, Mr. Parker," she said coldly. "Please just leave."

"Now, Alina, maybe we should hear him out," Katie interjected. "I know this man, and it ain't like him to be such a jackass. I'd like to learn how this happened."

Alina whirled to face her friend, her hands on her hips. "He will tell you he made a mistake, that my dress and my presence behind the bar led him to the wrong conclusion. That I can understand. What I cannot forgive is his refusal to listen to me, to believe me when I told him I was only a bookkeeper." She turned on Beau. "I shudder to think what would have befallen me, were I not capable with a weapon." Her eyes blazed like blue flames; her breath came quickly with the force of her anger. "I have nothing to say to him, nor will I ever." She twisted to look at Katie, as if daring her to argue.

Katie shrugged. "Suit yourself, honey."

Alina nodded, then strode out the door.

Emerald sniffed. "Ah gots work awaitin' me in my kitchen." Her withering glance caused Beau to shift uncomfortably. She marched after Alina and the door closed, hard. Katie sighed, then turned back to her desk.

"Ya might as well sit and have some coffee, Beau." Katie waved at a chair as she sank into hers. She reached for her cup. Beau set his hat on the red velvet sofa by the door and shrugged out of his duster. He took the pot and filled a cup from the tray, as well as Katie's cup when she held it up to him. He settled in the chair Alina had vacated and sipped his coffee.

"What the hell were ya thinking of, Beau? I know ya better than that. I told everyone to stay away from her." Her gaze was piercing. "What happened?"

"It was Madeline, I guess, and too much whiskey."

Katie's eyes narrowed. "What does that spoiled little bitch have to do with this? I'd heard ya were sparkin' on her, but I didn't believe it. Figured ya had more sense than that."

Beau raised his eyebrows and tried not to smile. Katie was not one to mince words. A man always knew where he stood with her. It was one of the many things he liked about the gregarious saloonkeeper.

"You probably know that her father hosted a small gathering last night, before the grand ball at the hotel."

Katie nodded. Only the most elite of Laramie's small society circle had been invited to Richard Petrie's opulent mansion. She took a quick swallow of coffee. "I think my invitation got lost," she said with a smile.

Beau's lips curved. "I wish mine had been lost. I'm sorry I went."

"No offense, Beau, but how'd ya get invited? Your brother's spread isn't that big, and ya aren't some kind of big shot."

Beau bent one leg to rest the ankle on his other knee. "Petrie wants to buy Ambrose's land, though I've told him I'll not sell. And Madeline acts like she likes me, sometimes. Hell, Katie, I don't know." His head came up as he realized he had uttered a profanity. "My apologies, ma'am."

Katie waved her hand with a laugh. "Hell, Beau, I swear all the time. Don't worry yourself about it. But ya still haven't told me what that blackhearted woman did."

"Let's just say she made suggestions that she never planned on following through." Beau was uncomfortable with the topic. "Then I came here and drank too much, and when Alina refused me, I thought she was playing Madeline's game." He set his cup on the desk and looked at Katie. "I didn't hear you warn us away from her. I thought she was the most beautiful woman I'd ever seen." He paused. "I still do," he murmured.

"So Madeline played the tease and Alina paid for it," Katie commented dryly.

An embarrassed flush darkened Beau's face, but he said nothing.

"I don't need to remind ya to behave yourself when you're in my place from now on, do I, Beau?"

"No, ma'am," Beau answered stiffly. He stood. "I apologize to you, also. It won't happen again."

"Hell, I know it won't." Katie stifled a yawn as she pushed herself out of her chair. "Stay away from Madeline Petrie, Beau, for your own good. I'm telling ya, like I told your brother before ya, God rest his soul. Those blond curls and that bouncy body hide the soul of a viper."

Beau thought Katie's assessment of Madeline was severe, but all he said was, "Some of us are slow to learn."

He could not get the vision of flashing blue eyes and luxuriant black curls out of his mind. "Do you think Alina will allow me to call on her the next time I come to town?" he asked as he reached for his duster.

"I doubt it, honey. If I know Alina Gallagher at all, I know she's a determined and strong-willed woman. She don't strike me as the kind to easily change her mind, and her feelings toward ya were pretty clear. It's a damn shame."

Alina Gallagher. Now he knew her complete name! "Tell me about her, Katie," Beau pleaded.

Katie again tightened the belt of her dressing gown. "There's not much to tell. She's been working for me almost a month now, and she's a hard little worker. Damn smart with them ledger books, she is. Real helpful to Emerald, too, even if she don't know her way around a kitchen. She's willing to learn. Not a snob at all, though I think her upbringing was privileged. She won't say where she came from, or talk about her life. I think she's running from something, or someone. I do think the world of that gal." Katie had become pensive. She mentally shook herself. "I'm sure she don't want me talking about her."

Katie picked Beau's hat up from the sofa. There was a twinkle in her eye as she handed it to him. "I've always liked ya, Beau Parker. If I'da met ya when I was younger, I'da had a run at ya myself."

An affectionate smile lit Beau's tired face. "And I would have been pleased if you had caught me. I would have run real slow." He leaned forward and placed a soft kiss on her cheek. "Happy New Year, Miss Katie." He left, pulling the door closed behind him.

Katie sighed and pushed at her tousled hair. She needed more coffee. She loaded the used cups on the tray and picked it up, balancing it against one hip, then headed for the door.

"Alina, girl, I'm gonna have a talk with ya," she said to herself. "That is one hell of a man."

Chapter Four

Alina stepped out of Johnson's Mercantile and pulled her cloak more tightly around her. She clutched a parcel to her chest. Heavens, it was cold! All this because Katie had a craving for oyster stew! Alina was almost sorry she had volunteered to make the trip to the store for Emerald, but she would have felt worse if the old cook had gone herself. Alina had found it hard to believe fresh oysters were available in Laramie City. Mr. Johnson had explained that the oysters were shipped live from the East Coast, packed in barrels of ice and cornmeal, and that they fed off the meal as the ice melted. Amazing!

She pulled her hood over her head, then squinted as she started down the deserted street. The wind, combined with the sunlight glinting off the ground snow, made her eyes water. The Satin Slipper seemed far away. She trudged on.

It was the middle of February, over six weeks since the scene in the office. Katie's numerous attempts to defend Beau Parker exasperated Alina to no end, as did the fact that he seemed to haunt her. Memories plagued her, of the waltz, of the feel of his arms around her, of his eyes sparkling with humor or flashing with anger, of his lips on hers. She had finally asked Katie not to mention his name again, but she had not been as successful at silencing her own mind. The memory of Beau Parker continued to torment her.

Delilah was also causing trouble. She verbally attacked

Alina at every opportunity, when Katie or Emerald were not around. Alina sensed that the Satin Slipper was being divided into two camps: those who supported Delilah, and those who did not. It bothered her that she was contributing to a problem for Katie, even though she avoided Delilah and her friends whenever she could. She wondered, as she often had in the past weeks, if it was time to change her plans.

Perhaps it was time to move on, to backtrack to the East coast. She could stay with Jenny for a while in Philadelphia, then go on to Susannah's home in Charleston. Perhaps it was best to keep moving. The longer she stayed in one place, the better chance Cordelia and Donovan had of tracking her down. She had been lulled into a false sense of security here, thanks to Katie's friendship, but now the situation was getting awkward. If only Conor could be found, or her father returned! Alina said a silent prayer for both men as she burrowed her chin deeper into the muffler wrapped around her neck. It was as cold here as it was in Chicago in the winter!

"Miss Gallagher!"

Alina turned. A young man unknown to her was hurrying toward her. He repeated her name. She backed up warily as a powerful warning rushed through her. A nagging sense of foreboding had been with her all morning, and she now knew that it had something to do with this man approaching her. Suddenly, hard arms encircled her from behind and she was lifted off the ground.

"You didn't really think you could escape me, did you?"

Alina's heart jumped when she recognized Donovan Randall's gloating voice. She struggled against him and dropped her package as she twisted out of his grip. He lunged at her and caught one of her arms in a cruel hold before she could get away.

"You'll regret your little adventure, Cousin." Donovan pulled her along the boardwalk. Alina's hood fell back from her head as she tried to pry his fingers from her arm.

"Donovan, stop!" she cried. "You are hurting me!"

"Good God, Randall, there's no need to manhandle her!" The other man stepped in front of Donovan, forcing him to halt. Donovan moved his arm to Alina's waist and jerked her against his side. Her continued struggles were futile.

"Your services are no longer needed, Buchanan. Come by my mother's suite this afternoon and we'll have your payment. Now, get out of my way." He shoved the man with his free arm and would have moved forward again when a cold voice stopped him.

"Release the lady."

Donovan turned to find a tall man with furious eyes staring at him. "This is none of your affair, Mister, so I suggest you mind your own business," Donovan snarled.

In one swift move, Beau Parker grabbed Donovan's arm and twisted it away from Alina's body, then pulled her behind him. Relief and a strange joy filled her. She touched Beau's arm and peeked around him.

"I make it my business when I see a woman mistreated, especially when the lady in question is a friend of mine." Beau's voice was low and dangerous. "What's going on here?"

Donovan leaned against a post and held his aching arm, his florid features twisted in fury. "You'll regret this, cowboy!"

The other man came forward. "I'm Frank Buchanan, of the Pinkerton Detective Agency. This is Donovan Randall, who, with his mother, hired me to find this young woman." He glared at Donovan as he rubbed his hands together and blew on them. "He told me she was his cousin, and that she had been kidnapped."

"I am not his cousin," Alina said sharply. She moved to Beau's side. "And I was not kidnapped, as he well knows. I ran away!"

Donovan pushed away from the post. "I'm not going to stand out in this goddamned wind and argue with you. My mother is her legal guardian and awaits us at the hotel. She's been very concerned about her ward." He reached for Alina.

Beau knocked Donovan's arm away. "You don't seem to understand, Randall. Miss Gallagher does not wish to accompany you. And don't swear in front of her."

A throbbing rage roared through Donovan, but he was reluctant to push the cowboy. "I'm going to get the marshall. The law is on our side, Alina. You'll be sorry you defied us." He waved his arm. "Go wait in your saloon. I know where to find you." He stomped off. Frank Buchanan spread his hands apologetically, then followed Donovan.

Alina retrieved her parcel from the snowy boardwalk and faced Beau, her features pale. "I never thought I would be happy to see you, Mr. Parker." She shivered as she pulled her hood to cover her hair. "Thank you for your assistance."

Beau shook his head. "No thanks are needed, Miss Gallagher. May I escort you to the Satin Slipper?"

Alina nodded, her mood somber. "I would be grateful."

Beau took the package from her and offered his arm. She gripped it tightly. They did not speak. Alina appreciated his silence. Her heart still pounded and her stomach felt sick.

When they reached the saloon, Alina left Beau at the bar and went to the kitchen. She found Moses and Emerald at the long oak table, peeling potatoes. Alina handed Emerald the package of oysters and turned to Moses.

"Do you know where Katie is?" Alina pushed her hood back. Her face was waxen and her eyes had a hunted look about them.

"She be upstairs, Missy. Ah just took some wood up for her."

"Mr. Parker is with me and I don't want to take him to her room. Will you please get her?" Alina pulled off her gloves.

" 'Course Ah will, Miz Alina." He stood up. "Everthin' be all right?"

Alina shook her head in the negative, but did not explain. "We'll wait in the office." She disappeared through the swinging doors into the saloon. Moses and Emerald looked at each other in concern.

"Somethin' be terrible wrong, Emmy," Moses said as he passed her chair. Emerald nodded, her usually cheerful features clouded with worry.

Alina led Beau into Katie's office. She threw the muffler and gloves on the sofa, followed by her cape, then rubbed her cold hands together as she walked over to stare out the window. A heavy weight of dread and fear settled in her stomach. The Randalls had found her! For the first time in her life, Alina knew genuine terror and panic. She glanced over her shoulder at Beau. He was watching her, his handsome face filled with concern. The expression in his eyes warmed and confused her. She turned again to the window, surprised to realize that she was glad for his presence. He exuded strength and confidence, two attributes she desperately needed right now.

Beau eyed her for a minute longer, then set his hat down and took off his coat. He stirred the coals in the fireplace.

Katie rushed in. "What's wrong, girl?" she demanded as she closed the door. She was breathless from her flight down the stairs. Her eyes flew from the woman to the man. She wondered in the back of her mind why they were together.

Alina turned from the window. "I'm in trouble, Katie." She was trembling.

"Ah, honey, nothing can be that bad." Katie went to put an arm around Alina's shoulders. She glared at Beau in passing, but he shook his head. The problem was not him, then. Katie was glad of that. She led Alina to one of the chairs facing the fire and sat on the edge of the other as she took the younger woman's hands in her own. "Now tell us."

"I fled a serious situation at home." Alina's voice was flat and spiritless. "It is a long and dreary tale, but suffice it to say that those I sought to escape have found me. I do not know what to do."

"Who are they, honey?" Katie squeezed her hands.

"Distant relatives, if they can be called that, who wish to control my father's estate, and me with it."

"How distant?" Beau asked.

"Cordelia Randall was married to my father's brother when she was very young. Uncle Bruce died not long after the wedding. Cordelia later married a man named Randall, who was Donovan's father. He died, also, and left his family in desperate straits. My father took Cordelia and Donovan in, and has supported them ever since."

"That's pretty distant," Beau commented.

Katie's fingers tightened on Alina's hands. "What of your family? Is there anybody ya can turn to?"

Alina shook her head. "My mother is dead, both of my brothers are dead, my father is on an extended voyage, and my Aunt Elizabeth is with her dying cousin in San Francisco." Alina sighed. "Actually, Elizabeth is my mother's aunt. She's my great-aunt. I have a cousin, a true cousin, but my father's solicitor has not been able to locate him." She pulled her hands from Katie's grasp and hid her face. "Listen to me ramble on! There is no one! What am I to do?"

A knock sounded at the door. Alina's head came up, her eyes wide with fear. Again, she was grateful for Beau's presence. He strode to the door and opened it to reveal Deputy Sam Trudeau, who stood with his hat in his hands. Alina was relieved to see that the man was alone.

"How do, Beau," said the deputy. "I wondered if it was you that arrogant jackass was talking about."

"Sam." Beau stepped back to allow the lawman to enter, then closed the door. They shook hands. Sam Trudeau was not quite as tall as Beau, but he was as lean. He was an attractive man with thinning brown hair and laugh lines around his eyes. He had just passed his fortieth birthday, and had been in law enforcement for most of his adult life. There were times he did not enjoy his job, and he knew this was going to be one of them.

"Miss Gallagher, this is Sam Trudeau, the deputy marshall." Beau made the introductions. "Miss Alina Gallagher, Sam."

Sam and Alina nodded to each other, then Sam spoke. "I've just come from a meeting with Cordelia Randall and her son over at the Laramie Hotel. Are you acquainted with them?"

"Yes, sir," Alina whispered.

"Mrs. Randall informed me that she is your legal guardian. Is that true?"

Alina closed her eyes. "Yes, sir," she repeated.

Sam glanced at Beau, then Katie. He twisted his hat. "Mrs. Randall wants you to accompany her and her son back to Chicago. As your guardian, she has the right to insist, and I have the obligation to ensure your cooperation." He watched Alina's pale face with sympathy.

"I cannot go back." Alina's words were barely audible.

"I'm sorry, Miss, what did you say?" Sam leaned forward.

Alina opened her eyes and looked at him. "I said, I cannot go back." Her voice was now clear and strong.

Sam sighed. "Please don't make this more difficult. Mrs. Randall is acting within the confines of the law."

Alina came to her feet. "You do not understand, Deputy." Two red spots had appeared on her white cheeks. "My safety will be endangered if I go back." She looked at Katie, her eyes huge and pleading. "Help me get out of town," she begged. "Get me on the train to California, to my aunt. I have my ticket." She turned to the deputy. "Look the other way for just a while, and I will be gone. I implore you, sir."

Sam shook his head with regret. "I can't do that, Miss."

"Calm down, now, honey, and tell us why ya think you're in danger." Katie's voice was soothing.

Alina walked around the chair. "They want me to marry Donovan, and he has threatened me with physical violence if I do not agree."

"If all he's done is threaten, Miss Gallagher, there's nothing I can do. It's not against the law to make threats."

"He accosted her on the street," Beau interjected brusquely from where he leaned against the wall.

Sam looked at him, then back to Alina. "Did he strike you?"

"No."

"Has he ever struck you?"

"No. At least not yet."

"Miss Gallagher, the man can't beat you and drag you to the altar, nor can Mrs. Randall force you to marry her son. Perhaps you're not keeping this in perspective."

"There is nothing wrong with my perspective, sir," Alina snapped, her eyes blazing like blue flames. "I am not a hysterical female. Mr. Randall has stated that he will force himself upon me and, if necessary, create a child, to ensure that I marry him. I believe him capable of such an act."

Katie gasped. Alina stepped toward the lawman, her hands clenched at her sides. "Listen carefully, Deputy. *I will not return with them.*"

Sam could not meet her burning eyes.

"Well, Sam, now what are ya going to do?" Katie stood up to face the unfortunate man. "Ya can't make her go back to that."

Sam threw his hat to the sofa and rubbed his eyes. "The westbound train is scheduled to leave at one-thirty."

"Oh, thank you, sir," Alina breathed as Katie hugged her.

"That will only put off the inevitable," Beau said. All eyes turned to him as he pushed away from the wall.

"What do you mean, Mr. Parker?" Alina demanded.

"I mean they will track you down again. They will find you, Alina, perhaps where you have no friends to help you." He did not notice that he had used her Christian name.

"This is the only chance I have," she said stubbornly.

"No, we have to think this out," Beau insisted. "This woman is your guardian until when?"

Alina turned from Katie to walk the floor. "That is what is so maddening. Her guardianship ends on my twenty-first birthday, which is in May. I need only a few months."

"Then you are free of her?" Beau asked.

"Not entirely. She is trustee of my father's estate until I reach twenty-five, I marry with her permission, or my father returns."

"Your father returns from where?" Sam queried.

Alina hesitated only a moment. "China," she answered. "It is hard to know when he will be home for sure, but he could be back at any time."

"He's been in touch with you, then?" the deputy asked.

Alina looked at the floor. "Not for a while."

"Does he know about your situation?" Sam persisted.

"No." Alina read the skeptical look on Sam's face. "I know he is alive, Deputy, and that he will come as soon as he can." Her voice held a note of desperation.

The other three looked at one another.

"Alina, honey, Beau might have a point here." Katie spoke with caution. "Even when that witch isn't your guardian any more, how can ya expect to protect yourself from Donovan? If he's ready to resort to rape, what would stop him from coming after ya anyway?"

"Aunt Elizabeth will help me," Alina answered, with more confidence than she felt. Her aunt would do all she could, but there was no way to know how successful Elizabeth would be. "She will force the judge to make her my guardian and trustee, which is how it should have been in the first place." She managed a tremulous smile. "Aunt Elizabeth is not a woman to be trifled with."

"That will take too long," Beau interrupted, his voice firm.

Alina whirled on him. "Well, I don't hear you coming up with any brilliant ideas!" She resumed her pacing.

No one spoke for a few minutes. Beau looked down at the floor and tucked his thumbs in his belt. Tumbled thoughts ran around in his head; of Alina in her robe, holding his gun, her hair falling to her waist, her splendid, angry eyes flashing at him; of the small ranch he had inherited from his brother, the small cabin he lived in; of his own uncertain and perhaps dangerous future. Then he thought of Donovan Randall and the cruel determination he had seen in that man's face. His jaw tightened. The brute would not have her. Beau raised his eyes and stared at Alina until she returned his gaze.

"Marry me," he said quietly.

Sam and Katie turned to him in astonishment. Alina was the first to find her voice.

"This is no time for jokes, Mr. Parker." Her hands were at her hips. "I have a serious problem here."

"I'm not joking, Miss Gallagher."

"Then you must be mad, sir!"

"Nor am I mad," Beau said calmly. "It's the perfect solution."

"Perfect for whom? Certainly not for me! You are no better than Donovan!"

"Now, Alina, that's not fair," Katie admonished. "I've never met this Donovan, but I know Beau's a hell of a lot better man. Let's hear him out."

Alina stared unbelieving at her friend, but the warning in Katie's eyes persuaded her to remain quiet. She sank into a chair and stared at her clasped hands resting in her lap.

Katie nodded at Beau.

"If we marry, the Randalls will have no power over her." Beau glanced at Alina. "I mean a marriage in name only, at least until her birthday, and perhaps until her father returns. Then the marriage can be annulled. Chances are they will give up on her, and if not, I can protect her."

"And who will protect me from you?" Alina retorted. She turned her face to Katie. "How can you even consider this? Have you forgotten what this man tried to do to me?"

"Alina, I'm tired of hearing about that," Katie snapped. "It's over and done with. The man made a mistake and has done all he knows to do to make it up to ya. Now he's offering to marry ya, to give ya his name and protection, and you're acting like a child. Maybe he oughta reconsider."

Alina was overwhelmed by a powerful sense of betrayal. She rose from the chair with hurt dignity and went to the window, where she stared at the winter landscape with unseeing eyes. Her thoughts raced. Where could she go? She would not have the element of surprise in her favor if she disappeared again. If she made it to the train, the weather could still halt her journey. Beau was right about having friends. If she got to California and her great-aunt, how could Elizabeth protect her from Donovan? Alina leaned her head against the window frame. *Like a rat in a cage,* she thought despairingly.

Katie watched the younger woman. "What do ya think, Sam?" she asked in a low voice.

Sam shrugged. "Seems to me Beau's willing to go to a lot of trouble for this woman and she doesn't even like him. But if she marries, she's no longer the responsibility of Cordelia Randall. It's probably the best choice, especially since there's just no time to plan anything else. They're waiting for her now. They want to catch the eastbound tonight."

Alina turned from the window. "I am confused by your sudden nobility, Mr. Parker. Why do you care what happens to me?" Her voice was cold and emotionless.

"I still feel obligated to you for my behavior that night." Beau glanced at Sam with some embarrassment, but the lawman only raised a curious eyebrow.

"So this is to ease your conscience." She crossed her arms.

"I guess that's part of it." Beau shifted his feet.

"Do you realize that if I marry without Cordelia's approval, I will be cut off from all financial support until my father returns or I come into my inheritance at twenty-five?"

Beau flushed. "I don't want a penny of your family's money," he growled. "I take care of my own."

"Make up your mind, girl," Katie said harshly. "It looks to me like Randall will have ya, sooner or later, or ya can have Beau here, for a while, anyway. Decide!"

Alina looked from Katie's angry face to Beau's neutral one, then her gaze quickly traveled over him. She noticed the easy grace with which he carried his tall, lean frame, even as he stood still. His thick hair curled around his collar in an annoyingly appealing way. She met his eyes but could not bear the intensity she saw there, and closed her own. *Beauregard Parker or Donovan Randall.* Was the choice really so difficult? Her heart pounded. What was it about Beau Parker that frightened her? Her eyes flew open and she stared at him, resentful that she had to choose at all. But she did have to choose, and the choice was not difficult. After a moment she spoke. *"In name only."*

"Agreed," answered Beau, "but only we four will know that." He saw the instant suspicion on Alina's drawn face. "Otherwise, your guardian can have the marriage annulled, Alina. You have to trust me."

"No, Mr. Parker, I do not." She looked at Katie. "Send for the preacher." She marched from the room, her head held high.

Katie stared after Alina as if she did not know her. "I'm not sure that I don't feel sorry for ya, Beau," she said as she went out the door.

Beau ran a hand over his hair. "Well, Sam, will you stand up with me?" At Sam's nod, Beau reached for his coat. "I've got to go to the mercantile, then to the livery for the wagon. I'll be back shortly." He was gone.

Sam spied a decanter on a side table in the corner. It was early, but a brandy was in order. He sloshed some of the liquid into a crystal tumbler and took a seat by the fire.

"Miz Kate tol' me everythin'," Emerald announced as she entered Alina's room. Her white teeth sparkled in her dark face. "My Moses went for the justice of the peace, and Ah come to help yo' get ready. My, my, a weddin'! This worked out jus' fine!"

"Worked out fine, Emerald? I feel like I'm jumping from the frying pan into the fire!" Alina paced the floor.

"Don't yo' be silly, Miz 'Lina. Ah heared jus' good things 'bout Mr. Parker. Miz Kate wouldn't set yo' up with someone bad. 'Sides, it seems to me that other man is who to stay shy of. Land sakes, yo' hair is a sight! Turn 'round here and let me brush it out." Emerald chuckled as she pulled the pins from Alina's hair. "Somebody gonna be real unhappy 'bout this, though."

"You mean besides me?" Alina asked forlornly.

"Ah means Madeline Petrie. Mr. Parker, he been seein' her last fall, serious-like. 'Course, winter's been bad, so he ain't been to town much. Set yo'self in this here rockin' chair so's Ah can pin this back up. Yo' have such pretty hair, Miz 'Lina."

"Well, she can have him, whoever she is."

"Madeline Petrie be the daughter of the richest land-owner in these parts. Ol' Richard Petrie owns most the valley, and he just keep buyin' up mo'. Miz Madeline, she used to gettin' her own way. Wish Ah could see her face when she finds out. There. Yo' hair all fixed now."

Alina stood and smoothed the skirt of her plaid wool dress. Emerald placed her hands on her hips and eyed the simple garment with skepticism. The dark greens and blues complemented Alina's coloring, but the dress was plain. The high neckline and long straight sleeves did nothing to show off her figure to advantage. Why, the girl wasn't even wearing a bustle!

"Yo' ain't gonna marry in that ol' dress."

"There's no time to change, Emerald," Alina said firmly. "This will do. Mr. Parker is not dressed up, either."

Emerald shook her head. "Ah helped yo' make that dress, and Ah knows there be plenty o' room under that skirt for a small bustle. Yo' get it out here this minute." Alina knew better than to argue with Emerald when she was in such a mood. She rolled her eyes, but pulled the bustle from a drawer and handed it to the cook, then lifted her skirt.

"If'n yo'd wear a corset, Ah'd have somethin' to attach this to," Emerald complained as she struggled to tie the laces.

"Please don't make it so tight!" Alina was short of breath,

as well as patience. "My papa says corsets are unhealthy, and I say they are uncomfortable!"

Emerald adjusted the position of the bustle and pulled the skirt back into place. "Yo' is just lucky yo' doan need one, Missy," she retorted. She stepped back to examine her handiwork. "That's better. Now, put a lace collar on yo' neck, and yo' mama's cameo brooch'll look real nice. This be yo' weddin' day, for heaven's sake. And wash yo' face and pinch them cheeks, 'cause yo' is too pale, even for a white girl."

Alina did as she was told. When her face was scrubbed, she moved to the dressing table and looked in the mirror. Emerald had arranged her hair in a becoming style. Her features were now pink, her eyes huge and haunted. She had never given it much thought, but this was not how she had imagined her wedding day would be. Her gaze fell on the pictures of her parents and tears came to her eyes. "I'm really scared, Papa," she whispered. "But I don't know what else to do."

"What'd yo' say, child?"

Alina blinked rapidly and brushed at her eyes. "Nothing, Emerald." She dabbed rose water on her forehead and on the back of her neck, and rubbed a little into her hands. "Let's get this over with."

Chapter Five

The ceremony conducted by the thin, red-nosed justice of the peace took only a few minutes. Alina held herself stiff and erect, refusing to meet Beau's eyes. His responses were spoken in a strong, clear voice; she was surprised when he slipped a narrow gold band on her finger. She stared at her hand and wondered where he'd gotten the ring. Her own answers to the justice's questions were spoken with reluctance. Love, honor, and obey? Although the reasons for the marriage were understood, she was deeply disturbed to make the sacred vows with no intention of honoring them.

Did it bother Beau? The words "You may kiss your bride" penetrated her thoughts. Beau's hand was at her waist. He bent and placed a gentle kiss on her unresponsive lips. It was done. The documents were signed, the justice left, and Katie opened a bottle of champagne. Alina wanted no part of the little celebration, but the silent admonition on Katie's face convinced her to accept a glass.

"To the bride and groom." Katie held her champagne high.

"Here, here," Emerald chimed in.

Alina took a sip and set her glass on the desk. "What now?"

"We talked it over while ya was upstairs," Katie replied. "Sam'll head on over to the hotel and tell the Randalls you'll be along shortly. He's not gonna say anything about the wedding. We'll let ya tell them yourself." She emptied her glass. "Ya go on upstairs and pack your things."

"Pack?"

"Ya got to go live with your man, Alina. Did ya think to stay here?" Katie's tone was impatient.

"No, I guess not. I didn't think about it." Alina hesitated. "What about my job? Who will keep your books?"

"Ya got all me caught up. I'll get along. When ya come to town, ya can check and see how I'm doing. But ya gotta go to the ranch, girl, or she'll have the marriage annulled. Surely ya see that."

Alina's shoulders sagged. "Just don't call him my man," she muttered.

Katie ignored her remark. "Get on upstairs. Beau here will help ya."

Without another word, Alina left. Beau drained his glass and followed her to her room. He closed the door and locked it, then drew the curtains.

Alina's stomach twisted. "What are you doing?"

"Making sure we won't be disturbed for a while." He read the fear and distrust in her eyes. He sighed. "I'll keep my word, Alina. I'll not touch you. What do you have to do?"

She tried to hide her relief. "Just pack. There's not much. It won't take long."

"Is there anything I can do to help?"

"No." Alina pulled her clothes off the hooks along the wall and threw them on the bed. Beau sat quietly in the rocker and watched her. The room, and the woman, brought back memories of New Year's Eve. It seemed like a long time ago.

One by one, Alina emptied the drawers. She paused when she opened the last drawer. The blue ballgown rested there, wrapped in tissue. She bit her lip. What to do with Katie's lovely Christmas gift? Only pain was associated with it now. Alina slammed the drawer closed. She wouldn't need the dress while living on a ranch.

She began to fold the garments, then hesitated when she

came upon her dove-gray traveling suit. It was much warmer than the dress she wore.

"Please leave the room, Mr. Parker. I want to change. I'll call you when I am ready."

"I'll turn my back."

"I insist that you leave!"

Beau turned the chair to the corner. He did not respond.

Alina whirled in frustration. She could not undress with a man in the room, especially *that* man! After a moment, she glanced over her shoulder; he still faced the corner. Biting her lip, she quickly undid the buttons down her back and pulled the dress off over her head. It was a struggle to loosen Emerald's knot on the bustle strings, but at last it came free. She defiantly threw the bustle into the open trunk, then hurried into a high-collared white flannel blouse and shook the wrinkles out of the lined wool skirt. She settled the skirt over her hips and fastened the waist buttons. The brooch was again pinned at her throat, and she tucked back a few strands of hair that had come loose.

"May I turn around now?" Beau asked politely.

How did he know she was finished? "Yes, Mr. Parker, you may." Alina's tone was sharp. When all the clothes were packed, she reached for the items on the dressing table. The room was silent until she closed the trunk lid and secured the latch. "I'm ready," she announced.

He eyed the trunk and the single hatbox that sat next to it. "Is that all you have?"

"I did not bring much with me. I had little time to plan my escape from Chicago, and I did not want to draw attention by emptying my closets." For some reason his question irritated her. "Can we go now?"

"We have to wait awhile." Beau continued to rock.

"Why?"

"It's too soon to go, Alina. Please trust me."

"You keep saying that, Mr. Parker," she snapped. "This is a business relationship, nothing more."

"I'm well aware of that. But it is important to trust one's business partner, is it not?"

Alina did not answer. She sat on the edge of the bed, her hands in her lap. She twisted the ring. "This was not necessary," she said after a moment.

Beau shrugged. "The ring will make the marriage more convincing."

"Where did you get it?"

"At the mercantile. I stopped there on the way to the livery." He hesitated. "Does it fit?"

"It is rather loose," Alina admitted.

"Bert told me we could exchange it. I need to get my supplies before we leave, so we'll take care of it then."

Alina nodded, and they lapsed into an uncomfortable silence. After several minutes Beau cleared his throat.

"You left Chicago to escape a forced marriage to a man who threatened you, and now here you are, forced to wed another man who at one time also threatened you."

Alina raised her eyes to his, surprised at his perception and train of thought. "Yes."

"It must be very difficult."

"It is. It is also infuriating. Had I been born male, there would have been none of this trouble." She clenched her hands into fists. "I am just as intelligent as any man, just as capable, but because I am a woman, society and the law have decided that I cannot handle my own affairs."

"I would say you are more competent than most men I know," Beau commented. "And I, for one, am glad you are a woman."

"Don't start your blarney with me, Mr. Parker," Alina warned. "I repeat, this is a business arrangement. Please do not forget that."

"No, ma'am." Beau's smile was forced. "I'm certain you won't let me forget it. But since I am now your husband, at least in appearance, I suggest you get used to calling me by my given name."

She did not respond. After a few more minutes of awkward silence, she spoke. "Where in Virginia are you from?"

Beau seemed surprised by her question. "Louden County," he answered. "West of Washington, about fifty miles. My family has a plantation near Middleburg."

Alina cocked an eyebrow, genuinely curious now. "Whatever brought you to Wyoming Territory?"

He shrugged. "My older brother homesteaded here. I came out and decided to stay for a while."

"Don't you miss Virginia? It is so green and beautiful there, especially compared to here!"

"No. Memories of the war are still too fresh."

Alina sobered at the mention of the war. "I guess they would be. But what of your family?"

"My mother and my younger brother are all that's left. I do miss them," Beau admitted. "My father died before the war." He glanced toward the curtained window. "I've always been thankful he didn't live to see his country torn apart."

Alina nodded, twisting her hands. "I miss my family dreadfully, too," she said softly. "But unlike you, I cannot wait to go home."

Beau looked at her, a strange, guarded smile on his face. "Then we'll hope your father returns soon." Alina was startled by the bitterness in his voice. He stood up. "We can go now."

Alina slipped into the tailored gray redingote and reached for the hatbox. She buttoned the redingote with one hand as she left the room. Beau shouldered the heavy trunk and followed her down to the saloon. Some of the women, including Delilah, were seated at a table near the stove, involved in a game of cards. A few customers leaned against the bar, and Jake was drying glasses. It seemed he was always drying glasses, Alina thought idly.

Beau returned from loading the trunk and the hatbox in the wagon out front, blowing on his hands. He thanked Emerald as she gave him his duster. He slipped into it, then held Alina's cloak for her. She nodded her thanks and tied the neck strings. She heard a noise and looked up the stairs. Her mouth fell open.

Katie slowly descended, her bearing majestic. She was dressed in opulent, almost gaudy finery. Her bright red walking dress sported a huge bustle in back, and was cut daringly low in front, so low that her generous bosom seemed in danger of escaping. The gown was decorated with black lace and fringe and she wore black gloves. A jaunty little hat perched on her burnished curls, highlighted with two red ostrich feathers that bounced with every movement. Her lips and cheeks were lightly painted, and her eyes sparkled with humor. She reached the saloon floor and executed a slow pirouette. Not a sound was heard.

"Well, what do ya think?" she demanded.

Alina gulped and glanced at Beau. He seemed as much at a loss for words as she was. He blinked.

"You look, uh, stunning, Miss Katie," he managed to say. Alina could only nod.

"Oh, get on with ya, Beau!" Katie cried. "I look overblown and overdone, like a madam, which is what I want! If ya don't mind, I'd like to tag along and have me some fun with this snooty witch that's trying to hurt my girl here!"

Alina covered her mouth with her hand, but a giggle escaped anyway. "You will certainly get their attention."

Katie sobered. "Do ya think it's too much, girl? I don't want to embarrass ya, but they just make me so damn mad!"

Alina went to her friend, her hands held out. "You could never embarrass me." Katie took Alina's hands and knew all was well between them again.

"Everything will be just fine, honey," she whispered as Emerald threw a cloak over her shoulders. "I promise, ya needn't fear Beau."

Alina nodded, but her stomach tightened. *We'll see.*

Katie eyed Alina's travel suit. She raised her eyebrows and looked at Beau, then back to Alina. "Ya changed?"

Alina blushed. "This is much warmer, Katie. I thought with the wagon trip and all . . ." her voice trailed away.

Katie nodded wisely. "Of course, honey." Her eyes twinkled.

"If you are ready, ladies, I suggest we go." Beau held the door open, then followed the two women outside. He offered an arm to each lady. "I swear, I am the luckiest man in the world," he declared, as they set off down the street.

The day had warmed a little. Katie and Beau chatted, but Alina's thoughts were elsewhere. Her feelings were a confusing mix of relief and trepidation. The knowledge that the Randalls could not hurt her now was elating. The fear and worry of the past two months were gone, but new and different fears had replaced them, all centered on the man who walked beside her. *Her husband.* She felt again the strange excitement she was beginning to associate with Beauregard Parker. She glanced at him from the corner of her eye. He looked like a simple cowboy, but she now knew he was much more. As she had suspected, he came from a privileged background, and she would bet he had fought in the war. It did not matter to her, but she wondered if he had fought for the Union or the Confederacy.

He was telling Katie about someone he called Pike. They both laughed at one of his statements. He had a nice laugh, Alina decided, then silently scolded herself. Too much about him was nice; his eyes, his body, his voice, his strength, and now his laugh. She shook her head and forced herself to remember every detail of that night in her room with him, to remember how frightened she had been. Perhaps it had been easy to chose Beauregard over Donovan, but that did not mean he posed no threat to her. Her fingers tightened involuntarily on his arm at the thought. She did not notice Beau look down at her with curiosity.

They entered the plush lobby of the Laramie Hotel. Katie patted her hair and ignored the stares of the people in the room.

"I'll check with the clerk," Beau said, but before he could move, Frank Buchanan came up to them, holding his bowler hat in his hands.

"Miss Gallagher, may I please speak to you for a moment?" He eyed Beau with some nervousness.

"Of course, Mr. Buchanan. I would like to present my friend, Miss Katie Davenport, and you are already acquainted with Mr. Beauregard Parker. Katie, this is Frank Buchanan, of the Pinkerton Detective Agency."

"Ma'am." Frank nodded respectfully to Katie and held his hand out to Beau. "I prefer meeting you under these circumstances, Mr. Parker."

"I agree, Mr. Buchanan." The men shook hands. Buchanan turned to Alina.

"I want to apologize to you, Miss Gallagher. I was appalled by Randall's treatment of you on the street this morning. I only recently learned some of the truth regarding your flight from Chicago, when Mrs. Randall explained the situation to the deputy. Had I known the true circumstances, and the true character of Mr. Randall, I never would have accepted this case." His expression was sincere and remorseful.

"You had no way of knowing, Mr. Buchanan. Please do not trouble yourself."

"I will never forgive myself for leading that madman to you," he stated flatly. "Is there any way I can help you now?"

"All is well, sir," she assured him. "Mr. Parker and I were just married. The Randalls no longer have any power over me."

Buchanan looked from Alina to Beau. "Married? Oh, that is capital!" He pumped Beau's hand with vigor. "Congratulations, sir! And to you, ma'am! Are you going to tell them now?"

Beau nodded. "Do you know which room is theirs?"

"Second floor, around the corner to the left. Suite 201. The deputy is with them." Frank noticed Alina's cloak. "Leave your coats with me," he suggested. "I'll wait over there." He pointed across the lobby to a chair that sat next to a potted palm. "I would be most anxious to learn how this meeting goes, if you won't mind telling me."

Alina handed him her cape. "We should not be long."

They followed Buchanan's directions to Cordelia's suite. Donovan answered Beau's knock.

"It's about time," he snarled. "You better have your things with you. We're leaving on the evening train." He made a move to grab Alina's arm, then noticed Beau's forbidding face. His hand fell to his side. "Get in here," he ordered.

Her heart pounding, Alina walked past him. Donovan looked down his nose and started to close the door in Katie's face, but Beau pushed it back open.

"We're coming in, Randall."

Donovan stood his ground. "You will not bring that woman," he pointed at Katie, "into my mother's presence."

"Now, Donovan, don't be rude," Alina scolded as she came to take Katie's arm. "Katie is as much a lady as your mother is, and she is also a *very* dear friend of mine. I'm sure Cordelia would *love* to meet her!"

Donovan sputtered as Katie sailed past him, followed by Beau. He could do nothing but close the door.

Arm in arm, Alina and Katie swept around the corner into an elegant sitting room. Cordelia waited on an overstuffed camelback sofa, her hands folded in her lap. Her eyes glittered with triumph and fury. Not a hair was out of place, and her costly silk gown shimmered in the sunlight that streamed through the window. Sam Trudeau stood by the fireplace, absorbing the warmth from the roaring flames.

Katie sauntered around the room with her hands on her hips. "Just look at this place. Alina, honey, Mrs. Randall here sure likes spending your papa's money. Howdy, Sam."

Sam tried to keep a smile from his face as he nodded at Katie. He was not entirely successful.

Cordelia flushed. "Who is this creature, Alina? I want her out of here!"

Beau led Alina to a chair. "Forgive me, Cordelia," she said sweetly as she arranged her skirts. "Where are my manners? I am pleased to present Miss Katie Davenport, owner of the Satin Slipper Saloon and Dance Emporium, where I have been employed of late. She has become one of my closest friends. Katie, dear, this is Cordelia Randall, my former aunt-by-marriage. The sullen man over there by the window is her son, Donovan Randall."

"Charmed, I'm sure," Katie said with a wide grin. She nodded to Cordelia, then Donovan; the red feathers danced. "Alina has told me *all* about ya'll, and I do mean *all.*" Katie settled into a chair near Sam and fussed with her neckline. "Say, ya don't have anything to drink, do ya?"

Cordelia glared at Alina with a look that promised revenge. Alina smiled up at Beau as he came to stand beside her. "And this," she said softly, "is Mr. Beauregard Parker. Beau, this is Cordelia Randall, and you have already met Donovan."

Beau nodded at Cordelia, but did not say anything. The room fell into silence.

Cordelia looked at the handsome cowboy with disdain. He was tall and lean, dressed in boots and denim and a white shirt. He wore a leather vest with a blue bandana knotted at his neck. His dark hair was clean and combed, his thick mustache neatly trimmed. A gunbelt was strapped low on his narrow hips. He watched her with irritatingly confident brown eyes.

She cleared her throat. "It was very nice to meet your friends, Alina, but I'm afraid we must prepare for our journey. Say your farewells and show them out." She stood up. "Thank you for your help, Deputy. I find it unfortunate that you had to be drawn into our domestic affairs."

"Cordelia," Alina interjected. "I have indeed come to say my farewells, but to you and Donovan, for I shall not be returning to Chicago."

Cordelia whirled. "I will tolerate no more of this nonsense, Alina! Deputy Trudeau has explained the legalities to you. I am your guardian, and you will do as I say!"

"But you are not my guardian, Cordelia, not any longer," Alina corrected calmly. She rose to stand next to Beau.

"When I introduced Mr. Parker, perhaps I forgot to mention that he is my husband." She slipped her hand into his, and he looked down at her in a loving manner. She was startled by the warmth in his eyes. His fingers tightened on hers.

Cordelia stared at them. Donovan started forward.

"What the hell are you talking about?" he bellowed. "You are mine!"

"Never!" Alina vowed. Beau kept hold of her hand and his other arm encircled her waist.

"You . . . are . . . *mine!*" Donovan's eyes bulged from his mottled face as he stormed to the center of the room.

"Shut up!" Cordelia screamed, her hands at her temples. For an instant, her gaze fell on Katie's face, which was covered with a smug, satisfied smile.

Cordelia turned on Alina and Beau. "I don't believe it!"

"Oh, we are wed, Mrs. Randall," Beau assured her. He brought Alina's left hand to his lips for a kiss, then held it out. The simple gold ring twinkled in the light. "A little over an hour ago. Actually, I have your son to thank for my bride. If not for him, I would've had to wait awhile longer. It's all legal, and I have the marriage certificate as proof." He patted his shirt pocket.

"I demand to see it this instant!"

Katie jumped out of her chair. "Let me show her, Beau. I wanna show where I signed." She took the paper from him. "See? Me and Sam were the witnesses. Right there." She pointed as she waved the document in Cordelia's face. She sighed. "It was a lovely ceremony. Brought tears to my eyes. Too bad ya'll weren't there." She folded the paper and returned it to Beau.

Cordelia turned to the deputy. "Is this true?"

Sam nodded. "Yes, ma'am. And legal."

She advanced on him. "How could you allow this?"

"I had no grounds to stop it, Mrs. Randall. It's not illegal to wed. I told them you wouldn't like it, but you know how love is." He spread his hands helplessly.

"I am her guardian!"

"She's over eighteen, ma'am."

"Why didn't you tell me?" Cordelia's voice had risen again to a scream.

"It wasn't my place, ma'am." Sam's tone was firm.

Cordelia stalked back and forth. Suddenly she stopped. "I'll have this ridiculous marriage annulled."

"On what grounds?" Sam demanded.

"On the grounds that my ward married without my permission and that the marriage has not been consummated," Cordelia answered triumphantly.

Beau spoke. "Excuse me, Mrs. Randall, but Alina doesn't need your permission to marry, and as I said before, the ceremony took place over an hour ago." He paused; a lazy smile curved his lips as his hand moved up and down Alina's arm in a slow caress. "Where do you think we have been since then?"

Alina blushed a deep red as all eyes turned to them. Now she understood why he had insisted they wait in her room. The fact that she had changed her outfit, as innocent as it was, had aided in the deception. Not even Katie knew for certain that nothing had happened between them. She was deeply embarrassed by his insinuation, and at the same time she felt a grudging admiration for his cleverness.

Cordelia sank onto the sofa, speechless.

"You *slut!*" Donovan advanced toward Alina. "You refused me, thought yourself too good for me, and while we waited here, you were lying with this . . . this goddamned *cowboy?*" Spittle flew from his lips.

In one smooth movement, Beau stepped away from Alina and his fist connected with Donovan's jaw, knocking him to the floor. "If you ever address my wife by anything but her name again, I swear, Randall, I'll tear your head off!" His hands clenched and unclenched at his sides. "Her name is Parker now." He emphasized each word. "Mrs. Beauregard Parker. And I warned you about the profanity."

Donovan glared at the enraged man standing over him. He touched his throbbing jaw and silently swore that

Beauregard Parker would die one day for this insult. His hate-filled eyes fell on Alina. He would have his revenge on her, too.

Cordelia appeared to be unconcerned about her son's injury. "Do you know, Mr. Parker, that Alina's family is quite wealthy?"

"I know," Beau snapped as he returned to Alina's side.

"Because she married without my approval or permission, do you also know that she will not have one cent from her father's estate until she turns twenty-five, over four years from now?"

"I know," he repeated with impatience.

"I am prepared to offer you a great deal of money if you will end this farce of a marriage immediately."

Alina's eyes widened with dismay. She glanced uncertainly up at Beau's impassive face.

Cordelia continued. "I don't believe you have tender feelings for my ward, nor she for you. Perhaps you've acted out of some misguided sense of chivalry." She eyed his clothing. "I doubt you have the means to support a wife, at least in the style to which Alina is accustomed. I also doubt her ability to make you the kind of wife you need. Somehow, I cannot envision her cooking and cleaning, or," her lip curled in derision, "carrying your screaming brat around on her hip. Be practical, Mr. Parker." Her tone became harsh. "The situation between Alina, my son, and myself is none of your business, and I resent your interference. I believe it would be in your best interests to reconsider your impulsive act. Take the money, and let us all get on with our lives."

The air was thick with tension. Donovan struggled to his feet and stood next to his mother.

After a long moment, Beau spoke. "I'm curious, Mrs. Randall. Since you bring up the subject of children, what if, as a result of our union this afternoon, Alina already carries my child?" His voice was deceptively soft. Donovan choked in frustrated fury. Alina blushed again and stared at the rug, wondering why Beau would ask such a question when there was no possibility that a child had been conceived. She also wondered why the idea of someday carrying his child was not distasteful.

Cordelia shrugged. "There are ways to be rid of an unwanted child, before or after birth."

Beau's grip on Alina's arm tightened. She raised her eyes to his face. A muscle in his cheek twitched as he clenched his teeth, and she hoped he never had cause to look at her with such rage. She trembled. Beau glanced down at her and relaxed his fingers, rubbing her arm apologetically.

"It is you who are misguided, Mrs. Randall." His tone was low and dangerous. "You are also beneath contempt. Your offer is insulting to both Alina and me, and I think it best we leave, before I forget that you are a woman." He took his hat from the table next to Alina's chair and guided her toward the door. Katie and Sam moved in the same direction.

Beau stopped and faced Cordelia and Donovan. "Alina has told me all the two of you have done. Mark my words. Stay away from her. She is my wife now. If you dance with her, you dance with me, and I guarantee you won't like the tune."

He followed Alina out the door.

"It sure was nice meeting ya'll," Katie called brightly, as she stepped into the hall. "Sam, honey, are ya coming?"

Sam took his hat and coat from a hook near the entryway. "The Eastbound Express is scheduled to leave at seven-thirty tonight. In view of Mr. Randall's threats concerning Mrs. Parker, it would be best if you both were on that train. Good day." He closed the door behind him.

As they walked down the hall, Katie let out a whoop of laughter. "I wouldn't have missed this for anything!" she cried. "Sam, come back to the Slipper with us! Drinks are on me!"

Sam smiled. "I'd like to, Kate, but I have a meeting with Mr. Ivinson, over at the bank. I'll come later, maybe for some supper, if you can sweet-talk Emerald into cooking for me."

They descended the carpeted stairs into the lobby. Frank Buchanan rose from his chair. "How did it go?" he asked eagerly.

"They were not pleased, Mr. Buchanan, but there was nothing they could do." Alina felt shaky and weak.

"Beau here nailed Randall right in the chops," Katie announced happily. "It was a wonderful sight to see. I wanted to hit that Cordelia. She is nasty! Say, Frank, come on over to the saloon with us."

Buchanan shook his head as he held Katie's wrap for her. "Thank you, Miss Davenport, but I'm going to try catch the 12:35 freight to Cheyenne. I need to get back to Chicago." He turned to Alina. "I'm relieved all has turned out so well. I hope you can forgive my part in this mess."

"There is nothing to forgive, Mr. Buchanan," replied Alina.

Beau settled her cloak around her shoulders and held his hand out to Buchanan. "Have a safe trip."

"Thank you, Mr. Parker, and again, my congratulations. You have a lovely wife."

Beau pulled his duster on. "I think so," he said with a grin. At Beau's words the color rose in Alina's cheeks. The party stepped outside.

"Deputy." Buchanan nodded at Sam and left.

Alina held her hand out to Sam. "I appreciate your help, Deputy Trudeau."

Sam took her hand. "It was my pleasure, Mrs. Parker. See you, Beau, and good luck to the two of you. Kate, I'll be by later." He touched the brim of his hat and walked off toward the bank.

Katie, Beau, and Alina turned in the opposite direction. No one spoke on the way back to the saloon. When they arrived, Beau checked the harnesses on the two horses that waited patiently with the farm wagon.

"Will ya have a bite before ya leave?" Katie invited hopefully.

"We can't tarry, Kate. Pike will already be wondering where I am. I don't want to worry him," Beau answered.

Disappointed, she turned to Alina. "Well, girl, come on in here out of the cold 'til he's ready and we'll have Emerald fix something for ya to take with ya." Katie ushered her silent friend through the saloon and into the kitchen. Now that the leavetaking was upon them, both women felt a sharp sadness.

They sat at the table while Emerald wrapped thick slices of bread and cheese in a clean cloth. She filled a jar with hot coffee and secured the lid. Moses placed two bricks that he pulled from the oven in a burlap bag.

Alina plucked at her skirt. "Should I explain what I've done in the ledger, Katie? I hate to leave on such short notice."

"Thanks, honey, but there's no time today. I think I'll show those figures to Sophie and see if she can make sense out of them. Her and Jake are all excited about each other all of a sudden, and he doesn't want her mingling too much with the customers any more." Katie rolled her eyes. "Love!"

Beau came in, stamping his feet. He looked at his new wife. "Are you ready?"

"Yes," she answered quietly.

They moved out into the saloon.

"Say your goodbyes while I get this contraption off my head," Katie ordered as she hurried up the stairs. "I'll be right back."

Alina went to the bar. "Thank you for all your kindness to me," she said to Jake.

"Ah, wasn't nothin', Miss Alina," he said shyly. "I'll miss you around here, but you married a good man. Congratulations."

I'm tired of everyone telling me he's a good man, Alina thought peevishly. "Thank you," she said. "And good luck to you and Sophie. I think you two are good for each other."

Jake nodded, his face suddenly touched with a pink tinge.

She turned to find that Delilah had left the card game and now stood beside her.

"What did you have to do to get the poor bastard to marry you?" she taunted in a low voice, so that only Alina could hear. "Did you just bat those big eyes at him and cry?"

"I have nothing to say to you." Alina turned away.

"I'm just glad you're leavin'," the other woman jeered.

"I won't miss you, either," Alina snapped over her shoulder.

Delilah laughed and walked around Alina. She moved close to Beau and put her hands on her hips as she insolently examined him from head to foot. "It's a shame she trapped you," she said, her voice silky. She shifted her shoulders so that her robe slipped down her arms and exposed her camisole. The garment stretched across her large breasts, and her dark nipples showed through the thin material. She passed the tip of her tongue over her lips. "When you get tired of bouncin' on her skinny bones, you remember me. I promise I'll make you forget all about her." She reached up and trailed a finger along Beau's jaw.

He flinched away from her touch. There was no expression on his face, but a slow anger built in his eyes. "I don't think so." His gaze fell on Alina. She stood tall and proud, her face flushed, her lips pressed in an angry line. He was struck again by her beauty, and by the underlying strength he sensed in her. "No one could make me forget her."

"We'll see, cowboy." Delilah turned to Alina, her expression contemptuous. "We'll see if you don't feel different when she's fat with your whelp, and after she's been workin' in the sun and the wind for a while. I've seen what ranch life does to a woman. She's not always gonna look like that." She sidled up next to Beau and slipped one hand inside his vest. "That's why all the boys like me so much. I know what a man wants."

Beau grabbed her errant hand and pushed her away. "You don't know what this man wants."

Delilah laughed again as she pulled her robe up on her

shoulders. "Time will tell, handsome. Just remember—I'm Delilah." She breathed her name, then laughed again as she sauntered back to her table.

Katie came down the stairs and jerked her head in Delilah's direction. "Is she causing trouble?"

"It doesn't matter anymore," Alina said through gritted teeth. "Maybe things will settle down for you now."

Katie snorted. "I'd rather it was her leaving. Here's your wages for this week." She closed Alina's fingers over the bills and her voice dropped to a whisper. "Take it. I know ya got some stashed away, but ya might need more. A woman should have her own money."

Alina swallowed her protest and smiled. She slipped the folded currency under the cuff of her jacket sleeve. "Thank you," she said softly.

Katie hooked her arm with Alina's as they walked outside, then enveloped her in a tight hug. "I'm gonna miss ya like the dickens, gal." She blinked rapidly. "But remember what I said. Beau's a good man, and he'll take care of ya, if ya'll let him."

"Thank you for everything, Katie." Alina's eyes filled. "You gave me a job when no one else would, and I meant what I said about you becoming my dear friend."

"Ah, hell, listen to us." Katie pulled a lacy handkerchief from her cleavage. "It's not like we'll never see each other again. Beau'll bring ya in." She dabbed at Alina's eyes with the dainty piece of cloth, then at her own, and muttered something about the "damn wind."

Alina hugged Moses, then turned to Emerald. "Thank you, too, Emerald. I will miss our mornings in the kitchen."

Emerald grabbed her in a hard embrace. "And Ah'll miss yo', child. Ah slipped somethin' in with that bread and cheese, somethin' yo'll be needin'." She released Alina and stepped back. "Yo' bring her by, Mr. Beau, or yo'll answer to me!"

Beau laughed. "Yes, ma'am!" he said as he helped Alina up onto the wagon seat. "I wouldn't want you mad at me."

His eyes softened when he turned to Katie. "Thank you, for more than I can say." He gave her a quick hug.

"Don't go gettin' all sweet on me, Beau Parker," Katie admonished. "Ya're a married man now. Ya just take good care of my girl there."

"I will," he promised. He climbed up next to Alina.

Moses came around the wagon and settled the burlap bag under her feet, then set the package of food on the seat and handed her the jar of coffee. "It'll keep yo' hands warm if yo' hold it."

"Thank you, Moses." Alina's voice was quiet and sad.

Beau took up the reins. "Keep your eyes and ears open, Kate. I don't think the Randalls will give up this easily."

"I'll watch, Beau. Sam will, too. Stay in touch. And bring Pike with ya next time."

Beau lifted his hand in acknowledgment, then slapped at the horses lightly with the reins.

Alina looked back over her shoulder. "Goodbye, Katie! I'll see you soon!"

The three on the porch waved, then hurried back into the warmth of the saloon. Alina faced forward again and pulled the hood of her cloak up over her head. She did not say anything until the wagon approached the mercantile.

"Why did you ask Cordelia what she would do if I was carrying your child?"

"I wanted to know how far she was prepared to go." Beau pulled the wagon to a stop in front of the store.

"She would have given you a lot of money."

Beau stared at her. "Like I told you, Alina, I don't want *any* money." He wrapped the reins around the brake stick and jumped to the boardwalk. "Did you think I would even consider her offer?"

Alina had the feeling her answer to Beau's question was very important to him. She shook her head. "No," she answered honestly. Beau nodded and held his hand up to her. He helped her down from the wagon and they entered the store.

"Howdy, Beau." Bert Johnson was a plump man of about thirty-five, with receding brown hair and a pair of spectacles that clung precariously to the end of his nose. He had friendly brown eyes, and an apron was tied at his neck and waist. "Your supplies are over there by the door." He looked at Alina with curiosity. "Do you need more oysters, ma'am?"

Alina shook her head.

"Bert, I'm proud to announce that Alina is my new wife." Beau was not surprised to realize that he genuinely was proud.

"Well, well, well!" Bert came around the counter and grabbed Beau's hand. "I didn't know you were going to use that ring so soon! Congratulations, Beau! Ma'am!"

"We need to exchange the ring. It's too big for her."

"It's a hard thing to judge, that's for sure. Well, come on over here and pick what you want." Bert led the way to a glass case that held an assortment of rings, pocketwatches, brooches, and ornamental hair combs. Alina handed the ring to him. He pushed at his glasses as he eyed her finger, then leaned over the case.

"Here." He selected an identical ring. "This is smaller. See if that will work." Bert gave the ring to Beau, who reached for Alina's hand and slipped the gold band on her finger.

"Is that better?" he asked. Alina pulled from his grasp and twisted the ring with her other hand.

"Yes." Her voice was a whisper.

Beau took her hand again, and without taking his eyes from her face, placed a gentle kiss on the ring. Her face warmed at the romantic gesture and she avoided his intense gaze. In addition to getting tired of everyone telling her what a good man Beauregard was, she was also getting tired of blushing.

"This one will do, Bert." Beau released her and moved to his stack of supplies. He picked up a sack of coffee beans and a tin of tobacco. "I'll load this, then settle with you. Get anything you want, Alina." He disappeared out the door.

Alina wandered about the store. There was nothing she wanted that she'd let him buy! He was acting like her husband! At the counter, she found a display of scented soaps. She picked up a bar and held it to her nose. It smelled of roses. She handed the bar to Bert.

"I'll take this." She pulled the money Katie had given her from her sleeve. Her eyes scanned the shelves against the wall. "And a tin of the British tea, if you please."

"Anything else, Mrs. Parker?"

"No, thank you." She held out a bill and wondered if she would ever get used to her new name.

"I'll just put this on your husband's account."

"I would prefer to pay for it myself," Alina said firmly as Beau came to her side.

Bert peered at Beau over his spectacles. Beau shrugged.

"Yes, ma'am." Bert took Alina's money and gave her the change. "Here's your statement, Beau." He handed Beau a slip of paper. "That includes the ring."

Beau pulled a wad of bills from his pocket and counted out the necessary amount. "Thanks, Bert. See you next trip."

"You bet. I wondered why you came all the way into town for those few supplies, especially with the snow. Now I know." He looked at Alina with a warm smile. "You're a lucky man." He followed them out the door.

"I am that," Beau agreed. He helped Alina into the wagon and climbed up next to her.

"Wait up there a minute, Beau," Bert ordered. He backed into the store and returned in a few minutes to give Beau a wrapped bundle. "Here's a little something for your wedding supper tonight, since Mrs. Parker won't get any of Emerald's stew. Don't let it freeze."

"Thanks, Bert. That was real nice of you."

"Yes, thank you, Mr. Johnson," Alina added as she tucked the heavy package under the lap robe.

"Congratulations again! Say hello to Pike for me!" Bert called as the wagon pulled away. Beau waved in farewell.

Neither of them spoke until they were on the outskirts of Laramie City. The snow-packed road led east across the prairie, toward distant, tree-covered hills.

"How long will it take to get to your ranch?" Alina asked in a small voice.

"Because of the snow, about two hours. We're on the Cheyenne Pass Road now." He pointed ahead. "The ranch is in the Black Hills."

Alina looked at him, suddenly concerned. "I thought the Black Hills belonged to the Indians."

"The Black Hills in Dakota Territory do. This is a different, much smaller range. Much closer, too," he added with a smile.

"Oh." Alina was relieved. After a moment she asked, "Do you have any neighbors?"

"Not many. Union Pacific land borders part of the ranch, as does a timber tract belonging to Richard Petrie, and then there's a homestead owned by a family named Freeman." He fell silent.

Alina pulled the muffler up over her mouth. The sound of a train whistle echoed across the frozen, windswept valley. How she wished she were on that train, wherever it was going! She glanced at the silent man next to her. His cheeks were red from the cold and his breath made a white cloud. He seemed to feel her observation of him, for he turned to her, his warm brown eyes intense and questioning. She dropped her gaze and twisted the ring on her finger through her glove. It felt strange to her. She sighed and squinted against the sunlight reflecting off the snow. It would be a long, cold trip to Beau Parker's ranch, and her new life.

Chapter Six

It seemed an eternity had passed before Alina felt the wagon finally stop. Her eyes were closed against the glare, her nose buried in her muffler, her hands and feet numb. She opened her eyes a crack; the wagon was parked in the shadow of a cabin. She lifted her head out of the muffler. Beau stood beside her.

"This is it." He held his hands out. "Let me help you down."

Alina fumbled with the lap robe and reached for his hands. When he set her on the ground, her stiff legs refused to hold her, and she fell against him. He put an arm around her shoulders to steady her. Again, she found his strength comforting.

"It's about damn time ya showed up, Beau." A querulous voice came from the direction of the cabin. "I feared I'd have ta set out and search for ya, and ya know these old bones of mine just don't like this damn cold . . ." The voice stopped abruptly.

Alina squinted toward the covered porch of the cabin. A man with a bushy gray beard and matching hair stood in front of the open door, his eyes wide with surprise. A blush covered his weathered cheeks.

"Beg your pardon, ma'am, for my cussin'. I didn't see ya there." He pulled his hanging suspenders up over his faded undershirt.

Alina managed a weak smile. Beau escorted her around the wagon and up to the porch.

"I know we've caught you by surprise, Pike," Beau said apologetically. "We're a little surprised ourselves." He pushed through the door and guided Alina toward a massive stone fireplace. Pike watched from the door while Beau pulled a chair from the table and set it close to the fire. "You just sit here and warm up, Alina. We'll be in directly, after we see to the horses and unload the wagon."

Alina nodded and pulled her cloak more tightly around her. Beau grabbed a coat from a hook by the door and tossed it to Pike, then closed the door behind them.

She huddled in the chair as warmth returned to her limbs. The ticking of a mantel clock on the stone shelf over the hearth and the crackling of the fire were the only sounds she could hear. She pushed her hood back and looked around. The room seemed small, the few pieces of furniture rough and old.

Alina stood and laid her gloves near the clock. A stack of books and a freestanding framed picture were the only other items on the stone mantel. She picked up the picture and bent to the firelight.

The formal family portrait showed a middle-aged woman seated on a chair, surrounded by two men and a boy. The two men were dressed in officers' uniforms of the Union Army; she recognized one of them as Beau. They were a handsome family.

She returned the picture to its place and eyed the rifle that rested on two large nails protruding from the stones of the chimney. It was an old flintlock Kentucky rifle, in excellent condition. She rubbed her hands together and was startled to rediscover the alien gold band.

Alina peeked through a door to the left of the fireplace. The long room held a narrow, unmade bed; a shirt hung on a nail by the door and other articles of clothing were strewn on the floor. She realized that the fireplace went through the wall and opened into this room as well. A pair of crutches leaned against the wall beside the bed, and an upended wooden crate held a coal-oil lamp and a book, upon which rested a pair of wire-rimmed spectacles.

She crossed the main room, her eyes on the kitchen, such as it was. A narrow counter was built along the wall, with dishes and pots stacked below. Shelves on either side of a curtainless window held supplies, while a short pump hunched over the tin sink embedded in the counter.

Alina's nose wrinkled appreciatively at the savory smell coming from a covered cast-iron pot on the new stove that stood between two doors on the back wall. Her stomach growled. The few bites of bread and cheese she had eaten earlier had not been enough to satisfy her for long.

She looked through the door to the left of the stove and found another bedroom. The double bed was pushed into the corner and neatly made up with two pillows and a comforter. A small table next to the headboard held a lamp, and an old dresser with a mirror rested against the far wall next to another naked window. She wondered which bedroom belonged to Beau, and which would be hers.

Alina backed away from the door and turned to the main room; despair washed over her. The primitive cabin was not filthy, but there were dirty dishes in the sink, a shirt was thrown over the arm of the faded sofa, and the floor needed a good sweep. There were no curtains at the windows, no rugs on the floors, no pictures on the walls, nothing to make the atmosphere homelike. Cordelia would laugh to see Alina's tiny new home. She sank onto her chair and stared at the fire through tear-filled eyes.

"Oh, Papa," she whispered. "I didn't plan this too well. I don't know how long I can last here." She wrapped her arms around herself. The cabin was so small! It would be very difficult to avoid Beau Parker in this place, and yet avoid him she must, as much as possible. He presented a danger to her.

Alina was startled by the thought. *Danger? How?* She straightened her shoulders and dropped her hands to her lap, then closed her eyes. She searched her heart for a warning about the cowboy. None came.

Her eyes flew open and focused again on the flames as the realization struck her: the danger was in the way he looked at her, in his voice, in the warmth that surged through her at his touch. The danger was in her growing and unwanted fascination with the man. The true danger was within her. *Like the moth to the flame,* she thought bitterly. *And here I am, trapped in this tiny cabin with him.*

A fierce determination drew her mouth into a tight line. The Randalls would not defeat her; neither would Beau Parker. She would live here for as long as it was necessary, and she would resist him. And she would pray for her father's return.

Outside, the two men worked silently as they stacked the supplies for the house on the porch. Neither spoke until they were leading the team across the yard.

"So, are ya gonna tell me what's goin' on?" Pike's breath came out in a frosty cloud. He helped Beau turn the team and back the wagon under the shelter next to the barn. They released the harnesses and lowered the wagon tongue to the ground.

Beau did not answer until he had opened the barn door and led the horses inside. "When we go back to the cabin, I'll introduce you to Alina. I apologize for not doing that sooner, but I wanted to tell you in private that she is my wife."

"Your *wife?*" Pike's eyes bugged. "Damn, Beau, I didn't even know ya was sweet on anyone, 'cept for maybe that snotty Madeline Petrie. I'm glad ya got over that one." He unbuckled the harness on one of the horses.

"That seems to be the general consensus," Beau said dryly as he pulled the harnesses away from the animals. He hung the heavy pieces of leather on the wall while Pike grabbed a worn blanket that was draped over the top board of a stall and began to rub the nearest horse.

" 'Course, that would explain why ya insisted on goin'

inta town when we didn't need anythin' urgent-like." He glared at Beau over the horse's back. "Ya coulda told me, ya know."

Beau reached for another blanket and went to work on his horse. "I swear I had no idea we'd marry, Pike."

"Well, who is she? And where'd ya meet her?"

"Her name is Alina Gallagher, and she worked at the Satin Slipper. I met her New Year's Eve."

Pike scratched his beard. "Thought ya was at Petrie's on New Year's Eve, then at that fancy party at the Laramie Hotel." He put his blanket back on the stall fence.

"I started at Petrie's, but decided to go to the Slipper instead." Beau looked up and found Pike's sharp, knowing eyes boring into him.

"Madeline didn't have nothin' ta do with that decision, did she?" the older man asked, as he led the horse to a stall. Beau did not answer. "So ya met her. Why'd ya marry her?"

"She was in some trouble, Pike."

Pike snorted. "And are ya sure that ya're the one that got her in trouble?"

"No, no, it's nothing like that. She was Katie's bookkeeper. Not all women who work in saloons are whores, you know." Beau's lips curved in a cynical smile. Alina should be proud that he had learned his lesson.

"So, why'd ya marry her?" Pike repeated.

"It's a long story." Beau led his animal to its stall and filled the feedbag with oats. He fluffed the hay and made sure the water in the bucket was not frozen, then faced his friend. "Alina's guardian wants to control her inheritance. The plan was to force Alina to marry the guardian's son. I caught the brute manhandling her on the street and offered to marry her myself. She accepted."

"Mighty noble of ya, Beau, but it seems a little drastic ta marry a woman ya hardly know, no matter the reason."

Beau shrugged. "I owed her. I also thought she was the most spirited, beautiful woman I'd ever met." His grin was sheepish. "I should have known you'd figure I was going to town for more than supplies. I did hope to see her again."

"Ya did a heap more than just see her."

Beau shrugged again. "I'm glad I was there, Pike. She needed help." He closed the barn door, and they crossed the yard. "Bert at the mercantile says hello, and so does Katie." His voice dropped. "Katie also mentioned that Alina doesn't know much about cooking," he warned as they stomped their feet on the porch. Pike rolled his eyes.

Alina started when the door opened. She stood as the men came in laden with supplies. Beau set his load on the counter while Pike set his, which included Alina's hatbox, on the table. Pike hung his coat on a hook next to the door and waited. Alina's eyes widened slightly when she saw that the older man's right leg from the knee down had been replaced with a wooden pegleg.

Beau set his hat on the bag of coffee beans, then tugged at his gloves. "Alina, I would like to introduce you to my friend and business partner, Mr. Sebastian Amadeus Pike. Pike, this is my wife, Alina." There was an unmistakable ring of pride in his voice. Alina blushed and held out her hand.

"I am pleased to meet you, Mr. Pike."

"Likewise, ma'am," Pike responded as he crossed the room to take Alina's cold hand in his. His old blue eyes twinkled. "Beau wasn't exaggeratin' none when he said ya was real pretty." Alina's cheeks turned an even deeper red. "Welcome ta the Parker Ranch. We're pleased ta have ya." He released her hand and adjusted his suspenders, suddenly self-conscious. He cleared his throat and thumped around Alina to pull the wrinkled shirt from the sofa, then retraced his steps. "Thank ya for the tobacco, Beau. 'Scuse me, ma'am." He nodded at Alina, grabbed the tin of tobacco from the table, and disappeared through the door by the fireplace.

Beau carried her trunk into the other bedroom and deposited it at the foot of the bed. He hung his coat next to Pike's, then turned to her. "May I take your cape?"

She handed him the garment and watched as he hung it

on the third and last hook. He stood for a moment, his hands at his sides.

"Welcome to my home," he said simply. She did not know what to say. At her silence, he continued somewhat awkwardly. "It's yours for as long as you need it."

"Thank you," she said, her voice a whisper. She cleared her throat. "Will that be my room?" She gestured toward the back bedroom.

"Yes." Beau walked by her. "I suppose you'll want to get unpacked." She took the hatbox from the table and followed him. He opened one of the dresser drawers. "I'll make room for some of your things in here." He pulled out a neat stack of folded clothing, then another, and walked out to lay them on the sofa. He waved at the empty drawer. "I know that's not much space, but it's a start. I'll get more hooks in here and we'll make do." He glanced at her tight face. "I could use some coffee," he said, and left her.

Alina sighed. One drawer and—she glanced at the wall—two hooks. Most of her things would have to stay in the trunk. She set the hatbox on the bed and caught a glimpse of herself in the dresser mirror. Her eyes were bright with unshed tears, her shoulders slumped in fatigue and discouragement.

She shook her head dejectedly as she slipped out of the gray redingote. Katie's roll of currency fell to the floor. She retrieved the bills; they would be hidden with the rest of her savings at the bottom of the trunk. Alina thought of Katie and Emerald; she missed them already. Somehow, the stay at the Satin Slipper seemed like a lifetime ago.

It did not take long to arrange a few clothes in the drawer and on the two hooks. She decided to leave the porcelain dove and her father's chess set safely packed in the trunk. The dove, at least, would not come out until she was home again. She set the pictures of her parents and her brush on top of the dresser, along with the bottle of now frozen rose water. There was something disturbingly intimate about the sight of her things next to Beau's bottle of bay rum and his hairbrush. She hoped he moved his belongings soon.

She sank onto a chair by the window. Whereas the bed in Pike's room had been a crude affair of boards nailed together, this one had a headboard almost as tall as she was, and the matching footboard rose a full twenty-four inches over the mattress. Both end pieces were beautifully carved, and the wood, which she guessed to be oak, was well polished. The lovely bed was strangely out of place in the otherwise rough cabin.

There were no pictures in here, either, but it was a nice enough room. Curtains were the greatest necessity. She twisted to look out the window. The sun, almost down behind the tree-covered hills, spread long shadows on the ground. She shivered as she eyed the simple white cotton comforter that covered the bed and hoped there were many blankets hidden beneath it.

"The coffee's ready, if you'd like some," Beau called.

Alina pushed the hatbox under the bed and pulled a black shawl from the trunk. She wrapped the warm wool around her shoulders and went into the main room. Pike lit the lamp on the battered table under the front window, then brushed at the covering of crumbs before he straightened and turned around. Alina murmured her thanks when Beau handed her a mug of steaming coffee. Her eyes widened in astonishment when she looked fully at Pike. His hair was now neatly combed and lay flat against his head, no doubt with the aid of some kind of hair tonic. Alina thought she could smell its clean scent from where she stood next to the stove. His beard had been groomed, and he wore a fresh shirt that was buttoned up to his throat.

"Hello again, Miz Parker." He bowed. "I hope ya will forgive my appearance and my language when we first met." He cleared his throat nervously.

Alina smiled at him. "There is nothing to forgive, Mr. Pike. You were simply being comfortable in your own home. I hope my presence here does not change that." She sat on the sofa, avoiding the stack of Beau's clothes, and sipped her coffee. It felt good to be warm.

"No, ma'am." Pike took the iron poker and stirred the coals in the fireplace.

Beau picked up a parcel from the counter and held it out to Alina. "I think Emerald meant this for you."

Alina set the mug on the floor next to her feet and accepted the package. It was lightweight and soft. She unwrapped the flour sack towel to reveal one of Emerald's long white aprons. Her eyes filled with tears when she saw the delicate embroidery along the bottom. She held it to her face, catching a faint scent of the lavender Emerald had kept in her drawers. The thoughtful gift filled her with a tremendous sense of longing for her friends at the Satin Slipper.

"I put your tea tin up on the shelf with the spices." Beau gave her the bar of scented soap and unwrapped the last package. "Bert sent along a bottle of French wine and some fresh oysters for our gift, Alina." He turned with the bottle in one hand, a grin on his face. "Do you like oysters?"

Alina nodded and reached for the mug at her feet. She had no desire to celebrate this pretense of a marriage, but Bert's intentions had been kind. And she loved oysters. She glanced at Pike as he went by with an armload of wood from the back porch. She hoped Beau had told him the truth about their arrangement so she would not have to play the loving wife here. Pike would learn soon enough when Beau moved into his room.

"He even threw in a lemon," Beau continued happily. "With that stew of yours, Pike, this will make a real feast."

"Well, I'm hungry now," Pike commented. "I'll just doctor this fire, then I'll mix up some cornbread and we'll eat." He paused and turned from the fire, the look on his weathered face one of pensive uncertainty. "Maybe ya'd rather eat alone, this bein' your weddin' night and all."

"No, Mr. Pike." "No, Pike." Alina and Beau spoke at the same time. They looked at each other.

"Pike, Alina and I would be honored if you will join us for our wedding supper," Beau invited solemnly.

"Are ya sure?" The older man watched the couple with suspicion. "Ya're not just sayin' that?"

Alina stood up. "We insist, Mr. Pike. We'd not have it any other way."

"Well, if ya're sure . . ." Pike threw one more log on the fire and stepped back to survey his handiwork. "That'll do," he muttered, as he rubbed his hands together. "Now for some muffins." He took two smaller pieces of wood with him to the stove.

"May I help?" Alina asked.

Pike shook his head. "Nope. This is your weddin' supper. Ya don't make your own weddin' supper, not where I come from, anyways. Beau'll shuck them oysters and open that wine, and I'll take care of the muffins." He looked at Alina apologetically as he slammed the stove door. "If I'd known about this, I'da planned a real special meal, but all I have ready is this here antelope stew."

Alina sank back down on the sofa. "It smells divine, Mr. Pike," she assured him, and she meant it. "I've never had antelope stew."

"You're in for a treat, Alina," Beau said from the counter where he was vigorously pumping water into a large tin bowl. "Pike's not much for making curtains or," he glanced at the crumb-topped table, "cleaning up, but he makes a great stew."

"I haven't noticed ya making no ruffly window curtains your own self, Beau Parker, and ya can sweep just as damn good as I can—beg pardon, ma'am." He moved toward a barrel that sat on the floor at the end of the counter, deliberately bumping into Beau as he passed. Alina brought the mug to her lips in an effort to hide a smile.

The two men continued their good-natured bantering as they worked. Their voices faded in Alina's mind as her eyes fell on the lamp in front of the window across the room. It was almost completely dark outside now, and her thoughts flew far away. She needed to write to Elizabeth immediately, as well as to Seamus Percival. Her brow furrowed at her troubled contemplation of the past several weeks. She had not been in touch with Elizabeth for over a month, and Percival had not heard from her since she had sent him a wire telling him she was safe. She was relieved that she could now communicate openly with both of them. She wondered if there was any news of her father.

Alina jumped when the oven door clanged shut. She looked up to see Beau and Pike watching her, the latter holding a steaming muffin tin with a cloth. If those muffins were cooked already, she had been quiet for a long time.

"Are you all right?" Beau asked with concern.

"I'm fine, thank you." She managed a tight smile. "I'm just tired." The two men did not appear convinced. "You must admit it has been a long and unusual day," she added.

"Damn!" Pike dropped the hot pan on the counter and blew on his fingers. "Beg pardon, ma'am."

Alina's smile was genuine now. She rose and placed her empty cup in the sink. "Please allow me to set the table."

Pike nodded to a dented tin can on the counter that held an assortment of flatware. "Utensils are there," he said as he carefully freed the muffins from the pan. "Bowls are down on a shelf, on the left, and since we got no glassware, I reckon we'll have ta drink that fancy wine from cups. They're on that high shelf next ta the coffee grinder. Plates are next ta the bowls."

Alina ducked into the bedroom and stuffed the apron and soap into her full drawer, then returned to the kitchen. After Beau wiped the table off with a cloth, she arranged the dishes and stood back. She would eat her "wedding supper" from a speckled blue enamel bowl with a wooden spoon and drink French wine from a chipped porcelain mug, at a table with no cloth, and, most likely, no napkins. She pulled her shawl more tightly around her.

Beau came from the back bedroom with the chair and picked up the other chair that still sat in front of the fireplace.

They joined the remaining chair at the rectangular table, one in front and one on each end. He set a pie tin filled with lemon wedges and oysters in half shells on the table. Pike handed Alina a small crock of butter and a wooden bowl of warm cornmeal muffins, then carefully wrapped a cloth around the handle of the pot and followed her to the table.

Beau pulled out the center chair. "Mrs. Parker," he said with a gallant flourish.

"Thank you," Alina responded as she sat down. Beau and Pike took their places.

"If'n ya don't mind, I'll say grace," Pike offered. When Beau and Alina nodded, he put his hands together and dropped his eyes. "Thanks for the food, Lord. It sure looks good. Amen." Alina smiled at the brief prayer. Beau poured the wine while Pike pulled the cloth from the handle of the stew pot and tucked it into his collar, then eyed the oysters expectantly. "Beau, put some of them oysters on each plate, will ya? I'll serve the stew after that."

When Beau divided the oysters, Pike picked up his mug and cleared his throat. Alina glanced at him, and when he nodded at her mug, she picked it up.

"I can tell this marriage feels strange ta both of ya, and I know it happened too fast, but I hope the two of ya are just as happy as ya can be." His eyes were shining with sincerity as he hit his mug against both of theirs.

"Thank you, Pike," Beau said.

"Yes, thank you," murmured Alina. So Pike knew at least some of the story, she thought as she sipped from her mug. The wine was excellent.

The oysters did not last long and the stew was as wonderful as the aroma had promised. Perhaps the wine helped, but Alina enjoyed the dinner. Pike and Beau entertained her with tales of their adventures on the ranch, and by the time her hunger was satisfied and the wine bottle empty, she felt warm and relaxed.

In a spirit of comradeship, they worked together to clear the table and wash and dry the dishes. Pike pulled his coat on, lit a lantern that hung by the back door, and announced he would take the covered stew pot to the smokehouse, where it would stay cool through the night, and check on the animals.

The silence between Beau and Alina stretched as they finished the last of the dishes. Finally she spoke.

"How do you usually pass the evenings?"

"We read, write letters, sometimes play cards. We go to bed pretty early and get up early." He reached over her to place a clean mug on the shelf and caught the faint scent of roses.

"I'd like a cup of tea," Alina said as she dried her hands on the cloth Beau handed her. "If you and Mr. Pike care for some, I'll make a pot."

"Thank you. Tea sounds good to me, but I know Pike would prefer coffee. And don't be surprised if he adds a little something to it from that bottle up on the top shelf." Alina looked up and saw a tall bottle in the corner against the wall. The label read "Brandy."

She pulled a pan from the low shelf and pumped water into it, then remembered she did not have a teapot. The leaves would have to go in the pan. She took the tea tin down, along with the three cups Beau had just put away.

Pike came in the front door and blew on his fingers. "Lordy, it's cold out there! I think somethin's blowin' in." He thumped by Alina to hang the extinguished lantern on its nail. "We keep this here by the back door in case we need ta use the necessary in the middle of the night," he informed her, not noticing her deep blush. "Ya may not relish using a chamberpot. Matches are in that box." He pointed to a black iron matchbox that was nailed to the wall next to the lantern. He pulled the coffeepot onto a burner and checked the fire level, then retraced his steps to hang his coat.

"That gash on Bay's leg is healing up fine, Beau. We can let him out for a short run tomorrow, but I think it's too soon ta leave the bandage off, so I rewrapped it. He don't seem ta be worryin' it much. First thing in the mornin', we'd best ride out and check on the herd. We may need ta haul some hay out to 'em. Somethin's comin' in."

"How soon?" Beau took a book from the stack on the mantel.

"I'd say by tomorrow night. This water here is boilin', Miz Parker."

Alina spooned tea leaves into the pan and removed it from the burner. "Would you like some tea, Mr. Pike?"

Pike shook his head. "Thanks, but that stuff ain't strong enough for me. I'll just stick with my coffee here." He eyed Alina as she retrieved her shawl from the back of her chair. He reached for the brandy bottle, then jumped when she spoke.

"Please feel free to add whatever you wish to your coffee, Mr. Pike, and to smoke, also." She turned to face him. "This is your house, and I want you to be comfortable here. Mr. Parker may have mentioned that I worked at the Satin Slipper, as a bookkeeper, mind you, but still in a saloon. Not much will shock me." She came over to him, her expression earnest. "Mr. Parker did me a great service by offering me the sanctuary of his name and home, and I am grateful for it, but I would be terribly distressed if my company causes either of you any discomfort."

"Well, thank ya, ma'am. I don't want ta distress ya none." He held up the bottle. "Would ya like a dollop in your tea?" he offered with generous innocence.

"Alina told me she doesn't drink hard liquor." Beau spoke from his seat at the table. Alina glared at him.

"How 'bout ya, Beau?"

"No, thanks. I'll just have tea."

Pike fixed his coffee to his liking and put the bottle back on the shelf. He held his cup to his nose and sniffed with appreciation. "There ain't nothing like this on a cold night," he commented, as he set it on the table. He went into his room and returned a moment later with a book in one hand and his pipe in the other. His reading spectacles were perched on his nose. He settled into his chair.

Alina put a cup of tea in front of Beau. "Thank you," he said. "There's a tin of sugar on the spice shelf, if you want it, Alina."

"No, thank you." She disappeared into the bedroom and came back out with a wooden letter box, then grabbed her cup.

Beau stood and pulled her chair out for her. Pike half rose from his chair and abruptly sat again, never taking his eyes off his book.

Alina lifted the lid of the beautifully carved box and removed an ink bottle, a sheath of paper, and a pen. Her hand lingered on the lid as she closed it. The box had been a gift from her father. She shook the bottle to see if the ink had frozen like the rose water had. She glanced at Pike, her curiosity compelling her to speak.

"Excuse me for interrupting your reading, Mr. Pike, but how can you tell there will be a storm tomorrow?"

Pike looked at her over his spectacles. "I can feel it, ma'am, in my leg." He snorted with laughter. "What's left of it, that is. And this old leg is a pretty fair forecaster, ain't it, Beau?"

"That it is, Pike. I can't remember it ever being wrong."

"Anyways, ma'am, that's how I can tell."

Alina's face was a deep red. "Forgive me, Mr. Pike." She could not look at him. "I did not mean to draw attention to your . . . injury."

"Ah, hell, ma'am, beg pardon, don't worry yourself 'bout it. Ain't no sense pretending it didn't happen. Lots of good men gave more than a leg in that damn war, beg pardon." Pike awkwardly patted her hand.

Alina's heart lurched. *Like my brother gave his life.* She looked at Pike and managed a small smile.

Pike was startled by the sudden, devastating grief in Alina's eyes, and instinctively he knew she had lost someone. He had seen that anguish all too often. He patted her hand once more, and his look was one of warm understanding.

Beau watched them curiously. He knew he had missed

something, but they spoke no more. Alina sipped her tea, then unscrewed the lid to the ink bottle and took up her pen. The room settled into a comfortable silence, broken only by the sounds of Alina's pen as it scratched across the paper, and by an occasional log breaking apart on the hearth.

At last, Pike closed his book and removed his spectacles. "This fellah Dickens sure can tell a story, but my coffee's gone, my pipe's cold, and I'm done for the day." He rose and gathered his things.

Alina looked up from her letter. "I am happy to know you, Mr. Pike."

"Likewise, ma'am." He set his cup in the sink, then headed toward his room. "Good night, Miz Parker. 'Night, Beau."

"See you in the morning, Pike," Beau answered. The door closed, leaving them alone. Alina heard Pike's peculiar gait as he crossed his room.

She glanced at Beau and saw that he had returned to his book. Her letter to Elizabeth was already pages long, for she had poured her heart out to her great-aunt, but there was a little more to tell. She stifled a yawn as she dipped the pen.

After a few minutes, Beau closed his book. "That's it for me, too." He stood and stretched, then grabbed his coat and headed to the back door. "I won't be long."

Alina nodded distractedly and put the finishing lines to her letter. She was forcing the folded missive into an envelope when Beau returned. He hung the lighted lamp on the nail, returned his coat to its place, and walked to the bedroom door. "Turn the lantern off if you don't need it." He disappeared into the dark bedroom. A moment later, light flooded from the room.

Alina looked at the lantern as a deep blush again colored her cheeks. These men were too familiar with their comments on personal bodily functions, she thought with stubborn hauteur. But she really did need to make the trip across the yard. She replaced the lid on the ink bottle and arranged her papers in a tidy pile, the letter on top. Percival's letter would have to wait until tomorrow.

She stepped out onto the back porch and held the lantern high. A path between tall, neat stacks of firewood led off the porch and across the yard to a privy some distance away. It was every bit as cold as Pike had said, and the wind had picked up. Alina thought with longing of the heated, indoor water closet in her father's house as she trudged over the hard-packed snow.

Before long, she was retracing her steps. Her eyes were drawn to the lighted window of her room. She watched as Beau pulled his undershirt off over his head, exposing a muscled chest covered with dark hair. Her heart jumped. She wished he were not so handsome, then was surprised that her cheeks could feel hot when it was so cold. Curtains were the first thing she would insist upon, without a doubt.

She was shivering by the time she returned the lantern to its place. She crossed the room and held her hands out to the fire, wondering if Beau planned to sleep on the floor out here or in Pike's room.

He came from the bedroom, wearing a dressing robe over a long nightshirt. "I'll bank the coals here, if you want to get ready for bed."

Alina nodded and moved to the bedroom door, then paused. "Mr. Parker, I haven't been particularly gracious to you today." She twisted her hands together. "I want you to know that I do appreciate what you did for me. I would be on the train to Chicago if not for your intervention, and I thank you."

"You're quite welcome, Alina. And please call me Beau."

"I'll try," she promised. She closed the door behind her.

The bedclothes were pulled back, exposing clean sheets. Weariness suddenly washed over her. What a day this had been! It did not take long to change into her nightdress. Alina hung the skirt, blouse, and shawl on an already laden hook and placed her folded petticoats in the trunk. Her underthings went into the stuffed drawer.

She pulled the pins from her hair and massaged her scalp before she picked up her brush. A yawn escaped as she sat on the edge of the bed, then there was a light knock at the door.

"May I come in?" She could barely hear Beau's quiet request. Her eyes narrowed with suspicion. Whatever game he was playing, she'd have none of it! She jumped off the bed.

She gripped the brush with one hand and opened the door with the other. "What is it, Mr. Parker?" she asked in a tense whisper.

"I'd like to come to bed, if you're ready," he replied in the same low tone.

Her mouth tightened. "You said this was my room!"

"It is, Alina. Your room and mine."

"No! We had a deal!"

Beau's face flushed with anger. He pushed his way into the room and closed the door. "Keep your voice down!" he commanded in an irritated whisper. "You'll wake Pike."

"I'll wake the *dead* if you don't leave this room right now!" Alina promised heatedly, but she dropped her voice.

For an instant, Beau's gaze fell on the glossy curls that had fallen forward over her shoulders, a startling contrast to her white nightdress. The curls clung to the mounds of her breasts and moved up and down in time with her breathing. With an effort, he looked away and pulled the robe from his arms. "Our agreement was that I would not touch you," he ground out between clenched teeth. "And I won't. But you are my wife, for the time being, at least, and my wife sleeps in my bed."

"Not *this* wife!" Alina yanked the door open only to have Beau force it closed again. He grabbed her shoulders.

"I have agreed to this charade, Alina, but I'll not allow you to make a fool of me, in my community or in my home. As far as the world is concerned, with the exception of Katie and Sam and probably Pike, because he's too smart, and your family, *no one* will know this is a marriage of convenience." His eyes bored into hers. "A marriage for *your* convenience, I might remind you. As long as we're married, in public you will play the role of my wife, and you will sleep in my bed if I have to tie you to it. You'll learn that I keep my word, including the promise that *I will not touch you.*" His voice was low and determined. Alina blinked. He let go of her shoulders.

He pulled his gun from the holster that hung over the corner of the headboard and cocked it. Alina watched as he rotated the cylinder to be sure each chamber was loaded. She wanted to ask if he always kept the gun near, but the expression on his face was forbidding and she did not speak. He carefully released the hammer and returned the gun to the holster.

His eyes followed her as she set the brush on the dresser and quickly plaited her hair. He wished it was his own fingers that moved through the long strands. When she finished, she stared into the mirror for a long moment.

"Are you ready?" Beau finally questioned in a hard whisper.

She nodded.

"You will sleep next to the wall," he ordered.

So you can pen me in, she thought furiously, but she remained quiet. She crawled across the foot of the bed and into her place, then pushed close to the wall. She could not suppress a shiver as she pulled the icy sheets to her chin and lay back on the pillow. Beau extinguished the lamp. He tugged the bedclothes up over his arms and turned his back to her.

He stared into the darkness, acutely aware of the woman next to him. The vision of her in her nightdress, with her hair free and falling to her waist, tormented him, as did the faint scent of roses. He began to doubt his wisdom in insisting on this sleeping arrangement. He had dreamed of her for weeks, wanting her in his bed, but not like this! He had sworn not to touch her! He ground his teeth in frustration and closed his eyes, determined to sleep.

She lay still a long time. Every nerve was stretched taut.

Her ears strained to catch any sound he might make; her fists clenched as she waited for him to make a move. Eventually his breathing slowed and deepened, but she did not let down her guard. It was very late when she finally slept.

Chapter Seven

The aroma of coffee awakened Alina from a fitful sleep. She was alone in the bed, snuggled in the middle. She hoped she had not moved close to Beau in her sleep. Judging from the pale light at the window, it was very early. She yawned. What a miserable night she had spent! She had awakened at every sound, every movement, constantly on her guard against Beau. This arrangement was not going to work. She'd never get any sleep! She yawned again and crawled from under the warm covers. After pulling on a thick pair of socks and her wrapper, she opened the bedroom door quietly.

"Mornin', ma'am," Pike greeted her cheerfully. His hair was again neatly combed, and his cheeks were pink, either from the heat of the stove or from a recent scrubbing, or both. His peg thumped as he moved from the stove to the counter and filled a mug with steaming coffee. He handed it to her as she ventured into the room. Beau was nowhere in sight. She accepted the coffee gratefully.

"Thank you, Mr. Pike. This smells wonderful."

Pike nodded. "I hope I didn't wake ya too soon. I tried ta be quiet, but Beau and me have ta get outta here. There's a plate of hotcakes in the oven for ya. Butter's on the table; maple syrup, too. If ya want ta lighten that coffee, there's a tin of milk here, and I think ya know where the sugar is." He wrapped several pieces of bread in a flour sack cloth and put them into a small burlap bag. He searched through the contents of a small barrel on the floor next to the flour barrel and finally straightened with two wrinkled apples in one hand. "These'll have ta do," he muttered, as he placed them in the bag.

Beau came in the front door. "Are you ready, Pike?" He saw Alina standing by the stove. "Good morning," he said with a stiff nod.

"Good morning," she responded softly. He wore his coat and hat, and there was no trace of stubble on his red cheeks. She wondered if he was still angry with her, then decided she didn't care if he was. She tossed her long braid back over her shoulder. She would not accept his decision about their sleeping arrangements without a battle, even if he had won the first round last night.

Pike reached for his coat. "I'm sorry ta take your husband away from ya so soon, Miz Parker, but we gotta check on the stock. I'll bring him back as soon as I can." He winked at her.

Alina blushed and looked down at her cup.

"We may be gone all day, Alina." Beau walked past her to the back porch and brought in a large armload of firewood. He deposited it next to the hearth. "Make yourself at home." He pointed to the books on the mantel. "If you like Shakespeare, Dickens, or Cooper, you are welcome to those."

It dawned on Alina that she would be alone. What if the Randalls had not left? What if Donovan came to the ranch? She swallowed hard, but did not voice her fears when she spoke. "Is there anything I can do to help while you're gone?"

"Like what?" Beau demanded.

"Like feed chickens, or check on the animals in the barn, or start supper."

Beau looked at her. "Do you know how to do any of those things?"

"I can learn," Alina said defiantly.

"I fed the chickens and checked on the animals, and we'll

have the remains of the stew for supper. I didn't bring you here to work. You've made it very clear that yesterday was a trying day for you, so why don't you just rest today?" Beau grabbed the lunch bag from the counter and disappeared out the door. Pike stared after him as Alina dropped her head in embarrassment.

"He's cranky sometimes first thing in the mornin', Miz Parker. Maybe he didn't sleep too well last night," Pike said without thinking. His cheeks reddened. "Uh, don't worry on it." He pulled a battered hat on his head. "Do ya know 'bout horses?"

"I'm not an expert, but, yes, I know about horses."

"Ya can check on the bay in the barn 'bout noon, if ya like. Make sure his water ain't frozen, and that he hasn't tore the bandage off his hock."

"I'd be happy to, Mr. Pike." She flashed him a grateful smile. "What happened to his leg?"

"He cut it on the ice, crossin' the river last week. Cut it good, too."

"What's his name?"

Pike looked at her with a puzzled expression. "Whose name?"

"The horse, of course." She laughed, a light, musical sound. "I want to call him by his name."

Pike shrugged. "Never thought about it. Ambrose just called him Bay. I guess that's his name."

"Who is Ambrose?"

"Beau's brother." Pike wrapped a brown knitted scarf around his neck.

"The one who owns this place," Alina guessed. "Is he the other officer in the picture?" She pointed to the mantel.

Pike squinted in the direction of her hand. "Yeah, that's Ambrose. And before ya ask where he is, he's dead. Are ya always this full of questions first thing in the mornin'?"

Why didn't Beau tell me his brother was dead? Alina set the cup on the stove and hurried to put a hand on Pike's arm. "I didn't mean to pry, Mr. Pike. Please don't be angry with me. I could not bear it if you were angry, also."

Pike relaxed. "I'm sorry, little lady." He patted her hand. "I oughtn't snap at ya. I was real close ta Ambrose."

"Did he die in the war?" Alina asked softly.

Pike's voice became hard again. "He was murdered, ma'am. Shot in the back while riding his own land, just last summer. That's what brought Beau out here from Virginia. His brother's murderer has never been caught."

Alina stepped back, her eyes wide. "How awful!"

"Pike!" Beau's voice came through the closed door.

"We'll be in the south pasture. No one can approach by way of the road without passin' us, and the snow is too deep for travel in the hills. Ya'll be safe here." He opened the door and was gone.

Alina moved to the window and watched Pike cross the yard to the fence and let himself through the gate. He was amazingly quick and agile with that wooden peg. Pike climbed up into the seat of a strange-looking wagon that sat on runners instead of wheels. Beau rode a restless buckskin. They spoke for a few minutes, then Pike slapped at the horses with the reins. The wagon slid easily over the snow-covered ground. In a matter of minutes they were out of sight.

Alina turned away from the window with a sigh. This plan was not going to work. She did not want to be here any more than Beau and Pike wanted her here. Once she was certain Cordelia and Donovan were gone, maybe she could go back to the Satin Slipper.

After quickly eating her breakfast, she filled the washbasin from the water reservoir on the stove and took it to the bedroom.

The chill in that room contributed to the speed with which she washed. She slipped into the plaid wool dress and decided that if she stayed here for any length of time, she would need more simple clothes. Her fingers pulled through her hair to release the braid and the brush followed, then she twisted her curls into a knot at her neck and secured it with pins. She tied Emerald's apron around her waist, determined to show Beau that she could carry her own weight.

An hour and a half later, the small cabin looked different. The changes were subtle. Nothing was moved, nothing had been added, but everything was neater and cleaner. Even Pike's bed was made.

"Not bad for a city girl, Mr. Beau Parker," Alina said with satisfaction as she rinsed her hands. She returned to her room and pulled a long, narrow package wrapped in canvas from her trunk. She laid the package on the bed and slowly unwrapped it, catching her breath in anticipation. The canvas fell away, and she pushed aside a piece of oilcloth to reveal a beautifully engraved Colt revolving rifle. She ran her hand lovingly along the length of the unmarred barrel and turned the weapon over to read once again the inscription on the underside of the polished walnut stock. *"Presented to Miss Alina Gallagher, with Love from her Father, upon the Occasion of her Eighteenth Birthday. May 22, 1869."* She took a box of bullets from the trunk and filled the six chambers. When she was here alone, she'd not leave the cabin for any length of time without a means to defend herself.

She put on her cape and gloves, then went outside, cradling the rifle in her arms. The day was clear and cold, but the wind was not as strong as it had been yesterday. She moved to the center of the yard and studied the layout of the ranch.

The homestead itself was nestled against a pine-covered slope. The land to the south and east was an open valley, dotted here and there with rolling hills covered with trees, rocks, and snow. She thought she heard the faraway sound of a train whistle. Somewhere in that direction was the Dale Creek trestle bridge, and she knew from her own trip to Laramie City that the train sounded the whistle when it approached the trestle.

Not far from the house, a mostly frozen creek wound its way to the plains, crossed by a simple wooden bridge. A rail fence surrounded a pasture and formed a corral near the solidly built barn. An overhang to the right of the barn protected the wagon she had arrived in yesterday, as well as a black buggy. On the other side of the barn, a plank fence enclosed a chicken yard, with the coop built up next to the wall. She assumed the small building that stood some distance to the left of the chicken yard was the smokehouse, and when she had turned in a complete circle, she was looking at the cabin once more. The homestead was simple but nice, and the location was beautiful. She again looked out over the valley to the south and breathed deeply of the bracing air. It seemed impossible that a storm was coming.

She trudged to the barn, following the path made by the men. Beau had left the heavy bar off the door. The interior was dim and smelled pleasantly of hay and animals. She made her way down the corridor between the stalls to the second one on the left. A fine bay horse nickered a welcome.

"Hello, yourself." Alina rested the rifle against a post and slipped in next to the horse. She held one gloved hand up for him to inspect and patted his neck with the other.

His thick winter coat was of a deep, burnished red, and his mane and tail were black. He was magnificent.

"You *handsome* boy," she breathed. She moved along the horse's side to his back left leg. A neat bandage was securely wrapped around the hock. It had not been disturbed. She patted his rump. "Good for you." A thin sheet of ice covered the contents of the water bucket that hung from a nail. Alina pulled her glove off and broke up the crystals with the tip of her finger. "Brrr. That's almost too cold to drink." She reached under her cape and extracted a withered apple from her apron pocket. "Here, sweetheart." She held the treat out to the horse. He sniffed her offering and daintily took it into his mouth.

Alina patted his neck one more time and backed out of the stall. "Bye," she whispered. "I'll see you again, and maybe you'll take me for a ride when your leg is healed."

She held her rifle under one arm as she pulled her glove

on and stepped into the sunshine. The glare from the snow was blinding. She closed the barn door and headed toward the smokehouse, shading her eyes with one hand. As she passed the chicken yard, she saw that someone had pushed the snow from the center of the enclosure. A few hardy hens were pecking at the remains of scattered feed. The sound of their contented clucking was comforting. She spied a marker of some kind on the hillside overlooking the homestead. She hiked her skirts and pushed through the snow, grateful for her warm, knee-high boots.

The marker of carved stone sat nestled among the trees. Alina brushed the snow from its face, then stood back to read it.

Ambrose Elijah Parker
Beloved Son, Brother, and Friend
Born December 14, 1839
Died August 7, 1871
Rest in Peace

Sadness washed over her. She knew what it was to bury a brother who had died before his time. Compassion for Beau filled her. She turned again to view the wild beauty of Ambrose's land, then made her way down the hill. She retrieved the stew pot from the smokehouse and returned to the cabin.

"Married!" Madeline Petrie stormed past the startled butler holding the door. She tore the stylish hat from her head and threw it across the entry hall. The butler closed the door and edged around his mistress. He scooped up the discarded hat and stood in silence, his face expressionless.

"The bastard got married!" she screamed, and pressed her gloved hands to her temples. She paced the wide hall for several minutes, then finally threw open the double doors that led into the parlor. "Send for Latham this instant, Beckett," she snapped over her shoulder.

"Yes, Miss," he replied, thankful that he'd had the foresight to lay a fire in the parlor. He disappeared down the hall.

The sound of breaking glass reached Ross Latham's ears when the butler opened the front door in answer to his knock. The cowboy rolled his eyes, then entered the parlor. Beckett closed the doors behind Latham, who stepped quickly to one side to avoid a missile. The china vase narrowly missed his head and shattered in a spectacular fashion against the door. The frantic woman searched for another object to throw.

"What's happened, Madeline?" Latham demanded as he crossed the room. "Calm down!" He grabbed her shoulders and shook her. "Tell me what has happened!"

Madeline turned glazed eyes to his face. Her pretty features were twisted into a mask of rage. When he shook her again, the fire faded from her eyes. She blinked and took a deep breath as she pulled from his grasp. She peeled her gloves off and threw them on the loveseat, then paced the rug in the center of the room while she tugged at her pale blond hair with one hand, making a mess of the once elaborate style.

"I just came from Trabing's." Her voice was flat. "That damned Katie Davenport was there. I can't believe Gus lets women of her kind in his store!" Latham hooked his thumbs in his gunbelt and remained quiet.

"She told me Beau Parker married one of her girls yesterday, her *bookkeeper!*" Madeline's breath quickened. "The bastard married a goddam saloon girl! And that bitch Katie just had to tell me all about it! I could have killed her!"

Latham eyed the distraught woman unsympathetically. "I guess you won't be marrying him, then, will you, Madeline? Your father will have to find some other way to get control of Ambrose Parker's land." He chuckled. "Those Parker men haven't been very good at doing what you want them to. First Ambrose wouldn't marry you, and now Beau won't, either."

Madeline grabbed a book off the shelf next to the fireplace and threw it with unerring aim. The volume knocked Latham's hat off and grazed his temple. A slow trickle of blood coursed down the side of his face.

"My father wants the Parker ranch, and by God, Ross, he will have it." Her voice was ragged as she made her vow.

Latham strode across the room to take her chin firmly in one hand. "That's fine, Madeline. Your daddy can have anything he wants. But don't you *ever* raise your hand, or anything else, to me again." He twisted her head up so that she was forced to look at him. The fury in his eyes frightened and excited her. She raised one hand and traced the trail of blood on his temple, then deliberately licked the tip of her finger.

"I'm sorry I hurt you, Ross," she murmured.

The man turned away from her. He retrieved his hat from the floor. "Will there be anything else, Miss Petrie?"

"Find out about the bitch he married. I want to know everything. How long she's been here, where she came from, how they met. I'd swear he wasn't involved with her on New Year's Eve. Maybe he knocked her up. Just find out."

Latham left the room with no further word, closing the doors behind him. A grim smile curved Madeline's full lips. "You will regret the day you married, Beau Parker, and so will your little wife," she whispered.

Alina spent the afternoon quietly; she wrote a long dispatch to Mr. Percival and wondered how soon she would be able to post her letters. She laid down for a short nap, then awakened refreshed and read from Beau's copy of *The Last of the Mohicans* that she'd found on the mantel. The wind picked up and the sky clouded over. The first flakes were falling when she heard the men return. She was thankful they were home.

"It sure is good ta come home and have the house all warm and," Pike looked around the room meaningfully, "clean and have supper ready. It's a nice thing, a woman's touch." He moved a spoonful of stew to his mouth.

Alina smiled her thanks for his compliment. "The next time we go to town, I'll want to get material for curtains. You are losing a lot of heat through the windows. A few rugs would be nice, also."

"Thank you for your efforts, Alina, but I told you I didn't bring you here to work." Beau did not look up from his bowl.

"And how do you expect me to fill my days, Mr. Parker?" Alina's voice was sweet, but edged with steel. "Call on my lady friends, discuss the latest fashions, perhaps sip tea and nibble on sweets while the servants see to the house?"

Beau flushed. "No, but you don't have to work your fingers to the bone."

She set her spoon down and held out her hands. "My fingers are fine, Mr. Parker, as you can see. I am very aware that you did me a favor by marrying me, and I insist that I be allowed to contribute to this household. I do not have a lot of experience as a domestic, and none as a cook, so you will have to bear with me, but I will not be beholden to you any more than is necessary. Have I made myself understood?" Her hands were now in her lap.

Beau's angry eyes rested on her face. "Perfectly, madam."

Pike cleared his throat as he rose. "It was a fine meal, Miz Parker. Thanks for all ya did around here today." He took his dishes to the sink. "I think I'll read in my room for a while, then hit the hay early." He refilled his cup and added a generous portion of brandy. "The two of ya need some time alone." He thumped across the room and disappeared behind his bedroom door.

Alina stared down at her hands in mute embarrassment. Beau sighed and leaned back in his chair.

"I'm sorry, Alina." He ran one hand over his hair. "I do appreciate all you did. Pike was right; the place looks very nice. But I feel uncomfortable about you working like this. You did not hire on as a domestic, and I don't like my wife working like one."

His use of the word "wife" disturbed Alina. "Need I remind you again that our arrangement is for business purposes, and temporary?" Her tone was sharp.

Beau stiffened. "No, ma'am," he snapped.

"Then please do not try to treat me as your loving wife."

"No, ma'am," Beau repeated, and stood. He was no longer hungry. He took his bowl to the stove.

Alina braced her elbows on the table and buried her face in her hands. She wasn't saying anything right. She listened as Beau scraped the remains of his stew back into the pot. She straightened. "I apologize for my rudeness, Mr. Parker."

Beau was silent. "Please sit down," she invited, her tone carefully polite. He grabbed the coffeepot and joined her at the table. At her nod, he filled her cup, then his, and set the pot on the table. He watched her and waited.

She pushed her half-empty bowl away and reached for her coffee. "This is a difficult situation for both of us, Mr. Parker. Yesterday, this marriage seemed to be my only option, but now we are both uncomfortable. Perhaps it would be best to end it immediately. I can return to the Satin Slipper, perhaps even continue on to California."

Beau stubbornly shook his head. "We've discussed that, Alina. It isn't safe."

"It is if the Randalls believe I am here," Alina argued.

"They won't give up this easily. There is too much at stake, and now Randall's pride is involved. He won't forget that you refused him, and I took his woman."

"I was never his woman!"

"In his mind you were." His tone softened. "I've seen his kind before. I know you don't like me to say this, but please trust me on this."

Alina looked at him. His brown eyes shone warm in the light of the lamp. She sighed. "Very well. But there are a few things we need to settle."

He nodded. "Go on."

"First of all, you must let me contribute to our lives here.

I will go mad with nothing to do all day." She looked down at her cup. "As I mentioned before, I'm not very experienced with actual housekeeping duties and cooking, but I'll do my best, and I promise not to work my fingers to the bone."

Beau smiled. "Agreed. And I'll buy material for curtains and get some rugs. In fact, make a list of anything you want."

"When can we go to town? I would like to mail my letters as soon as possible. I'm certain my aunt is worried about me."

"We'll go as soon as the weather clears, but that could take a few days. We may be snowed in, if Pike's leg is right."

Alina nodded. Beau watched her carefully. She was so beautiful in the soft light. Curls played around her face and her long lashes seemed to touch her cheeks as she kept her eyes down. He realized she was nervous. "Is there something else?"

Alina took a deep breath. "Our sleeping arrangement."

Beau's face hardened. "I've explained my feelings on that issue."

"Well, I haven't," Alina retorted. "The arrangement is totally unacceptable, Mr. Parker. If you're not willing to give me the bedroom, then I shall make something up out here. We cannot continue sleeping in the same bed as if we were wed! It isn't seemly."

"But we *are* wed, Alina, and to my mind, it would be far more unseemly for a married couple to sleep in separate rooms."

"It is not unseemly to sleep apart, nor uncommon at all!"

"It is unacceptable to me," Beau said flatly. "I don't want to have this argument each night, so please accept that I won't compromise on this. I will do almost anything in my power to make you as comfortable as possible during your stay here, but I insist on this." He pushed away from the table, wondering if he had lost his mind. Was it only his pride that refused to allow him to back down? He knew his stand on the issue made no sense, especially if he wanted to sleep.

"But why do you insist on it?" Alina demanded. "Are you hoping to wear down my resistance, and eventually seduce me? If so, Mr. Parker, I assure you it won't work!"

Beau glared at her. "I gave you my word on that, and I'm getting tired of repeating myself!"

Alina dropped her gaze and spoke in a calmer tone. "If you tell Mr. Pike the truth about our agreement, it won't matter if we sleep separately. He won't tell anyone."

"Pike already knows the truth about our agreement, except for what happened in your room the night we met, and you're right, he won't tell anyone." He took the coffeepot to the stove, then turned to face her. *"My wife sleeps in my bed."* He stared at her, his hands on his hips.

Alina clenched her teeth in frustration and remained silent. Beau crossed the room to his coat. "I'll check on the animals one last time. I won't be long." He lit the lantern and stepped out the door, letting in a whirl of snow. Alina shivered as she carried the dishes to the sink.

She was drying the last spoon when Beau blew in the back door. His face was red and his mustache was crusted with ice.

"I've run a line from the porch post to the privy, one to the smokehouse, and another from the front porch to the corral. If you have to go out for anything, use the rope. It is surprisingly easy to get lost in a blizzard, even in your own yard."

She nodded and folded the towel. He allowed her the use of the bedroom first. The uncomfortable silence between them continued until Beau reached from under the blankets to extinguish the lamp.

"Goodnight, Alina," he ventured in the dark.

"Goodnight, Mr. Parker," she returned in a small voice.

He sighed. "Please call me Beau."

"Goodnight . . . Beau." She turned her back to him. The cabin was quiet except for the howling of the wind, but it was a long time before either of them slept.

Beau was aware of Alina's every movement. He knew

when she finally fell asleep. He dozed off periodically, only to awaken again if she shifted her position, or if a particularly strong gust of wind shook the cabin. In the early hours of the morning, when the room had begun to lighten, she drew closer to him in her sleep, her nose buried under the covers close to his shoulder.

He glanced at the top of her dark head and cursed himself for a fool. Her delicate scent assaulted him; the curves he knew were hidden under the soft material of her nightdress enticed him; the memory of her standing up to Cordelia, Donovan, Delilah, and yes, even himself, delighted him. He longed to free her curls from the imprisoning braid, to see her glorious hair spread across the pillow. He wanted to cover her lovely face with kisses until she opened those blue eyes; he wanted to bury his own face in the valley between her breasts and explore all the other hidden treasures of her body.

Beau groaned and rubbed his eyes. He must have been mad to think he could sleep next to her each night and not touch her. He was only punishing himself. He sat up and swung his feet out from under the covers. Alina stirred. He looked over his shoulder at her. She slept peacefully, her long lashes resting on her cheeks. Stray curls played about the side of her face.

Something twisted deep in Beau's gut and he turned away from her. Who was he trying to fool? She did not want him, and even if she did, what did he have to offer a woman like her? He had been lost since the end of the war, drifting aimlessly through his life with no real direction.

Through the material of his nightshirt, he absentmindedly stroked the long scar that ran along his ribs. To the casual observer, he wasn't drifting. He had helped his younger brother manage the plantation. He had held a high-powered position in the Grant administration until his brother's death had brought him out here, and he still had a promising future in Washington, if he wanted it. The problem was that he did not know what he wanted; nothing truly satisfied him.

It was Ambrose's death that had shown him how lost he truly was. The murder of his brother was the first incident he had allowed to touch his heart since the June day in 1864 when a desperate Confederate officer's saber had come down on him. The saber had torn him open, then had killed Jonathan Kirk, his best friend, who had thrown himself in the way of that merciless weapon.

Beau closed his eyes against the memories. Now here he was, resigned from his government job, going through the motions of running his dead brother's ranch, driven by an obsessive desire to find the murderer. But when he did, and justice was served, he had no plans for the future. He glanced back at Alina, shaking his head sadly. He had nothing to offer a woman, this woman, except his name and his protection, for as long as she needed it. One thing she didn't need was him in her bed. He hated to back down, especially after he had been so stupidly insistent last night, but she had won.

He dressed quietly and let himself out of the bedroom. He built up the fire in the stove and the fireplace, then prepared a fresh pot of coffee. After bundling up, he went out into the storm, careful to find the rope before he stepped off the porch.

A half an hour later, Beau struggled back through the front door, dragging something behind him. Pike was slicing bacon into a pan. He dropped his knife and hurried to help Beau.

"Damn, Beau, what the hell are ya doin'?"

Beau did not answer. When they had the wooden contraption inside, Beau slammed the door and leaned against it.

"Ain't this Ambrose's old bed?" Pike demanded.

Beau shrugged as he pulled his gloves from his hands. "It is. Now I need it."

Pike crossed his arms and tried not to smile. "And what's wrong with the bed ya already got?"

"It's too crowded," Beau mumbled. He took a handful of

nails from the pocket of his heavy coat and laid them on the table, followed by the hammer he pulled from his belt.

"I could swear ya told me your wife would share your bed, and that ya wasn't gonna touch her."

"I changed my mind!" Beau snapped as he hung his coat.

Pike sauntered back to the stove and picked up the knife. "Well, I sure hope ya get more sleep out here. Ya've been as ornery as a grizzly with a toothache, and it's gettin' tiresome!"

Beau glared at his friend's back as he crossed the room. He pulled the sofa away from the wall and positioned it in front of the fireplace, then dragged the battered bed frame across the floor.

Alina opened the bedroom door, tying the belt of her robe.

" 'Mornin', Miz Parker," Pike said cheerfully.

"Good morning, Mr. Pike." Alina rubbed one eye and stifled a yawn.

Beau shoved the rope bed up against the wall and shook one end of the wooden frame. The bed swayed drunkenly. He stomped over to the table and grabbed up the hammer and several nails, his boots leaving a trail of melting snow. Alina watched silently as he hit the nails with inspired strength. Finally she turned to Pike in bewilderment.

"He's fixin' up his bed!" Pike shouted helpfully over the noise. Alina whirled back to Beau, astonished.

Beau stilled the hammer. "You win, Mrs. Parker," he ground out as he reached for another nail. "The bedroom is yours, but I will ask that I can keep my clothes and such in there." He pounded at the unfortunate nail.

"But why?" Alina asked. Beau did not hear her. She moved to his side and leaned down to place a gentle hand on his wrist. The hammer paused in midair. "Why?" she repeated.

Beau pulled away from her touch. "I changed my mind," he said flatly, and continued the pounding.

Alina turned back to Pike, who shrugged and raised his

bushy eyebrows. She sighed and retrieved the washbasin from the wall, then filled it with warm water. She returned to the bedroom and closed the door, setting the basin on the dresser. Steam rose from the water, causing a mist to form on the part of the mirror it touched. The relief she felt because he had given her the bedroom was clouded by a tiny, troubling sense of disappointment. She pushed strands of hair away from the sides of her face and leaned forward to examine her tired eyes in the mirror, resolutely refusing to explore her feelings. It was hard to see in the dim light. She would have to light a lamp in order to wash her face! Why *had* those men gotten up so ridiculously early?

Chapter Eight

The storm lasted for three days, and once Beau got settled in the main room, the time was spent in relative peace. Twice a day, the men made their way to the barn to check on the animals. Pike did the cooking, with Alina watching at his shoulder. She made notes of which spices he added to the meats he cooked, to rice and potatoes, to stewed apples. They took turns reading aloud, and by the time the snow stopped, they had finished *The Last of the Mohicans* and had begun *The Deerslayer.* Pike and Beau had been thrilled to learn of Alina's chess set. Her heart caught in her throat to see the familiar pieces, but she enjoyed the games the three of them played. Beau promised to make a table for the set and brought an oak board when he returned from one of his excursions to the barn. Alina watched in fascination when he cut the wood to size and began to sand the edges. She had expected him to nail planks together, as was done for his new bed; she wondered what this chess table would look like.

She awakened on the fourth day to a strange silence and realized the wind was no longer blowing. She jumped from under the covers to peer out the window. The early morning sky was clear. The men were moving about in the kitchen, so she hurried into her black skirt and white blouse, then walked out the bedroom door as she tied a black ribbon to the end of her braid.

Pike looked up from the pan he was tending. "Mornin',

ma'am," he said with a grin. "Your cup's yonder," he nodded over his shoulder toward the counter, "and this here side pork'll be done in two shakes. Biscuits'll be out in a minute, and Beau opened a jar of peaches."

Alina returned his smile. "You are always so cheerful in the morning, Mr. Pike. But you'll have to start sleeping later if I'm to take over the cooking. You're up before me every day."

"I been thinkin' on that. Why don't ya let me handle the breakfast cooking? I kinda like doin' it, and I tend ta get up early anyways. If ya took care of dinner and supper, that would be real nice."

"Agreed," Alina answered.

Beau looked up from the table. "I think I got the best deal here."

"Don't be too sure, Beau," Pike warned. "We ain't tried Miz Parker's cookin' yet." He winked at Alina.

"That's true," she said with a giggle. "We may all regret this, myself included."

Beau watched her as she filled her cup. He liked the sound of her laughter, the healthy glow on her cheeks, and the way the tail of her braid danced around her hips. He enjoyed having her in his home, but he had known from the first night he met her that he would enjoy her company under any circumstances. Many times over the last three days he had caught himself staring at her face, marveling at its delicate perfection, losing himself in the sound of her lyrical voice as she read the stirring words of James Fenimore Cooper, delighting in the way her brow wrinkled as she contemplated some chess move. He knew he enjoyed her company too much, for she had made it very clear that she would stay no longer than was necessary.

Alina stood at the stove and sipped her coffee. Although she missed Katie, Emerald, and Moses, she was far more at ease here than she had been at the Satin Slipper, especially now that the bedroom was hers. She looked at Beau, taking in his handsome face and thick hair, and was glad the cup hid her lips when they curved in an involuntary smile. Many a woman would happily have shared his bed. She wondered what her feelings toward him would have been under different circumstances, but the memory of that first night would not let her forget what he was capable of. She also could not forget that their marriage was a business arrangement, one she had entered reluctantly, one he had entered to ease his conscience. Her face sobered at the thought.

Beau wondered what had chased the pleasure from her lovely features.

Pike handed Alina a plate piled with crisp salt pork and followed her to the table with a bowl of biscuits.

"We'll have to take hay out to the herd again today, Alina." Beau slathered butter on a steaming biscuit. She nodded, her mouth full of peaches. He continued. "We'll probably head on over to the Freemans while we're out and make sure they got through the storm all right."

"Neighbors ta the southeast," Pike explained at her questioning look, as he stabbed at a piece of pork.

She nodded again, remembering that Beau had mentioned the family the day he had brought her here.

"You'll like the Freemans," Beau said. "They are about the nicest folks you'd want to meet. This is their first winter here, like it is mine, so we kind of check on each other." He looked at Pike. "Let's throw a few extra bales on the wagon, in case David can use them."

"Sounds good. Let's get at it." Pike drained his mug.

"Leave the dishes, Mr. Pike," Alina said when he reached for his empty plate. "I'll clean up and pack some lunch while you hitch the horses."

Pike nodded and made his way to the door. Beau followed him out.

Alina cleared the table and wrapped the remainder of the pork in the only clean towel she could find. She cut the last of the bread into two thick slices and fished out two of the best apples and placed the food in the burlap sack. Someone would have to make more bread, and the laundry was piling up. She had no idea how to make bread, but maybe she could work on the laundry after the men left. She poured the rest of the coffee into a ceramic jug and placed a cork in the neck, then hesitated.

Although the day was clear, it was very cold, and the men were going to be working outside all day. Alina reached for the bottle of brandy and carefully poured some of the liquor in with the coffee. That would help warm them, she thought with satisfaction. She gathered the jug and the sack and stepped out onto the porch as Beau reined the buckskin to a halt in front of her. She moved into the sunshine at the top of the steps.

"I doctored that coffee some," she warned when he took the food. She pulled her shawl more tightly around her shoulders. She mouthed the word "brandy" at Beau's questioning look.

He smiled and winked at her. "Thank you. I'm sure we will appreciate your gesture in a few hours."

"Will the coffee still be warm in a few hours?"

"No, but we won't care." He secured the sack in one saddlebag and the jug in the other. "Thank you for the trouble you took to prepare this meal for us. And remember our agreement."

She looked at him, puzzled. He leaned far out of the saddle and grasped one of her cold hands. "Don't work them to the bone." He lightly squeezed her hand and released it, noticing that a most becoming blush kissed her cheeks.

He turned the horse's head and rode to join Pike. Alina waved after the men and scurried back inside. As she closed the door, she saw that Beau's bed was made. She made her own bed and straightened the kitchen. A smile came to her face when she poked her head into Pike's room and saw that his blankets were smooth and neat, and his clothes were all hung on hooks. She went to the back porch and pulled the heavy, four-legged wooden washing tub into the middle of the room. She lifted the lid and dubiously eyed the paddle inside. It could not be that hard to wash clothes, she thought.

All she had to do was turn that paddle and put the clothes through the attached wringer.

After she filled the tub, Alina took advantage of the clean water and washed her hair first, twisting the wet strands into a braid that hung down her back. She then reached for the pile of clothes she had gathered on the floor.

Two hours later she held one hand to her stiff back while she pushed at a stray wisp of hair with the other. She felt a sense of pride as she viewed the many garments hanging on the rope she had strung back and forth across the room. Never would she have guessed that doing the wash was such hard work. She felt a new appreciation for the laundry maids in her father's house, and for the Chinese family she had taken her laundry to while living in Laramie City. Now she stared at the large washtub with dismay and rubbed her aching arm. There was no way she could drag the tub outside to dump the dirty water. She would have to either empty it as she'd filled it, one bucket at a time, or wait until the men returned to help her.

She wiped up the trail of water that ran from the sink, where she had rinsed the clothes using the pump, to the tub in the middle of the room and was just wringing out the rag when she heard a wagon pull up in front of the house. She dried her hands on her apron as she stepped out onto the porch and was startled to find herself looking up at a woman on a wagon seat. Two children sat in the back of the wagon and stared unblinking at her. Alina returned her gaze to the woman.

"You must be the new Mrs. Parker," the woman said cheerfully. "I'm Cynthia Freeman."

"Well, hello, Mrs. Freeman. Mr. Parker was just telling me about you this morning. Won't you and the children come inside?" Her heart sank at the thought of laundry hung across the room. She patted her hair self-consciously.

Cynthia hesitated. "I don't know if Beau explained to you that my husband is a colored man, Mrs. Parker. I mean no offense, but before I get down, I want to be certain that my children are welcome, too."

Alina blinked. For the first time she noticed that the children's faces were several shades darker than that of their mother. A baby let out a yell; an older child in the back rocked the infant soothingly. "For heaven's sake, Mrs. Freeman, let's get these beautiful children in out of the cold."

Cynthia smiled in relief. Alina stepped off the porch and moved to the side of the wagon bed. "Give me that baby," she ordered, and took the fidgeting child in her arms. She cuddled the bundle against her breast and looked down into two curious dark eyes. She smiled, then moved to the end of the wagon to assist the other two children to the ground.

"Tanya, you help Mrs. Parker, and make sure your brother minds," Cynthia called from the seat. "I'll take the team over to the barn, if that's all right, and be in directly." At Alina's nod, she slapped the reins and the wagon moved away.

Alina guided the children into the cabin and closed the door. She pulled the blanket away from the baby's face, and when she looked up, she found Tanya and her younger brother staring at her. She shifted the baby's weight to a more comfortable position on her hip. "Please forgive the mess in here." She moved into the room and with her free hand pushed the drying laundry to the far ends of the rope to clear a place in front of the fireplace. "Why don't you take off your coats and come closer to the fire?"

Tanya unwrapped the scarf from her head and unbuttoned her coat, then helped the boy as Alina set her squirming bundle on Beau's bed. She loosened the blanket that enveloped the baby and straightened the yellow calico dress. The little girl cooed and kicked her fat legs, relishing her freedom.

"Where would you like me to put the coats, ma'am?" Tanya asked shyly.

"If you'll watch your sister for a minute, I'll take them." Alina draped the coats over the footboard of her bed, then glanced in the mirror. Lordy, she was a sight. Her cheeks were a bright pink, her still-damp hair was untidy and coming loose from the braid, and her blouse and apron both wore splotches of wash water. She pushed back the unruly curls that framed her face and pinned the long braid into a knot at her neck. She would just have to make the best of the situation.

Alina heard steps on the porch and opened the door to admit Cynthia. "Please forgive the room." She waved sheepishly at the laundry and took Cynthia's coat into the bedroom.

"Think nothing of it, Mrs. Parker," Cynthia said warmly. "I know we caught you by surprise. When Pike and your husband came by and Beau announced he had married, I was so excited I just had to come calling." She set a jar and a burlap bag on the table and moved around the sofa. Alina saw Cynthia eye the bed with curiosity as she picked up the baby, and was thankful that her guest did not comment on it.

Cynthia was a tall, thin woman with dark brown hair pulled into a bun at the back of her head. Her plain dress was of green plaid shot through with yellow bands, and when she turned, Alina saw that her large brown eyes sparkled with good humor.

"This here is Tanya." Cynthia dropped her free arm around her daughter's shoulders. "She's my oldest at seven." Tanya's young face promised great beauty. She had lovely eyes and long, thick, curly hair that was pulled back into a braid. She shyly executed a curtsy, holding out the skirt of her simple wool dress.

"Pleased to meet you, ma'am."

Alina nodded at her with a smile.

"My oldest boy, David Earl Junior, insisted on helping the men. He just turned six; you'll meet him later. This is Lincoln."

"And I'm gonna be four," Lincoln announced. Tanya nudged him and the boy hastily bowed.

"And this one here is Margarite; she's just ten months," Cynthia finished as she jiggled the baby. "Children, this is Mr. Parker's new wife. You can call her Mrs. Parker."

Alina smiled. "I am very happy to meet you."

"Now you children get your pencils and paper out of this bag and sit here in front of the fire while Mrs. Parker and I have a nice talk." Cynthia took a chair at the table and handed the burlap bag to Tanya.

"Would you like some tea?" Alina asked.

"That would be lovely." Cynthia settled the baby on her lap and waved at the jar. "I brought you some chokecherry jelly. I put it up last summer." She planted an affectionate kiss on the top of Margarite's curly head. "I don't know how long this little squirmer will sit here, but maybe she'll surprise me." The baby laughed and pounded one little fist on the table.

Alina set the pan of water on to boil. "I've never heard of chokecherry jelly," she said as she reached for the tea tin.

"Chokecherries grow mostly along creekbeds and in the lower mountains. The Indians use them in their pemmican, or so Pike told me. They're a small, very bitter cherry, mostly seed. But they make up into wonderful jelly and syrup."

"I wish I had some bread so we could try the jelly, but I sent the last of it along with the men for their noon meal."

Cynthia glanced at the counter, then at Alina. The bread was gone and Beau's new wife had no dough rising? "I think the men are planning to come here for lunch. At least, that's the way I understood it when we left David Junior with them."

Alina's eyes widened. "Coming here?" she croaked.

Cynthia was puzzled by the anxiety on Alina's face. "Is something wrong, Mrs. Parker?"

Alina came over to the table and sank onto a chair. She twisted her hands in her lap. "I have a confession to make, Mrs. Freeman," she said in a low voice.

Cynthia leaned over the table conspiratorially. "Please

call me Cynthia," she whispered, "and tell me what's wrong."

Alina smiled. "My name is Alina, and I can't cook a lick. Mr. Parker and I married suddenly, and I had no time to prepare for my new role as wife."

Cynthia sat back. "Fiddlesticks, Alina, is that all?" She did wonder about Alina's background, though. Why hadn't her mama taught her to cook? "There's nothing to it. Show me what you have, and we'll throw something together. The men aren't too fussy." She stood up. "Tanya, honey, you keep an eye on your sister, and make sure she doesn't drive Lincoln crazy, or crawl in the fire. Mrs. Parker and I are going to get to cooking."

"Yes, Mama." Tanya came to take Margarite from her mother.

Alina stood up and moved to the back door. "Let's see what we have in the smokehouse." The two women crossed the yard.

"Alina is such a pretty name," Cynthia commented. "I've never heard it before."

"It's an old Celtic name." Alina struggled with the latch to the smokehouse. "My family is Irish, and Papa said the name goes back generations. It was my grandmother's name." She opened the door, and the women stepped into the small building.

"Here's a nice haunch," Cynthia pointed out. "It looks like venison." She touched the meat. "It's frozen, but we could shave off some of the meat. If you have potatoes, and maybe an onion, we could fry it all up and it will make a filling meal."

Alina nodded. "I also have apples we could stew. That I know how to do," she added with a smile. She ran back to the house for two knives and a plate, then Cynthia showed her how to shave the meat off the bone.

Back inside, Cynthia helped her rehang the laundry in Pike's room. Together they dragged the washtub out the back door and dumped the water off the porch.

"If you have the makings for bread, I can show you how to get your dough rising," Cynthia offered. "It's not hard at all."

Alina flashed her a grateful smile. "That would be wonderful."

Cynthia rolled her sleeves back. "I want you to tell me how you lassoed that Beau Parker, though you're so pretty, I'll bet it wasn't hard to do." Her warm eyes twinkled with anticipation.

Alina hesitated, hating to lie. "Well, I guess you could say he swept me off my feet."

Cynthia laughed. "I'll bet he did. I'm just so glad he didn't hook up with that Madeline Petrie. I was afraid she'd get her claws into him like she did his brother for a while, and he's just too good a man for her. Of course, Ambrose was too good for her, too, rest his soul. Beau told me you were a bookkeeper at the Satin Slipper. I've heard that's a real nice place."

Alina was surprised that her new friend was not disturbed by the fact that she had worked in a saloon. She could just imagine the reactions of some of her friends in Chicago to learn that interesting bit of news, which, she thought grimly, Cordelia would be certain to share.

With Cynthia's cheerful and efficient help, it was not difficult to prepare the huge meal and get a batch of bread dough rising. The two women passed a pleasurable hour talking about Laramie City, the Satin Slipper, and themselves. Alina learned that Cynthia was from Kansas, and that her husband was a former slave who had fought for the Union Army during the Civil War. He had been wounded, and they had met when he was brought to a hospital where she was a volunteer.

It was almost noon when Alina looked up from the pot of stewed apples she was stirring to see the three men and the boy troop into the cabin.

"Alina, this is my husband, David Earl Freeman," Cynthia said proudly. David was slender, like his wife, and only a little taller than she. "David, this is Alina, Beau's new wife." Margarite crawled to her father. David swung the baby into his arms and held out one hand.

"Pleased to meet you, Mrs. Parker." His teeth were a startling white against the dark skin of his friendly face. Alina grasped his hand.

"And I am pleased to meet you, Mr. Freeman." She looked to the boy that stood at the man's side. "This must be David Junior."

"Yes, ma'am," he answered shyly as he bowed.

"Is anyone hungry?" she asked.

A chorus of hearty cheers filled the room. Alina caught Beau watching her over the crowd. His eyes were warm with pride. She blushed and turned back to the stove. "Sit where you can find room," she instructed, "and we'll serve you."

After the hectic and, to Alina, surprisingly delicious meal, the men went back outside and Cynthia helped her clean up. All the children pitched in to dry the dishes. Cynthia checked the bread dough one more time. "Let this rise all day. Tonight, before supper, punch the dough down, divide it into loaves, and let it rise through the evening. Then bake it for about forty minutes, until it's brown on top and sounds hollow when you knock on it. You have to play with your oven to get the heat right," she warned. "Each oven is different, and it can be frustrating, so be patient."

"I had no idea it took so long."

"Usually what I do is make the dough up after supper, let it rise through the night, then bake it in the morning." Cynthia's smile was encouraging. "Before you know it, you'll be able to do this in your sleep."

Alina raised a skeptical eyebrow. "I don't know about that."

David stuck his head in the door and said that it was time to go. On an impulse, Alina took down the tea tin and tied a generous amount of the fragrant leaves in a clean cloth. Shyly she held the small bundle out to Cynthia. "I'd be pleased if you would take some of this tea."

"Why, thank you, Alina." Cynthia accepted the package with a warm smile. "This is a real treat. We'll enjoy it." They all filed out onto the porch. As the men loaded the children in the wagon, Cynthia set the tea on the seat and turned to Alina, holding out her hands.

"I am just so happy to have you for a neighbor," she said sincerely. "I hope we see a lot of each other. You come by anytime you want to."

Alina took Cynthia's offered hands. "I feel the same."

Cynthia gave her a quick hug. "Don't let the cooking scare you," she whispered. "You'll do just fine."

"Thank you," Alina whispered back.

"Lord, Beau, they're telling secrets already," David said as he rolled his eyes. "Come on, woman, I can't stand here holding this young'un all day."

"Yes, dear," Cynthia responded sweetly. She released Alina and accepted Pike's help into the wagon. David handed her the baby, then climbed up next to his wife.

" 'Bye, Alina!" Cynthia called, as the wagon pulled away. "You remember all I told you! Congratulations, Beau! You got a real nice wife!" Her voice drifted away on the wind and the children waved until they could no longer be seen. Pike headed to the barn, and Beau followed Alina into the cabin.

"I'm sorry we couldn't warn you about the company, Alina. We met down by the pasture. They were coming to check on us; Cynthia said the kids had cabin fever and would drive her to distraction if they didn't get out, and when she learned that I had a wife, she had to come and meet you. I hope you didn't mind."

"It's all right," Alina answered as she sank onto the sofa. "She's a lovely woman, and I am very happy to have a new friend." She laughed. "This place was a disaster when she got here. My wet hair was hanging down my back, I had laundry hung all across the room, and the washtub was in the middle of the floor. It didn't seem to surprise or offend her."

Beau looked at her in amazement. "You did laundry, too?"

Alina nodded, her eyes sparkling. "Tell Pike to watch his head when he goes into his room. We moved the clothes in there."

Beau watched her in silence. Under his intense stare, she sobered. "What is it?" she asked.

"You did me proud today," Beau said quietly. "You made my friends welcome and set out a fine meal, and I thank you."

Alina was uncomfortable with the praise. "Cynthia is really the one who cooked, Beau. I panicked when she told me you were coming here to eat. She showed me how to do everything." She waved in the direction of the stove. "She even made up a batch of bread dough."

"I'm sure you helped." Beau headed to the door. "The stock fared well through the storm. I don't think we lost any. We want to check the fence further along the road, so we'll be gone for a while yet." He paused with his hand on the latch and looked back at her. "I am proud to introduce you as my wife," he said, and closed the door behind him.

Alina stared at the door for a long time, surprised and touched at his words.

Chapter Nine

A succession of blizzards over the next few weeks made the trip into Laramie City dangerous. Beau went in once with David for supplies and mail. By then Alina had a handful of letters for him to mail, letters to Elizabeth, Mr. Percival, and her friends Jennifer and Susannah. She also sent along a letter to Katie. Much to her disappointment, he brought no mail back for her, but he did bring greetings from Katie and Emerald, and a collection of rugs. He explained that he wanted her to pick material for the curtains herself, as there was a large selection to choose from, so they fashioned temporary window coverings from flour sacks.

Alina, Beau and Pike settled into a comfortable routine with each other. Beau treated her with polite respect, although she sometimes caught him staring at her, his eyes burning with the familiar intensity that brought color to her cheeks.

Lately she had found herself staring at him as well. In the quiet of the long evenings, when he worked on the little table for the chess set, or when he took a turn reading from the Leatherstocking Tales in his deep voice, her eyes would devour his attractive features and eventually come to rest upon his sensuous lips. She would remember the first gentle kiss he had given her that night so long ago at the Satin Slipper. She wondered how she would feel if he kissed her again, but he did not try.

Finally the weather cleared enough for them to go to town. They stopped at the Freemans and invited the family along. Pike drove the wagon, and the women and children packed into the back and snuggled together for warmth. Beau and David followed on horseback.

In town, the men took the boys to Ingersoll's Livery, where David wanted to look for a new milk cow. Alina, Cynthia, Tanya, and Margarite went to Johnson's Mercantile.

Little bells tinkled when Alina pushed the door open. She led Tanya in, and Cynthia followed with the baby in her arms.

Bert pushed at his spectacles as he looked up from the bolt of cloth he was showing to a well-dressed woman. His face broke out in a wide grin. "I'll be with you in a few minutes, Mrs. Parker," he called to her. "Howdy, Mrs. Freeman."

Cynthia smiled and Alina nodded. "Take your time, Mr. Johnson." The woman at the counter looked over her shoulder. Her eyes narrowed with malevolence before she turned back to Bert. Cynthia nudged Alina with her elbow.

"You've heard of Madeline Petrie?" she whispered.

Alina nodded. Cynthia inclined her head in the direction of the counter. "That's her."

Alina eyed the woman with curiosity. She couldn't tell much from the back, but she could see that Madeline had a tiny waist and blond hair. She wondered how strong Beau's feelings were for the woman. He had never mentioned her, although many others had. She shrugged and looked down at Tanya.

"I need material for curtains. Will you help me?"

Tanya nodded eagerly. "Yes, ma'am." Cynthia wandered toward the back of the store.

Alina and Tanya made their way to a table piled high with bolts of colorful fabric and marveled over the selection. They narrowed their choices down to a yellow material with a floral pattern and a cheery blue gingham. They discussed the merits of each and tried to ignore the rising voices of Bert and the woman at the counter.

"I can't do that, Miss Petrie."

"You will, or I'll take my business to Gus Trabing."

"You already trade at Gus's, ma'am."

Madeline flushed. "He'll have my business exclusively from now on if you don't get that woman and her half-breed children out of here this minute! I won't be in the same room with them!"

Bert reached for the bolt of satin and began to roll it. "In that case, you are welcome to leave, Miss Petrie."

Madeline gasped and stared at the man in disbelief. "How dare you!" she spat. "I will *never* shop here again, nor will any of my friends. I'll see you ruined, Bert Johnson!" She turned and flounced toward the door.

Alina looked down at the now silent child beside her. She took Tanya's hand into her own and squeezed it comfortingly.

Madeline stopped at Alina's back. "So you're the new Mrs. Parker." Her voice was ugly.

Alina slowly turned and pushed Tanya behind her. "Yes, I am," she said sweetly. "And you must be Madeline Petrie. I've heard so much about you."

The two women stared at each other. Alina saw a pretty woman with a perfect hourglass figure dressed in a costly burgundy walking costume that would have been fashionable on the streets of Chicago. Her blond hair was arranged under a matching hat, and she carried a frilly parasol. Anger and resentment poured from her large brown eyes.

Madeline's feelings intensified when she saw how lovely Beau's bride was. Alina was dressed in a pale gray traveling suit with a high-collared white blouse graced by a simple cameo. She wore an old-fashioned black cape over it, and carried a serviceable umbrella. Her black curls were pulled up under a jaunty hat, and her blue eyes were as icy as the air outside.

Madeline tossed her head. "Beau never struck me as the

impulsive type. I was distressed to hear of his marriage, as he and I had an understanding. How did you force him to marry you?"

Alina's chin rose a notch. "Marriage was his idea. Perhaps you should ask him," she suggested coldly. She turned away in a dismissive gesture.

Madeline grabbed her arm. "Don't turn your back on me, you hussy! I know you worked in a saloon, and I know you're running from something in Chicago. I'll find out what it is, and I'll ruin you!"

"I must insist that you keep your hands to yourself." Alina pried the woman's grip from her arm. Sparks flew from her eyes. "You will be kept very busy, ruining me and Mr. Johnson and whoever else crosses you, won't you, Miss Petrie? Now, if you'll excuse us." Alina guided Tanya toward the counter.

"Beau Parker is mine," Madeline swore vehemently. "And I always get what's mine."

"Perhaps at one time he was yours, Miss Petrie." Alina did not bother to turn around. "He is no longer, by his choice." She continued to walk away, holding Tanya securely by the hand.

Madeline fumed in impotent rage, then stomped out, slamming the door behind her.

Bert came around the counter. "I apologize for that disgraceful display, ladies." He bent down to look into Tanya's solemn face. "I'm especially sorry you had to hear that, little one. Don't you listen to that nasty woman." He held out his arms. Tanya released Alina's hand and allowed Bert to pick her up. He carried her behind the counter to a row of jars filled with brightly colored sweets. "I think you should choose a piece of candy."

Tanya hesitated and looked to her mother.

"Go ahead, honey," Cynthia encouraged.

Still Tanya waited, and finally she whispered something to Bert.

"You're right," he said approvingly. "I think your brothers would like a piece, too. And maybe a soft piece for your little sister, if that's all right with your mother."

Cynthia nodded with a smile, then her face sobered. "How badly can she affect your business, Bert?"

"Miss Petrie? Not much. She doesn't come in here that often. She usually orders her dress goods from New York or Chicago." Bert set Tanya on the floor.

"What about her father, or her friends?"

"Richard Petrie doesn't do much business with me, either, and Madeline doesn't have any friends. Now, let's forget about her. What can I get for two of my favorite customers?"

"Alina, you go first," Cynthia offered. "I haven't decided on everything yet."

Alina nodded. "I need some material for curtains, and I think I'll go with the blue gingham, if Tanya agrees."

Tanya looked up from her candy. "The yellow is too flowery for Mr. Pike and Mr. Beau," she pronounced.

Alina smiled and turned back to Bert. "Here is my list, and I'd like to look at your collection of cookbooks."

A half an hour later, Bert set a bag of coffee beans on top of a barrel of cornmeal. "If that's all you think you'll be needing, ladies, I'll add the bills and we'll settle up when your men come for the supplies."

"That'll be fine, Bert." Cynthia shifted the sleeping baby on her arm and held out her right hand. "Thank you for standing up for me and my kids. It means a lot to me."

Bert took her hand and patted it. "You're surely welcome, Mrs. Freeman, though no thanks are needed. We just fought a terrible war to make this country free for everyone, and I'll not have the likes of Madeline Petrie keeping old hates alive, at least, not in my store."

"The old hates are still alive, and doing quite well, I assure you," Cynthia commented softly, sadly.

"I know," Bert answered. "But not in my store."

Cynthia pulled the blanket over Margarite's face, then turned to Alina. "Shall we go look for those men?"

Alina nodded. "We should also think about getting something to eat, and I want to visit Katie and Emerald. We'll see you later, Mr. Johnson," she called, as she pulled the door closed. They stood on the covered porch and looked up and down Second Street. The shrill sound of a train whistle echoed between the buildings. There was no sign of the men.

"Do you think they're still at the livery?" Alina asked.

"It wouldn't surprise me. David can be real particular when he gets it in his head to buy an animal."

Alina reached for Tanya's hand and they started up the street. The day was pleasant, without much wind, for a change, and the sun shone brightly. After a few minutes of silence, Cynthia spoke.

"How is it you have no prejudice against people of color, Alina?"

Alina looked at her friend. "How is it you have no prejudice against the Irish?" she countered with a smile.

"What difference does it make if you're Irish?" Cynthia asked, genuinely puzzled. "Many of the old settlers came from Ireland and Scotland."

"In some places, it makes a big difference, like Boston or New York City, for instance. Colored people are more welcome there than an Irishman is. Perhaps too many of us came during the Potato Famine." Alina shrugged. "That's when my parents came. They endured terrible prejudice at first, and therefore would allow none of it in our home. My brothers and I were taught that we were no better, and no worse, than any other. The prejudice is what drove my father west to Chicago. He felt he would have a better chance to make something of himself."

"Did he?"

Alina nodded. "Yes. He has been successful, but he worked very hard for what he has."

"That's why we came to Wyoming Territory," Cynthia said, as she shifted the baby up onto her shoulder. "It is one of the most liberal places in the country, the Madeline Petries of the world notwithstanding. Can you imagine women having the right to vote? It all started here. And there are several Negro families in the Territory. We'll make a good life here for our children."

Alina looked at her friend with a smile. "I think you already have."

A commotion in the street ahead caught their attention. A big man had a grip on a struggling boy about Tanya's age.

"That boy is the son of the Chinese couple who run the laundry," Alina said through tight lips.

"And the man is Log Carter, one of Richard Petrie's men, and a bully besides. David had a run-in with him." Cynthia shifted Margarite to her other hip. "That poor boy."

Alina looked at the few people on the street. No one seemed concerned about the child, although one man watched the proceedings as he leaned nonchalantly against a hitching post.

Alina dropped Tanya's hand. "Wait here with your mother."

"What are you going to do?" Cynthia asked nervously.

"I don't know yet, but I'm not going to stand here and watch that child be terrorized." She stepped off the boardwalk.

"Oh, be careful," Cynthia called after her. She turned to Tanya. "Run to the livery as fast as you can," she said urgently as she pushed at her daughter's shoulder. "Get Mr. Parker and your pa." Tanya took off down the street.

Alina approached the cowboy at the hitching post. "Do you know that man?" She waved her umbrella at the man in the street.

"Yes, ma'am," Ross Latham answered.

"Then please stop him from harassing that boy."

Carter had the boy facedown on the ground, his knee pressing into the child's back. He pulled on the boy's pigtail with one hand and brandished a hunting knife in the other.

"I don't tell Log what to do, lady," Ross responded.

Alina's eyes widened with disbelief. She glanced around and saw no one who appeared the slightest bit sympathetic.

"Well, I'll tell him what to do," she muttered. She picked up her skirts and marched into the street.

She stopped beside the big man and tapped his shoulder with her umbrella. Her nose wrinkled at his pungent and unpleasant scent. "Unhand that boy," she ordered. Carter looked up at her; his mouth opened in surprise, displaying rotten teeth.

"This ain't none of your business, lady," he snarled, and placed the knife under the boy's queue. Alina's umbrella came down on the top of his head and crushed his hat. A few of the onlookers laughed.

"I said unhand him!"

Carter's ugly face flushed. "I'll deal with you as soon as I'm done with this China-boy," he promised threateningly.

Alina's umbrella descended again, knocking his hat to the ground. "You'll deal with me now," she said through clenched teeth, as she brought her weapon down yet again, this time across the arm that held the knife. The umbrella bent from the force of her blow.

Carter dropped the knife and fell off the boy with a howl of rage and pain. Alina pulled the child to his feet and thrust him behind her. The big man got up, rubbing his forearm.

"I'll deal with you now," he agreed.

Alina brandished her bent umbrella. "Go to that lady holding the baby," she whispered to the frightened boy without taking her eyes from Carter. "Go on, now." The boy ran to Cynthia when she beckoned to him.

Alina was aware of the increasing number of spectators and hoped to use them to her advantage. "Are you going to show everyone what a big man you are by hitting a woman, Mr. Carter?" she taunted in a loud, clear voice. "The same way you demonstrated your prowess against a little boy?"

Carter shook his head. He didn't understand most of her last sentence, but he understood the first. "No woman hits ol' Log and gets away with it. You hit me, I hit you," he said with an evil grin. "It's as simple as that."

People in the crowd muttered disapprovingly, but no one

stepped forward. Her heart pounding, Alina stood her ground as the man approached, his big, dirty hands clenched into meaty fists. She gripped her umbrella with both hands and held it up over her shoulder. Her mouth was set in a determined line.

The man from the hitching post spoke. "That's enough, Log."

Carter stopped a few feet from her. "This ain't none of your affair, Ross," he warned. He did not take his eyes from Alina's face. "And I'm gettin' goddam tired of tellin' people to stay outta my business." He took another step toward her.

Alina caught a glimpse of a woman in a burgundy dress on the boardwalk across the street. She recognized Madeline Petrie and saw the fiercely joyous look on the woman's face. She turned her attention to Carter again.

He reached for her and Alina swung her umbrella with all her might. It caught him across the face, the bent wires scratching his skin. She stepped back, still clutching her weapon, her breathing ragged. Carter wiped his hand over his cheek; when his hand came away smeared with a small amount of blood, his eyes bulged. With a roar of anger, he lunged at her. Alina sidestepped him, but he caught a handful of her skirt. His other hand closed on her shoulder, then he froze at the sound of a gun being cocked.

"It's one thing to have a little fun with a China-boy, Log, but I draw the line at hitting women." Ross Latham's drawling tone was conversational. "Let her go." He still leaned against the post, but his pistol was in his hand and his steel-gray eyes were hard.

Carter pushed Alina away. "Another time, Miss Nosy Britches," he promised, his jaw tight with fury. "I'm not finished with you." He stomped over to retrieve his knife and hat from the street.

"Thank you, sir, for your assistance." Alina felt shaky and weak.

Latham slid his gun into the holster and straightened. "You're welcome, ma'am." He touched the brim of his hat, admiration glinting in his eyes. Alina nodded, then walked back to join Cynthia. She dropped to one knee next to the boy and pulled her handkerchief from her sleeve.

"Are you all right?" she asked softly.

The boy nodded, his dark eyes huge and tear-filled. Alina rubbed at the dirt on his cheek. She reached around his neck and pulled his queue over his shoulder. "He didn't cut your hair."

"Thank you, ma'am," he whispered. There was a noise from the street. Alina rose, one arm around the child's shoulders. The boy's father came running from one direction, while Beau and David came from the opposite direction. Ross Latham and Log Carter crossed the street to join Madeline.

The boy pulled away from Alina and ran to his father as Beau and David approached.

"Are you all right?" Beau took Alina's shoulders in his hands and looked her over for signs of injury.

She nodded. "I'm fine, Beau, really I am." She tried not to show how happy and relieved she was to see him.

He draped one arm across her shoulders and pulled her against his side. He stared across the street at Log, Ross, and Madeline. "What happened? I couldn't make sense of what Tanya was trying to tell us."

"Log Carter was accosting the boy. He intended to cut off his queue. No one was going to stop him."

Beau's hold on her tightened. "So you did?"

"I couldn't stand by and do nothing, Beau. I didn't think he'd attack me, not in front of everyone." She watched as the boy excitedly told his father, in Chinese, what had happened. He turned and pointed to her. The man straightened and, holding his son by the hand, came up to them.

"T'ank . . . you for . . . helping my . . . son," he said, and formally bowed.

"You are welcome, sir." Alina bowed her head in return.

The slight man turned and walked away. The child looked

back over his shoulder and shyly raised his free hand in farewell. Alina waved at him with a smile.

Pike pulled the wagon to a halt in front of them. David Junior, Tanya, and Lincoln watched from the wagon bed with wide eyes.

"What's goin' on here?" Pike demanded.

"Alina stood up to Log Carter, Pike," Beau answered, his arm tightening on her again. He took the destroyed umbrella from her and held it up. "She won."

Pike looked down at her incredulously.

Alina nodded across the street toward Ross Latham. "Without that man's help, I don't know what would have happened. He wouldn't do anything to help the boy, but he wouldn't let the brute hurt me. What an unusual code of ethics."

"Log Carter is lucky he didn't hurt you," Beau said through gritted teeth.

"You would have been here before he could have done much, even without Ross Latham's help," Cynthia assured him.

"And I wouldn't have minded another chance at Carter myself," David added as he took Margarite from Cynthia.

Beau eyed the group across the street. "Wait here for just a minute." He tossed the umbrella to Pike, then moved around the horses and started across the street.

"Why did you interfere, Ross?" Madeline demanded furiously.

Latham looked at her with a mixture of amazement and disgust on his face. "Like I told Log, Madeline, I draw the line at hitting women." He hesitated a moment. "Usually," he finished meaningfully.

Madeline was about to say something else when she saw Beau approaching. A smile instantly covered her face.

"Hello, Beau," she said, her voice soft.

"Madeline." He nodded curtly. He turned to Latham. "Thank you for coming to the aid of my wife."

Latham raised his eyebrows. So that courageous, handsome woman was the new Mrs. Parker. No wonder Madeline was so angry. He shrugged. "No problem, Parker."

Beau turned to Carter. "You're lucky Latham stopped you. Had you harmed her in any way, you'd have answered to me."

"I'll still answer to you." Carter's features were ugly with resentment. "Maybe I can teach you how to control yore woman. She needs to learn to keep her nose outta other folks' business." He started forward.

Madeline placed one hand on Beau's chest and glared over her shoulder at Carter. "There will be no more fighting, gentlemen, not in front of me. I find such behavior abhorrent." She shivered delicately. "It's in poor taste to engage in public brawling, and in the middle of the street, no less. I can't imagine what your wife was thinking, Beau."

Beau backed away from Madeline's hand. "She had her reasons," he said bluntly, not taking his eyes from Carter. "Stay away from my wife."

Carter did not answer.

"Madeline." Beau touched the brim of his hat.

Madeline fumed as he walked away. "Get the carriage, Log," she ordered. The big man lumbered off. She tapped one hand with her parasol, her eyes narrowed in thought. "I think I may take a trip to Chicago, Ross. You did well, but I need more information. I might find a conversation with Mrs. Parker's former guardian most enlightening. Yes, I think that's what I'll do." She turned to Latham. "Get me a ticket on the next train that has a first-class compartment, then meet me at the house."

Carter pulled the team to a stop in front of them. Latham helped Madeline into the conveyance. "Get a ticket for yourself, too, Ross," she said as she arranged her skirts. "I can't travel such a distance all alone, and Father did hire you as my bodyguard." Latham nodded, ignoring the gleam in Madeline's eye. He stared after the departing carriage for a moment, then turned to go. His eye fell on the group across the street. Beau Parker was a lucky man. He trudged toward the railroad station.

Beau placed a protective arm around Alina once again. "What you did was very brave, and I'm proud of you. But next time, wait for me."

"Next time, don't dawdle," she retorted, but she did not pull away from him. It felt good to have his arm around her.

Lincoln hung over the top of the wagon. "I'm hungry, Mama."

Pike spoke up. "The boy has the right idea. Kate's invited all of us ta the Slipper. And Emerald threatened me with terrible bodily harm if we don't get Miz Parker over ta see her, so I suggest we head that way." He took up the reins. "All aboard, or you'll walk."

A few minutes later, Katie opened the double doors herself when the wagon stopped in front of the Satin Slipper. "Come in, come in," she cried. "Let's get these kids outta the cold." She herded everyone inside.

"Alina, girl, ya're a sight for sore eyes," she sighed, and the two women embraced. "And Beau Parker, so is your handsome self." She left Alina and held out her arms to Beau. Emerald came running from the kitchen and threw her arms around Alina. The Freemans stood in silent awe and looked around the elegant saloon. The few patrons eyed the newcomers curiously.

Katie turned to David and held out her hand. "Ya must be Mr. Freeman. Welcome to my establishment."

"Yes, ma'am," he answered with a wide smile, and shook her hand. He put his other arm around Cynthia. "This is my wife, Cynthia, and she's holding our youngest, Margarite."

"How do, Mrs. Freeman," Katie said cheerfully. "Alina told me all about ya and your family in a letter. I'm pleased ta meet ya."

Cynthia shifted the baby and held out her hand. "I've heard of you, too, Miss Davenport. Thank you for inviting us to your place."

Katie shook Cynthia's hand. "For heaven's sake, call me

Katie." She turned toward the kitchen. "Emerald has fixed a nice meal for all of us. Let's see if I can guess which of these gorgeous children is Tanya. I'll bet she's the prettiest one. And I know one is David Junior and one is Lincoln."

Lincoln pulled at her skirt. "I'm Lincoln."

"So ya are, child," Katie laughed. She held out her hand to him and they led the way into the kitchen.

The conversation was lively throughout the meal as the adults caught up with the happenings in each other's lives. When the bowls and plates were empty, Alina and Emerald cleared the table. Emerald pulled two warm pies from the oven and cut them while Alina found a stack of small plates.

"Ross Latham's been around, digging for information about Alina," Katie commented. "He's gotten real cozy with Delilah."

Alina turned to look at her. "Who is Latham, and why would he want to know about me?"

"He's the one who stopped Carter today," Beau answered. "He works for Richard Petrie."

"So why does he want to know about me?" she repeated as she carried plates of pie to the table.

"My guess is Madeline put him up to it," Katie said. "She was mad as hell when I told her about the two of ya weddin' up." She glanced at the children, her attractive face suddenly flushed with embarrassment. "I apologize for my swearing," she whispered. Tanya and David Junior giggled. "And what's this about Carter?" Katie continued. "Ya're not talking about Log Carter, are ya?"

"The same, Katie." Beau picked up his fork. "Alina got into it with him today." He took a bite of the canned-peach pie and closed his eyes in ecstasy.

"Beau Parker, don't ya dare leave me hanging like this! What d'ya mean, she got into it with him?" Katie turned to Alina. "What did ya do, girl?"

Alina shrugged as she returned to the table with two more plates. "I hit him over the head with my umbrella," she said casually, and sat down.

Katie rolled her eyes. "Here we go again," she muttered. "Just like when ya shot the knothole outta the wall."

Beau choked on his pie.

"You shot a knothole out of the wall?" Cynthia asked with delight.

"Cynthia, you tell Katie what happened with Carter," Alina suggested, her face bright red.

Cynthia moved her pie plate from Margarite's reach. "Log Carter was bullying a Chinese boy, the one whose folks run the laundry over on First Street. He was going to cut off the boy's pigtail, and you know how the Chinese set store by their hair. Anyway, Log had his knife in his hand, and this poor child on the ground, and Alina told him to stop, but he wouldn't, so she hit him with her umbrella."

"Well, I'll be d—" Katie caught herself.

"Log turned on her, and Ross Latham stepped in. Then Beau and David got there, and it was all over," Cynthia finished.

"Alina, girl, ya watch your step," Katie warned. "Stay away from Log Carter, 'cause he has a long memory, and he's mean through and through. He likes to beat up on women. He hurt Grace real bad. I won't let him in here anymore."

Alina nodded, feeling weary and depressed all of a sudden. It seemed she had made another enemy. She could eat no more. She pushed back from the table and carried her pie to the counter. "I also met Madeline today," she said over her shoulder. Beau and Katie exchanged glances. "She doesn't seem to like me much, either."

"No, Ah don't guess she would at that," Emerald interjected as she rose from her chair. "Yo' is too pretty, and yo' got the man she fancied."

Katie cleared her throat. "Why don't ya men take your coffee and these boys into my office? Ya can smoke in there if ya've a mind to, and us girls will clean up this mess."

At that, everyone moved away from the table. Beau came up behind Emerald, leaned around her, and planted a kiss on her dark cheek. "Thank you for a delicious meal, Emerald."

"Don't yo' be trying that sweet stuff with me, Mr. Beau," a pleased Emerald retorted. "Yo' and yore tickly mustache. How can yo' stand to kiss him, Miz 'Lina?"

Alina blushed as Beau glanced at her.

Emerald continued her tirade. "And with my man in the room, and yo' woman, and all these young'uns. Yo' get on outta my kitchen, now." She shooed at the laughing Beau with her apron. "All yo' menfolks get outta my kitchen, and leave us women in peace!"

"I guess we got told, huh?" Pike grumbled good-naturedly as he picked Lincoln up and followed the rest of the men through the door.

Suddenly Katie gasped. She grabbed a flour sack towel from the counter and rushed out of the room. She returned in a minute without the towel, a sheepish grin on her face. "Those boys are in that office, and I forgot about the naked-lady lamp on the desk," she explained in a whisper, with an eye on Tanya, who was helping Emerald at the sink. Alina and Cynthia exchanged smiles.

The women spent an enjoyable hour in the warm kitchen, then Beau poked his head in the door.

"I realize I am taking my life in my hands by invading your kitchen, Emerald, but it's getting late, and we must head home."

"We have to pick up our supplies, and the cow, if David found one," Cynthia added.

"He did," Beau confirmed, and disappeared. A minute later the kitchen was full again, and the noise was great as coats were handed out and children were bundled up.

The wagon pulled away a few minutes later as a chorus of goodbyes filled the air. After hurried stops at the mercantile, the post office, and the livery, where the protesting cow was tied to the end of the wagon, they headed toward home.

Alina opened the new umbrella Beau had purchased for her and positioned it against the sun. Tanya was snuggled next to her and Alina knew the child would soon be asleep.

Cynthia watched her friend with affection. "Katie and Emerald sure are nice. Do you miss them?"

"Terribly," Alina admitted. "But it has helped, now that I have found you, and they will be able to visit when spring comes." She grew thoughtful. "I am glad I don't live there anymore, though. I am much more comfortable at the ranch."

"Of course you are," Cynthia agreed. "Especially with that handsome husband of yours."

Especially with that handsome husband of yours. Cynthia's words echoed in Alina's head. Her eyes fell on Beau. He and David followed the wagon once again, speaking quietly. Beau rode the bay, sitting tall and graceful in the saddle. Alina watched him for a long time, her eyes shaded by the umbrella.

Chapter Ten

Cordelia Randall slowly descended the curving staircase of Neil Gallagher's home, her lips pursed in thought as she examined the calling card in her hand. Her striped satin dress rustled softly with her movements. She paused before the doors to the parlor and threw the card on a side table, then swept into the room. A lovely young woman in an elaborate lilac carriage outfit rose from the sofa to face her.

"Miss Petrie? I am Cordelia Randall." Cordelia made her way to the fireplace and pulled on the bell rope that hung beside the chimney. She waved her hand in a silent invitation to sit.

"I'm pleased to meet you." Madeline sank back on the sofa, resting her gloved hands on the handle of her braced parasol. Cordelia settled into a low-armed chair, careful of her large bustle, and eyed her guest with curiosity. Miss Petrie did not fit Cordelia's idea of a female from that god-forsaken Wyoming Territory. Her costly outfit was in the latest style, and she was obviously well mannered. The butler appeared at the door.

"Yes, madam?"

"Davis, bring tea and a light refreshment for us."

The man bowed and backed out of the room, closing the doors as he went.

"Now, please explain the purpose of your visit, Miss Petrie. Your letter was intriguing, but uninformative. I don't quite understand how you think we can be of use to one another."

Madeline leaned her parasol against the sofa and pulled at her gloves. She set them on the low table in front of her and after smoothing her skirt, clasped her hands in her lap. "If my sources are correct, an event occurred in Laramie City this February past which you found as distressful as I did."

Cordelia's eyes narrowed. "Go on."

"I am referring, of course, to the marriage of your ward to a local rancher named Beauregard Parker. I believe you had set your sights somewhat higher as far as a match for your ward is concerned, and the ungrateful girl refused to honor your wishes."

Cordelia dipped her head in agreement. "Your sources are very accurate, Miss Petrie. Pray explain why this disgraceful match was so distressing to you."

"Mr. Parker and I had an understanding. It was my intention to marry him myself, thus fulfilling my father's wishes." Madeline's pretty face wore a downcast expression.

Cordelia snorted in a most unladylike fashion. "Surely a woman of your obvious breeding and background could not wish to marry that cowboy."

"It's what my father wishes." Madeline shrugged her dainty shoulders. "Mr. Parker's land adjoins my father's, and Father feels an alliance would be advantageous. As for myself, my first duty is naturally to my father. However, I must admit I do find Mr. Parker somewhat attractive, in a barbaric sort of way."

Cordelia snorted again, but was prevented from responding by a knock at the door. "Enter!" she snapped impatiently.

Davis delivered a silver tray to the low, marble-topped table in front of the sofa. He arranged everything within Cordelia's reach and waited until she spoke.

"That will be all, Davis."

"Very good, madam." The butler silently left the room.

Cordelia reached for the teapot. "So my ward's little

arrangement upset your plans as well. I still don't see what assistance we can offer each other. Do you use sugar and milk?"

"Yes, thank you." Madeline leaned forward. "Mrs. Randall, perhaps I've not made myself clear . . . I am devoted to my father, and am determined that his wishes be honored."

Cordelia handed Madeline a cup and caught a flash of furious determination in the younger woman's eyes.

Madeline nodded her thanks as she took the cup and continued. "I'm here to discuss possible ways we could work together for our mutual benefit. The marriage must be ended."

Cordelia sampled her tea, then spoke. "I understand how the dissolution of the marriage would benefit you. But what makes you think I care any longer? Alina has made her choice."

Madeline stared coldly at her. "Mrs. Randall, I have learned that the right combination of cash and persuasion can uncover the most interesting information. Therefore, let us not play games. Your position is fine, for now, but I know that upon Alina's twenty-fifth birthday, you'll have to give all this up." She waved a hand to indicate the lavish room. "Somehow, I don't think she will invite you and your son—Donovan, isn't it?—to remain with her."

Cordelia set her cup down on the marble-topped table with such force that the saucer cracked. Her dark eyes glittered with a dangerous anger.

"Oh, come now, Mrs. Randall," Madeline soothed. "There's no need to get upset. You see, we understand each other perfectly. You want Alina for your son, and for her money. I want Beau, for myself and for his ranch. It's really quite simple."

Cordelia leaned back in the chair, now unmindful of her bustle. She rested her elbows on the arms of the chair and made a tent of her fingers. "What do you have in mind?"

Madeline sighed. "That is the problem. I don't know what to do at this point. The marriage is legal; I checked on that."

Cordelia nodded as she rose. "As did I." She pulled the bell rope again. The women were silent until Davis knocked lightly on the door.

"Ask Mr. Donovan to join us immediately."

The butler nodded and withdrew.

"My son may have some thoughts on the matter," Cordelia said as she returned to her chair.

"An excellent idea. I look forward to meeting him." Madeline sipped her tea.

A few minutes later, Donovan stormed into the room without knocking. "Really, Mother, I hope this is important. I was just on my way . . ." He halted in mid-sentence. "I beg your pardon. I didn't know you had a guest." He eyed the attractive woman on the sofa with interest as he threw his coat on a chair. He advanced to Cordelia's side and kissed her cheek.

"Donovan, I would like to present Miss Madeline Petrie. Miss Petrie, my son."

Donovan bowed over the hand Madeline held out to him and gallantly brought it to his lips. "I'm delighted to make your acquaintance, Miss Petrie." He could not take his eyes from Madeline's lovely face. A becoming blush covered her cheeks; she dropped her lids and extricated her hand from Donovan's eager hold. His gaze swept over her, lingering on her full bosom.

"Please join us," Cordelia invited. Donovan settled next to Madeline.

"Miss Petrie has come from Laramie City with a very interesting proposal." Cordelia briefly related their previous conversation. "We've asked you to join us because we have no plan," she concluded, "and we thought you could help us."

"Actually, I had one idea, but I don't think you'll agree to it." Madeline toyed with the decoration on her overskirt.

Donovan smiled at the sound of her sweet voice. "And what is that, Miss Petrie?"

"For my purposes, the most logical answer is to kill Alina."

Donovan laughed. His mother did not. She saw the look in Madeline's eyes and knew the girl was deadly serious. Cordelia repressed a shudder.

"However," Madeline continued, "murder can be so messy, and one always runs the danger of getting caught. Besides, that solution would not be advantageous to you unless you were next in line to inherit the estate. As you are related by marriage only, and there is the old aunt who would inherit, the idea probably won't do at all." She sighed.

"Mother, she is a delight!" Donovan cried.

Cordelia watched the woman with fascinated concern. How did the chit know so much about the legal situation? She cautioned herself to proceed with the utmost care. She sensed that the pretty Miss Petrie could become a dangerous acquaintance.

"Of course that won't do, my dear," Cordelia admonished lightheartedly. "Let's be serious, now. What shall we do?"

"We could kill Parker," Donovan suggested with a grin.

Madeline turned to him, her eyes frosty, her features tight. "That won't do, either," she said with great coldness.

The smile fled Donovan's face. "I was joking, Miss Petrie. Forgive me."

Cordelia glared at him, then shifted her gaze to Madeline. "How long do you intend to stay in Chicago?"

"A week, perhaps. I hope to visit some of the shops while I'm here."

"And where are you staying?"

Madeline pouted. "When I was here a year ago, I stayed at the Palmer House, but it burned in that inconvenient fire, and I fear my quarters are less than satisfactory."

"But you must stay here, with us. Mother, I insist that she remain as our guest." Donovan looked hopefully at Cordelia.

"Of course you must stay, Miss Petrie. Our fair city is

sadly changed from the time of your last visit, and I fear you will find many of the shops gone. It will be much easier if you allow me to act as your hostess and guide during your stay. Surely we'll think of some plan before you return home."

Madeline pursed her lips. She had not anticipated this turn of events. She would be far more comfortable here, but it would be decidedly more difficult to entice Ross Latham to her bed, and she was determined to have the resistant cowboy. She glanced at Donovan from under lowered lids. He was attractive enough, and displayed more enthusiasm for her attentions than Latham ever had. Perhaps Mr. Randall would prove a most intriguing diversion. She made her decision; Ross would have to wait.

"I can't express my gratitude at your generosity, Mrs. Randall. And you, Mr. Randall, have certainly made me feel welcome. I accept your kind invitation." She gave Donovan the full force of her charming smile.

"I insist you call me Donovan, my dear," he said as he took her hand. "I have the feeling we will become fast friends."

"Then you must call me Madeline." She looked at Cordelia. "Both of you."

Cordelia stood. "Very well, Madeline. Are you traveling with a companion?"

"Oh, my, no." Madeline's tinkling laughter filled the room. She ignored Cordelia's disapproving expression. "One advantage of life in the Territory is that women are allowed much greater freedom. I haven't traveled with a chaperon since I left the schoolroom. One of my father's men has accompanied me as a guard, but he will stay at the hotel. I'm sure I will be quite safe with you." She squeezed Donovan's hand as she spoke.

"Donovan, please make arrangements to have Miss Petrie's things brought from the hotel. I'll alert the staff that we have a guest." Cordelia swept regally from the room.

Donovan's lips curved in a sly smile. "I think this next

week will prove most interesting. Don't you agree, Madeline?"

Madeline raised knowing eyes to his face. "Yes, most interesting, I'm sure. Just don't forget that our primary relationship is one of a business nature. I am quite determined that Beau Parker's marriage to your dear Alina be ended, and I always get what I want." There was a steely edge to her voice that gave Donovan pause. Then he shrugged.

"Whatever you say." He stood and reached for the bell pull. He was certain he could handle the enchanting woman from Wyoming Territory. He did not notice the calculating gleam in her lovely brown eyes.

Alina opened the door for the third time in ten minutes and peered into the night. The lantern she had hung from a rafter of the porch roof swayed in the wind, casting its light in a small moving circle. She pulled her shawl more tightly around her and stepped out onto the porch. Her ears searched for the sound of an approaching horse as she strained to see down the road. She heard and saw nothing. Worry sat like a rock in her stomach.

"I know it's the second week of April, but the wind don't know it's spring yet!" Pike roared from inside. "Get in here and close that door, woman!"

Alina smiled and obeyed his command. "It's been four days now, Mr. Pike." She shivered and walked over to stir the pot of stew that bubbled merrily on the stove. "Ever since he got that letter from Washington last month, he's been acting strange, and . . . secretive, and he's been gone so often. Are you sure you don't know where he is?"

Pike looked up from the boot he was polishing. "I told ya I don't know," he said stiffly. "I ain't his mother, and I wouldn't lie ta ya." He maneuvered his chair to face the fire and turned away from her.

Alina was filled with remorse as she flew to his side. "Oh, Mr. Pike, I'm sorry! I know you'd never lie to me. It's just that he's never been gone this long." She dropped to her knees and sat back on her heels, twisting her wedding ring. "Forgive me?" she pleaded.

"Ya know I do," Pike answered with gruff affection. He thought for a minute. "He could be hunting the varmint that killed Ambrose. He's sworn ta find the bastard, beg pardon, no matter what. It eats at him. He ain't had a moment's peace, not really, since he got here, and he ain't leavin' 'til the murderer is caught."

"How does he know the murderer is still around here?" Alina asked. "Maybe it was some drifter."

Pike shook his head. "A drifter would've taken Bay and the guns. No, Ambrose's death was a message." He paused. "Ya know, Beau used ta work for the government in Washington. Maybe that letter had somethin' ta do with that," he said, almost to himself.

Alina smiled. So Pike wondered what was going on, too.

Pike eyed the boot critically. "Don't worry so about Beau, ma'am. He can take care of hisself."

"Like Ambrose could?" she asked softly. Pike's gaze riveted on her face. She shrugged. "I can't help thinking about that."

Pike did not answer. He rubbed the boot with fierce strength. After a few minutes of silence, Alina spoke again.

"Will you tell me something straight, even if I won't like the answer?"

The old man nodded. "Ya know I will."

"Do you think he's with Madeline Petrie?"

Pike looked at her in astonishment. "Whatever would make ya think such a thing?"

Alina dropped her eyes, an embarrassed flush reddening her face. "I don't know. She's just so pretty, and she seems to really want him." *And I've told him I don't.*

"I know ya and Beau have a strange set-up, Miz Parker, but he'd never be with another woman when he's married ta ya," Pike said firmly. "I'm sure he has a good reason for bein' away, and he'll tell us when he wants us ta know."

Alina was not convinced. She got up and moved toward the door. Pike watched her.

"Beau'll be here when he gets here. Standing on the porch lookin' for him, with the damn door wide open, beg pardon, ain't gonna get him here any sooner."

Alina guiltily glanced back at him. Pike winked at her. "You're right," she sighed, and returned to her stew.

"It couldn't be that ya're beginnin' ta feel sweet on the man, could it?" Pike asked nonchalantly as he returned to his chore.

Alina whirled around. "Of course not! But I do care for his safety. He has been a good friend to me."

Pike nodded, a wise expression on his weathered face. "Yep, he's a good friend, all right."

The sound of hoofbeats reached their ears. Alina ran to the door and again let in an icy draft.

"Damn," Pike complained, "beg pardon. A body could freeze ta death in his own house."

Beau pulled up at the porch and leaned out of the saddle to take the lantern from its nail. "Thanks for the light. I'll be in directly." He turned the horse toward the barn. Alina closed the door, a relieved smile on her face.

Pike had moved his chair close to the fire. "Do ya feel better now?" he asked without looking up.

Alina took bowls from the shelf. "At least I know how many places to set," she replied tartly.

"Beau'll be touched ta know that ya worried about him."

Alina dropped the bowls on the table with a clatter. "Don't you dare tell him," she warned, her hands on her hips.

"Or ya'll do what?" A wide grin covered Pike's face.

Alina stomped over to grab the tin of flatware. "Or I'll, I'll . . ." She turned to the table in frustration. Pike laughed. An idea came to her. "I'll call you Sebastian Amadeus for the rest of your life," she finished triumphantly.

Pike rose out of his chair. "Ya wouldn't do that ta me!"

"I would," Alina promised. Her eyes sparkled with humor.

"Ya're a heartless woman," Pike groaned.

"Desperate times call for desperate measures, Mr. Pike," Alina said sweetly as Beau came through the door. She continued to set the dishes around the table.

"Who's desperate?" Beau asked innocently. He pulled his gloves from his hands.

"Mr. Pike is. He's desperate to eat, so you're lucky you got here now. There may not have been anything left."

"It sure smells good, whatever it is," Beau commented as he hung his coat and hat.

Pike carried his chair back to the table and sat down. "Miz Parker's turning into a right decent cook."

"Thank you, Mr. Pike, but don't exaggerate." Alina came from the stove with the heavy pot of stew, a cloth wrapped around the handle. "I do all right with simple dishes, but that's it. I still can't make biscuits worth a hoot."

"It'll come, Alina," Beau assured her. He took his seat.

"Does it feel cold in here ta ya?" Pike asked Beau with a twinkle in his eye. Alina shot him a warning glance and mouthed the word "Sebastian."

Beau missed their exchange. "Not after riding in that wind for a few hours. But I'll build up the fire, if you like."

"We'll just eat," Alina said firmly, and reached for his bowl. "We were concerned when you didn't come home." She did not look at his face as she set his full bowl in front of him.

"I got tied up. There was no way to get word to you." He took a mouthful of stew. "This is good."

Alina stole a glance at him. There was a stubborn set to his features, and she could see that he was exhausted. He was not going to explain his absence, at least not tonight.

The next day he was up early again. He ate quickly and left to saddle his horse. Alina went out to the porch.

"Would you like me to make you a lunch?" she asked.

"No, thank you." Bay's reins were draped over the porch

rail. Beau stood beside the horse and tightened the cinch. "I'm heading into town. I'll get a bite there. Give me any letters you want mailed."

Alina went back inside, a frown covering her face. He was going to town without asking if she wanted to go? Without asking Pike? She pulled a bundle of addressed envelopes from her letter box and returned to the porch. He was in the saddle now. She silently handed him the letters.

Guilt washed over Beau when he saw the troubled look on her lovely face, but he pushed it away and placed the bundle in his saddlebag. "Do you need anything from the mercantile?"

"I'm getting low on writing paper and envelopes."

Beau smiled at her. "You do write a heap of letters." He turned Bay's head toward the road. "I'll be home by supper."

"Say hello to Katie if you see her!" she called. He waved in acknowledgment as the horse clattered over the bridge. Alina crossed her arms and stared after him until he disappeared from view.

She went inside and dropped dispiritedly into a chair. Perhaps he was getting bored with the whole situation, she thought. She couldn't blame him; she consistently treated him with distant politeness, allowing nothing else to develop. Those had been the terms of their agreement, and it was best to remember that her stay here was temporary.

Alina looked around the room. It was very different from that first day. Simple curtains made from the cheerful blue gingham hung at the windows and from the countertop, a serviceable tablecloth covered the battered table, and colorful rugs dotted the floor. A framed Currier and Ives print hung over Beau's bed, and the finished chess table stood between the sofa and the fireplace with the treasured chess set in place.

She marveled at the beautiful table. Beau had engraved the pedestal with a pattern of leaves and vines, and the top and base were smooth and polished. She had enjoyed watching the table take shape, although she had sometimes envied the wood for the skilled touch of his long fingers.

Alina pressed her hands to suddenly hot cheeks. What was she thinking? She mentally shook herself and stood to clear the table. She had no business longing for the touch of his fingers, and the man owed her no explanation for his actions. She had done well these last two months, resisting the pull of his eyes, and she would continue to do so. She rose and marched over to the sink.

Before long, the few dishes were washed and a batch of rising bread dough sat in its cloth-covered bowl on the counter. Restless, Alina went again to the porch. The day was clear and almost warm, the wind no more than a breeze. Conditions were perfect for target practice.

She went back inside to the bedroom. Curtains now hung at that window now, too, and a few more hooks had been added to the wall. Her eyes fell on the carved footboard and she reached out to caress the fine wood finish. Had Beau made this bed? She reached under the bed for her rifle and the box of cartridges.

Alina followed the sound of Pike's hammer across the yard, scattering chickens as she went. He was pounding on a metal wheel rim at the forge. He looked up at her; his eyes widened with surprise and interest when he saw the rifle.

"Are ya gonna shoot me?" he teased. "I swear I didn't say nothin' ta Beau about how ya're sweet on him."

Alina managed a small smile. "I'm not sweet on him, Mr. Pike, any more than he's sweet on me. You know the situation. Is there a place I can practice without scaring the stock?"

"Beau and I usually set up cans and such on the fence 'round back of the barn when we practice. I'll show ya. I need ta take a break from this old wheel anyways. It's fightin' me." He laid the hammer on the anvil and wiped his forehead with his sleeve. "Outta curiosity, when are ya gonna drop that 'mister' ya insist on puttin' in front of my name?"

"When you drop the 'Mrs. Parker' and call me Alina," came the quick retort.

A grin creased Pike's weathered face. "Fair enough, Alina. Wait here a minute."

She smiled to herself. Pike always knew how to make her feel better. He crossed the yard, his peg making its peculiar track in the soft ground, and returned with an assortment of cans in various stages of rusting. He led the way through the barn and out the back door.

He eyed Alina's rifle. "Don't think I've ever seen a rifle like that. What kind is it?"

"It's a Colt sporting rifle," Alina said proudly. "My father ordered it from Samuel Colt himself, in 1859. He later gave it to me, on my eighteenth birthday. I treasure it."

"Can ya hit anything with it?"

"I can."

"Wait here," Pike ordered. He crossed the pasture to set a number of cans on the rail fence, then retraced his steps.

Alina loaded the rifle and held it out to him. "Go ahead. Look at her. Shoot her, if you like."

Pike took the gun from her with reverence. "Her?"

Alina smiled sheepishly. "I call her Betsy."

Pike's eyes twinkled. "Do ya have ta have a name for everything?" he teased. "Horses, guns. Ya've probably named those damn chickens, beg pardon."

Alina shook her head, her grin widening. "Not yet."

Pike winked at her. "I'm just funnin' with ya, girl." He examined the weapon with wonder. "A revolving rifle. Would ya just look at that. And see that fancy engraving on the barrel and the plate." He turned the weapon over and read the inscription on the bottom of the stock, then settled the butt against his shoulder. "Let's see what Betsy can do."

He gently squeezed the trigger and a can jumped off the fence. "Nice. Not much kick to her at all." He handed the rifle to Alina. "Now let's see what Alina can do."

She took the rifle and aimed. Another can flew from the fence. In quick succession she pulled the hammer, aimed, and fired, and in quick succession four more cans fell. She crouched down to the box of cartridges on the ground and reloaded.

Pike scratched his beard. "Not bad, girl, not bad at all."

Alina squinted toward the fence. "I'd guess that's only about fifty yards, Mr., uh, Pike. It would be difficult to miss at that range." There was no hint of boasting in her tone.

Pike looked at her in amazement. Alina did not notice. She straightened and took aim at a long dead pine tree halfway up the hillside another fifty yards beyond the fence.

"What are ya aimin' at?"

"The branches on that dead tree up there."

"That tallest one?" Pike gaped.

"Yes," Alina breathed as she squeezed off a shot.

A branch vanished. "I'll be damned," Pike whispered. He forgot to beg pardon as he watched five more branches disappear. "That must be a hundred yards. Do ya ever miss?"

"Not often."

They took turns with the rifle until the box of cartridges was almost empty. Alina massaged her right shoulder.

"It must be near to noon. I've got to check on my dough. If you're hungry, I'll put some food on the table."

Pike nodded in agreement. He handed her the rifle. "Give me a few minutes ta wrestle with that wheel rim, and I'll be in. I'd be interested ta watch how ya clean Betsy there."

Alina nodded. "I'll save that for later, then." They walked through the barn. "Thank you for spending some time with me, Pike. I enjoyed myself."

"Well, girl, so did I. Just remind me ta not make ya mad." He winked at her and headed back toward the forge.

Alina slowly walked to the cabin, her eyes wandering over the land. There was a fresh beauty to this wild place that she loved. She breathed deeply of the clean air. Chicago seemed like another world now, one that was far away and long ago, one to which she was no longer sure she wanted to return. She missed the people she loved, but not the life. That was somehow disturbing, for this was Beau's home, not hers, and she feared she was wearing out her welcome.

Several hours later, she was pulling the last loaf of bread from the oven when she heard the sound of an approaching horse. She set the hot pan on the counter and walked out onto the porch, pushing a stray curl from her cheek.

Beau climbed down from the saddle. He held one arm at his waist in a strange position. "Howdy," he said. He looked at her and his heart lurched. He saw her beauty as if for the first time again. Her outfit was simple: the black skirt, the white blouse with the sleeves rolled up to her elbows, the white apron tied around her narrow waist. Wispy curls kissed the sides of her face and hung against her neck. Her lovely eyes seemed to shine. She was more beautiful to him now than she had been that first night, when she had worn the elegant ballgown.

"Beau, why are you staring at me?" she asked with a laugh. Her hand flew self-consciously to her cheek. "Do I have flour on my face or something?"

Beau swallowed and rubbed the side of his neck. "You just look so pretty, Alina."

She blushed and looked down for a moment, then raised her eyes back to his. The moment was broken by a muffled yipping sound.

"Oh, I brought you a gift." Beau turned away from her and fumbled with something in his coat. He undid the buttons and pulled out a squirming mass of golden fur. "I hope you like dogs. This little guy needs a home."

Alina gladly reached for the pup. "I love dogs!" she cried as she cuddled the creature to her chest. A cold nose poked at her chin, followed by a warm tongue. She giggled. "How old is he? Where did you find him?"

Beau flung the saddlebags over his shoulder. "I think he's about three months. Bert found him hanging around the railyard. He's a little skinny, and he could use a bath."

Alina set the wiggling puppy down and watched him sniff

around the porch. He tumbled down the steps and wandered off a short distance, then squatted.

"That's right, little one. You'd best do that outside." Alina followed Beau into the cabin, leaving the door open.

"There's nothing like the smell of freshly baked bread," Beau said as he emptied the saddlebags on the table. "Here's your paper goods, and the mail, and a bottle of brandy for Pike."

"I'll get the money I owe you."

Beau sighed. "You don't owe me for the paper, Alina."

"Yes, I do," she said firmly as she disappeared into the bedroom. "This is no different than the umbrella, and I paid you back for that. Remember our agreement." She did not see the flash of anger in his eyes.

"Are you going to insist on paying me for the pup as well?" His voice dripped with sarcasm.

Alina came to the bedroom door, surprised. She stared at him. "I will if you want me to," she answered stiffly.

"Of course I don't want you to! Why won't you allow me to present you with a gift?"

Alina opened her mouth to answer, but he held up his hand. "I know, I know. The agreement. Then you'd better add fifty cents for the hair comb I got you." He turned to the open door.

"Beau, wait. What are you talking about?"

He waved at the table. "I thought of you when I saw the comb, and I wanted to give it to you."

Alina approached the table and saw a small wrapped package next to a stack of letters. She glanced at his face; his features were set and hard, almost defensive. She saw the hurt in his eyes and suddenly felt ashamed. "I apologize, Beau." She was reluctant to look fully at him.

He stared at her for a moment, then leaned over the table and picked up the parcel. He handed it to her and watched as she unwrapped it with trembling hands. Her breath caught. Along the back of the tortoise shell comb was glued a row of pink porcelain roses, a large one in the center with two smaller ones on each side. The delicate roses were perfectly formed. She blinked suddenly teary eyes.

"I thought of you," he repeated softly. "You remind me of a rose." His fingers touched her cheek. "My Irish Rose."

Alina looked up at him, startled. His eyes, usually so intense, were filled with tenderness and longing. She leaned into his hand. After a moment she spoke. "The comb is beautiful, Beau. I shall treasure it."

"You'll accept it without trying to pay for it?" he asked suspiciously.

She nodded. "Thank you."

His hand fell away from her face. "What about the paper?"

Alina looked down at the comb. "I asked you to get that for me. Please allow me to pay for it." Her voice was quiet.

Beau sighed. "Very well, since you accepted my gift." He gently lifted her chin so that her eyes met his. "I don't like to argue with you."

"I don't like it, either." She did not lower her gaze.

His hand again moved to caress her cheek, and he felt he was losing himself in the depths of her blue eyes.

A yip came from the porch. They both turned to the door and saw the puppy scramble up the last step. He pranced into the room, very proud of himself.

Alina laughed and bent to scratch his ears. "Very good, sir." The puppy looked up at her expectantly. "I'll get you some water, but if it's food you want, you'll eat when the rest of us do."

"I'll take care of Bay." Beau moved to the door.

"Supper will be in about an hour. Will you let Pike know? He was at the forge the last I knew. He's been working on that wheel all afternoon."

Beau nodded. Alina positioned the comb in her hair, high on the left side. "How does it look?" She turned her head for his inspection.

"Lovely, as I knew it would, especially against your black

hair." The admiring glow in his intense brown eyes brought a shy smile to her lips.

"Thank you again." Her voice was little more than a whisper. She picked up the paper from the table and took it to the bedroom, the puppy close at her heels. Her voice carried back to Beau. "There's time enough to give you a bath before dinner, you scamp." He smiled at the affection in her tone.

Beau led Bay toward the barn, the smile still upon his lips. She had not pulled away from his touch. He would swear he had seen some tenderness or feeling of some kind in her eyes when she had looked at him. He could not stop his foolish heart from soaring with hope.

Later, when the dinner dishes were clean and put away, Alina brought her rifle to the table with a bottle of oil and several rags.

Pike closed his book and turned up the lamp. "Time ta clean Betsy, huh? Beau, have ya seen Alina's rifle?"

Beau looked up from where he sat on the floor, engaged in a tug-of-war with the puppy over an old sock. "No, I didn't know she had a rifle."

"Well, she does, and it's a beauty. She can shoot with it, too. Say, where'd ya get that gewgaw ya're wearin' in your hair? I don't recall seein' that before."

Alina did not look up from her task as she replied in a soft voice, "Beau gave it to me."

Pike made no comment, but he smiled with satisfaction and puffed on his pipe. Beau stood and dusted the seat of his pants. He crossed to the table and leaned over Alina's shoulder as she removed the chamber piece. The faint scent of roses reached his nostrils. He would never again be able to smell roses without thinking of her.

"Are you as good with that rifle as you are with my pistol?" Beau teased.

"Better," Alina retorted. She hoped Pike didn't notice the blush that suddenly covered her cheeks.

"When did she shoot your pistol?" Pike demanded.

"Not long after we met." Beau was sorry he'd brought up the subject. If Pike learned that Alina had taken his gun from him, he'd never live it down. "That surely is a beautiful piece."

"Alina calls her Betsy," Pike explained helpfully. "And she nailed dead branches at a hundred yards."

"A hundred yards?" Beau repeated, disbelief in his tone.

Pike nodded. "It was something ta see. She may not be the best cook in the world, but I'd like her at my side in a scrape, let me tell ya."

Alina smiled as she snapped the chamber barrel back in place and ran the oiled cloth over the stock. "I only shoot targets, Pike, not people." She glanced up at Beau, her eyes twinkling. "Although I've been tempted, at least once that I can think of."

Beau chose to ignore her remark. "May I see Betsy?" Alina handed the weapon to him. He inspected the rifle, obviously impressed. "Very nice." He sighted down the barrel. "I've heard that one of the reasons revolving rifles never caught on was because they weren't too accurate, that it was difficult to line up the chambers with the barrel."

Alina shrugged. "Papa said something about that. But Samuel Colt himself made this one. She's very accurate, and I've never had a problem with her shaving bullets."

"I'd heard about that, too. Where have you been keeping her?"

"Under the bed."

Beau walked over to the fireplace, careful to avoid the now sleeping form of the puppy. He examined the stonework of the chimney. "If I put a couple of braces here, we can keep her with Killdeer. A beautiful piece like this should be displayed." He turned to Alina. "Would you like that?"

She nodded. "Did you say 'Killdeer'? Wasn't that the scout's rifle in *The Last of the Mohicans?*"

Beau waved at the old rifle that already hung above the fireplace. "That's what Ambrose called it." He smiled. "I told you he loved those Leatherstocking Tales. This rifle belonged to our great-great-grandfather, and dates to before the Revolution."

"Ambrose liked ta name things, just like you do, Alina," Pike commented. "Ya would have liked him."

"I'm sure I would have," Alina agreed softly. She turned to Beau. "Betsy will be in good company. Let me load her before you put her up there."

A short while later, Alina looked up from the letter she was reading. Beau settled her rifle on the two braces he had forced into the stonework. She was touched to see the gun resting there, as if it belonged in this house.

"Thank you, Beau."

He nodded. "Someday I'd like you to show me how well you can shoot."

"Perhaps," she said with a smile.

"I'll escort the little one outside, in case he has any business to take care of. What will you name him?"

"I'm not sure yet. I want to choose the perfect name."

Pike snorted as he rose from his chair. "I'll just call him Dog. That's what he is."

"No! I'll think of something special. Don't you dare call him Dog."

"Well, whoever you are, let's go," Beau said as he opened the door. The puppy raced after him.

The door to Pike's room was closed, and Alina, wearing her nightdress and robe, was seated on the sofa when Beau returned. She took down her hair while he changed in her room. She held the comb in her hand and stared at it in the firelight. It was one of the most beautiful things she owned, and she did not want to admit how thrilled she was that it had come from Beau. She set the comb on the chess table and ran the brush through her hair, deep in thought. He still had not explained what was taking him away from the ranch, but perhaps, judging from his actions today, he was not too tired of her presence in his home. Her eyes fell on the puppy curled on a blanket in front of the fire and she smiled.

She was pleased with both of his gifts. He opened the bedroom door.

"Where did you intend the puppy to sleep?" she asked as she braided her hair.

"He's your dog. Where do you want him to sleep?" Beau moved to his bed and pulled back the blankets.

"With me," Alina answered promptly. She walked into the bedroom and set her brush, hairpins, and the hair comb on the dresser. "Then maybe the bed won't seem so lonely," she added without thinking. She clapped a hand over her mouth and stared wide-eyed at her image in the mirror. Oh, she hoped Beau hadn't heard that!

Beau did not say anything, so she moved to the bedroom door. He was sitting on his narrow bed, staring at the dying flames in the fireplace. Surely he hadn't heard her.

"One of the letters you brought me today was from my aunt," Alina said brightly.

Beau looked up at her. "How is she?"

"Her cousin has at last died. The poor thing lingered for so long."

"I'm sorry. Did you know her?"

"No, I never met her." Alina moved to the sofa and settled into one corner, drawing her feet up underneath her. "I'm concerned about how Elizabeth is taking it, but from the sound of her letter, she is fine. She will help settle the estate, then return to Chicago, and another bad situation with Cordelia. She wants to stop here for a few days on her way home. Will that be all right with you?"

Only if she doesn't take you away with her. "Of course. I look forward to meeting her. She sounds like a wonderful lady."

"She is. You and Pike will both like her."

"Will she like us?"

Alina smiled. "Oh, yes. She will like both of you very much." She pulled her long braid forward over her shoulder and thoughtfully stared at the fire.

Beau watched the rope of hair rise and fall with her breathing. His fingers itched to touch those shining locks. He clasped his hands tightly together and concentrated on her face, lovely in the firelight. He cleared his throat. "There's something I wanted to ask you."

"What is it?" Alina stifled a yawn.

"You probably heard that the McAllister brothers' barn burned last week."

"Yes." This time Alina yawned outright.

Beau hesitated, surprised at how nervous he felt. He was grateful for the dim light. "They're planning a barn-raising in a few weeks, and Pike and I will be going to help out. Barn-raisings are a lot of work, but they're also a lot of fun. The women bring food and Pike takes his fiddle. There's dancing and the children play games all day. Anyway, I was wondering if you would like to go with us."

Alina's eyes widened with happiness, but she did not look at him. "I didn't know Pike could play the fiddle." She paused. "Will I be expected to dance with you?"

Beau stared at his hands and frowned. "Since you're my wife, it will seem strange if you don't. So, yes, you probably will have to dance with me."

Alina kept her eyes on the fire. "Then I would be delighted to go with you," she said quietly.

Beau nodded to himself, a small smile touching his lips. "Good," he answered. After a moment of self-conscious silence, he stood up. "He's had a full day," he said, indicating the sleeping puppy with a wave of his hand.

Alina moved her feet to the floor. "It seems a shame to wake him."

"I'll carry him in." Beau bent down and gathered the puppy in his arms, blanket and all.

Alina followed him into the bedroom and watched in surprise as he settled his burden on the blankets near the foot of the bed. "How did you know I wanted him on the bed?" she asked suspiciously.

Beau shrugged, his expression neutral. "My dog always slept on my bed when I was a boy. Would you rather he slept on the floor?"

Alina shook her head. Perhaps he really hadn't heard her comment about the lonely bed.

They both watched as the puppy roused himself and pushed the old blanket around with nose and paw. Finally, he walked in a circle and plopped down, his head resting on his front paws. He eyed them for a moment, then sighed deeply and blinked. His eyes slowly closed.

"I think he's satisfied with his quarters," Beau remarked. He looked at Alina, who was still watching the puppy, a smile curving her lips. She nodded in agreement.

"Thank you for the puppy. I love him already." She turned to Beau.

"You're welcome," he answered, his voice husky. Her eyes seemed to sparkle in the light from the bedside lamp. He could not stop his hand from reaching out to touch her cheek. He caressed that softness for only a moment, then his hand fell to his side. "Goodnight, Alina."

She stepped back to allow him to pass through the door. "Goodnight, Beau." She closed the door behind him and leaned against the wood. Her hand moved to her cheek. His touch still made her feel warm. And he had asked her to a barn-raising! She turned to the bed with a happy smile.

Beau settled into his uncomfortable bed and watched the pattern of the flickering firelight on the ceiling. So she found her bed lonely. What did that mean? She had certainly been anxious enough to get him out of it. He sighed. Despite his determination to resist her, the woman was wrapping her rose-scented fingers around his heart.

Chapter Eleven

May came, and at last the promise of spring was fulfilled. The sun spread its warmth over the land; green grasses and adventurous wildflowers poked their heads through the earth to greet the new season.

Alina stood on the top porch step with the empty egg basket in her hands and breathed deeply of the early morning air. How she had come to love this place! She crossed the yard, the puppy at her heels. She filled a tin from the huge feed bag in the barn and made her way to the coop. After throwing handfuls of seed over the ground outside the enclosure, she opened the gate. Hungry chickens rushed past her to argue over breakfast.

"Watch yourself, Sundance," she warned the interested pup. "You've been pecked once already." She had named the puppy after Pike made a comment about how the sunlight seemed to dance on his golden fur. A smile came to her lips at the memory of the heated but good-natured discussion that had followed the announcement of her decision. Pike pronounced the name too "fluffy" and accused her of taking advantage of his poetic moment of weakness. Beau had suggested that "Barney" might be more suitable, but Alina had remained firm.

She slipped inside the henhouse and shooed two stubborn hens off their nests, then searched the straw. There were four eggs altogether, enough for a cake if she felt brave enough to attempt one.

Alina returned the feed pan to the barn as Pike led his saddled buckskin from its stall. They walked out into the sun together.

"Where are you off to this morning?" she asked.

Pike looped the reins over the fence by the water trough and adjusted the cinch. "Thought I'd take a ride along the property line through the hills and make sure Petrie's loggers ain't crossed onto our land." He lowered the stirrup. "The damn fools, beg pardon, would cut every tree if they could. They don't know nothin' about carin' for the land. And sometimes they don't appear ta know much about fences and property lines, neither."

Beau came from the cabin to join them. He handed Pike a canteen and a cloth bag. "There's a couple of apples and a chunk of bread in there, in case you don't get back for lunch."

Pike nodded his thanks and hung the canteen over the pommel. He put the food in a saddlebag, retrieved the reins, then swung into the saddle. He leaned down to secure the end of his peg in the small boot that had been designed especially for him.

"Watch your back, Pike," Beau warned soberly.

"Always do." Pike raised a hand in farewell as the buckskin trotted over the bridge and disappeared into the trees. Sundance raced after them for a distance, then returned to plop himself on the porch, his sides heaving, his tongue hanging.

Beau and Alina strolled toward the cabin. "Is that why Richard Petrie wants to buy this place?" she asked. "Because of the timber?"

"I'm sure that's part of it. The demand for wood is so great. But they mow down every tree. You should see what they've done to Sheep Mountain, on the other side of the river. Ambrose wouldn't allow anyone to harvest the forest on his property. Petrie can't seem to understand a love of the land. He didn't understand why Ambrose wouldn't sell, just as he doesn't understand why I won't." They climbed to the porch. "There are some things you can't put a price on."

For a minute they silently drank in the beauty of the valley spread before them, glorious in the morning light.

"This is a long way from Virginia," Alina commented. "How did Ambrose end up way out here?"

Beau did not take his eyes from the view. "Ambrose and Pike were here even before the railroad. I know Ambrose was deeply affected by the war. He was an officer, and Pike was his sergeant. They saw four years of almost constant battle. Ambrose survived physically, but he was never the same. I think he came out here searching for peace. He wrote that he had found it. Then the railroad came."

"And Richard Petrie."

"And Richard Petrie," Beau echoed, his features grim. They entered the cabin, Sundance at their heels. Alina moved to the counter with her basket while Beau filled his cup one more time from the coffeepot. The puppy curled up on his blanket in front of the fireplace and promptly went to sleep.

"You were in the war, too, weren't you?" Alina rolled back the cuffs of her plaid dress and reached for the wash-basin.

"Yes." He took his rifle down from over the front door.

"How did it affect you?"

"Not as severely, I guess." He settled into a chair at the table. "I was an officer, too, but I was attached to General Grant's command after he took over the Army of the Potomac and I spent a lot of time in Washington. I didn't see nearly as much combat as Ambrose and Pike did. War affects everyone, some worse than others. Pike did all right, even with losing his leg, and I've been able to put it behind me, for the most part, but it seemed that Ambrose was damaged to his very soul." He sipped his coffee, then removed the shells from the rifle casing.

"War also affects those who never see a battlefield. Many

souls are damaged." Alina blinked at her sudden tears and piled the plates in the wash water.

Beau stared at her slender form. "Who did you lose?" he asked gently. He held his breath, afraid that she would shut him out, as she had done every time he had asked about her family.

"My brother Joseph," she whispered. She cleared her throat. "At Gettysburg." Her voice was stronger now. She scrubbed at a plate.

"Tell me about him."

"He was ten years older than me, and very handsome, with black curly hair and blue eyes like mine. He was gentle and intelligent, and he had a wonderful singing voice. He was only twenty-two when he died." She wiped at her cheek with a sleeve.

"I'm sorry, Alina." Beau wanted to go to her, to hold her, but he stayed seated, afraid she would push him away.

She shrugged. "Tell me about Ambrose. He was older than you, wasn't he?"

"By two years. He, too, was a gentle man. He loved animals—really had a way with them. With wood, too. He built the bed in your room."

Alina smiled. "I thought you made it, after the lovely job you did on the chess table."

"Ambrose was killed before it was done." Beau's voice grew hard. "I finished the engraving and polishing." He rammed an oiled cloth down the barrel of the rifle with a rod.

Alina looked at him, her eyes soft with sympathy. "Please tell me what happened."

Beau's jaw tightened. "He suspected loggers were cutting his trees, so he went out one day to check the property boundaries. Bay brought him back that afternoon with two bulletholes in his back. He had been tied in the saddle. We were never able to learn where it happened. Pike and I suspect Petrie had a hand in it, but there's no evidence." He wiped the barrel with the cloth.

"Did the law do anything?"

"They tried. Sheriff Boswell and Sam Trudeau launched a full-scale investigation, but there was nothing to go on. When I got here last August, after Pike sent the telegram notifying us of Ambrose's death, I myself rode every inch of this ranch, and even into the surrounding property, but never found anything."

"How agonizing for you! I would think the not knowing would be the hardest part of it, especially for your poor mother."

Beau reloaded the rifle. "She took it hard." His voice was flat. "We all did." He stood and returned the weapon to its place, then took his cup to the sink and reached for a clean cloth. He took a dripping plate from her hand. "Didn't you have another brother?"

Alina nodded. "Sean. He died in a boating accident, a little over a year ago. He was different from Joseph. He had our father's coloring; lighter hair, darker eyes. And he had the most wonderful sense of humor! Always teasing and telling jokes. I still miss him." She tried to swallow the lump in her throat. "We were very close, especially after losing Joseph, and our mother. She died in the fall of '66. She never really recovered from Joseph's death." A tear ran down her cheek and she impatiently wiped at it with the back of one wet hand.

Beau set the plate down and placed a hand on her shoulder. She turned to him and he dabbed at her cheek with the towel. His act of gentle kindness caused Alina's eyes to overflow. "I was in England," she cried. "I knew something was going to happen, but my warning didn't reach him in time. I never got to say goodbye to him."

Beau dropped the towel on the counter and pulled her into his arms. She buried her face against his shoulder and let the tears come. He held her close, one hand cradling the back of her head. Her arms moved to encircle his waist.

"There, now," he murmured. "It wasn't your fault. How could you have known?"

"I just knew," she sobbed, her voice muffled against his shirt. Alina cried for her brothers, for her mother, for her missing father, for her lost home. After a few minutes, her crying eased. He stroked her hair.

"I'm so sorry about your brothers," Beau whispered.

Alina sniffled. "I'm sorry about Ambrose, too. I wish I could have known him."

Beau moved his hands to cup her face and brushed at the tears on her cheeks with the pads of his thumbs. She raised her eyes to his. The sadness he saw there tore at his heart. He bent and kissed each cheek, his mustache soft against her skin.

"Will you be all right?" he asked. She nodded. He could not take his gaze from hers. One hand moved to her shoulder, while the other moved to brush a stray curl from her temple. "I've got chores waiting for me in the barn, and you mentioned at breakfast that you were going to do the wash."

She nodded again, then managed a watery smile when he lifted her chin and winked at her.

"You're sure you'll be all right?" Beau asked as he walked around her to the back door.

"Don't worry about me. I probably needed that cry." She dumped the contents of the washbasin down the drain.

He called to her from the back porch. "It's so nice out here, Alina. Would you like me to leave this tub on the porch?"

Alina moved to the door, drying her hands on her apron. "Yes, that's a good idea. Will you string a line to that tree for me? I'll hang the clothes there."

"You bet." He saw the now-awake puppy peek from behind Alina's skirts. "Sundance, you come with me. Your mom is going to do laundry today, and she doesn't need your help."

Alina smiled at his term for her. Her eyes fell on the grave on the hill, then on the man and the dog as they walked toward the barn. Beau carried his lean frame with an easy grace that Alina found fascinating. His tenderness and understanding had surprised her. She felt a new bond with him, a closeness that had not been there before. A new dimension had been added to their already confusing relationship. She went back inside.

Several hours later, Beau came from the barn, brushing at the sweat on his forehead. The stalls were cleaned and loaded with fresh straw, his saddle was soaped and polished and he had started oiling harnesses. He crossed the yard to the water trough and pumped fresh water over his head, then cupped his hand and drank deeply. As he straightened, he tossed his head back, sending a spray of water in an arc behind him.

Refreshed, he ran his hands through his hair and walked along the side of the cabin. Fat hens scolded him as he passed. He rounded the corner and watched Alina adjust a wet petticoat over the rope he had hung for her.

"Let me know when you're ready to dump the tub, Alina," Beau called to her.

She turned to him with a smile and pushed her hair from her forehead with the back of one hand. "Thank you, I will. I'm almost done."

He marveled at her. She never complained about the unending chores. It was as if she thrived on her life here. The thought struck him that maybe she *liked* living on the ranch.

"I'll set out some lunch," he said, and disappeared into the cabin. She joined him in a few minutes. It seemed strange to eat without Pike. Although the meal was simple, it was somehow more intimate.

Afterward, he dumped the laundry tub for her and returned to the barn. He sat on a barrel and reached for a harness, a frown marring his countenance at the thought of her great-aunt's impending visit. Would Elizabeth want Alina to return to Chicago? Over the past few weeks, it had been easy to forget that their arrangement was temporary. Maybe Alina would want to leave. The idea saddened him, for he could no longer imagine life here without her. It was difficult to imagine life *anywhere* without her.

The afternoon shadows were long when Alina heard the pounding of approaching hoofbeats and Sundance's excited barking. She set the potato she was peeling in the sink with the others and walked to the front porch. Pike was not alone.

"This man tells me he has come a long way ta find ya, Alina." Pike jerked his thumb at the stranger.

Alina's eyes went to the tall man in the duster on the chestnut horse. It was difficult to make out his features under the brim of his hat, but she saw brilliant blue eyes, and a handsome face split in a wide grin.

Her breath caught. "Conor?" she whispered.

The man nodded and stepped out of the saddle.

"Conor!" Alina flew from the porch into her cousin's welcoming arms. The man held her tightly to his chest.

Beau heard Alina's cry and came from the barn to see his wife in another man's arms. His lips formed an angry line as he stalked across the yard.

Alina raised her eyes to Conor's weary face. She placed a hand on his stubble-covered cheek, blinking at tears of joy. "It is so good to see you," she whispered, and hugged him again.

"And you, Alina. You are more beautiful than ever, and a glad sight for these tired eyes." Conor kissed the top of her head.

Alina turned in Conor's arms as Beau approached. She did not notice the jealous anger in his eyes. "Beau, this is my cousin, Conor O'Rourke. Conor, this is Beauregard Parker, my husband."

The tension drained from Beau's face at her words. He held out his hand. "I've heard a lot about you, Mr. O'Rourke, and I know my wife is delighted to see you. Welcome."

Conor kept one arm around Alina's shoulders and shook Beau's hand. "And I want to hear more about you, Mr. Parker. From what I could make of Percival's letter, I owe you a debt of gratitude. You helped my cousin out of a tight spot."

"I was glad to do it," Beau responded. "There is no debt." His gaze traveled from Alina to her cousin. They did not resemble each other except for their striking blue eyes. Conor's were clouded with fatigue. "You look done in, Mr. O'Rourke. I'd be glad to see to your horse if you'd like to go inside with Alina."

Conor turned to his animal. "Thank you, but Charlie and I have been through a lot together, and I consider it a privilege to care for him. I'd prefer to see to him myself, if you'll show me where he'll stay. And if you want to drop the 'mister' we're calling each other, it's all right with me."

Beau nodded.

"Charlie?" Pike questioned as he dismounted. "Does namin' things run in your family?"

"Charlie is a better name for a horse than Tumbleweed," Alina retorted. Her eyes fell meaningfully on Pike's buckskin. Pike turned his suddenly flushed face to Beau.

"Ya told her!" he accused.

Beau held his hands up. "I swear, I didn't," he laughed.

"I heard you call him when you were trying to corner him in the corral last week," Alina said sweetly. She climbed the porch steps. "I'll start supper." She turned to Conor. "Would you like a bath?"

Conor's tired eyes lit up. "Oh, yes." He ran a hand over his chin. "And a shave, and some coffee, if you have it."

Alina nodded. "I'll get the bathwater heating, and by the time you're finished with the horses, there'll be fresh coffee."

"I think I'll set up the bathing tub on the back porch, Alina," said Beau. "It's relatively private, and you won't have to leave the house."

"Good idea." She disappeared into the cabin.

After the horses were stabled, Beau carried pails of hot water from the stove to the back porch, filled three cups with fresh coffee, then closed the door. Pike entered a moment later and grabbed the bottle of brandy from the shelf. He winked at her as he pulled the door closed again. Alina smiled. She liked the sound of the masculine voices, the occasional laughter, as three men who were important in her life got to know each other.

She looked up from lighting the lamp when the men finally filed in the back door. Pike carried a rough plank stool.

"We don't have a fourth chair," he explained.

"I'll make a real bench tomorrow," Beau offered. He pulled the table away from the wall, and Pike set the makeshift stool in place under the window.

Alina's eyes fell on Conor. He was too thin, and his fatigue was evident. His shirt and denim pants, fresh from his saddlebag, were worn and wrinkled, but clean. His dark wet hair was combed back from his face and fell to his shoulders. His handsome face was clean shaven now, and his blue eyes, so uncannily like hers, sparkled at her.

"It's so good to see you, Cousin," he said softly.

She went to his open arms for yet another hug. "Oh, Conor, thank you for coming." After a long minute she moved away from him. "I'd better set the table."

Conor wandered over to the fireplace. "Isn't this your father's gun?"

"It was, but it's mine now." Alina glanced over her shoulder as she struggled to open a jar of peaches. "Read the inscription on the stock."

Conor took the rifle from its resting place and turned it over. "Are you any good with it?"

"She is," Pike chimed in. "She's damn good, beg pardon."

"It must run in the family, Conor, because Papa told me you were pretty good with a gun yourself." Alina eyed the gunbelt strapped around his narrow hips.

Conor shrugged. "Everybody's good at something." He replaced Alina's rifle and admired the old flintlock.

"Please take your seats, gentlemen." Alina set a bowl of fried potatoes and onions on the table. Pike and Conor argued over the rude stool, and finally Pike told Conor it was bad manners to argue with a man in his own house and would he please shut up and take the chair. Conor smilingly obliged.

Alina giggled as she forked a thick antelope steak onto each plate. She refilled coffee cups and took her seat. "Tonight I'd like to say the prayer."

"Just don't make it too long," Pike warned.

"I won't." They bowed their heads. "Thank you for bringing my beloved cousin here safe, Lord. Guide us all through what lies ahead. And thank you for the food. It sure looks good. Amen." Beau tried not to smile.

Pike eyed her suspiciously over the lamp in the center of the table. "Wasn't that last part my prayer?" he asked as he tucked one of the new napkins Alina had made from leftover curtain material in his collar.

"It was." Alina handed the bowl of potatoes to Conor. "Where did Mr. Percival finally find you?"

"His letters caught up with me in Santa Fe."

"Santa Fe! We thought you were in Texas."

"I was, for a while." He passed the bowl to Pike. "I headed up here as soon as I heard." He looked at Alina, sorrow in his eyes, and covered her hand with his. "I didn't know about Sean. I was so sorry to learn that."

She squeezed his fingers. "I know."

"How long did it take you to get here?" Beau asked.

"Almost a month. There's no railroad in New Mexico, so me and Charlie just headed north along the mountains. We picked up a railroad in a town called Pueblo in Colorado Territory, and came up through Denver to Cheyenne, then on over here." He cut a piece of steak. "Charlie doesn't think much of riding on a train, but it sure is a fast way to get somewhere." The bite of meat disappeared into his mouth.

Alina had many questions to ask Conor, but she could tell he was hungry, so she held her tongue. She couldn't keep her eyes from him, though. It was hard to believe he was here. It felt good just to look at him.

When the plates were emptied, Alina stood and gathered

them. She held up a hand to Beau when he made to rise. "You men stay out of my kitchen."

"Ya sound just like Emerald," Pike complained as he thumped into his room. He returned a moment later, his pipe in hand.

"Who is Emerald?" Conor asked. He leaned contentedly back in his chair.

"Only the bossiest woman ya'll ever meet, especially in her own kitchen." Pike settled again on the stool. "Do ya mind if I light up this here pipe, Alina?"

Alina smiled. "No, Pike, but thank you for asking." She looked at Conor. "Emerald is a friend of ours, and she *is* bossy in her own kitchen, as a woman has a right to be." She brought the coffee pot to the table and refilled the cups. "If you saved any of that brandy, Pike, I'll get it for you."

Pike looked at her in surprise. "Well, thank ya, Alina. It's on the back porch there, by the tub."

Alina set the coffeepot on the stove and retrieved the brandy, which she handed to Conor when she returned to the table. Conor poured a little in his cup and passed the bottle to Pike. When the brandy came back to Alina, she poured a tiny bit in her cup as well, much to the surprise of the men. She forced the cork in the bottle and looked around the table. "We're celebrating," she explained, a little defensively. She turned her eyes to her cousin and held her cup in the air. "Welcome, Conor."

"Welcome," Beau echoed, and raised his cup.

"Glad ya came, son," Pike said around his pipe, and knocked his cup against Conor's.

"Glad to be here, sir," Conor responded. They all drank.

"Don't be startin' that 'sir' stuff with me," Pike warned. "I ain't your grandpa, though I'm probably old enough ta be. No 'mister,' neither. It's just Pike."

"All right, Pike," Conor agreed with a smile. He settled his gaze on Alina. "What happens now? Do we go to Chicago?"

Beau stiffened and looked from Conor to Alina.

Alina shook her head. "Aunt Elizabeth will be here sometime in the next few weeks. We'll wait for her, then decide."

"So her poor cousin finally died?"

Alina nodded and took a sip of coffee. "Elizabeth is doing well, from the sound of her letters. I'm so anxious to see her again." She glanced at her exhausted cousin. "But we can speak of this tomorrow. I think you should get some rest."

Conor did not argue. He drained his cup. "I'll spread my bedroll in the barn, if that's all right."

Alina looked helplessly at Beau. She did not want Conor sleeping in the barn, but they had no accommodations for a guest.

"It ain't all right, not at all." Pike's voice was firm. "Ya're plumb tuckered out. Anybody can see that." He stood and headed to his room. "Ya'll sleep in here, where ya can get some real rest." He reappeared at his door with a thick blanket over one arm and his crutches under the other. "Since I get up with the chickens anyways, I'm gonna sleep in the barn, and tomorrow Beau'll be knocking together a bed as well as a bench."

Conor shook his head. "Pike, I'll not take your bed. Your barn will be one of the nicer places I've slept over the past few years."

"What did I tell ya about arguin' with a man in his own house?" Pike thundered, his bushy eyebrows drawn together in a scowl. "Hand me my cup, woman."

Alina placed Pike's cup in his free hand. He emptied the receptacle, thumped over to set it in the sink, and grabbed the lantern from the wall near the back door. He made his way to the front door, then paused.

"Sleep well, son," he said to Conor. "Ya need it."

"Thank you, Pike," Conor replied.

"Alina, thank ya for the fine meal. Beau, open this here door for me. My hands are full. Come on, dog. It won't kill ya ta keep me company tonight." His tail wagging, Sundance followed Pike out the door.

"Good night, Pike," Beau called as the old man crossed the yard. He closed the door and sat down again.

"Did I offend him?" Conor asked, worried.

"Not at all," Alina assured him.

Beau shook his head. "Pike gets gruff when he thinks you're going to argue with him. He's concerned about you, as we all are. You're dead on your feet, man."

Conor nodded. He stood and leaned over to kiss Alina's cheek. "It was a fine meal, Cousin. I didn't know you could cook. Tomorrow we'll talk about how you've become a pioneer." He walked around Alina's chair and held his hand out to Beau. "Thank you for everything, Beau. Good night."

Beau pushed out of his chair and shook Conor's hand. "Sleep well."

Conor retreated to Pike's room and closed the door.

Alina rose and carried Conor's cup and hers to the counter, a happy smile on her face. Beau followed with his own cup, his expression troubled. The coming of her family could mean that he would lose her, and the thought caused his heart to sink.

Chapter Twelve

The next morning Beau went to work on the new furniture. By late afternoon, a sturdy bench sat under the window on the fourth side of the table. He also constructed a simple bed frame of pine that now occupied the empty corner in Pike's room; Pike had insisted upon sharing his quarters, on the condition that Conor not complain about occasional snoring. From empty, clean feed bags Alina fashioned a case to be used as a mattress, and she and Conor took it to the barn to stuff with fresh straw. The task escalated into a good-natured battle, and they later came from the barn flushed and laughing, with bits of straw stuck to their hair and clothing. The sight of the happy cousins brought a powerful sense of sadness to Beau.

"I wish she felt as comfortable with me as she does with Conor," he remarked to Pike. They stood on the porch and watched the two approach, carrying the new mattress between them.

"She has surely come alive since he got here," Pike observed. "I'll miss that gal somethin' awful if she leaves." He glanced at Beau from the corner of his eye.

Beau's jaw tightened, but he did not respond.

Conor easily settled into life on the ranch. He was a hard worker, and insisted on earning his keep. He turned a good-sized patch of earth for a garden next to the cabin under the kitchen window, and Beau promised they would put a fence around the little plot when Alina had it planted, so the rabbits would not eat the fruit of her labors.

Late one morning, Alina was toiling in her garden. She wore a simple blue cotton skirt she had constructed specifically for chores such as this, and Beau had lent her one of his work shirts. She had also borrowed his leather gloves and Conor's hat. The hat slipped once again down over her eyes and she pushed it back with irritation.

"The very next time we go to town, I'm getting a straw hat," she muttered. She glanced at her hands where they grasped the hoe handle. Beau's gloves were also much too large. "And my own work gloves." She pulled one of the gloves off and opened the top button of the shirt. It was warm in the sunshine. Damp curls hung around the sides of her face and down her neck. She slipped her hand back into the glove and returned to her chore.

Alina had never had a garden, and she dreamed of the day when she would see tiny green shoots. She liked caring for her little patch of earth and was proud of her straight, neat rows. She didn't mind the labor or the dirt.

She did not hear the approaching horse until it entered the yard. She watched as the animal trotted past the cabin and came to an abrupt halt in front of the garden. The nervous mare pulled an ornate buggy, in which was seated Madeline Petrie.

Alina's heart sank. What on earth was the woman doing here? Madeline looked cool and elegant, the feathers on her hat fluttering in the breeze. Her skirt and jacket were expertly tailored, and not a hair was out of place. Alina felt grimy and dowdy in her work clothes. She unconsciously straightened her shoulders and waited, her hands supporting the upright hoe.

Madeline looked disdainfully at Alina. How could Beau have chosen that bitch over herself? Good God, the woman was a common serf! But she was an irritatingly lovely one. How did she manage to be so attractive in a dust-covered skirt, with what seemed to be only one petticoat, wearing a man's oversized shirt and a man's hat? And those damned blue eyes!

"I'm here to see Mr. Parker," Madeline snapped. "Send for him at once."

Alina stiffened. Her eyes narrowed and she stared coldly at Madeline for several moments before she spoke. "You forget yourself, Madam."

Madeline's eyes widened in surprise. "What?"

"*I* am mistress here, and you will not order me about. If you wish to speak with my husband," she emphasized the last two words, "you will find him in the barn." With that, she returned to her hoeing.

Madeline flushed with fury. She jerked cruelly on the reins and struck the unfortunate horse with the buggy whip. The animal skittered and jumped away in the direction of the barn.

Alina did not raise her head when she heard Madeline shout Beau's name, but after a moment she glanced toward the barn. She saw Beau come from the recesses of the big building. He had taken his shirt off, and even from where she stood, Alina could see the definition of the muscles in his chest and arms. Her breath caught. He was beautiful to her eye. And it was that damned Madeline, cool and lovely Madeline, who he smiled at, who he lifted from her fine carriage.

Alina attacked the dirt with a vengeance. She had a fine carriage, too, in Chicago. She had pretty, stylish clothes, in Chicago. She could be fresh and composed, even on the warmest of days, when she wasn't cooking and cleaning and washing clothes in a tub and hoeing in a garden, of all things!

She stopped her frenzied motions and leaned on the hoe, her gaze returning to the barn. Beau and Madeline disappeared inside, and a moment later Conor came out. He ran his hand over the mare's rump, a frown on his face, then led the animal toward the water trough by the corral fence.

Alina stared at the entrance to the barn with troubled eyes. She was stunned to realize that she was jealous! There had been a time she'd have welcomed another woman's interest in Beau, but she felt that way no longer. When had her feelings changed?

Conor tied a long lead from the fence to the horse's harness, leaving the animal free to drink, then crossed the yard toward the woodpile on one side of the smokehouse. His shirt was hanging open in the front. "I'll chop wood for a while," he said as he passed Alina. She watched him pull the ax from a chopping stump and the sound of splitting wood filled the air. With a sigh, she resumed her hoeing.

Madeline could not take her eyes from Beau's naked chest. And that scar along his ribs! It was all she could do to keep from touching him. The thought of lying with him on the soft piles of straw overhead in the hayloft sent shivers down her spine. She licked her lips with the tip of her tongue and raised her eyes to his handsome face.

"Oh, Beau," she sighed.

Beau watched her with curiosity. At one time he'd have swept her into his arms if she'd looked at him like that, but now he was having trouble remembering why he had wanted her so badly.

"What is it, Madeline? Why did you want to see me?" His tone was businesslike. Madeline frowned.

"I want to talk about your ridiculous marriage, Beau. I thought you'd have had the courtesy to come to me, to explain yourself, but you haven't. I know it isn't seemly for a lady to call on a gentleman, but I could bear it no longer." She batted her eyelashes, affecting a very distressed expression.

Beau sighed. "There's nothing to explain. Alina and I are married. That's it."

"Beau, I know something was growing between us! Surely I was not mistaken."

"I was attracted to you, yes," Beau admitted. "But after the way you treated me New Year's Eve, I thought you had no special feelings for me." He shook his head and rested his hands on his hips. "What is the point of this? I'm married now, and I doubt that you are broken-hearted over it."

"But I am! That's why I'm here! I had hoped that you and I would one day be lovers, be husband and wife." Madeline gazed at him wistfully, then turned to pace the dirt floor. "I can't believe your heart is attached to that . . . disgraceful woman you married! You found her in a saloon, Beau! She's an embarrassment to you! Brawling in the streets, befriending whores and niggers, working in the dirt like a common fieldhand!"

Madeline paid no attention to his clenched jaw or the building rage in his eyes. "I know you married her to protect her from her guardian. Your action was noble, but you were mistaken, Beau. She lied to you about the Randalls."

"What do you know of them?" Beau demanded.

"I know more than you do, for certain. I visited them in Chicago. Cordelia has only Alina's best interests at heart. Alina is a deeply troubled woman." Madeline shook her head in mock concern. "She refuses to accept the fact that her father is dead, even though his men saw him washed overboard in a typhoon."

Beau's eyes narrowed in confusion. *Alina's father was lost at sea?*

Madeline did not notice his reaction. "Her father's ship has returned to Chicago," she continued, "and he's been reported missing and feared dead. Alina claims to know, by unholy means, that her father is alive."

"What do you mean, by unholy means?" Beau asked dangerously, suspiciously.

Madeline finally took warning from his attitude. She gentled her tone. "Those are Cordelia's words. Rumor has it that Alina's mother knew when awful things were going to happen, that she was a witch. Cordelia fears that Alina suffers under the delusion that she, too, 'knows' things."

The memory of Alina's remark about knowing that her brother Sean had been in danger before his death flashed in Beau's mind.

Madeline warmed to her subject. "She is deranged, Beau! I beg you to annul this marriage and return her to her guardian. Cordelia understands Alina, and knows what is best for her."

"Cordelia thinks that marriage to her brute of a son is what's best for Alina," Beau retorted. "Cordelia also thinks that control of the Gallagher estate is what's best for Cordelia. And what of Donovan, Madeline? Surely you must have met the charming Mr. Randall."

Madeline pushed aside the memory of the violently passionate nights she had shared with Donovan while in Chicago. "He is indeed charming, and was a perfect gentleman. I don't know why you would call him a brute. He cares deeply for his troubled cousin, Beau, and wishes to marry her, even as disturbed as she is. He, too, understands her, and will take care of her."

"He's not her cousin," Beau snapped, "and Alina despises him."

"The Randalls believe Alina isn't capable of judging what's best for her. Perhaps they're right," Madeline suggested gently. "You must remember that the courts agreed." She laid a dainty hand on his forearm. "You were wrong about me, Beau. I *do* have special feelings for you, very deep feelings. That's why I'm here today. I couldn't bear to see you hurt, or to see your reputation damaged any more than it already has been." Her brown eyes were wide and sorrowful.

Beau stared into those eyes and, for the first time, sensed something that made his skin crawl. He could not put a name to it. He moved away from her touch and crossed his arms over his chest. "And of course, this ranch has nothing to do with your tender feelings for me."

Madeline started, managing to bring tears to her eyes. "How can you think such a thing, Beau?" She blinked rapidly and pulled a lacy handkerchief from her sleeve.

"Spare me the tears, Madeline. I know you were involved with my brother. I find it ironic that you could grow to care so deeply for both of us when the only thing we've ever had in common is this land. I don't know what game you're playing with me, but I suspect it all boils down to that. Your father wants this ranch, and he's willing to do anything to get it."

"My father has no idea I'm here! I came because of my feelings and concern for you!"

"I don't believe you." Beau turned toward the door.

Madeline grabbed desperately at his arm. "Beau, you can't remain tied to that witch-woman!"

Beau raised his forefinger to her. "Do not *ever* disparage my wife again."

She opened her mouth to speak.

"Not one word," he warned. "It would be best if you leave now." He gestured toward the yard.

Madeline's nostrils flared; her eyes flashed with fury. Her hand snaked out and struck him forcefully across the face. "You bastard! Cordelia was right! You're nothing but a goddamned cowboy!" She stomped to the open door, then whirled to face him again. "You and that pathetic, one-legged old man won't keep this godforsaken piece of land from my father! Like me, he always gets what he wants!"

Beau turned away as Madeline stormed out of the barn. He rubbed his stinging cheek, his brow furrowed in a troubled frown. Alina's father was missing and feared dead? Why hadn't she told him? Her casual explanation that her father was on an extended sea voyage had not been the complete truth. Beau dismissed Madeline's claim that Alina was unbalanced, but he could not escape the thought that Alina did not trust him.

He sighed and reached for the pitchfork. Perhaps she had not forgiven him for New Year's Eve. Perhaps she never would. Should he ask her about her father, or wait until she saw fit to tell him? He stomped into one of the stalls. What did he care if she trusted him or not? She'd be leaving as soon as she could. *Let sleeping dogs lie.* He stabbed ferociously at a pile of straw in the corner of the stall.

Madeline ran from the barn to the buggy and awkwardly climbed in. She took up the reins and jerked the horse's head. The animal squealed in pain. Because of the lead Conor had attached to its halter, the horse could not move. Madeline grabbed the buggy whip from its socket and lashed out repeatedly and unmercifully at the mare.

Alina watched for a moment in horror, then dropped her hoe and ran across the yard. Conor's hat fell off the back of her head and hung from her throat by the tie. "Stop it!" she screamed, and tried to catch the frantic animal's halter. Conor came running from the woodpile as Beau raced from the barn.

An evil grin twisted Madeline's features when her glazed eyes fell on Alina. She leapt from the buggy and raised her whip.

Alina cried out as the lash came down across her back, but she did not release her hold on the horse. From behind, Beau caught Madeline around the waist with one hand while his other grabbed her wrist as she raised the whip to strike again. Conor shielded Alina with his body and reached for the harness.

Beau wrested the lash from Madeline's grip and pushed her against the buggy wheel. His breathing was harsh and ragged.

"Alina! Are you all right?" he demanded, not taking his furious gaze from Madeline's unrepentant face.

"I'm fine," Alina called in breathless response. "This poor creature is not, though." Her heart ached for the distressed mare. She ran her hand down the length of the trembling animal's neck as Conor released the traces.

Beau took Madeline's upper arm in a tight grip and forced her to accompany him to the porch. He pushed her to a sitting position on the top step. *"Don't move!"*

Madeline stared sullenly at the ground. She did not move.

Beau returned to Alina and grabbed her arms. "Are you truly all right?"

"Truly, Beau. Conor's hat saved me from any real harm."

She attempted a smile. "I don't know how his hat fared, though."

Beau pulled her into his arms and spoke to Conor over her shoulder. "Bay is harness-trained." He waved at the horse that stood in a corner of the corral. "If you'll hitch him up, I'll see to this one. Madeline can't be trusted with any animal; one of us will have to take her home."

"I'll do it," Conor offered. "You stay here with Alina."

Beau nodded gratefully. He took the lead from Conor and led the mare to the barn, his other arm still around Alina's shoulders. He guided the horse into a stall and ran his hand over the welts on her back. A few were deep enough to warrant treatment. His jaw tightened at the discovery of old scars covering the animal. "She has been beaten before," he said through clenched teeth. Alina patted the horse's neck in sympathy. "Stay with her," he instructed. "I'll get the salve."

Alina nodded and pulled the gloves from her hands. Beau jerked his saddle and saddle blanket from their stand and left the barn. Conor had Bay in the traces and was securing the harness.

"Do you know how to get to town?" Beau asked, as he threw the saddle and blanket in the buggy box.

Conor nodded. "Sure do." He buttoned his shirt and tucked it into his faded denim pants, then adjusted his gun-belt.

"The Cheyenne Pass Road will take you into Laramie City. It comes into town at Eighth and South F Street. Follow Eighth to North A—it's about eight blocks—and turn left. Petrie's home is on the corner of North A and Fifth. You can't miss it." Beau crossed the yard and pulled Madeline from her seat. He led her to the buggy and lifted her in, then continued speaking to Conor; his still furious eyes passed over Madeline as if she wasn't there. "Tell Petrie he can send for his horse in a few days."

Alina stood at the barn door with Conor's hat in her hand and his leather vest draped over one arm. Her cousin walked to her and took the battered hat.

"Are you sure you're all right?" Conor asked.

Alina nodded. "I found your vest hanging on one of the harness hooks."

Conor examined his hat ruefully, placed it on his head, and slipped into the vest. "Thank you." He winked at her and returned to the buggy. "I'll be home by supper," he said to Beau as he took up the reins.

As the buggy clattered across the bridge, Madeline glanced calculatingly at the handsome man next to her. She wondered who he was. "I appreciate you driving me home, sir," she said softly. "I feel very distraught. I can't imagine what came over me."

Conor did not take his eyes from the road. "Save your speech, lady."

Madeline fell back against the seat, her arms folded across her chest, her lips pressed in an angry line. The rest of the trip passed in silence.

Beau watched the buggy until it disappeared around the stand of trees. He felt like he needed a bath, just to wash away Madeline's presence. He turned to Alina; she still stood in the doorway of the barn. Most of her hair had fallen from its arrangement. She had dirt on one cheek where she had rubbed her face. Her simple skirt was covered with dust, as was his ridiculously big workshirt. He compared her in his mind to Madeline, then to every woman he had ever known, and he knew she was the only woman he would ever want. Perhaps one day she would grow to trust him, and perhaps one day he would be ready to plan a future with her. For now, he would just kiss her.

"I'm going to kiss you, Alina Parker, just so you know," he called. He covered the distance between them in a few long strides.

Her eyes widened with surprise at his words, and a thrill of excitement chased itself around her stomach. She watched him come, the sun shining off his naked shoulders. She noticed a scar that curved across his left side, interrupting the pattern of fine hair that covered his chest. The look in his eyes caused her to tremble. He stopped in front of her. He caressed her upper arms and pulled her close, then lowered his mouth to hers. Her eyes closed. At the touch of his lips, it was as if a bolt of lightning shot through her. She couldn't seem to find her breath. His mouth moved slowly, wonderfully, over hers as his arms encircled her body. Her arms crept around his waist while her lips responded to his of their own accord. She reveled in the feel of his naked back under her hands. When the kiss ended, he moved one hand to brush her hair from the side of her face.

"What was that for?" Alina asked breathlessly.

"To tell you that I'm proud of you." His eyes searched her face, the need to kiss her again so strong that he was afraid he could not stop himself. But he did not want to push her; he would not be able to bear it if the fear and distrust she had felt in those early months returned. He took a shaky breath and smiled at her, then turned to guide her into the barn. "Let's see to that poor horse."

"You didn't get the salve," Alina reminded him, wondering how she could remember it herself, after that kiss.

A sheepish grin covered his face. "I'll be right back."

He trotted across the yard to the cabin. Alina watched him go, a thoughtful frown wrinkling her brow. She moved one hand to touch her trembling lips.

Conor pulled the buggy to a stop in front of Richard Petrie's opulent mansion. Madeline jumped out of the vehicle and flew up the steps, screaming for her father. Conor paid no evident attention to the three cowhands who came from behind the house, nor did he look up from his task of releasing Bay from the buggy harness when Richard Petrie stormed from the house, followed closely by Madeline.

"What is the meaning of this, young man?" Petrie shouted as he came down the steps. He was a tall, imposing man, his expensive clothes tasteful and understated. He wore his fifty-plus years well. Conor slipped Beau's bridle over the bay's head.

"I demand an answer, sir! My daughter says that Beau Parker stole her mare." The three cowhands moved menacingly closer.

Conor looked at Petrie. "If that's what your daughter told you, then, in addition to being an animal abuser, she is also a liar," he said calmly. He led Bay from the traces and around to the back of the buggy.

Madeline gasped in outrage. "Father," she whined, and clutched at his arm. Petrie shook her off and approached Conor.

"Explain yourself, sir," Petrie demanded.

Conor pulled the saddle blanket from the buggy box. "Your daughter was beating her mare," he spat out, "and it's not the first time. That horse is covered with scars. She also raised her whip to Beau's wife." He heaved the saddle onto the horse. "Beau Parker said to tell you that you can send for the mare in a few days, when she's healed."

Petrie turned on Madeline. "Is this true?" he thundered.

"Father, the horse wouldn't go," Madeline whimpered, backing up a few steps.

"The horse was tied to the fence," Conor said sharply as he tightened the cinch. "She *couldn't* go."

"I warned you about mistreating that mare, Madeline. You won't be entrusted with any of the horses from now on."

"But, Father—" she cried, stepping forward again.

"Silence!"

Madeline cringed.

"If one of the men can't drive you, you'll walk, or stay home." He turned to Conor. "Do you work for Parker?"

Conor held the reins in one hand and hitched his other hand in his belt. "I'm staying on for a while to help out. Alina Parker is my cousin."

"What's your name?"

"Conor O'Rourke."

"I'll sell you the mare for five dollars, O'Rourke."

"Father, she's mine!" Madeline cried. "She's worth much more than that! You can't sell her!"

Petrie ignored her.

Conor was astonished. He shrugged. "I don't have five dollars on me, Mr. Petrie."

"How much do you have?"

Conor pulled his timepiece and a collection of coins from his vest pocket. "Three dollars and two bits."

"Sold. Come with me. I'll give you a receipt." Petrie climbed the porch steps. "You men get that buggy to the stable!" he shouted to the cowhands, then lowered his voice. "Madeline, go to your room." He did not look at her. "I'll talk to you later." He stomped into the house.

Conor tied the reins to the hitching post, then took off his hat as he followed the dejected woman into the lavish entryway. He did not miss the hate-filled look Madeline gave him as she climbed the stairs. The butler closed the front door.

"Mr. Petrie awaits you in his study," Beckett informed him. "Please follow me."

Petrie was seated at an impressive mahogany desk. He wrote quickly and finished with a flourish. He handed Conor a piece of paper, which Conor accepted and read. He put the paper in his shirt pocket, then retrieved the coins from his vest and set them on the table.

"Good day, Mr. O'Rourke," Petrie said coldly.

Conor settled his hat on his head. "Good day, Mr. Petrie. I'll let myself out." He made his exit, glad to be free of the house. He heard the roar of Richard Petrie's voice as the man shouted for his daughter. Conor untied the reins and swung into the saddle. "Let's get on home, boy," he said. Bay broke into an easy lope.

At dinner that night, Pike complained that he was never around when anything exciting happened.

Conor looked up from the trout he was enjoying. "I'm mighty glad you were out catching these fish, rather than here."

"The only excitin' thing that happened ta me today was that silly mutt fell in the river. It's lucky he can swim, 'cause I wouldn't have gone in after him."

Alina looked at the puppy, who was heartily eating his own dinner of deboned fish and rice. "Don't you believe him, Sundance," she said soothingly. "He doesn't show it, but he likes you."

"Ah, woman, why'd ya go and tell him that?" Pike moaned. "Now he'll never leave me alone."

Everyone laughed, and Beau caught Alina's eyes. The warmth he read in her gaze caused his stomach to flop, as the fire in his eyes brought a blush to her cheeks.

Conor spoke again. "Alina, I'll give you that mare, if you'd like her. I don't need another horse."

Alina's shining eyes fell on her cousin. "Oh, Conor, really? I'd love her! She's so sweet. I'm glad she doesn't have to go back to that woman."

Pike rolled his eyes. "Now we gotta get ya a saddle of your own, and I suppose ya gotta name her, don't ya?"

"I've already named her Lucy."

"That ain't too bad, I s'pose."

"It's better than Tumbleweed," Conor retorted, and again everyone laughed.

When the meal ended, Alina filled the water reservoirs, so that by the time the dishes were dried and put away, there was enough hot water for a bath. She had scrubbed her face and hands before dinner, and had brushed and pinned up her hair, but she longed for a good soak. She ached from head to foot. The men had washed the dirt of the day from their bodies at a pool in the creek; however, Alina preferred a warm bath, with lots of soap. She lit the lantern and stepped onto the back porch. If she bathed out here, the men could stay where they were.

She hung the lantern on a nail embedded in the post and pulled the bathing tub from its leaning position against the cabin wall. She stepped back inside and filled a pail from the water reservoir. Beau set his book down and rose from the table to take the pail from her hand.

"I'll bring the tub in for you," he offered.

"No, it isn't that cold outside. Besides, then you all won't have to leave the room." She waved her arm toward the sofa where Pike sat, involved in a game of chess with Conor.

Conor looked up and pushed his chair back from the chess table. "We don't mind, Alina."

Alina shook her head with a smile. "Thank you, but I can take my time out there. Stay where you are."

"Well, let me fill the tub for you then," Beau said. "You look tired."

Alina flashed him a grateful smile. "Thank you. The bucket did seem awful heavy tonight." She went to her bedroom and removed her boots and stockings, then gathered a couple of clean flour sack towels, her scented soap, the bottle of rose water, and her nightclothes. She returned to the porch as Beau dumped a final pail of water into the tub.

"Test the temperature," he suggested.

She draped her nightdress and robe over the porch railing and bent to trail her fingers in the warm water. "It's fine. Thank you."

Beau watched the lantern light play off her face.

"Beau?" she asked, puzzled at his intensity.

He blinked, then turned to the door. "I'll fill this so you'll have rinse water." A minute later he set the full pail within reach of the tub. Alina put the soap and the rose water down next to the pail. "Call if you need more water," Beau said, and reluctantly closed the door. He ran his fingers through his hair as he returned to the table and his book. It would not be easy to dispel from his mind the imagined picture of his lovely wife in her bath.

Alina stretched her stiff back and unbuttoned the workshirt. The time she had spent in the garden had taken its toll on her muscles, and on the tender skin of her palms. She let the shirt hang open and examined her hands in the lantern light. Beau's gloves had helped, but blisters had been raised.

She sighed and slipped the shirt off, wincing as the material passed over her right shoulder. She dropped the garment to the floor and examined the painful spot. An ugly welt ran at an angle along the top of her shoulder, the skin scraped and bruised. Madeline's whip had found its mark after all, at least partially. Alina was thankful once again for Conor's hat. She could have been hurt far worse. The skirt and petticoat joined the shirt on the floor; they all needed to be washed. She pulled the pins from her hair and ran her fingers through the mass of curls. Even her hair smelled of dust.

Dressed only in her camisole and drawers, Alina glanced around the dark, silent yard, suddenly self-conscious. She moved the lantern from its nail to the floorboards and lowered the flame as much as she could, then quickly slipped out of her undergarments and into the tub. She closed her eyes and leaned against the tall back with a heartfelt sigh of relief and pleasure. The warm water just covered the tips of her breasts, and the air that touched her exposed skin was cool and refreshing. She felt she could go to sleep just like this.

But she did not sleep. Her mind was suddenly filled with the picture of Beau, shirtless in the sunshine, striding to take her in his arms, his eyes on fire. She remembered the feeling in her stomach when he kissed her; a trace of that excitement returned now, just at the memory. She remembered the muscled expanse of his naked chest and wondered what it would be like to run her fingers through the fine dark hair, to touch the long, pale scar. It troubled her to think of him sustaining an injury severe enough to leave such a mark. A sudden thought struck her.

Alina opened her eyes and sat up straight. She looked down. The water now came only to her ribs. The cool breeze caressed her wet skin, causing her nipples to tighten. Would Beau find her chest as appealing as she found his? A frown drew her arched brows together. She lifted a leg from the water and straightened it, examining its length critically, then did the same with her arms. Would her body please him?

With a sigh, she lowered her leg back into the warmth of the water and clasped her hands over her breasts, twisting the golden ring. Innocent though she was, she knew enough to know that Beau wanted her. He behaved as a gentleman, but his eyes were not so polite. He wanted her body, but he had given no indication that he wanted her as his wife, as his *true* wife. He had not asked her to stay on, to make her life with him.

Deeply troubled, Alina reached for the soap. She carefully washed her injured shoulder, then ran the silky bar over the rest of her body. Her tired mind betrayed her with the tantalizing idea of Beau's fingers replacing the soap.

"Alina Gallagher!" she scolded herself, her cheeks warm. "What has gotten into you?" Her voice was a whisper. She sighed again, knowing full well what had gotten into her. She leaned forward and pulled her hair over her head, then wet and lathered the long tresses. When she grabbed the handle to the pail, she found she could not lift it from that position. Her arms were more sore than she had thought. With a sigh, she rinsed her hair as best she could in the tub; perhaps after she was dressed one of the men would help her. She had just finished twisting the excess water from her hair when Beau's voice came through the door.

"Do you need more water?"

"No, thank you." She hesitated. "Beau?"

"Yes?"

Alina leaned forward and grabbed one of the towels. She draped it over her shoulders and pulled her hair forward. "Will you come here, please?"

Beau tried to keep a smile from his lips as he came to her side. In the dim light, he could not tell that her upturned face had flushed hot. "What can I do for you?"

"My arms are surprisingly sore, and I could not lift the bucket. Will you help me rinse my hair?"

"Of course," he answered gladly, and knelt beside the tub.

She leaned forward, her face and the front of her body hidden behind the curtain of her hair. The small towel covered her shoulders and soapy water concealed her from the middle of her back on down. The expanse of wet skin that was exposed seemed to glow.

"Please pour the water slowly over my head," Alina instructed. She worked her fingers through her hair as he followed her instructions. He reached across her to be sure the water rinsed the right side of her head as well, and the bucket brushed her injured shoulder. She flinched.

"What is it?" Beau demanded as he set the pail down.

"Nothing serious." She again twisted the excess water from her hair, holding it up out of the bathwater.

Beau was not convinced. He grabbed the lantern and turned up the wick, then pulled the towel from her shoulders.

"Beau, what are you doing?" Alina cried. Her hair fell back into the water as she crossed her arms over her breasts.

He held the lantern over her head with one hand and with the other gently brushed damp strands of black hair away from her right shoulder. His jaw tightened when he discovered the wound.

"You said you were not hurt!"

"It isn't that serious," she retorted. "I didn't know about it myself until I took the shirt off. Now, I insist that you go back inside this minute."

Beau ignored her. He ran his free hand over the entire surface of her back. She gasped in outrage, then winced when his fingers found another painful spot, this one on her left side, below the water line. Beau swore under his breath as he stood and hung the lantern on the nail. He disappeared into the cabin.

Alina wrung her hair once again and deftly wrapped the damp towel around her head. She was now shaking with cold, and furious that he had left the lantern turned up. She was about to rise when Beau came back out the door.

"Leave me!" she ordered through chattering teeth, her arms again protecting her modesty.

Beau stood at the side of the tub and held up a clean blanket, high enough to cover his face. "Stand up, Alina."

"Not while you're here," she snapped.

He lowered the blanket to look at her. "If you do not stand, I will lift you from the water myself."

Alina's shocked eyes met his determined ones. He raised the blanket again. She braced her hands on the sides of the tub and rose to a standing position. Beau wrapped the blanket around her shivering body and easily lifted her into his arms, ignoring her cry of protest. He kicked the partially closed door open and carried her to her room, speaking as he went.

"Pike, I left the salve in the barn. Please get it."

"What's wrong?" Pike demanded as he jumped up from the sofa. A few chess pieces toppled. Conor rose so forcefully that his chair almost fell over.

"Madeline's whip did some damage," Beau ground out as he laid Alina on the bed. Pike crossed the room, grabbed the lamp from the table, and was out the front door without a word.

Conor entered the bedroom to stand at the foot of the bed. Alina held the blanket in a desperate attempt to keep her body covered. "For heaven's sake, it's not that bad!" she cried in exasperation. "Will you leave me be?"

Beau sat on the bed next to her. "Turn over, honey," he instructed, his tone now gentle. Alina rolled her eyes. She could see that Beau was not going to give up, and one look at Conor's concerned face told her that he would not be her ally in this. She struggled to do as Beau had asked and still maintain her dignity, but it was difficult, wrapped up as she was. Beau helped her. The towel fell away from her head as she settled herself on her stomach. Beau arranged her damp hair on the far pillow and pulled the blanket down to her waist. Alina hid her face in embarrassment. The front door slammed and Pike came into the room, followed by Sundance, who promptly jumped up on the bed. Conor grabbed the puppy and placed him on the floor as Pike handed the tin of salve to Beau. The three men stared at Alina's naked back.

"There's not much we can do about this," Beau remarked as he gently traced the bruise on her lower back with his forefinger. "The skin's not broken. But the shoulder's bad enough that there could be a danger of infection." He looked back at Conor. "Thank God for your hat."

"Amen ta that," Pike responded. "I'll get her things."

"Did you wash the shoulder, Alina?" Beau asked.

"Yes." Alina's voice was muffled.

Beau opened the tin and, after dipping out an amount of salve with two fingers, set the container on the bedside table.

Pike returned and draped her nightclothes and the dry towel over the footboard, then placed the bottle of rose water on the dresser. "Ya don't need me gettin' in the way, and ya don't need this here dog tryin' ta help, neither." He scooped a squirming Sundance up into his arms. "Holler if ya need anythin' else," he said, as he closed the bedroom door.

Alina flinched at Beau's gentle touch upon her bruised skin.

"I'm sorry," he murmured. "Conor, will you tear off a strip of that towel? I want to wrap this."

Conor did as he was asked and handed Beau the material. "I'll wait in the other room with Pike," he said, and slipped out the door.

Beau lifted Alina's shoulder from the mattress, careful not to expose her breast to his view. He lightly wound the piece of towel under her arm and over the wound a few times, tying the two ends in a knot. He paused, his eyes wandering over the expanse of her back. His left hand moved of its own volition to caress the soft skin. Alina held her breath. Beau suddenly realized what he was doing. He cleared his throat as he pulled the blanket up to her shoulders, then reached for her nightdress. "I'll help you into this," he offered.

Alina looked back at him, then struggled to a sitting position, holding the blanket around her. Beau guided her head and arms into the appropriate openings. She worked the hem under her hips and Beau caught a flash of slender, shapely legs as she pulled the garment down to her feet. She buttoned the front opening, then draped the damp blanket over the footboard. "I think you overreacted, but thank you for tending to me." She maneuvered under the bedclothes and sat facing him.

Beau shrugged as he replaced the lid on the tin of salve. "There's no sense risking infection." He looked at her, his features somber. "I'm sorry you were hurt, Alina. She was upset with me and took it out on you, and that poor mare."

Alina took up the towel and patted at her hair. "Why was she so angry?" she asked without thinking, then caught herself. "I'm sorry. That's none of my affair."

"Actually, it is." Beau shifted his weight on the bed. "She came to urge me to end our marriage."

"What business is it of hers?" Alina's eyes flashed. "That woman has a lot of nerve."

Her response pleased Beau, but he kept his expression neutral. "She's been to Chicago."

Alina's eyes widened in sudden fear. "Why?"

"To visit the Randalls. I think they've joined forces. The Randalls want you and your inheritance, Madeline wants me and this ranch."

"What did you tell her?" Alina twisted the towel in her hands.

Beau's features softened. "What do you think I told her?" A tender smile played around his lips.

"Is everythin' all right in there?" came Pike's querulous voice through the door.

Beau sighed and moved to open the door. "Everything is fine, Pike."

"I made Alina some of that tea she likes ta drink, so get on outta my way, Beau." Pike pushed past Beau and came to set a steaming mug on the bedside table. Conor leaned against the doorjamb, and Sundance once again jumped on the bed. After greeting Alina with a wagging tail and a wet tongue, he snuggled contentedly next to her legs.

"How do you feel, Cousin?" Conor asked.

"I'm fine, really." Her gaze traveled affectionately over the three men. "I just hope I never get badly hurt. You'll kill me with your care! Now, will one of you nurses please hand me my rose water?"

Beau grabbed the bottle from the dresser and passed it to Pike, who gave it to Alina.

"Thank you," she said sweetly. They all continued to watch her. Finally she pointed to the door in exasperation. "Out!"

"She's still mighty bossy, so she can't be feelin' too bad," Pike commented to Conor as they disappeared into the other room.

Beau paused. "Call if you need anything." At Alina's nod, he left the room, pulling the door closed behind him.

Alina poured a little of the rose water into one hand before she set the bottle on the bedside table. She worked the scented liquid through her hair. Again her thoughts turned to Beau. Today he had defended her, held her, kissed her, and cared for her injury. Surely there was more to his feelings than just honor, duty, or guilt!

And what of her feelings for him? The distrust and fear had fallen away over the last months, to be replaced with friendship and affection, and other, deeper feelings. Alina thought of his fingers on her back and longed to know his touch again. She leaned forward and stroked Sundance's soft head. She would be glad when Elizabeth arrived; she needed someone to talk to.

Chapter Thirteen

Alina glanced at the clock on a shelf in Mrs. Simpson's dressmaking shop and sighed. It was only a little past eleven in the morning; her great-aunt's train was not due for another hour. She dropped her eyes to the material she had been examining and tried to still her impatience. Her hand caressed the soft calico. The tiny pink flowers that danced over the burgundy background were the same color as the porcelain flowers on her hair comb, which was why she had chosen that particular fabric. She could picture the lovely dress the material would make, with lace trim at the neck and cuffs. She desperately needed more casual clothes, and hoped Mrs. Simpson would not take long to make up the dress, the two skirts and the three blouses she had ordered today. Now that Elizabeth was on her way, Alina felt more comfortable spending some of her hoarded money.

"That calico will be enchanting on you, Mrs. Parker." Mrs. Simpson draped the tape measure around her plump neck.

"Thank you. When can I pick up my order?"

Mrs. Simpson squinted at the calendar from the T. D. Abbott Bookstore and News Depot that hung on the wall behind her counter. "I can have everything finished by the end of the month. Will that be soon enough?"

"That will be fine." Alina pulled on her gloves and moved toward the door. "Good day, Mrs. Simpson."

The distracted woman paused at the entrance to the back room, her arms filled with Alina's material. " 'Bye now, Mrs. Parker." Her eyes fell on a hat displayed in her window on a head mannequin. "Mrs. Parker, wait!"

Alina hesitated, a patient smile on her face. Mrs. Simpson hurried toward her, struggling to keep all the material in her arms. A wisp of fine gray hair waved over her shoulder as she moved. "That hat, the one with the pink ribbon, would be lovely with your new dress." Her hopeful eyes squinted up at Alina.

Alina looked at the wide-brimmed straw hat. It was indeed lovely. The finely woven straw had been bleached to a soft cream color, and a wide pink ribbon surrounded the base of the crown, tied in a bow at the back with streamers hanging down. Delicate silk flowers of pink and burgundy played along one side of the crown.

"You are absolutely right, Mrs. Simpson." Alina fingered the pink streamer. "The hat complements the calico perfectly. I'll have that as well; I'll pick it up when I get the rest of my order." She smiled at the short, plump woman. "Thank you for pointing it out to me."

"It was my pleasure, to be sure." Mrs. Simpson beamed. "Good day now, ma'am."

"Good day, Mrs. Simpson." Alina opened her umbrella as she stepped into the sunshine. She glanced up and down the street, uncertain of what to do next. She had already been to the Satin Slipper and to Johnson's Mercantile. There was nothing else she wanted or needed. Conor was to meet her at the depot at eleven forty-five. Although it was early, she decided to await her great-aunt's train at the station, and set off in that direction.

At the appointed time, Conor came through the back door of the depot. Alina stood on the platform between the train station and the tracks, her eyes fixed on the horizon to the north. A smile came to Conor's face at the sight of his pretty cousin.

"Any sign of the train?" he called.

Alina turned to him and shook her head. "I didn't hear your approach," she said. Conor took her hand and led her to a bench that rested along the depot wall.

"Did you get all the supplies?" Alina asked.

Conor nodded. "The wagon is loaded and out in front."

"And did you mail your letter?" Alina eyed her cousin, her curiosity evident. This was the second letter he had sent to a law firm in Pennsylvania in the short time he had been here. He had not explained who he was writing to and why, nor had he yet received any return mail.

Conor nodded again, his expression shuttered. He was quiet for a minute. "Will you go to Chicago with Elizabeth, Alina?"

Alina hesitated. "I don't know," she said finally. "We should see what Elizabeth thinks is best."

Her cousin looked at her searchingly. "Do you want to leave?"

Alina dropped her eyes. "A few months ago, nothing would have kept me from returning to Chicago with Elizabeth." She gazed down the track. "But now I don't know. I don't miss my life there. I have grown to love this land."

Conor stretched his long legs out and leaned against the wall. "Have you grown to love Beau as well?"

Alina fixed troubled eyes on her cousin's face. "I don't know, Conor. My feelings for him are confusing. Our relationship got off to a rough start, before he rescued me from Cordelia's clutches. Part of me can't forget that. And what of the future? What will happen when my father returns? I don't know what Beau wants of me, in the long run."

"What do you want of him in the long run? To live in Chicago with you? To ask you to stay here?" Conor eyed her thoughtfully. "Would you stay if he asked?"

"I don't know," she repeated, her voice a whisper.

The faraway sound of a train whistle reached their ears. Alina jumped up and closed her umbrella. They both moved closer to the rails and watched the slow approach of the powerful engine. Neither spoke until they saw their great-aunt wave to them from the window of a passenger car.

"Aunt Elizabeth!" Alina called. Conor swept his hat from his head and stood back when Elizabeth stepped onto the platform. She held her arms out to Alina, and as the women embraced, Alina was surprised to feel her eyes tear. The past six months had been fearful at times, and often depressing and filled with anxiety. All her hopes had rested upon the slight woman she now held. The sense of relief was almost overwhelming.

"Let me look at you, girl," Elizabeth said briskly after a moment. The women stood back from each other, still holding hands. To Alina, Elizabeth looked smaller and more frail than she remembered her. Elizabeth's hair was completely white, and her face was lined with the tales of sixty-five years, but she carried herself proud and straight, and her aged blue eyes had not lost their fire.

Elizabeth turned to Conor. "Conor O'Rourke," she said with a smile. "I'd know you anywhere. Give your old aunt a hug." Conor gladly did as he was instructed.

Elizabeth looked at him, her gaze piercing. "How have you been these last years, my boy? I've been concerned about you."

Conor shrugged. "I'm still alive, Aunt." He put his hat on his head and adjusted the string. "I'll check on your luggage." He walked off.

"And you?" Elizabeth asked Alina.

"I'm fine, Aunt Elizabeth. But these last several months have been hard. I'm so happy that you're here. I'll be glad to have this whole mess settled."

"Indeed. And we *will* get it settled." The two women strolled out of the bright sunlight into the crowded depot.

Conor joined them a few minutes later. "Did you have only one trunk?"

Elizabeth nodded. "I sent the rest of my things on to Chicago last week."

"We've reserved a suite for you at the hotel," Alina said.

"I would prefer to stay with you, Alina. If I understood your letters, your husband's ranch is some distance from town, too far to make it practical to travel back and forth every day, and you are the one I am here to see."

Alina and Conor shared a glance, then Alina spoke. "Our cabin is comfortable, Aunt, but it is not what you're used to."

"Nonsense, girl. Don't forget that I shared many a ship's tiny cabin with the late Captain Hammond in our voyaging days. I've lived under primitive conditions and done quite well, thank you. Now let's be on our way." She hooked one arm with Alina and the other with Conor. "As you are both adults now, I think it's time we drop the 'aunt.' It makes me sound old." She laughed at her own words and guided them toward the door.

The trip to the ranch passed quickly. Alina shared the shade of her umbrella with Elizabeth and pointed out the landmarks along the way. Sundance barked a welcome and ran happy circles around the wagon as they pulled into the yard. Beau and Pike came from Alina's garden, where they had been sinking posts for the fence. They took off their hats.

Conor lifted first Elizabeth, then Alina, from the wagon onto the porch. Elizabeth eyed Beau's tall frame approvingly as Alina made the introductions.

"Elizabeth, I would like to present Mr. Sebastian Amadeus Pike and Mr. Beauregard Parker. Gentlemen, our great-aunt, Mrs. Elizabeth Hammond."

Elizabeth gave her hand first to Pike. "Mr. Pike," she murmured, then turned to Beau. "So you are the man to whom I am so beholden," she said with a smile as he took her hand in a firm grip.

"Not at all, ma'am. It was my pleasure, I assure you." His warm gaze fell on Alina, a gesture Elizabeth did not miss.

"Elizabeth would prefer to stay with us, Beau," Conor said, as he lifted the trunk from the wagon. "I figured we'd put her in our room, if that's all right with Pike."

" 'Course it is," Pike asserted. He opened the door to the

cabin. "Won't take us long at all ta clear outta there. We'll just bunk down in the barn."

"No, she should have my room," Alina protested.

"Ya do have the best bed, Alina," Pike admitted, stroking his beard thoughtfully. "Mrs. Hammond'll have your room, we'll move ya into our room, and me'n Conor'll still sleep in the barn." He clapped his disreputable hat on his head and lifted one end of the trunk. Conor took the other and they disappeared into the cabin.

Elizabeth looked at Alina. "Is your room large enough to share?"

Alina nodded. "Yes. Well, at least the bed is." She glanced at Beau, her cheeks touched with pink.

"Do you mind sharing with me?" Elizabeth asked.

"Not at all," Alina responded quickly.

"Good. Then no one will sleep in the barn," said Elizabeth with satisfaction.

"I'll leave you ladies to get settled," Beau said. He replaced his hat and touched the brim. "It's a pleasure to meet you at last, Mrs. Hammond." He led the team toward the barn.

Elizabeth thoughtfully watched him go, then let her gaze wander over the vista spread before her. Alina crouched down to pet Sundance. "It is even more beautiful than you described, Alina," Elizabeth said finally. "I can see why you like it here." Her sharp eyes found Beau once more before she turned to her niece.

"This is Sundance," Alina offered.

Elizabeth leaned down and held out a hand to the dog. "Hello, there," she said with a smile, as Sundance joyously licked at her glove. Alina straightened. "It's good to see you, girl." Elizabeth hugged her again. "Now show me your cabin."

* * *

Alina cleared the last of the supper dishes from the table and refilled the coffee cups, then took her place next to Conor on the new bench. All eyes were on Elizabeth.

"Let me first express my gratitude once again to you, Mr. Parker, for the kind assistance you have offered my niece, and to you, Mr. Pike." She held up a hand as both men were about to speak. "No protests, please. The truth is that you helped Alina out of a dangerous situation, and those of us who love her," she nodded at Conor, "will be forever in your debt. Please allow us to express that."

"You are most welcome, ma'am, and you, Conor." Beau's tone was quiet. Pike stared into his coffee cup.

"Now," Elizabeth continued briskly, "we must decide what action to take from here." She looked at Alina. "I assume everyone knows the situation with the Randalls." Alina nodded. "Good. I will get to Chicago and learn what has happened in our absence. I have been corresponding regularly with Seamus Percival, and have instructed my own solicitor to offer Mr. Percival whatever assistance he can."

"And Alina and me?" Conor asked.

"I think it best that you both remain here for now, until I have a better idea of what we face. I don't want Alina anywhere near Donovan Randall, and you will be of more use here." Her sharp eyes went from Beau to Pike. "That is, if our friends don't mind sharing their home for a while longer."

" 'Course we don't mind," Pike blustered. Beau spoke at the same time. "They are welcome to stay as long as they want to."

Alina smiled her thanks to each man, then faced her aunt. "I will be twenty-one the day after tomorrow, Elizabeth. Cordelia's guardianship of me is no longer an issue. But she is trustee of Papa's estate until I turn twenty-five."

Elizabeth nodded. "I will try to have her rights as trustee revoked, although I'm certain she will fight me in court. She'll argue that you married without her permission, that she doesn't approve of Mr. Parker, that I'm too old, and that Conor is too unsettled. I fear this may drag out, and unfortunately, she has your father's wealth at her disposal. She can afford a lengthy court battle." She hesitated. "Do you know that the *Brianna* has returned?"

Alina nodded. "Mr. Percival has kept me informed."

"The *Brianna?*" Beau questioned.

"My father's ship," Alina answered.

"And what of your father, Alina?" Elizabeth asked quietly.

Alina stared into her great-aunt's kind eyes. "He lives, Elizabeth." Her voice was firm.

Elizabeth nodded with satisfaction. "Hopefully, we will hear from him, or he will return, before too much longer. But we cannot count on his presence in the near future, so we must make our own plans."

"Excuse me, Mrs. Hammond," Beau interjected. He turned to Alina. "I thought your father was lost at sea." At her startled expression, he spread his hands. "That's what Madeline said the Randalls told her."

"He was washed from his ship, but he is still alive."

"How do you know?"

Alina shrugged uncomfortably. "I just know. I saw him."

"You saw him where?" Beau persisted. Madeline's words nagged at him. *She thinks she 'knows' things.*

"In my mind," Alina answered reluctantly. She stared down at her hands clasped in her lap. The soft light from the lamp washed over her features.

"Ya mean, like a vision?" Pike asked, stroking his beard.

"Exactly, Mr. Pike, in this instance." Elizabeth spoke up. "We Irish call it the Gift of Sight. Alina's mother had it, as Alina does, to a degree. Usually she just gets feelings, warnings, I guess you could call them."

"And you accept this vision as fact?" Beau was skeptical.

"We do, Beau." It was Conor who answered. "My mother had the Gift as well. There's no real way to explain it. But I'll believe Uncle Neil is alive until Alina tells me different."

Alina turned to Elizabeth. "How soon will you leave?"

"Soon, girl." Elizabeth smiled with affection. "I'll stay a few days, but the sooner I return home, the sooner we can resolve this situation. When will you next go to town?"

"Friday, Mrs. Hammond," Beau replied. "We'll be leaving early. A rancher across the river lost his barn to fire a few weeks ago, and we'll be going to the barn-raising to give a hand." He wondered if Alina was looking forward to the day as much as he was.

"That will work out just fine," Elizabeth said. "We'll check the eastbound schedules, to be sure, but I think a train leaves around eight-thirty in the morning." She smiled at Alina and patted Conor's hand. "That will give us a few days together. And now, you must excuse me. These old bones are tired." Conor jumped up and pulled Elizabeth's chair out for her. Beau and Pike also rose, as did Alina.

"I'll bring you some wash water," Alina offered.

"That would be lovely, my dear." Her eyes fell on the stacked plates. "Mercy, what am I thinking? There are dishes to be done. I'll help with those first."

"No, you won't, Mrs. Hammond," Beau interjected firmly. "I will help Alina with the dishes."

Elizabeth capitulated with a smile. "Very well, Mr. Parker. Goodnight, Mr. Pike."

"Ma'am." Pike nodded at her.

She gave Conor a quick hug, then disappeared into her room. Alina followed with a basin of warm water.

Later, Beau stepped out onto the porch. Alina sat on the top step with Sundance snuggled at her side, watching the last bit of light fade from the valley.

"Would you rather be alone?" he asked.

"No." She smiled up at him. He sat down next to her. They were quiet for a few minutes, then Beau spoke.

"Why didn't you tell me the whole truth about your father?"

Alina stared at her hands. "I was afraid you would think I was crazy for believing that he is still alive."

Again Madeline's words ran through his head: *She's deranged.* He shrugged them off. "I guess I can understand that," he said. He looked at her curiously. "Can you really see things?"

Alina raised her eyes to his face, quickly, defensively. She found no mocking there. "Not usually," she answered. "As Elizabeth said, I mostly get warnings, powerful feelings that something is wrong. I knew Sean was in danger, and I knew it had to do with the Lake, but my cable did not reach him in time." She paused. "Mama knew the very minute Joseph was killed. I'll never forget it."

Beau turned to face her. "Tell me about it."

Alina stared straight ahead. "It was the summer I was twelve. We were in the parlor; she was making me practice my stitches. Suddenly she dropped her book and cried out, as if she were in terrible pain. She clasped her hands to her breast, sobbing Joseph's name over and over. She later said she had felt the bullets as if they had entered her own body. That day my happy childhood ended. Joseph died, and my mother began to die, too, though it took three years." Alina blinked tear-filled eyes. "But I did see Papa. I would know if he were dead, Beau, just as I knew Sean was dead long before Mr. Percival's cable reached me." She turned her head to look at him. "Do you believe me?"

He hesitated, then spoke quietly. "I believe that you believe, and that's good enough for me."

"Does my 'Gift' disturb you?" she asked.

"No. Should it?"

Alina shrugged. "It disturbs many people. People thought my mother was very strange. Well, the Irish didn't because they understand the Gift, but everyone else did. My childhood was happy, but often lonely. Besides my brothers, my only real friends were Susannah and Jennifer. We met each year in Narragansett, where our fathers took us for the summer season, and eventually we went to a finishing school in England together." She plucked at her apron. "Throughout my life, many people have found me strange."

"I don't find you strange at all. I find you lovely." Beau's voice was barely above a whisper.

Alina met his eyes, her own wide with surprise. His face was very close; he lowered his head and placed a soft kiss at the corner of her mouth. Alina could not stop herself from turning her head a little more to meet his lips. He sighed from deep in his chest and draped one arm over her shoulders, while his other hand moved to caress the side of her face. The familiar excitement grew in her stomach as Beau's mouth moved knowingly over hers. At the gentle insistence of his lips, she parted her own, allowing him access to her mouth. This time the sigh came from her. Never had she known such feelings! She worked her arm around his waist and nestled closer to him. When Beau finally raised his head, his breathing was ragged, and Alina was breathless herself. The fingers of her free hand moved through his thick, long hair as he searched her face with eyes that seemed on fire.

"Sweet woman," he murmured, his voice husky. He could feel the rise and fall of her soft, full breasts against his chest. "I knew you would taste sweet. Oh, Alina." His arm tightened around her. "My Irish Rose. I'm glad you won't be leaving with your aunt."

Alina was content to remain in his embrace. "I'll have to leave sometime, Beau. I have to deal with the situation at home." The thundering of her heart was beginning to calm.

"I know," Beau said, trying to keep the sadness from his voice. "I'm just glad it isn't now." They lapsed into silence.

"I can't believe it's time for you to leave already," Alina said sadly. She sat with Elizabeth on the bench outside the depot. Beau and Conor had said their farewells and had gone on to the McAllisters. Pike waited a distance away.

Elizabeth patted Alina's hand. "I know, dear. We'll see each other again soon. Your birthday has passed and you are free of Cordelia's guardianship. All will be well." She lifted Alina's chin with one finger. "We must talk about your young man."

"What about him?"

"I've been watching the two of you over these last few days. This is none of my business, but just how temporary is this arrangement?" At Alina's puzzled expression, Elizabeth continued. "You are married to each other. How intimate are you?"

Alina blushed a deep red and dropped her gaze. "You know we are married in name only, Elizabeth. We don't share a bed, and we have not become physically intimate."

Elizabeth looked at her wonderingly. "I can only marvel at your self-restraint, and his. You are legally married to that beautiful man, it is obvious that each of you has strong feelings for the other, and yet you resist the joys of love. I don't think I've ever seen two people try so hard not to love each other."

Alina glanced up and saw that her great-aunt's sharp gaze had not left her face. Elizabeth went on. "What do you intend to do with him when the situation at home is resolved?"

"The plan is to separate, to have the marriage annulled, as I told you when I wrote to you."

"That was the original plan. What will you do now? The man cares deeply for you, girl."

"Do you think so?" Alina asked doubtfully.

"Oh, yes. I can see it when he looks at you. He's a fine man, Alina. I think he would make you a good husband. And judging from how he is with animals, he'd be a wonderful father."

Alina blushed again. "Are you saying that you'd not object if we decided to remain married?"

"Heavens, no!"

"Do you think Papa would object?"

"Of course not. Why do you think he would?"

"Papa seemed to have great expectations for my eventual match."

"And you think he would not approve of a simple rancher and this wild land."

"I don't know, Elizabeth. I don't really know Papa very well. We haven't seen much of each other these last years. I don't think he would be so arrogant as to look down on Beau."

"Your father has not forgotten his own roots. He will be well pleased with your Beauregard."

The forlorn sound of a whistle heralded the approach of the train.

"Think about what I've said, Alina. Listen to your heart. For someone with the Gift of Sight, you can be very blind at times. Give the man a chance." Elizabeth stood and looked down at her silent great-niece. "Were I forty years younger, and that man's wife, I fear I would become quite wanton."

"Elizabeth!"

"The act of love between two people who truly love each other is one of God's greatest gifts to us, Alina. There is no shame in wanting each other. You have the potential of a glorious love right in front of you. Don't let it slip away." A fleeting wistfulness crossed Elizabeth's face, then she became businesslike again. "I will be in touch with you as soon as I have any information."

The noisy engine steamed to a stop in front of the depot. Alina walked with her great-aunt to the passenger car.

"Give me a kiss, my dear, and be off with you. I hate long farewells." Elizabeth held Alina in a tight embrace and the women kissed each other's cheek. Elizabeth turned to where Pike stood at the end of the platform.

"Thank you for everything, Mr. Pike," she called.

Pike came over to join them. He swept his hat from his head. "Ya surely are welcome, Miz Hammond. It was a pleasure ta meet ya."

"And you, sir. Watch out for my girl, here."

"Ya know I will, ma'am."

Pike took Elizabeth's elbow and escorted her up the steps to the car platform. With a cheery wave, Elizabeth disappeared into the passenger car. The wheels of the great engine began to turn once again, and the train moved down the tracks. Alina waved one last time. A deep loneliness settled over her.

"Let's go, girl." Pike slapped his hat back on his head. "They're needin' my help over ta the McAllisters."

Alina turned and hooked her arm through Pike's. They made their way to the wagon, and he helped her up to the seat. She was silent the whole way to the McAllister ranch. Pike respected her mood and did not try to carry on a conversation.

Chapter Fourteen

Alina watched Pike as he walked off to join the men, then reached into the wagon bed for the basket she had packed.

"Alina!" Cynthia waved as she hurried toward her. The two women embraced.

"Where are the children?" Alina asked.

Cynthia held a hand to the brim of her broad-brimmed felt hat as she searched the area. "They took off the minute David stopped the wagon. They're around here somewhere." The two women headed across the McAllisters' busy yard to where long tables and benches had been set up under two cottonwoods. Children laughingly chased each other, followed by a barking dog.

Several women were gathered about the tables, arranging baskets and bowls. Cynthia introduced Alina to those who returned her greetings.

"Is it my imagination, or are some of these people rude?" Alina whispered.

Cynthia set her basket on an empty table and pulled out a cotton tablecloth. "Some of them are rude," she whispered back. "I don't much notice anymore." The two women smoothed the cloth over the table. "I do hate it when they are rude to my children, though."

A short, rotund woman approached and set a heavy covered bowl next to Cynthia's basket. A dated hat with a bobbing bird sat on top of her tilted head, and she looked disapprovingly down her nose at Alina.

"Hello, Alva," Cynthia said cheerfully. "Have you met Beau Parker's new wife? Alina, this is Alva Murdoch. She and her husband have a spread north of town."

Alina smiled at the woman. "Hello."

"Are you the one that worked in the saloon?" Alva demanded.

The smile fled Alina's face. "Yes, I am."

"Now, Alva, whatever difference does that make?" Cynthia tried to keep her tone lighthearted. "You know lots of respectable women work in saloons and eating houses."

"My own sister does," Alva agreed, as she crossed her arms over her full bosom. "But most don't make enough money to buy a dress like that, unless they're selling more than beer and dances." She nodded at Alina's dark blue satin day dress. "And even if they did, they wouldn't show off by wearing it to a barn raising."

Alina self-consciously smoothed her skirt. Several of the women at the other tables were staring at her. She saw no warmth in their eyes. She raised her chin a notch.

"Fiddlesticks, Alva. Alina looks very nice in that dress." Cynthia waved her arm in a dismissive gesture. "I think your sister just arrived. Maybe you'd better go greet her."

"Don't be telling me what to do, Cynthia Freeman." Alva waved a fat finger in Cynthia's face. "You're no better than her, taking up with a nigger like you did. Your union is an abomination in the eyes of God." Alva snatched up her bowl and stomped off, the bird on her hat awkwardly bouncing in time with her graceless steps.

Cynthia's eyes closed; her mouth pressed in a tight line. Alina put a comforting arm around her friend's shoulders. "Don't listen to that woman, Cynthia. She's hateful."

Cynthia braced her palms on the table and leaned her weight on them. "It's nothing I haven't heard before, Alina, many times." Her voice was world-weary. Alina did not know what to say. Cynthia straightened. "But I won't let those self-righteous, narrow-minded biddies spoil this day." She turned to Alina with a determined smile. "Don't you pay them any mind, either." She hooked her arm with Alina's. "Let's lay out a blanket and give Tanya a break from her little sister. We'll sit in the shade and sew and have a nice visit."

"I thought this was to be like a party," Alina said as they walked off. "I was afraid this dress might be too fancy, but I wanted to wear something nice. I'm not showing off. This is my gardening hat, for heaven's sake!" One hand touched the wide brim of the simple straw hat, adorned only with a blue ribbon she had tied around the crown. Alina glanced back over her shoulder at the group of women gathered at the table. They were dressed much more casually than she was. Her gaze returned to her friend. Cynthia's dress was of a cheerful calico. "I should have worn my plaid wool dress."

Cynthia patted her hand. "Don't worry about it. They're just jealous because you're so pretty." Alina was not convinced.

They spread Cynthia's blanket in the shade of a box elder maple. Tanya brought a sleepy Margarite to her mother and ran off again to play with the other children. Alina searched for Beau among the many men hard at work on the new structure. She found him laboring next to Conor. They held boards in place while Pike and David pounded nails. As if he felt her gaze, he lifted his head and looked at her. His face broke into a smile and he raised a hand in greeting. She smiled and waved back.

"Did you bring anything to sew?" Cynthia asked.

Alina shook her head. "I didn't know I was supposed to."

Cynthia laughed. "You weren't 'supposed' to. You can do whatever you like, until it's time to set out the meal, around noon. The women serve the men, then the men go back to work. The children play, the women sew and gossip. It's very relaxed, at least for the women. Is this your first barn-raising?"

Alina nodded. She plucked at her skirt. "My father was

very successful, Cynthia. My family home is a mansion, far more grand than any residence in Laramie City. I am woefully unprepared for life here, as I'm sure you can tell." She raised sad eyes to her friend. "Perhaps I should have gone back to Chicago with my great-aunt. I'm not fitting in too well out here."

Cynthia shook her head. "You let that Alva get to you, Alina." She stabbed her needle at the napkin she was hemming. "The hell with her," she said vehemently. Alina was startled to hear Cynthia swear, but she was not offended. "The hell with all of them," Cynthia continued. "You just remember what's important, and it's not that bunch of judgmental hypocrites." Her eyes fell on her now sleeping baby. "This beautiful child was born of my love for David, and his for me, as all my children were. How can anyone call that love an abomination?" Cynthia blinked suddenly full eyes. She looked at Alina. "Remember what's important, Alina," she repeated. "Your man is important. Your cousin and your aunt are important. Pike and Katie are important. As long as the people who love you are satisfied with you, you don't need anybody else."

Alina reached for Cynthia's hand. "You are important," she said softly.

"Thank you." Cynthia squeezed Alina's fingers.

"Give me one of those napkins," said Alina. "I do know how to stitch a straight hem."

Katie arrived shortly before noon. Moses and Emerald accompanied her, as did a young woman named Mary who worked as a dancer at the Satin Slipper. Alina and Cynthia were the only ones who went to greet them.

"Land sakes, Cynthia, give me that young'un," Emerald ordered, as she handed her basket to her already-laden husband. "It's been too long since Ah held that lovely child."

"Hello, Emerald." Cynthia smiled warmly and transferred Margarite to the other woman's waiting arms. Emerald planted a noisy kiss on Margarite's cheek. The baby giggled.

After introducing Mary, Katie caught Alina in a boisterous hug. "Good to see ya, girl!" she boomed. "Did your aunt get on her way?"

"She did, Katie," Alina answered as they strolled toward the tables. Katie's sharp eyes caught the disapproving glares of some of the women.

"I see all the do-gooders are here," she commented dryly. Katie's bright green dress was far more elaborate than Alina's. The underskirt was of yellow shirred satin, the same color as the feather that decorated her flamboyant hat, and she held a green silk parasol in one hand. Alina silently wished Alva Murdoch would say something to Katie about *her* dress. It would be a pleasure to see Katie take on Alva.

"Howdy, ladies," Katie called. "Nice to see ya all again." None of the other women responded as the group made their way to the far table where Cynthia's and Alina's baskets stood alone.

Jason McAllister trotted across the yard toward them, a wide smile on his pleasant face. He came to a stop in front of Mary and took her hands in his. "Miss Mary," he breathed. "You came."

Mary's cheeks dimpled in a sweet smile. "I told you I would, Jason. We brought food, too." She nodded toward the basket she had set on the table.

"We'll be ready to eat real soon." Jason could not take his eyes from Mary's now blushing face.

"Jason, you're staring," she whispered, and pulled her hands from his grasp.

"I can't help myself," Jason gushed. "You're just so pretty." He turned to Katie. "Thank you, ma'am, for coming."

"Ya knew we would, Jason, after you and your brother helped when we reroofed the Slipper. Howdy, Beau." Alina looked up quickly from the basket she was emptying. Beau had joined them; his warm gaze was on her; a smile played around his lips. She shyly dropped her eyes.

Katie placed her hands on her hips and gazed at the

skeleton of the new barn. "Did ya ever figure out how the fire started?"

A scowl darkened Jason's brow. "No, ma'am. We figure it was no accident, though. Right after it happened, Richard Petrie sent that man of his, Latham, over with an offer to buy us out, though we'd refused him before. I think Petrie's the type of man who doesn't like to take 'no' for an answer." He turned to Beau. "Didn't you say he offered for your land, too, after your brother died?"

Beau nodded.

Cynthia turned from the table. "That's strange. David said Ross Latham approached him last week and offered to buy us out. Does Petrie want the whole valley?"

"Maybe he does," Beau said thoughtfully. "And if he does, I wonder why." He clapped a hand on Jason's shoulder. "We'd best go wash up, or these women won't feed us."

"That's right," Katie agreed. "We won't. Now get outta here 'til we call ya." She waved her umbrella in a threatening manner.

Alina watched Beau saunter toward the creek, her great-aunt's words sounding in her brain. *That beautiful man . . .*

The McAllister brothers joined Beau and his party at their table, along with two unemployed Irish railroad hands. Alina circled the table, filling coffee cups. The generous amount of food that had laden the table was quickly disappearing.

"Yo' men remember that us womenfolks ain't had our lunch yet," Emerald admonished as she cut into one of her famous pies.

A buggy pulled into the yard, followed by two men on horseback. All talk ceased as Ross Latham stepped down from his saddle and helped Madeline Petrie from the vehicle. As always, Madeline was beautifully dressed. She opened a dainty parasol and, taking Ross's offered arm, walked to the closest table.

"Log," she called to the other man, her voice sweet. "Please bring the basket from the buggy."

As Carter obeyed, two men jumped up and offered Madeline their places at the end of one bench. She smiled and gracefully sat down, careful of her skirts. No other woman was yet seated.

"Will ya look at those idiots?" Katie muttered. "They're all fawnin' over her like she's Queen Victoria. Robert, Jason, you boys better hold tight to your land deed. I doubt the fancy Miss Petrie is here outta the goodness of her heart."

Beau stood up. "Ladies, the meal was delicious. Gentlemen, let's get that barn up." His eyes found Alina. He smiled at her, then followed the rest of the men to the barn. The sounds of saws and hammers soon filled the air.

After the women ate and straightened the tables, they covered the remaining food with clean cloths. They then broke up into little groups; some went for a stroll along the river, some sat in the shade of the house working on a quilt, some rested with the younger children. Madeline held court in the shade of the cottonwoods, the sound of her tinkling laugh drifting across the yard. No one noticed that Ross Latham and Log Carter were nowhere to be seen.

Ross Latham piled the kindling high in the belly of Alva Murdoch's large stove. Log Carter handed him the base of a coal oil lamp, from which Latham unscrewed the wick. He poured the contents of the lamp over the kindling through one of the burner openings and made a circle with the oil on the wooden floor around the stove.

"Throw the rest of the oil around the front room, then put this back where you found it," he instructed, as he handed the lamp to Carter. Latham lit a match, then stood back and tossed the flaming stick into the stove. The coal oil ignited with a roar, the flames leaping high through the burner holes. The fire seemed to be alive as it blazed down the side of the stove and over the floor, devouring the spilled oil. Latham grabbed for the fluttering yellow curtains that hung at the window next to the stove and guided the material to the flames. He released his hold and jumped back as the fire raced up the length of cotton and licked at the ceiling.

"Let's get out of here, Log," he called over the roar of the flames. He heard Carter in the front room. "What are you doing, man?"

Carter appeared at the doorway to the parlor, a silver teapot in one hand.

"No, you don't," Latham warned. "We take *nothing.* Put it back."

Carter's face darkened. "I'm sick of you tellin' me what to do, Ross. There ain't no harm in taking some of this stuff. They'll think it burned."

The smoke was getting thick. Latham crossed the room and pulled the teapot from Carter's grasp. "It will tie us to the scene, and I'm not going down because of your greed. You know what the boss said . . . no booty." Latham ducked into the parlor and set the pot on an antique sideboard as Carter ran out the back door, coughing.

Latham pulled his neckerchief up over his mouth and nose. It was difficult to breathe. He made his way to the back door. A small mewing sound stopped him. He peered through the thickening smoke and saw that under the work table on the other side of the room was a wooden crate with a blanket hanging out of it. The sound came again, louder this time. A tiny kitten peeked over the top of the box, its claws dug into the blanket. Latham closed his eyes. His orders were to not move anything, to make the fire look as much like an accident as possible.

He backed out the door and closed it. Carter was mounted.

"Let's ride, man," Carter urged. "The smoke will be visible before long."

Latham placed a foot into the stirrup, then stopped before he was settled in the saddle. He swore under his breath as he stepped back to the ground. "You go on, Log. I want to be sure the whole house will go."

Carter did not need to be told twice. His horse jumped to

a gallop. Latham ran back inside and emerged a minute later, the wooden box in his arms. He glanced down and saw that the box held a mother cat and four very young kittens. He carried his cargo into the barn and crouched down to set it in a corner. A wry smile twisted his features as he scratched the mother cat's ears with a long gloved finger. "You and your babies may get me hanged," he muttered.

He rose and ran out to his horse. Flames were shooting from the upstairs windows now. The job was done.

Alina and Katie strolled in the shade. "I can't believe how fast that barn is going up," Alina marveled. "When we arrived this morning, nothing was standing." The two women stopped and admired the almost completed skeleton of the new barn. Only the frame of the back wall remained to be raised.

"Yeah, it is something, what can get done when everyone works together." Katie held her parasol high. "And I always enjoy it when these fine young men take off their shirts."

"Oh, Katie," Alina admonished with a smile.

"Take that cousin of yours," Katie continued, as if Alina hadn't spoken. Alina's eyes found Conor. He had removed his shirt and was perched high on one of the braces, pounding at a crossbeam. "He's a fine man. Always a pleasure to look at him. And Beau. Mm, mm. Some of the others, on the other hand, oughtta leave their shirts on." Alina giggled.

Katie came to an abrupt stop. "Now, what's she up to?" she murmured. Alina followed Katie's gaze. Madeline Petrie was approaching the barn, stepping daintily over boards and nails, holding her long skirts out of the dust. She made her way to Beau's side, and as Alina and Katie watched, laid a hand on his arm. Beau did not pull away from her. The two appeared to be involved in a deep conversation.

Alina sighed and turned away.

"Alina?" Katie hurried after her. "Are ya all right, girl?"

"I think I need some time alone," Alina answered softly. The smile she gave Katie was sad.

Katie put an arm around Alina's shoulders. "Maybe that's a good idea. Cynthia told me what that damn Alva Murdoch did this morning. On top of that, and your aunt leaving, ya don't need to watch that damn Madeline playing up to your man." She gave Alina a little push. "Go on, girl. There's a real pretty little creek out back of the house."

Alina straightened her shoulders and carried herself proudly as she passed the table of suddenly silent women. She disappeared around the side of the house. Katie marched over to where Cynthia rested in the shade, her napping children laid out around her.

"I'm gonna kill that Madeline Petrie," Katie whispered as she dropped her parasol on the quilt. She nodded toward the barn, her yellow feather waving with her movement.

Cynthia followed Katie's direction. She furrowed her brow at seeing Madeline and Beau together. "Alina's had a bad day, Katie. I've never seen her so unhappy. What can we do?"

Katie pursed her painted lips in thought. "I think Beau needs to know that his wife is upset," she said after a minute. A grim smile curved the corners of her mouth. "You talk to Beau, and I'll have me a talk with little Miss Madeline."

Cynthia nodded as she stood, then carefully stepped over the children. She and Katie headed in the direction of the barn. They saw Madeline leave Beau and move away toward Ross Latham, who crossed the yard from the opposite direction.

"Beau!" Cynthia called. He turned to her. She went to his side and hooked her arm through his, waving at David with the other. "I need to speak with you," she said quietly as she led him off a short distance where they would not be overheard.

Katie caught up to Madeline and took her wrist in a firm grip. "Let's go, missy. We gotta talk." Katie headed toward the McAllister house, pulling the stunned Madeline behind her.

Madeline finally found her voice. "Let go of me!" she shrieked. "How dare you?" She struck at Katie with her parasol. Katie stopped and turned without relinquishing her hold on Madeline's wrist. She snatched the parasol from Madeline's other hand and threw it to the ground, then continued toward the house without a word. Ross Latham ran up to them as Katie pulled Madeline up the porch steps. The women in the yard watched in shocked silence.

"Ya stay outta this, Ross," Katie warned as she yanked open the door. She pushed Madeline inside, then turned to Ross and shook a finger at him. "All I'm gonna do is talk to her, and if ya ever want to come into my saloon again, ya'll let me talk to her in private."

Latham held up his hands and stepped back. "I know better than to get involved in a cat fight. I'll just wait out here."

Katie nodded, then stepped into the house, slamming the door behind her.

"How dare you?" Madeline shouted again.

"Shut your mouth," Katie spat as she advanced on the younger woman. Madeline took a step back. "I'm only gonna tell ya this one time, so ya better listen real careful." Katie's brown eyes flashed. "Keep away from Beau Parker, Madeline, and keep your nasty, lying mouth closed about his wife. Got it?"

Madeline looked at her in amazed rage. "Who do you think you are?" she shouted. "No one talks to me like that! Have you forgotten who my father is?" She paced back and forth in front of the fireplace. "He'll have your precious saloon shut down before the month is out. I'll make sure of it. Do you think I'm going to let some *whore* tell me what to do?"

Katie's eyes narrowed; she placed her hands on her hips. "Yeah, I've whored at times in my life, when I felt there was nothing else I could do to keep body and soul together, but never have I been a slut, and that's what ya are, Madeline Petrie. Ya're a spoiled slut."

Madeline flushed. With an outraged shriek, her hand lashed out toward Katie's cheek. Katie caught Madeline's wrist in mid-air and twisted it in a tight grip. "Don't ever raise your hand to me again," Katie warned, "or so help me, I'll slap the piss outta you!" She pushed Madeline away. Madeline grabbed her wrist and stared at Katie, her eyes wide with fright and hatred.

"There's a difference between a whore and a slut," Katie said conversationally as she now walked back and forth. "A man always knows where he stands with a whore. Whores are honest, about one thing, anyways. A slut, now, that's another story. A slut plays a man along, teasing and holding out, and maybe finally giving in, when it suits her. And most men are too blind to recognize the game, especially when the player is as pretty as ya are." Katie stopped in front of Madeline. "But I'm not blind. I know *exactly* what ya are, and I'll not stand by and watch ya try to hurt my friends." She shoved her face close to Madeline's. *"Stay away from the Parkers."* Katie turned on her heel and strode to the door.

"I'll see to it that my father destroys you, Katie Davenport," Madeline vowed, her tone vicious.

Katie stopped at the door and laughed, a mirthless sound. She whirled to face Madeline. "If anything happens to my place or my people, or my business falls off sudden-like, I'll tell your pa about your past romps with some of his cowhands."

Madeline started, her eyes wide with only fear now. "What do you mean?" she squeaked.

"Ya ain't no blushing virgin. In fact, ya're real far from it. Would ya like your precious pa to know that?" Katie's hands found their way to her hips once again. She looked into Madeline's white face. "I didn't think so. If I was you, I'd just keep my pouty little mouth shut."

Katie opened the door and was gone, leaving a badly

shaken Madeline alone in the front room of Robert McAllister's house.

Alina had settled on the grassy bank of the stream that wound behind the McAllister house and was enjoying the peace of the afternoon. The water danced over the rocks, singing to itself on its eastern journey to the Laramie River. Here she was away from the staring eyes and mutterings of the women. She had heard the word "witch" as she had passed. She sighed. Perhaps it would be best for all concerned if she returned to Chicago as soon as possible. Her notoriety would eventually affect Beau, if it hadn't already.

She took her hat off and leaned back on her palms, raising her face to the warmth of the sun. She concentrated on stilling her thoughts, but it was difficult, as she could hear raised voices from within the house. She shook her head in annoyance and tried to ignore the sounds. Suddenly, a chill rushed over her, as if the sun had gone behind a cloud. Her eyes popped open. The sky was clear and blue. She searched the area around her, but could see no one. The feeling persisted, though, as if she were being watched. She grabbed her hat and stood up.

"Well, if it ain't Mrs. Nosy Britches." Log Carter's rough voice came from the bushes on the far side of the stream. He stepped from his cover and slopped through the water.

Alina ignored him and started walking toward the side of the house. Her heart pounded. Surely the brute wouldn't try anything with so many people so near.

"Hey!" Carter jumped at her and grabbed her arm. "I'm talkin' to you!"

Alina twisted from his grasp and continued walking. "I have nothing to say to you."

"Well, I got plenty to say to you, and you're gonna listen." He ran after her and wrapped his strong arms around her from behind. Alina kicked at him and opened her mouth to scream. As if he had read her mind, he clapped a big, dirty hand over her mouth. Her hat fell from her hand. Carter half-carried, half-dragged her back toward the stream.

"I told you that day in the street that I wasn't finished with you." He stopped momentarily to adjust his hold on her. The hand at her mouth tightened, and he deliberately ran his other hand over her breast as he positioned his arm around her waist. Alina fought like a thing possessed, but she could not escape him. "Maybe we'll have us a little fun," Carter grunted.

Suddenly Alina was wrenched from his grasp. She stumbled back, her eyes wide with relief and gratitude as she saw a furious Beau land a fist on Carter's jaw. Carter was knocked to the ground by the force of the blow. He shook his head and slowly got to his feet.

"Are you all right?" Beau demanded as he led Alina toward the side of the house. She nodded. "Then go find your friends." He heard Carter coming and turned, pushing Alina behind him. She backed away and watched, horror-stricken, as Carter struck Beau down.

Alina picked up her skirts and ran around the side of the house. Her frantic gaze fell on Katie, fresh from her discussion with Madeline, marching toward the barn.

"Katie!" she screamed. Katie whirled around. "Get Conor! Hurry!" Katie hesitated only a moment, taking in Alina's disheveled hair and the wild look in her eyes, then hurried on her way, shouting for Conor as she went. Alina ran back around the house. Both Carter and Beau were on their feet now, warily circling each other. Alina bit her bottom lip when Carter landed a solid punch to Beau's midsection, but Beau countered with a blow to Carter's head that sent the man reeling. Beau pressed his advantage and hit Carter again, knocking him to his knees.

Conor rushed up to Alina's side. He took her arm and pulled her further away from the battleground. She glanced around and saw that many people now watched the contest. Her eyes came once again to her cousin's grim face. "Help him," she whispered.

Conor shook his head. "It's Beau's fight. He won't want my help, nor do I think he needs it."

Katie came up behind Alina and put an arm around her shoulders. All eyes were now centered on the conflict in the yard. Carter was the heavier man, but Beau was taller and more agile. He also had the advantage of a blind, empowering rage. The few blows Carter landed did not affect him. His constant barrage was beginning to tell on Carter. Beau stepped in too close and Carter caught him in a back-breaking bear hug. The two men fell to the ground. Beau landed a right cross that broke Carter's nose and knocked him off to the side. Beau got to his knees and struck Carter again as the big man tried to rise.

Madeline came out the back door of the house, Ross Latham behind her. "Help Log," she ordered tersely.

"No, ma'am." Latham pushed his hat back on his head. "It's not my fight."

Madeline stared at him in disbelief, but Latham's eyes were on the battle.

Carter had struggled to his feet. He swung wildly and missed. Beau did not. Carter slammed against the trunk of a tree. His arms hung at his sides and blood poured down his face, from a cut over his eye and from his nose. There was a confused look in his bleary eyes. Beau hit him again, and again, first in the face, then in the stomach. The only thing keeping Carter on his feet was the force of Beau's punches.

Finally Conor stepped in and pulled Beau away. "That's enough, Beau! You'll kill him!" Carter slumped to the ground and did not move.

Beau stared down at Carter for a long moment, then turned to Conor. His eyes were wild, his breathing harsh and ragged. He allowed Conor to lead him back to Alina.

Robert and Jason McAllister pushed through the crowd. "What's going on?" Robert demanded.

"Carter attacked my wife," Beau said simply, his voice raw. He rested an arm across Alina's shoulders.

Robert's angry gaze went from Carter's inert form to Madeline and Latham standing on the step. "I don't know what purpose you hoped to serve by coming here today,

Miss Petrie, but you can tell your father that nothing will force me and my brother from our land. It'd be best if you and your men left now."

Madeline's eyes widened and her lips tightened. Without a word she swept off the step and around the far side of the house. Latham and two other men carried Carter from view. A few minutes later the sound of departing horses reached their ears.

Robert turned to Alina. "I'm awful sorry about this, Mrs. Parker. I guess he's still mad at you about standing up to him over that Chinese boy."

"How did you know about that?" Alina asked in surprise.

Robert smiled. "Everyone knows about that, ma'am. You've got a lot of grit. Beau ought to be real proud of you."

"I am," Beau assured him. His arm tightened on her shoulder as he smiled down at her. They walked toward the barn.

"No one's ever beat Log Carter in a fistfight, Beau. I've never seen the like," Jason said admiringly as he followed them.

"Maybe no one ever had the motivation I did," Beau muttered.

"Your hat is ruined, Alina." Katie looked at the crumpled object she had retrieved from the ground.

Alina shrugged. "I can always get another hat." She took Beau's free hand in hers as they walked. The knuckles were scraped and bleeding. "You need tending to, Beau." Her troubled gaze took in the bruises and cuts on his face.

"There's hot water in the stove reservoirs, Mrs. Parker," Robert said over his shoulder. Alina nodded her thanks.

"I'll get the water," Katie offered. "I've been in the house." She turned toward the front porch.

Beau wiped at the trickle of blood that ran from one corner of his mouth. "This isn't serious. We're almost finished with the frame; I'll clean up later, when the work is done."

"You'll sit at the table until I say otherwise." Alina's tone brooked no argument. Beau looked at her in surprise.

"Yes, ma'am," he said soberly, his eyes twinkling. He sank down on the bench with a weary sigh. He felt very tired all of a sudden. Lincoln pushed his way to Beau's side.

"Are you bad hurt, Mr. Parker?" The child rested his elbows on Beau's knee and looked up into his battered face. Worry puckered Lincoln's brown forehead.

Beau lifted Lincoln up to sit beside him. "No, but maybe you'd better stay with me, so I won't be all alone if Mrs. Parker hurts me with her fussing."

Lincoln frowned at Alina. "Is she gonna hurt you?" the boy asked in a low, serious tone.

"I don't know," Beau whispered. "You know how it hurts when your ma tries to clean up your knee when you've skinned it?"

Lincoln nodded.

"That's what I'm talking about. Everything would be fine if the womenfolk didn't fuss over us menfolk, but I guess it's in their nature to fuss."

Lincoln nodded solemnly. "I understand, Mr. Parker. I'll stay with you." His small hand worked its way into Beau's.

Alina watched the man and the boy with a smile. Elizabeth was right about another thing: Beau would make a good father. She dipped a clean cloth into the basin of warm water Katie had set on the table, then gently wiped the blood from his forehead.

"You've a gash just above the hair line, but it doesn't look too bad," she reported. "Emerald, do you think this needs stitches?"

Emerald leaned over Lincoln to examine Beau's scalp. "No, Ah don' think so. Mr. Parker, here, he got a hard head. It'll take more'n that fool Log Carter to do him any real harm."

"As long as he hits me in the head, huh, Emerald?" Beau asked dryly.

Alina's smile gave way to a frown as she continued to wash

his face. "This eye is swollen; I think it will blacken by tomorrow. And your jaw has a nasty bruise." She rinsed the rag and lifted his chin. She carefully cleaned the blood from the corner of his mouth. An almost overwhelming urge came over her to kiss the pain from his battered lips.

"Thank you for fighting for me," she said softly.

Beau stared at her. "Did you think I wouldn't?"

"No. I've always known you'd fight for me."

"Well, is his nose broken?" Pike demanded as he approached.

Alina looked at Beau's nose thoughtfully. "No, I don't think so. It's swelling, though."

Pike pulled at his beard. "Alina, girl, ya'd best dance with him tonight, 'cause he ain't gonna be too purty tomorrow."

"Thank you, Mr. Pike," Beau said sarcastically.

One at a time, Alina soaked Beau's hands in the water. "We'll put some salve on these when we get home," she murmured as she worked. Beau breathed in the scent of her hair. It had come loose in the struggle with Log and lay about her shoulders in disarray. She glanced up at his face.

"How is it that you keep getting more and more beautiful with each passing day?" he whispered, mindless of Lincoln's interested ears.

Alina blushed, but she could not keep her lips from curving in a pleased smile. "How is your stomach, and how are your ribs?"

Beau opened his shirt and pulled the tails from his pants. Alina ran her hands gently but firmly over his muscled torso, her touch light when she reached the scar. She had long dreamed of touching him like this, but not under these circumstances. "You'll have some bruises," she said, "but I don't think anything is broken."

"I don't think so, either. I know what broken ribs feel like." He pulled his shirt together. "Can I go now?"

"All right, go on with you, then," Alina laughed.

With a sigh of relief, Beau stood. He held one hand down

to Lincoln. "I might need help, now that I'm banged up. Are you game?"

Lincoln's eyes lit up. "Yes, sir!" He jumped off the bench and took Beau's offered hand. Alina watched them go, a soft look in her eyes. Cynthia and Katie nodded at each other with satisfied smiles.

The crowd broke into a cheer when the final frame was put into place. Robert and Jason decided that enough had been done for one day. The men trooped down to the river to clean up while the women made fresh coffee and set out a cold supper. After the meal, lanterns were hung from the frame beams, covering the fresh wooden floor of the structure with a golden light. Pike took his fiddle from its case and nodded in approval when one of the Irishmen pulled a harmonica from his pack.

Alina had washed her face and redone her hair before dinner. She looked at Beau's face across the table. The light of the table lantern showed the weariness in his features. The skin under his right eye had turned dark.

"We don't have to stay, Beau," she said softly. "You need to get some rest."

Beau shook his head. "And miss a chance to dance with you? You'll not get out of it so easily, madam."

"I'm not trying to get out of it," Alina retorted with a smile. "I just don't want you stomping on my feet because you're too tired to remember the steps."

The beginning strains of a waltz came from the barn floor. Most of the people had drifted over that way. Beau stood and held his hand out to Alina. "Come along, Mrs. Parker."

Alina gladly took his hand. "I've never heard a waltz played on a fiddle before."

"Pike does a good job." They stepped up onto the wooden floor. Beau took her in his arms and they began to dance. "I'm sorry some of the women weren't nice to you today," he said.

Alina's eyes found his. "They weren't nice to Cynthia, either. She and David put up with a lot."

Beau nodded. "They do. They are amazingly strong." His warm gaze devoured her face. "You are amazingly strong, too. And I think you look lovely in that dress. I'm very proud that you are my wife."

Alina did not know what to say. The dance came to an end and they stood looking at each other, their hands joined. Cynthia was right, Alina thought. Remember who was important, and everyone else, the world, for that matter, could go to hell.

Chapter Fifteen

Late one afternoon a week later, Conor led his horse into the barn. The animal's sides heaved from the brisk run he had just had. Beau threw a quantity of hay from the loft, then backed down the ladder, the pitchfork in one hand.

"That was a quick trip," he commented as he pushed the straw into a neat pile.

"Charlie likes to run." Conor pulled the saddle from the horse's back.

"Did you find the part you need for your rifle?"

"Sure did. I got Alina's order from the dressmaker and picked up the mail, too. It's at the house with Alina. There's a letter in there for you from Washington." Conor's face did not betray his curiosity as he began to rub Charlie down. Beau did not comment.

Conor continued. "The Murdoch house burned to the ground the day of the barn raising at the McAllisters."

Beau's head snapped up. "What?"

Conor nodded. "They lost everything. The chimney was the only thing left standing."

"What caused the fire?"

"No one knows. Something strange about it, though." Conor led Charlie to the back door of the barn and removed his halter. The horse trotted off into the sunshine. Beau rested his hands on the handle of the upright pitchfork and waited.

"Henry Murdoch told Sam Trudeau he found a box of kittens in the barn, a box Henry swears was under a table in the kitchen when they left the house that day."

Beau raised his eyebrows and rubbed his mustache with one hand. "An arsonist with a soft spot in his heart for kittens? That *is* strange." Beau leaned the pitchfork against the wall. "Was there any word of a house raising for the Murdochs?"

Conor shook his head as the two men crossed the yard. The sound of Pike's hammer reached them from the forge.

"There won't be one. Sam said Murdoch was barely making it as it was, and this ruined him. He sold out to Petrie. They're leaving tomorrow for St. Louis. I guess they have kin there."

Beau shook his head in regret as they stepped up onto the porch. "Damn," he muttered.

Conor took his hat off. "I don't care much for Murdoch's wife, especially after the way she treated Alina, but I do feel bad for her. I ran into her at the post office. She's taking it hard."

Beau nodded. "Yeah. I wouldn't wish such a tragedy on anyone." He opened the door and Conor followed him into the cabin. The men hung their hats and Conor headed for the coffeepot while Beau reached for the letter on the table.

Conor's eyes fell on Alina. She sat on the sofa, a piece of paper clasped in trembling hands that rested in her lap. He saw a trail of tears on each of her cheeks. He set the pot down.

"Alina?" Conor asked. He moved the dressmaker's bundle and sat next to her. "Alina, what is it? Was there bad news in that wire I brought you?"

Beau turned from the table, concern written on his face.

Alina raised her teary eyes, first to Conor, then to Beau. A faint smile tugged at the corners of her mouth. "It's from Elizabeth," she said, her voice just above a whisper. "Papa's alive. He sent her a cable from Hong Kong." She closed her eyes. "He's alive."

Conor's face broke out in a wide grin. He threw his arms around his cousin. "Just as you told us he was, Alina!"

Beau set his letter on the table and came to sit at her other side. He awkwardly patted her hand. "That's wonderful news, Alina," he said softly. Conor grabbed the wire from Alina's hand.

"It doesn't say much," he said, disappointed. "There's no explanation of what happened, or any indication of when he'll be home. It'll take months to get back from Hong Kong. But he's alive. That will help Elizabeth's case immensely. The judge might just throw out Cordelia's claim." Conor looked at Beau. "She's sending a letter to explain more."

Beau's heart pounded as the full import of the news sank in. He looked at Alina's bowed head with anguish. Their marriage was no longer necessary.

"Excuse me," he said quietly. He crossed the room and closed the door behind him. Conor and Alina looked at each other. Alina bit her bottom lip. She had recognized the full meaning of the wire immediately.

Beau stomped across the yard to the forge. Chickens clucked in irritation as they scrambled out of his way. He paced in front of Pike, running his hands through his hair. Pike pounded on a horseshoe a few more times, then set the hammer down. He pulled a faded handkerchief from his back pocket and wiped his face. He eyed Beau curiously.

"Well, are ya gonna tell me what's eatin' at ya or not?" he finally asked.

"Alina got a wire from Elizabeth," Beau ground out. "Neil Gallagher is alive, Pike."

"Just like Alina said he was," Pike marveled. "That's great news for the little lady. Them Randalls don't have a case now." Beau continued to pace. "So why aren't ya happy for her?" Pike ran the handkerchief along the back of his neck.

Beau stopped and looked at him. "But I am." He realized that his actions might not be conveying that message. "Truly, Pike, I'm real glad he's alive, for his sake and Alina's.

It will make everything easier for her. This whole mess can be set to right."

Pike's eyes lit up with sudden understanding. "But now she don't need ya any more."

"That's right," Beau spat.

Conor came around the chicken coop. "Am I intruding?"

Pike shook his head. "Nah. Beau's just got hisself a little problem. It'll be real interesting ta see what he decides ta do."

Conor leaned against a post and crossed his arms over his chest. "Because of Donovan Randall, I think Alina should stay here until Neil returns, and Elizabeth will probably agree with me. That could take months. Will you mind?"

" 'Course he won't mind," Pike chuckled. "That's the problem. He don't want her ta leave *ever.*" Beau scowled at him.

Conor dropped his eyes and raised a hand to cover his mouth. When he successfully wiped the smile from his face, he looked at Beau. "The way things are now, she's going to leave, sooner or later. What are you going to do about it?"

"What do you mean, what am I going to do about it?" Beau commenced his pacing again. "What can I do? She's never given any indication that she wants to stay permanently."

"Have you asked her?" Conor demanded.

Beau ran his hands through his hair. "I told her she could stay as long as she wants to."

"That ain't the same thing, Beau," Pike snorted. "For all your fancy upbringin' in that Virginia high society, and your education at that fancy college, ya don't know much about women. Alina's felt all along that ya married her ta do her a favor, and she's real uncomfortable about it. How's she ta know ya want her ta stay if ya don't tell her?"

Beau stared at the cabin with troubled eyes. "What if she says no?" he whispered.

"Ya better make damn sure she don't, 'cause I'll hold ya responsible if she leaves," Pike said firmly. Beau and Conor looked at him in surprise. He picked up the hammer and shrugged. "I don't want her leavin', neither. She's turnin' inta a mighty fine cook, and," he pounded at the horseshoe, "I'm sorta used ta havin' her around." He hit the shoe again. " 'Sides, if she goes, she'll probably leave that damn fool dog here, and then I'll have ta take care of him."

Conor laughed and Beau rolled his eyes. "This is serious, Pike. What if she says no?"

"I never took ya for a coward, Beau Parker." Pike shook his head in disgust. "Ya survived the damn war, ya've stood up ta Richard Petrie and that damn Log Carter, and here ya are, scared of a slip of a woman that only comes up ta your chin. I never thought I'd see the day."

Beau put his hands on his hips and glared at his friend. "Well, do you have any great ideas?"

"Court her," Conor interjected quietly.

"Court her!" Beau repeated in exasperation. "We're already married!"

"Did you ever court her?" Conor challenged.

Beau dropped his eyes to the dirt. He remained quiet.

"Alina hasn't told me exactly what happened when you two first met, but I understand there was some trouble. Thanks to the Randalls, you married before you had a chance to work things out." Conor leaned forward to emphasize his point. "You've never courted her, man."

"You're right," Beau admitted. After a minute his shoulders slumped. "Who am I fooling?" he muttered. Conor and Pike looked at him, puzzled. Beau continued. "I have nothing to offer her. I'm living a lie out here, gentlemen. I'm no rancher. I have no home, no plan for the future." He spread his hands. "All I am is an angry man bent on finding my brother's murderer. What kind of a husband will I make? I stepped in to help Alina because she needed help, not because I wanted a wife."

Conor eyed him thoughtfully. "Do you want a wife now?"

"I want *her*. But she deserves better."

"Alina deserves a man who loves her," Conor said harshly.

Beau was silent for a minute. "I do," he finally said.

"Then I'd talk ta her about it and quit gettin' myself all riled up." Pike thrust his handkerchief into a back pocket.

Beau nodded. His gaze roamed the yard, then came to settle on Conor's face. "She and I are doing fine now, as friends. Do you think she'll have me as her husband?"

Conor stepped forward and clapped him on the shoulder. "It wouldn't surprise me at all," he said with a grin.

"I know she's sweet on ya, Beau," Pike added.

"How do you know that?" Hope flared in his eyes.

Pike hooked his thumbs in his suspenders. "Maybe I saw it in a vision," he said mysteriously.

Once again Beau rolled his eyes. "Lord," he muttered. Pike and Conor both laughed.

Supper was a quiet meal. Neither Beau nor Alina spoke much. Alina pushed her food around her plate. She had been praying for months for the news that she had received today. Why was she not more happy?

She glanced at Beau from the corner of her eye. Was he relieved that she would be leaving now? The light from the lamp played over his face. Only a shadow of the black bruise remained under his eye. All the swelling was gone, but she suspected that his ribs were still sore from the way he moved. Somehow, that day at the McAllisters seemed like a long time ago.

Alina removed the plates and refilled the coffee cups while Pike retrieved his pipe from his room.

"Do ya mind if I smoke, Alina?" Pike asked politely, as he did every night.

Alina replied as she did every night. "No, Pike, but thank you for asking." She smiled at him as she resumed her seat.

Beau cleared his throat. "There's something I'd like to discuss."

"Well, go on," Pike urged, as he filled his pipe.

Beau cleared his throat again. His eyes fell on Alina. She watched him expectantly, waiting for him to speak. She was so beautiful in the lamplight. He realized his heart was pounding. Pike was right: he was scared of her. His black-haired, blue-eyed Irish Rose held his heart in her small hands, and she had the power to crush it.

"Now that we know Neil Gallagher is indeed alive, the situation for all of us will change. We'll know more when we get Elizabeth's letter." He turned again to Alina. "Conor, Pike and I think it best if you stay here for a while longer, perhaps until your father returns. There's no telling what the Randalls may do out of desperation, and we want to keep you as far from them as we can. Do you agree?"

Alina was startled. Beau didn't usually seem to care whether she agreed with him or not in such matters. "Yes," she said. "I don't want to be anywhere near the Randalls."

Beau nodded with satisfaction. He turned to Conor. "Until Captain Gallagher returns, I assume you will act as head of the Gallagher family."

Conor and Alina looked at each other, puzzled. At Alina's nod, Conor spoke. "I guess you could say that."

"Then I will address my next question to you, as the head of that family." Beau swallowed again. "During the past several months, I have come to know your cousin, Alina, and I have grown fond of her." His tone was formal.

Alina's eyes widened in surprise.

Beau glanced nervously at Alina, then continued. "Perhaps Alina has not had the opportunity to grow equally fond of me; therefore, Conor, if she is agreeable, I would like your permission to court her."

Alina gasped. Her eyes flew to Conor's face. His expression was serious, but a grin lurked around his mouth.

"Well, Cousin, are you agreeable to the idea of this man's attentions? The choice is yours." There was a definite twinkle in his eye.

Alina glanced at Pike, who puffed contentedly on his pipe,

a satisfied smile on his bearded face. "Don't look at me, girl," he said gruffly. "Like Conor said, it's your call. Do ya fancy the man or not?"

Alina turned her gaze on Beau. He stared at her, seeming to hold his breath. A warm light shone in his brown eyes. He was giving her a choice, giving her back some control over her life.

"I would be agreeable, Cousin," she answered softly.

"Then permission is granted." Conor finally lost the battle with the lurking grin.

"This calls for a spot of brandy." Pike thumped to the counter. He returned a moment later and poured a generous amount of the liquid into each cup. He remained standing and lifted his cup. "To Alina and Beau."

Conor stood also. "Here, here," he said, and clinked his mug with Pike's. Alina held her cup up with the rest. Her eyes met Beau's; they shyly smiled at each other.

Later, after Conor and Pike had gone to bed, Alina sat on the sofa in her nightdress, waiting for Beau to change. She had braided her hair and now stared at the dying fire, twisting the wedding band on her finger. Finally Beau opened the bedroom door. He pulled at the collar of his nightshirt as he came to sit next to her.

"It's getting too hot to wear this thing," he commented without thinking.

"What would you wear instead?"

Beau hesitated. "I usually sleep naked in the summer," he admitted.

She blushed. "So you've been wearing that for my sake?"

Beau nodded. Alina smiled as he stretched his legs out. A cool breeze blew in the open window over the table, causing the curtains to flutter.

"Why do you want to court me, Beau? Why now, after all this time?" Alina shifted her position to face him.

"Because I don't want you to leave," Beau answered, his voice low and gentle. "But it's no good if you don't want to stay. I'm hoping I can make you want to stay." He turned to her. "Conor was right. I never courted you. Every woman should be courted." He reached for the dark rope of hair he could see against the white of her nightdress and took the fragrant braid into his hand. He rubbed it along his cheek. "I should warn you, though . . . I've never courted a woman before, so be patient with me."

Alina smiled. "Not even Madeline Petrie?" she teased.

He groaned. "Let me explain about her," he pleaded.

"Beau, you don't have to." She touched his cheek.

"Yes, I do. This is important. I don't want anything between us." Beau dropped her braid and took one of Alina's hands in his. He stroked the soft skin as he spoke.

"Pike wired us the day after Ambrose's death, and I left Virginia that same day. I was crazy when I got here, Alina, half mad with grief and fury. I think I would have killed his murderer myself, had we caught him. I met Madeline shortly after I arrived. She and Ambrose had been involved, and she was as grief-stricken as I was, or so I thought. She was pretty and sweet, and she seemed so fragile and lost." His lips twisted in a self-deprecating grimace. "That's hard to believe, isn't it? I don't like to think I was so blind at one time that I couldn't see through her, but I was."

Alina squeezed his fingers. "I think Madeline is a very good actress."

Beau smiled at her. "And you are very kind. Anyway, by New Year's Eve, I had about convinced myself I was in love with her. I thought she returned my feelings, but that night she was just plain cruel. She played me for a fool." His long fingers tightened on hers. "I left her father's house in a rage, and went to the Satin Slipper. Then I met you."

Alina straightened. "That's why you were so upset when I told you to leave my room. You thought I was playing the same game."

He nodded. "It doesn't excuse my abominable behavior, but perhaps you can understand it a little better."

Alina smiled. "I can."

Beau put an arm around her shoulders and pulled her next to him. "Do you forgive me?" he whispered.

"I don't know if I should. You were boorish, and arrogant, and insulting, and unreasonable, and . . ."

"I know, I know," he groaned.

"And I forgive you," she finished softly. "It's much easier to forgive when you understand the reasons."

With his free hand, Beau raised her chin so that he could look into her eyes. He moved his hand to caress her cheek. "Thank you," he whispered, and lowered his mouth to hers. His hand moved once again so he could stroke her hair as the kiss deepened. Alina sighed deep in her throat and snuggled closer under his arm, her hand upon his broad chest. She welcomed his tongue into her mouth, then tentatively chased his with hers when he withdrew it. Beau shuddered with delight at her response. He had waited for her for so long!

Finally he raised his head. "We'd better stop now, woman, or I won't be able to stop at all."

Alina closed her eyes and tried to keep the disappointment from showing on her face.

Beau caught her hand in his. "We are courting now." His voice was ragged. "It's too soon. I want to be sure you will have no regrets." He pulled away from her and jumped up from the sofa. "I want to do this right." He bent and placed a hand on her cheek. She leaned into it, covering his hand with hers. Her wedding band flashed in the light. He slipped the ring off her finger.

Alina turned startled eyes to him. "Why did you do that?" she whispered, fear gripping her heart.

"Because you were not happy when I put this on your finger the first time." He kissed the small circle of gold. "I hope you will want it back soon." He looked down at her tenderly. Some of her hair had come loose from the braid, her lips were still wet from his kiss, her blue eyes held a confused, longing look. He reached for her hand and pulled her to her feet.

"To bed with you now," he said lightly, and guided her toward her bedroom. "Enjoy the solitude of your room while you may, for soon you'll share it with me again. And when I next sleep in your bed, Alina, it will be as your husband, in every way." He patted her bottom and closed the door behind her.

Alina climbed into bed and settled back on the pillow, his words running through her mind. For the first time, she seriously considered the idea of making her life here, in this cabin, with that man. She tried to remember what life in Chicago had been like. She realized, with surprise, that she had not really been happy there since her brother Joseph died. Things were never the same after that. It was as if the sun had gone out of her mother's life that day, and with her mother's death three years later, the sun had gone out of her father's life.

With the exceptions of Jennifer, Susannah, and Sean, before his death, Cynthia, Katie and Pike were the best friends she had ever had. Did she really miss the social life of the Chicago elite? Did she miss changing her clothes three times a day? Did she miss always watching her tongue, fearful of saying something strange or shocking? The answer was a definite "no." She missed Elizabeth terribly. She missed some of the comforts of home, such as having the laundry done, and she definitely missed the indoor water closet with running water. But Elizabeth could visit, and she had managed without the other comforts.

Alina looked around the small bedroom. If she was going to live here, she would ask Beau about enlarging the cabin. She knew nothing of his financial situation, and didn't care what it was. She was not even sure the ranch made a profit, but her father would settle a dowry on her. She realized with a smile that she was dreaming of her life here, that she was becoming excited about it. The thought of building a future with Beauregard Parker was exciting. She wrapped her arms around herself. And what of children? A shiver of anticipation ran through her.

She extinguished the lamp and snuggled down in the lonely bed. *He sleeps naked in the summer!* That was a thought sure to guarantee good dreams. She smiled in the darkness.

The next afternoon Beau returned from a trip to town with a strange-looking bundle tied to the back of his saddle. Alina came out onto the porch to greet him.

"Did you get your wire sent?" she asked as he stepped down from the saddle.

He climbed the stairs. "Yes, I did," he answered, and kissed the tip of her nose. "And I brought the mail, and I posted your letters, and I brought Pike a bottle of brandy, just as I said I would. I also brought you a present."

Alina smiled with pleasure. If he was trying to distract her from thinking about the wires he so often sent to who-knew-where, he was doing a good job. She watched with interest as he returned to Bay's side and loosened the ties on the strange bundle. He brought the package to the porch and set it down at her feet with a flourish.

Alina stared in bewilderment. "What is it?" she asked as she perused the damp burlap bag filled with dirt. Two dead twigs about eight inches long protruded from the neck.

"It's a rosebush," Beau explained. He frowned at the bag. "I guess it doesn't look like much right now, but Bert assured me it's alive. He doesn't know what color the blooms will be. I thought we could plant it right here in front of the house."

"Thank you, Beau," Alina said softly, genuinely touched. "I love roses, and I'm sure it will grow to be lovely. I'll plant it right now."

"Let me see to Bay, and I'll help you."

Alina nodded her agreement and watched as he led the horse to the barn, a smile on her lips.

Pike came from the house. He stopped and looked at the bag at Alina's feet. "What's that?" he asked, stroking his beard.

"A gift for the future, Pike," Alina answered dreamily.

Pike stared at her, his brow wrinkled with confusion. When she did not elaborate, he stepped off the porch and headed toward the corral. "Looks like dead branches in a bag of dirt ta me," he muttered, shaking his head. "I surely hope those two lovebirds don't go gettin' all mushy on us."

Alina and Beau worked together to plant the rosebush. Beau dug the hole and filled it in again around the roots as Alina steadied the frail stalks. They carried rocks from the creekbed and made a border around the tiny bush, then stepped back to examine their handiwork.

"It looks kind of silly," Alina admitted.

Beau nodded in agreement. "But it will grow," he promised. "I'll make a trellis and attach it to the rail."

"Do you think it will bloom this year?"

"I hope so, but I don't know much about roses." Beau put an arm around her shoulders. "I just know I like them." He kissed her ear. "I like roses a lot."

Alina tingled at his touch. The warmth in his voice reached a place deep inside her and she slipped an arm around his waist.

"Thank you for the gift, Beau." She rose to her toes and kissed his cheek.

"A rose for a rose," he said softly. "May it grow into something beautiful, like I hope our feelings for each other will." He pulled her more firmly into his arms.

"I think it will," Alina whispered as he lowered his mouth to hers.

The next three weeks passed as if in a dream. Alina could not remember ever being so happy. Beau was charming and funny, and always, sometimes to her disappointment, the perfect gentleman. She had no trouble falling totally in love with him, although she suspected she had not had far to go. He brought her handfuls of wildflowers when he returned from working with the cattle. He asked her to go with him on long, hand-holding walks in the evenings. Sometimes they sat under a tree, nestled in each other's arms, sharing long, deep kisses that left them both breathless.

One morning he woke her very early and told her to dress in her gray travel suit. He drove her into town, and after leaving the horse and buggy at the livery, escorted her to the train station. They took the eastbound eighty miles to Cheyenne and Beau led her to an outdoor roller-skating rink. Although Alina was an accomplished ice-skater, she had never skated on wheels. Beau taught her the basics, and they passed a lovely day together, then caught an afternoon westbound home. Alina had never felt so special or loved.

Each night he would see her to her room and kiss her goodnight at the door, and each night it was getting harder and harder for Alina to close that door. She lay awake one night late in June and thought over the last few weeks. Beau had done a masterful job of courting, she decided, for there was nowhere else she would now consider living, unless it was with him. How long would he wait before returning the ring to her? She was fully prepared to share her body and her life with him. She fell into a fitful sleep.

Sometime later, her eyes popped open. She lay motionless for a moment, disoriented. The grip of a terrifying dream was still upon her, a nightmare of fire and fear. She sat up. A feeling of uneasiness filled her, almost of dread.

Alina threw back the bedclothes and jumped out of bed. She opened the bedroom door and glanced at Beau's bed, his sleeping form barely discernible in the pale moonlight that came in between the curtains at the window. She did not want to awaken him. She quietly made her way across the main room to the front door, with Sundance right behind her.

"Shh," she whispered to the dog as she opened the door. They slipped out onto the porch.

The night was peaceful and cool. A breeze blew wispy clouds over the face of the almost-full moon, creating swiftly moving shadows across the valley. The tops of the tall pine trees bowed and whispered together, their soft voices comforting in the night. The creek gurgled nearby. A horse stomped in the barn.

Alina crossed her arms over her chest and leaned against the post. She glanced down at Sundance. The dog sat at her feet, ears up, nose quivering inquisitively in the cool night air. Alina looked out again over the valley. It was so beautiful here, she thought. Suddenly she stiffened. A faraway flicker of light caught her eye. She squinted. The tiny light seemed to bob and sway in time with an unheard melody as it moved steadily across the valley. It appeared the light was growing larger, but when it broke into several smaller lights, Alina realized it was getting closer. An errant breath of wind brought the sound of distant hoofbeats to her straining ears. Sundance growled, low in his throat.

Alina ran back into the house and made her way around the sofa to Beau's bed. "Beau!" she whispered urgently, then realized she did not have to be quiet any longer. "Beau!" she said again, louder. She shook his shoulder, surprised to find it bare and warm. He was instantly awake.

"What is it? Why don't you light a lamp?" He reached for the matches.

"No!" she warned as she grabbed his searching hand. "They'll know we are awake."

"Who?" Beau asked in bewilderment.

"A group of horsemen, headed this way." They both fell silent. The approaching horses were now audible even in the house. Sundance growled. Alina felt that her heart was pounding in perfect unison with the rhythm of the hoofbeats, and just as loudly.

Mindless of Alina's presence, Beau jumped out of bed and reached for his pants. She turned from his tantalizingly naked form in embarrassment and took her rifle from the chimney wall. "Pike! Conor!" Beau called. Conor stumbled out of the bedroom, his hair tousled, his gun in hand. Pike was behind him, on crutches. Both men wore only long underwear.

"We've got company," said Conor.

"That we do," Beau agreed, as he buttoned his pants. He pulled his pistol from the holster next to his pillow and stuffed it into his waistband, then pulled the table away from the front window and opened the latch. He pushed the windows wide open. "Pike, sit yourself here on the bench. There's no time to attach your leg, and here you'll have some cover. Try to keep Sundance quiet until they get here. I'll get your rifle." He headed into Pike's room, speaking as he went. "Conor, go out the back and circle to the south. Come up along the side of the cabin, and try to stay in the shadows." Both men did his bidding. Beau handed Pike his weapon, then took his own rifle down from over the front door.

"Alina, you stay in here."

"Beau, let me help," she pleaded. "I'm a good shot."

She could see him shake his head in the moonlight. "I'm sure you are, but I don't want you in any more danger than is necessary. Besides, you're our ace in the hole. If we get into trouble, you put Betsy to good use." He stared at her for a moment. "You'll have to shoot to kill, Alina. Can you do that?"

"I can do it," she said, her tone determined. "They'll not burn us out." She stood between the door and the window, Betsy grasped tightly in her hands.

Beau stepped out onto the porch. He did not close the door. Alina's breath caught as she watched him, silhouetted in the moonlight. He stood straight and tall, barefoot, with no shirt, his rifle cradled nonchalantly in one arm. She was filled with an almost overwhelming pride in him.

Beau retreated into the shadows and waited, the rifle cocked. The riders had slowed their mounts to a walk, and now entered the yard. They held their lanterns high; Beau saw that there were six. The lower half of their faces were covered.

"Someone go get them out here!" came a low, rough command.

Beau did not recognize the voice. He stepped into the lantern light. "I'm already out here," he said quietly, dangerously.

Someone swore. One rider nudged his horse forward.

"We have some advice for you and your wife. Where is the little lady?" a voice rasped, as if the speaker had something caught in his throat.

"I don't see where that is any of your business," Beau snapped. "State your business, then get off my land."

The leader straightened menacingly. "You've had a fair offer for your land. We advise you to take it. You and your witch-woman are not welcome here."

Beau snorted in derision. "You've had a long night ride for nothing, if that's all you've got to say." He decided to play a hunch. "Tell Petrie that I won't sell, and I won't leave."

"Never said I was speaking for Petrie." The man sighed regretfully. "I hoped you would make this easy, but I didn't really expect it." He raised his hand in a signal. The five other riders moved their hands to their pistols.

At that moment, Beau lifted his rifle and aimed it at the leader. The sound of guns being cocked filled the night. The men on horseback paused, their hands at their holsters. Moonlight gleamed off a rifle barrel that appeared through the open window. Another rifle seemed to grow from the open doorway. A pistol held in a steady hand shined from the side of the house. A dog growled, the sound low and threatening. No one moved.

"Gentlemen, it would seem we are at an impasse," Beau said conversationally.

"There are more of us," the leader pointed out.

"Perhaps," Beau answered. "But my gun is trained on you. You'll die for sure. Somehow, I don't think that was in your plans tonight."

The man held his hands out to his sides. "No, it wasn't," he admitted.

"Get off my land!" Beau lowered his rifle and aimed at the ground under the horses' feet, then fired two quick shots. Horses shied and jumped and bucked. One bolted down the road. Men swore. "We're not finished with you, Parker!" one shouted.

"Come anytime, boys!" Beau called out. "We'll be ready!"

Alina stepped from the cabin and stood beside him. Conor moved out into the yard, his pistol ready. Pike hobbled through the door, a crutch propped under his right arm, his rifle in his other hand.

"Ya damn cowards!" he shouted. "Ridin' in the night with your faces covered! Ya're all cowards!"

The last rider to leave the yard was a slight man. He rode slowly, glaring at them. Alina could feel the hate emanating from him. She shivered. The rider stared at them as he defiantly walked his horse from the yard, allowing the animal to run only after it crossed the bridge. The sound of hoofbeats faded into the night.

Chapter Sixteen

"Will you please hold still?" Alina begged. "Otherwise, I'll not be responsible for how you look."

Beau sighed and shifted on the chair. "I won't move again until you tell me I can."

"Thank you," Alina said. She combed out a thick dark lock and reached for the scissors that rested on the table. A moment later a small amount of hair floated to the floor.

Pike lowered his head and raised his eyes to look over the rim of his spectacles. "Why are ya even botherin', Alina? Ya're hardly taking off any at all."

Alina continued with her task. "I told you, I'm not very experienced at this. I'd rather take off too little than too much. Besides, I like his hair long." She glanced over her shoulder at Pike. "Read your book, or I'll turn the scissors over to you, since you seem to know so much about barbering."

"Please don't," Beau pleaded.

Alina smiled and stepped in front of him, pushing a strand of her own hair behind her ear. She had washed her hair earlier in the evening and had left it down to dry. The soft curls flowed down her back and swayed when she moved. Her skirts brushed against Beau's knees. She stared intently at his hair, studying the lengths over his ears. Beau caught the scent of roses as she leaned over him and snipped. Her breasts were level with his eyes. He fought a sudden urge to grab her trim waist and press his face to those soft mounds. His eyes closed. The courting had gone on for almost a month, and he was more than ready to return Alina's ring to her. But she hadn't asked for it yet, and he was determined that he would not push her.

"I ran into David Freeman out near the river today and told him what happened last night. Are we going to tell Sam Trudeau about our masked visitors when we go into town on the Fourth of July?" Conor spoke from his seat on the sofa.

"I think we should," Beau answered. "I'd like to know if anyone else has had the same problem. I suspect the McAllister and Murdoch fires were deliberate, and our callers were probably responsible. They are getting bold, coming as they did when they knew we were home. I sure would like to know what they had in mind that night."

"So you think they work for Petrie?" Conor asked.

Beau shrugged. "Everything points to it. He offers for the land, the owners refuse, something happens to their property."

"The sheriff should talk to Petrie," Alina suggested as she ran the comb through Beau's clean hair, wishing it was her fingers.

"Sheriff Boswell has spoken to him. Petrie swears he's not behind it. He admitted that he wants the land, but wouldn't say why. Boswell can't prove anything. If there *is* a mastermind behind these incidents, he's very clever. There's never any evidence."

"I just hope there ain't more bad news when we get ta town," Pike said as he closed his book. "I don't want ta hear about any more fires." He removed his spectacles and rubbed his eyes. "The Fourth is still a few days off, Beau. Do ya think one of us oughtta ride inta town tomorrow and let Sam know about this?"

"What do you think?" Beau asked.

Pike shrugged. "Seems like it might be a good idea. He may want ta keep an eye on Petrie and his men. Conor, what's your feelin' on this?"

Conor stretched his long legs out in front of him. "I'll feel a lot better about all of us being away from the ranch on the Fourth if Sam knows everything. Remember: the Murdochs were burned out on a day when it was known that everyone was going to be away from home."

"I was concerned about that myself," said Beau. "I'll go tomorrow; I have to send a wire, anyway."

"Hold still," Alina warned.

"Yes, ma'am!"

"How early was ya plannin' on going in on the Fourth?" Pike asked.

"I figure if we get there by early afternoon, we'll be in time for all the important events," he smiled, "like the shooting contest Alina is going to win, the dancing, and the fireworks."

"And how do you know I'm going to win the shooting contest?" Alina demanded. "You've never seen me shoot."

"Well, I have, and Beau's right—ya'll win." Pike stood up. "It's late. 'Night."

"Goodnight, Pike," said Alina.

"Are you finished with me, woman?" Beau inquired.

"Almost." She snipped a few more times, combed his hair again, and stood back. "There."

She stared at his face, then reached out to brush a lock off his forehead. "Your name fits you," she said softly.

Beau was confused. "Parker?"

"No, silly—Beauregard. That's French for 'good-looking.' " Their eyes met, then Alina looked down, suddenly shy.

Beau reached for her and pulled her onto his knee. Her arm went around his neck as she looked at him in surprise. "Thank you for the compliment," he said quietly.

Conor cleared his throat and stood up. "Pike had the right idea," he said, although he was not tired. "I think I'll hit the hay. You come with me, Sundance." He motioned to the dog, who was curled up on the hearth rug. "Goodnight."

"Goodnight, Conor," Alina murmured. The bedroom door closed.

Beau pulled her hair back from the sides of her face, delighting in its fragrance. "Kiss me," he whispered. His hand touched her cheek as she bent her head to meet his mouth. Now she gave in to her desire to run her fingers through his hair. She parted her lips for his questing tongue and sighed deeply.

Beau's hand caressed her back and side, moving slowly up her ribs until his long fingers brushed the underside of her breast. He nibbled at her bottom lip, then turned his head to kiss her neck.

"I'm glad you don't wear a corset," he whispered. His hand moved to cover her breast.

Alina caught her breath. Although she had never known a lover's caress, his touch seemed natural and right. A deep part of her was surprised that she felt no shame, while another part admitted that she had longed for him to touch her there . . . and other places. His hand moved slowly, his thumb brushing at her taut nipple through the material of her blouse. She shuddered at the sensations that rippled through her.

Beau pressed his face to her softness. His hand ran along the length of her thigh. "You feel so good," he murmured. His mouth found hers again, his lips insistent.

A warm feeling spread in her stomach, going ever lower. She shifted on his knee. She was on fire, and somehow she knew Beau was the only one who could put out the flames.

He lifted his head, pulling his lips from hers. His breathing was ragged, as was hers. Alina rested her forehead against the side of his head and tried to calm the pounding of her heart. She touched his cheek. He grabbed her hand and kissed it.

"You are bewitching, Alina. You make me forget that I am a gentleman." His voice was soft.

But I don't want you to be a gentleman. Ask to share my bed. She raised her head and looked at him, her kiss-swollen lips trembling.

Ask for your ring, Alina. Beau's plea was silent. Neither spoke.

Finally he sighed. "Up with you, woman." He patted her thigh.

Alina rose awkwardly and pushed her wild hair back over her shoulders. "I . . . I'd better get to bed."

Beau stood up. The fire in his eyes mellowed to tenderness. He touched her tumbled tresses.

She self-consciously smoothed her hair. "I must be a sight."

"You are an absolutely beautiful sight, Alina." His gaze was wistful and longing. He gently turned her toward their bedroom. "Off with you."

He did not move as she crossed the room. "Goodnight," she said quietly, then closed the door.

Beau ran his hands through his hair in frustration. Could she not feel how he wanted her, needed her? How much longer would she make him wait? He grabbed the lamp by its base and blew out the flame, then returned it to the table with a loud thump. The glass chimney rattled.

He stomped over to his narrow bed and sat down to remove his boots. Another sleepless night awaited him.

Pike heard Alina close her door, and he heard Beau moving around the other room. He snorted in exasperation.

"Conor," he whispered loudly.

"Yeah?"

"Those two are gonna drive me ta drink." He paused for a minute. "Say, ya don't think that us being here is puttin' a damper on their, uh, romantic urges, do ya?"

Conor smiled and put his hands under his head. "They do seem to be taking their time at this courting thing."

Pike pulled on his beard. "I think they need our help. Tomorrow, me and you'll go ta town and see Sam, and send Beau's wire, then we'll ride the ranch, checkin' fence. It'll take all day and we'll make damn sure that we'll be so far away come nightfall that we'll need ta camp out. That'll give those two lovestruck fools some time all ta theirselves."

"That's a good idea, Pike," Conor said as he rolled over and punched his pillow. "We'll set out right after breakfast."

Pike nodded with satisfaction. "And maybe I'll have ta explain ta Beau what the plan is, the lunkhead."

Early the next morning, Pike found Beau at the chicken coop. The sun had just peeked over the horizon. The day promised to be a fine one.

Pike eyed his friend. "Conor and me, we thought ta head ta town this mornin' and talk ta Sam, then we want ta ride the entire fence. We probably won't be back 'til sometime tomorrow afternoon."

Beau looked up. "I thought I was going to town. I told you I had a wire to send."

"We'll send it for ya if ya like. If ya don't like, can the wire wait 'til the Fourth?"

"It can wait." Beau emptied the pan of chicken scratch. "Why is it so important for you to go to town instead of me?"

Pike rolled his eyes. "Listen careful-like, Beau." He leaned forward and emphasized each word. "Because Alina will be here." He straightened. "Me and Conor'll get outta your hair for a day or two, so ya can do some real sparkin'." He hooked his thumbs in his suspenders and looked up at the sky. "My leg tells me this is a good day for a pic-a-nic, though it might rain a spell later on this afternoon, like it sometimes does."

Beau shook his head, but he could not keep a smile from curving his lips. "There's no need for you and Conor to leave." He headed to the barn.

"Oh, yes, there is," Pike assured him as he followed. "You two lovebirds don't seem ta be gettin' the hang of this here courtin'. Ya're takin' too damn long. Me'n Conor, we think that maybe with us bein' here, ya and Alina are stiflin' your natural urges."

Beau hung the pan on a nail over the feedbag. "We're not going to discuss natural urges," he said firmly. He hesitated, then continued in a soft, sad tone. "She hated me once, Pike. She despised and distrusted me, and with just cause. I couldn't bear it if that look ever returned to her eyes. So this courting will take as long as she wants it to. You and Conor have nothing to do with it."

Conor's voice sounded from the cabin porch. "Breakfast!"

Beau raised an eyebrow. "You let him cook breakfast?"

Pike shrugged. "It's hard ta mess up bacon." The two men crossed the yard. "I still think ya and Alina are just dancin' around each other. Whatever happened is long over. Tell her ya love her and give her the damn ring back."

Pike stomped up onto the porch and disappeared through the open door. Beau sank down on the top step, his gaze wandering over the valley. Sundance came from inside and settled next to him. He scratched the dog's ears, deep in thought. Maybe Pike was right. It was a lovely day for a picnic, and maybe if they knew they would be alone, both he and Alina could find the courage to say what was in their hearts.

Alina positioned the rose hair comb high on the left side of her head and examined the effect in the mirror. She nodded with satisfaction, then smoothed the skirt of her new dress. Mrs. Simpson had fashioned the burgundy calico into a lovely garment.

She lifted the new straw hat from the bed and gently placed it over her curls. She checked her reflection one last time. Her cheeks were flushed with excitement; her eyes sparkled. The idea of a picnic with Beau filled her with anticipation and pleasure.

The wagon stopped in front of the opened door as she pulled the folded quilt from the foot of the bed. She crossed the main room and stepped out onto the porch. Her eyes widened with surprise to see that Beau had hitched the bay to the two-man buggy.

"We're taking the buggy?"

Beau did not look up from the harness. "Somehow the wagon didn't seem appropriate for today." He finished his adjustments, then looked at her.

"You are lovely, Alina." He came to stand before her and reached for the quilt. His hand touched hers and caught it. "Is that one of your new dresses?"

Alina nodded. She could not pull her eyes away from his burning gaze. He raised her hand to his lips and placed a kiss there. "The hat becomes you, also," he added.

"Thank you," Alina said with a smile. She eyed his black broadcloth suit. "You look very nice yourself."

Beau dropped her hand and put the quilt behind the seat of the buggy. Alina went back inside and reemerged a minute later with a covered basket. Beau helped her into the buggy, pulled the cabin door closed, and took his place beside her.

"Where are we going?" Alina asked as the buggy rolled over the bridge.

"We'll follow the creek south. I know of a real pretty spot not too far away."

"I wonder whatever possessed Pike to insist on taking Sundance with him this morning," Alina commented. "It seems like a long way for the poor dog to run. He is still a puppy."

"Pike would never want me to tell you this, but when Sundance gets tired, he carries him on the horse with him."

Alina laughed. "Maybe I should be jealous. Sundance seems more like Pike's dog than mine."

Beau looked at her. "I think Sundance's heart belongs to you." *Like mine does.*

Alina smiled at him. They fell into a comfortable silence as the horse followed the winding creek.

Finally Beau pulled the horse to a stop. A grassy bank ran down to the water. Box elder maples and peach-leaved willows consorted with cottonwoods to create a cool, shady glade.

"This is just beautiful," Alina breathed as she took in the serenity of the place. He came around the buggy and helped her to the ground. She lifted her skirts and wandered around the glade, coming to a stop at the bank of the creek. The clear water gurgled and laughed as it poured over tumbled rocks of varying sizes. The sound was comforting. A large boulder jutted into the creek about ten yards downstream, creating a deep pool. Beau came to stand at her side.

"Do you think there are trout in that pool?" She pointed toward the boulder.

"I'm counting on it." Beau pushed his hat back on his head. "I plan to catch some for our supper tonight."

Alina looked at him, her eyes filled with tenderness. "Thank you for bringing me here."

"Thank you for coming with me." Beau touched her cheek. "Where would you like to spread the quilt?"

Alina's eyes traveled the glade as she considered his question. "How about under that maple over there?" She pointed to a tree a few feet away. Beau nodded in agreement. When the blanket was spread, it came almost to the edge of the water. He moved the basket next to the tree trunk and held out a hand to her. "Your quilt awaits, my lady."

Alina giggled and took his hand. She allowed him to lead her to the quilt, then sank to the ground and settled her skirts around her legs. Beau took his hat and coat off and sat down next to her.

They were quiet for a time, each content with their own thoughts. The late-morning breeze rustled the tops of the trees and blew a stray curl over Alina's cheek. She brushed at the tickling lock, then carefully lifted the straw hat from her head. She held the hat in her lap and closed her eyes, lifting her face. "The breeze feels good," she commented.

Beau watched her. The pink porcelain roses that decorated the hair comb peeked from her dark curls and matched the delicate bloom on her cheeks. His heart lurched. Everything he wanted in the world was wrapped up in the woman at his side. His hand strayed to her cheek. He prayed he was worthy of her. Alina looked at him with a questioning smile. He tucked an errant lock of blue-black hair behind her ear.

"What?" she whispered.

Beau shook his head. "Nothing. Would you like to explore the area?"

Alina nodded and placed the hat back on her head. He stood and held his hand out to her, then pulled her to her feet. He did not release her hand.

They spent the next hour wandering up and down the creek. They did not speak much. When they returned to the quilt, Alina took her hat off again and sat down. She removed her shoes and stockings and dangled her feet in the cool water. Her skirt was bunched around her knees. Beau admired her shapely calves and narrow ankles.

"The water feels wonderful." She kicked with one dainty foot, sending a spray of water across the creek. She struggled to her feet and waded into the water, holding her skirts high. Beau watched as she reached the other bank and bent over to pluck something from the streambed. Her skirts were now gathered in one hand, affording him a pleasurable view of her knees and the lower part of her thighs. She made her way back to him, using caution on the slippery rocks.

"Do you think this is gold?" She handed him a wet rock as she sank back on the blanket. Beau turned it over in his palm. The sunlight glinted off golden flecks imbedded in the stone.

"It's fool's gold."

"Fool's gold? What is that?"

"The scientific name is pyrite. One of my friends is a geologist; I heard him refer to it as 'fool's gold' one time."

"Is it worth anything?"

Beau shook his head. "But it's pretty to look at." He gave the rock back to her. "Like you are."

Alina smiled shyly. "Are you hungry?"

Beau looked pointedly at her bare calves, then nodded, his hot gaze devouring her. Alina blushed as she placed the piece of pyrite in the basket and handed him a slice of bread. They ate a leisurely meal, then Alina lay down on the quilt while Beau fished from the pool. In half an hour he had three good-sized trout on the bank. He moved a short distance away and cleaned the fish, then rearranged some rocks to form a small protected pool near the bank. He placed the gutted fish in the pool and rinsed his hands. As he stood he looked up at the sky. White and gray clouds moved languidly on the wind, sometimes covering the sun. There would be a rainstorm before long.

Beau returned to Alina. She was curled on one side, her head resting on her bent arm, her eyes closed. Her bare feet and ankles peeked from the hem of her skirt.

He sat beside her and stared at her for a long time. Eventually he stretched out, facing her, propping his head on one hand. He could not stop himself from touching her hair. Her long eyelashes rested on her cheeks. He watched the gentle movement of her breasts as they kept time with her relaxed breathing.

Alina stirred and opened her eyes. "Hello," she said with a sleepy smile. "I must have dozed off." She stretched a little. "Did you catch any fish?"

"I did," Beau whispered. His hand moved to her shoulder and he gently pushed her onto her back. "I can't wait any longer to kiss you."

A thrill went through Alina when she read the desire in his eyes. His lips were gentle and knowing upon hers. She wrapped her arms around his neck as he positioned his body over hers. The kiss deepened; her hands twisted in his hair. His mouth traveled from her lips to her ear, then down her throat, creating a trail of shivery excitement. He kissed the beginning swells of her breasts over the lace-edged neckline of her dress.

Alina moaned. His hand pressed against her breast, his fingers teasing her nipple to a tight bud. He reclaimed her mouth with his, while his hand left her breast and trailed down her ribs and stomach to her hip, then on down her leg. He pulled the hem of her skirt up and caressed her thigh through her cotton drawers.

A distant rumble of thunder pulsed across the sky. The bay nickered. Alina pulled her mouth from Beau's. Her breathing was ragged; her heart pounded. He looked at her questioningly, his eyes glazed with passion.

"What is it?" he whispered hoarsely.

Alina caressed his shoulder. "I just want to look at you." The sound of thunder reached their ears again. Beau's hand retreated from under her skirt and he pulled the material down over her knee. His long body trembled as he reluctantly rolled off her.

"We should go." He pushed her hair away from her face. "It's going to rain."

Alina sighed in disappointment. She ran her hand up and down his arm. "Will you bring me here again?"

He smiled. "Whenever you want." He leaned over and kissed her lightly. She clung to him for a moment, then allowed him to help her sit up. She reached for her stockings and shoes. The wind was rising and she could smell rain.

"Here," he said. The hair comb rested on his outstretched palm. One hand flew to her unruly hair, while she accepted the comb with the other.

"It would appear that you have a knack for disarranging my hair, Mr. Parker," she commented with a smile.

"It would appear that I do." Beau grinned as he handed her the straw hat. "And I thoroughly enjoy it." He pulled her to her feet. A few tiny raindrops touched her face.

They gathered the rest of their things and Beau assisted her into the buggy just as a loud clap of thunder announced that the rain would soon fall in earnest.

By the time Bay stopped in front of the cabin, the rain was coming down in torrents. The canvas top of the buggy had protected them to some extent, as had the quilt Alina had spread over their legs, but they were both damp and cold.

Beau lifted her from the buggy and set the basket on the porch, then led the horse toward the barn.

"I'll be in shortly," he called. She waved and disappeared into the cabin.

Once inside, she gingerly pulled her hat from under the quilt. A few of the flowers were flattened, but the hat had survived. She spread the wet quilt over the back of the sofa, then went into the bedroom and set the hair comb on the dresser. The rain pounded against the glass panes. Thank goodness she had closed the window that morning. She pulled the curtains closed.

A shiver raced through Alina's chilled body as she struggled with the hooks down her back. The beautiful dress fell to the floor at her feet, as did her damp petticoat, and she reached for her wrapper. After tying the belt at her waist, she slipped her shoes and stockings off. She hung the petticoat on a hook and draped the dress over the top of the bedroom door, then hurried to the fireplace.

By the time Beau came through the front door, a hearty blaze roared on the hearth. Alina looked up from her task of emptying the basket. "There's a clean towel on the counter for you." Her fingers closed on the chunk of pyrite. She crossed to the fireplace and set the rock on the mantel.

She turned and met Beau's curious gaze. "It's a memento of a lovely day," she explained.

Beau shrugged out of his dripping vest. "It *was* a lovely day," he agreed. Alina smiled shyly and went back to the bedroom. She sat on the edge of the bed and ran the brush through her hair, trying to figure out why she felt so lonely and sad. She looked at the bed that had seemed so big and empty these past few weeks. Her third finger still felt strange and naked without the gold band. Why was Beau taking so long to give the ring back? Surely he must know how she felt about him! Perhaps he was having doubts now. Every time the fires of passion had flared between them in the past several days, she had hoped he would truly make her his wife, but he had stopped. What was holding him back?

Alina winced as the brush pulled at a knot. She was reminded of another time her brush had pulled, and Beau's long fingers had freed her. She worked the brush out and set it on the dresser. Her eyes fell on the pictures of her parents. They had taught her to face her problems head on, to demand the truth. Determined to do just that, she turned and walked into the main room, her bare feet silent on the floor.

Beau had taken off his shirt and gunbelt. His boots rested next to his bed. His hands were braced on the fireplace mantel and he stared intently into the flames.

Alina's gaze traveled with pleasure over the muscles of his tanned back. His damp pants were molded to his taut flanks and hugged his long legs. The wistful yearning in her grew. She wrapped her arms around herself and tossed her head, throwing her hair back over her shoulders.

"What do you hope to find in the flames?" she asked softly.

Beau turned to her. The firelight played on his chest and highlighted the planes of his face. "I hope to find a way to make you want to stay, Alina." There was a sadness, a weariness, in his eyes.

Her breath caught in her throat. "What makes you think I don't want to stay?"

"You haven't asked for the ring."

Alina's mouth opened in astonishment. "You've been waiting for me to ask for the ring?" She took a step toward him.

He nodded.

"But I've been waiting for you to give it to me."

Hope flared in Beau's eyes as a grin split his handsome face. "Pike was right; we *have* been dancing around each other."

"He said that?"

Beau nodded again and held out his arms. "Shall we dance together for a change?"

Alina went into his embrace with a glad cry. She felt his

heart pounding against her cheek. Beau held her tightly for a moment, then released her. He pulled the ring from his pants pocket. The gold band rested on his open palm, sparkling in the firelight.

"You had it with you?" Alina asked wonderingly.

"I've kept it with me since the night I took it back." He reached for her left hand as his warm brown eyes searched her shining blue ones. "Will you stay, Alina Gallagher? Will you be my wife, my lover, the mother of my children?"

"I will, Beau," she answered lovingly. "Will you be my husband, my lover, the father of my children?"

"Oh, I will." Beau slipped the ring on her finger. His hands moved to cup her face. He stared into her eyes, then lowered his mouth to hers. His kiss was gentle and reverent. He raised his head to look at her again. "I love you, wife."

Alina threw her arms around his neck. "And I love you, husband!" she cried. She covered his face with little kisses. Beau laughed and wrapped his arms around her, lifting her off the floor. He turned in a circle, then set her down again. His lips found hers and claimed their softness with a new possessiveness. Alina leaned into his body, pressing herself against him. When their mouths separated, she felt weak with newfound passion.

"What day is this?" she asked breathlessly.

Beau closed his eyes and ran his hand down the length of her hair, coming to rest on her hip. "Tuesday, I think. Tuesday, July second. Why?"

Alina toyed with the hair on his chest. "Because this is our real wedding day, Beau. We will celebrate our anniversaries on July second."

His hand moved lower and cupped one curved buttock. He pulled her close against his body. Alina was thrilled to feel his hardened manhood pressing against her stomach. She held him tighter and, with a feminine instinct as old as time, moved her hips against him. He groaned and wrapped his hand in her hair.

"Beau, do we have to wait until tonight?" Alina whispered against his chest. She pressed her lips to his skin.

"I think we've waited long enough, Mrs. Parker," he said hoarsely, and swung her up into his arms. Alina clung to him as he crossed the room with long strides and carried her into their bedroom. He pulled the bedclothes back and laid her on the sheets. For just a moment, he disappeared into the other room, then returned with his gunbelt and draped it over the corner of the headboard. He sat down next to her and untied the belt at her waist, pulling the wrapper open to reveal her camisole and drawers. Alina waited, her hand caressing his thigh.

"It's too dark," he murmured as he reached for a match. "I want to see you." He lit the bedside lamp and turned the wick down low. A soft light filled the small room. The rain blew steadily against the window.

Beau took a handful of her hair and spread it across the pillow. "You were wearing this robe that night at the Satin Slipper." His voice was barely above a whisper. "Your hair was down, like it is now. I have dreamed of seeing you like this again for months, of seeing your beautiful hair on my pillow." He leaned across her, bracing his left arm on the mattress next to her hip. His other hand played with her hair, then stroked her cheek, then traveled down her throat and lower, until his fingers found the top button of her camisole.

Alina's breath caught when the tiny button slipped from its hole. Her nipples hardened as an aching excitement rushed through her. Beau's fingers moved lower. The fire grew in her belly, flaming higher each time his fingers moved down to the next button. Finally he opened the last one. His hand rested on the smooth skin of her stomach; his eyes searched hers with a warm tenderness. He leaned forward and placed a gentle kiss on her trembling lips, while his hand moved up over her ribs and finally covered her breast. Alina moaned against his mouth.

Beau's lips traced a river of fire down her throat and over

her chest. His hand pushed the camisole back. His soft mustache brushed her skin, and at last his lips fastened on the rosy peak of her breast. Alina gasped at the intense pleasure that washed over her. She shook her head restlessly from side to side.

"Oh, Beau," she breathed.

"You smell like roses," he murmured against her. His tongue teased and lapped at her.

He sat up and pulled her with him. "I want you out of these clothes." He pushed the robe off her shoulders. She freed her arms from the long sleeves. His hands returned to her shoulders and the camisole joined the robe on the sheets. He wrapped his arms around her and pressed his chest to hers. "I like the feel of your bare breasts against me," he whispered.

Alina nuzzled his shoulder and her hand dropped to the waistband of his pants. She tugged meaningfully at the material.

Beau laughed. "You're a lusty little thing, aren't you?" He stood up, but before he removed his pants, he reached behind her and pulled the robe and camisole out of the way. He gently pushed her back against the pillows and opened the button at her waist, then slipped her drawers off. He straightened. His eyes seemed to blaze as they roamed over her body. Alina shifted uncomfortably and fought the urge to cover herself with her hands.

"I knew you would be beautiful, just as I knew your mouth would taste sweet," he said softly. Alina smiled and held her arms out to him. He shed his pants and joined her. They clung to each other tightly, hungrily. Their mouths met, their legs entwined. Alina closed her eyes as Beau's gentle hands explored her body. Her breath came in short gasps. His fingers found her moist, mysterious softness. Beau settled himself between her thighs, his hard, eager manhood cushioned against her belly.

"I may hurt you this first time, darling," he warned, his voice low and husky.

Alina looked at him with love and trust shining in her eyes. "It will be all right," she whispered. Her hands stroked his back.

Beau groaned. His arms tightened around her. "I have wanted you for so long, my sweet woman." He shifted and pressed into her. Alina bit her lip and grimaced when he met her body's resistance. With one quick thrust he broke through and buried himself deep within her. He did not move, giving her body time to adjust to his presence. She held him tightly.

"Are you all right?" he whispered. She nodded against his shoulder. Beau began to move slowly, and the pain faded. She relaxed and met his thrusts, timing her movements to his. Her response fanned his passion, his ardor fanned hers. She cried out in surprise and pleasure when the aching promise of his loving was fulfilled. Beau shuddered and moaned her name. She could feel him trembling within her.

Alina clung to him. Her heart pounded and it seemed she could not get enough air. "Oh, Beau," she whispered. "I had no idea." She moved her hips, loving the feeling of him inside her.

He rested his weight on his elbows and looked down at her; a tender smile curved the corners of his mouth. One hand caressed her hair. He planted a quick, breathless kiss on her lips. "Nor did I."

Her brow wrinkled with doubt. "Surely this was not your first time also?"

He touched her cheek. "It was my first time with a woman I love, and beyond anything I could have imagined." He rolled onto his side, keeping her close, and pulled the sheet up over them. He sighed contentedly.

"It's good to have you in this bed again," Alina commented.

Beau nodded in agreement. "It's good to be here."

Alina rose up on one elbow. Her hair fell around her shoulders like a blanket. "I never understood why you insisted I share your bed in the beginning, when you had no intention of touching me."

Beau lifted a long black curl and played with it, deep in thought. "I think I just wanted to be close to you," he finally answered. "It was more than simple lust, although I felt that, too." He smiled wickedly. "I still do."

Alina playfully slapped his stomach. "Go on with you, Beau Parker."

Beau grew serious. His eyes met hers. "Your spirit touched me, Alina. You had a fire in you; you were *alive.* I wanted to be near that. Maybe I hoped some of it would rub off on me." He twisted the curl around his finger. "That was one of the reasons I wanted to marry you. I knew Donovan Randall would do everything in his power to break you, to destroy your spirit. I couldn't let that happen."

Alina's eyes softened at his words. "So it wasn't just your guilty conscious."

"Oh, no. I think I began to love you that first night, when you took my gun from me."

"I think I began to love you when you danced with me at Katie's. I couldn't get you out of my mind." Alina snuggled down next to him again, her breasts pressing against him, her head resting on his shoulder. She idly ran her hand over his muscular chest and found the scar.

"How did you get this, Beau?" she asked. Her fingers were light upon him.

"From a saber, during the war." Beau did not want to talk about the war, not now. His brow furrowed. "Does it bother you?" he asked.

"Only because it means you were badly hurt," Alina whispered. He was deeply touched when she moved over him and placed a gentle kiss on the scar, then returned her head to his shoulder. His lips brushed her hair.

Her hand again roamed his chest, coming to a stop over his heart. She felt the strong, steady beats, and rejoiced in his life. Never had she felt so close to another human being, so loved, so honored. "I love you, Beau," she whispered.

"And I you, my Irish Rose." His arms tightened around her and he pressed his lips to her forehead. The light of the lamp bathed them in a golden glow. The sound of the rain pounding on the roof and blowing against the window made the warmth of their bed seem like a sanctuary. They both drifted into a light sleep.

Chapter Seventeen

Alina stabbed at a piece of side pork sizzling in the cast iron skillet and flipped it over. For the third time since she had started breakfast, her eyes went to the porcelain dove that rested next to the pyrite stone on the mantel. She had taken it from the trunk the first thing that morning, after explaining to Beau that she had sworn to keep the treasure packed away until she was home. She was now home.

She turned the other pieces of pork, then glanced out of the window over the sink and saw Beau back out of the chicken coop. A soft smile touched her face as she wrapped her arms around herself. Never would she have dreamed that love could be what he had shown her last night.

When they had awakened from their short rest, the rain had stopped and it had been fully dark. Beau had insisted that she stay under the sheets while he made them something to eat. He had seen to the animals, then had returned to their bed with crisp pieces of cornmeal-coated fried trout and biscuits that had been left over from breakfast. They had fed each other with their fingers, and drank from the same cup of water. When their hunger for food had been satisfied, their hunger for each other had returned with a powerful intensity. He had pleasured her again, and yet again in the early hours of the morning, after she had been awakened by the feel of his lips on her neck.

Alina watched him cross the yard with long, easy strides,

swinging the egg basket. She felt loved and cherished and beautiful, and deliciously wanton.

His steps sounded on the porch, and Alina forced her attention to slicing a potato.

"Good morning, wife," Beau said as he set the basket on the counter. He stood behind her and nuzzled her neck. "You smell good." Alina set the knife down and leaned back against him as delightful shivers ran down her body.

"You've already told me good morning," she reminded him.

He turned her to face him, holding her close. Her arms circled his lean waist. "I did," he agreed, and planted a quick kiss on her lips. "I've already kissed you this morning, too, but I'm going to kiss you again." He did. "I don't think I'll ever get tired of kissing you," he sighed against her lips.

"Oh, I hope not," she murmured.

Beau lifted her chin and looked into her eyes. "Never," he said softly, and kissed her yet again, much deeper.

Alina was breathless when his lips released her. "You'll make me burn the pork, Beau." She pushed at his chest. "Put the plates on the table." Her sparkling eyes belied the severe tone of her voice.

"Yes, ma'am." Beau winked and moved to obey her. "This room sure looks bigger, now that my bed is out of here and the sofa is back against the wall," he commented as he set the plates down. "I did hate that bed."

Alina hid a smile and lifted the pork from the pan. Beau had rearranged the furniture that morning even before he had poured himself a cup of coffee. As for herself, she was entirely satisfied with the sleeping arrangements now.

Later that afternoon, Alina sat in a chair on the back porch, mending a tear in one of Beau's shirts. She looked up from her task every now and again to watch as Beau guided Bay down the hill behind the cabin. The horse pulled a huge dead tree behind him, straining when the branches caught on a rock or a pine. The man and the beast had just maneuvered the tree into position by the wood pile when the sound of Sundance's excited barking heralded the return of the fence party. Alina set the shirt aside and joined Beau. They walked hand in hand to the barn, where Pike and Conor had dismounted. Sundance ran in happy circles around them. Pike watched the approaching couple through the open door, his gaze speculative. He pulled the saddle from Tumbleweed and heaved it onto a support that protruded from the wall, then nudged Conor.

"They look mighty happy," he murmured out of the side of his mouth as he crossed his arms over his chest.

"Holding hands and all." Conor sounded pleased.

"Howdy, boys," Beau said as he and Alina stepped into the coolness of the building. "How's the fence?"

"The fence is fine." Pike stroked his beard. "How's the courtin'?"

A smile played about Beau's mouth. "The courting is finished." He draped his arm around Alina's shoulders, then took her hand and held it out so that the golden band twinkled in the light. "Alina has consented to be my wife, for real this time."

Pike let out a cheer and threw his hat in the air. Conor held his arms out to his cousin. Alina gladly went to him, while Pike pumped Beau's hand and clapped him on the shoulder. "Well done, Beau Parker, well done," Pike said, a grin splitting his grizzled face.

"Congratulations, Cousin," Conor said as he held Alina in a tight embrace. "I'm real happy for you, honey. He's a fine man."

Alina nodded. "I know." She turned to Pike. "Well, aren't you going to kiss the bride?" she asked him teasingly.

Pike blushed and hooked his thumbs in his suspenders. He leaned forward and pecked her cheek. "Congratulations, Alina," he mumbled.

Alina threw her arms around him. "Thank you, Pike. Thank you for everything."

Pike awkwardly patted her shoulder. "What're ya thankin' me for?"

"For being my friend, for being Beau's friend, for giving us some time alone."

Piké's face turned an even deeper shade of red. "Beau told ya that?"

"He didn't have to." Alina kissed his cheek.

Conor held his hand out to Beau. "I'm proud to welcome you to our family, Beau."

"I'm proud to be part of it, Conor. Thank you." The two men shook hands warmly.

"This calls for a celebration," Pike declared. "This'll be a real weddin' supper, and me'n Conor are gonna cook. Like I told Alina the first time, ya don't make your own weddin' supper." He shooed Alina and Beau toward the door. "The both of ya go on one of your romantic," he rolled his eyes, "walks or somethin'. Get outta our hair while we see ta these horses and get ourselves cleaned up."

"But I have Bay hooked up to that log," Beau protested.

"Well, go get him and turn him out into the pasture. Then ya take your lady and skedaddle for a spell." He waved them away. "Go on with ya, now. Me'n Conor got work ta do."

"All right, all right." Beau laughed as he held his hands up in surrender. He backed out of the barn, pulling Alina with him.

Pike dragged Alina's chair back with a flourish.

"Thank you, Mr. Pike," she said as she sank gracefully into the chair. She smiled up at him. His hair was slicked back and he wore his best shirt, a string tie at his collar. "You are looking fine this evening, I must say."

Pike's cheeks reddened, but he looked pleased. He cleared his throat. "Ya look mighty fine your own self, Mrs. Parker," he said gallantly. He turned to Beau. "I ain't gonna hold your chair, so ya might as well sit."

Beau laughed and took his seat. Alina breathed deeply of the enticing aromas that rose from the table. There was a baked chicken, a bowl of rice, and another of green beans.

Conor came from his room with a bulky package wrapped in brown paper and set it on the table between Alina and Beau.

"Pike and I got you a little something, in honor of your marriage."

Alina and Beau looked at him in surprise. Conor shrugged. "We were hoping the two of you would work things out. We gambled on it and got you a gift," he explained somewhat awkwardly. Pike hung back by the counter. "Go on," Conor urged. "Open it."

Beau nodded at Alina. She took the package and untied the string. She carefully pulled back the paper, then gasped with pleasure when a wineglass was revealed, then another. She continued to unwrap the paper until four glasses stood in front of her. The light from the lamp shined off the etched crystal. Alina's eyes filled with tears as her gaze met Beau's. He appeared to be as touched as she was. "They are beautiful," she whispered. "Thank you both." She reached for Beau's hand.

Conor removed the wrapping and string from the table, then took his seat.

"We know it ain't a real practical gift, 'specially for livin' out here," Pike explained, "but a lady shouldn't have ta drink French wine out of a chipped coffee mug." He came from the counter, a bottle in one hand. "We got some of that fancy white wine ya like, in case everythin' worked out. We didn't dare risk the oysters, though. There warn't no way ta keep 'em fresh, 'specially if ya was gonna take as long ta work things out as ya took a' courtin'."

He poured wine into each of the glasses, placing one in front of each plate, then moved to his place opposite Beau. He picked up his glass and cleared his throat. "I would like ta propose a toast to Mr. and Mrs. Beauregard Parker," he announced formally. Everyone took up their glass. "Congratulations on your marriage, and may ya have a long and happy life together."

"Here, here," Conor added. They gently touched glasses and each took a sip.

"Thank you, Pike. Thank you, Conor." Beau set his glass down. "You've made this a special evening for us."

Pike picked up a knife and a large fork and began to carve the chicken. "I poured a little of that wine over this here bird," he said as he cut off a drumstick. "It should be real tasty."

"It smells divine," Alina said.

Beau squeezed her hand. "Alina and I had a little discussion while on our forced walk this afternoon, gentleman, and we'd like to share our thoughts with you."

"Warn't forced, was only suggested," Pike argued.

"Strongly suggested," Conor added with a smile.

Beau nodded. "Since we are more or less a family now, it's time you know something. I told Alina this afternoon."

"So, get on with it," Pike muttered as he struggled to cut the wishbone out of the chicken and not break the bone.

"It's about my communications with Washington, and the trips I took away from the ranch in the spring."

Pike stopped carving and sat down. Conor leaned back against the windowsill behind his bench and waited, fingering the delicate stem of his wineglass.

"When I worked in Washington after the war, I became friends with a man named Clarence King. He's a geologist, and is now engaged in an extensive survey along the Fortieth Parallel, down in Colorado Territory. He'll be occupied with that very important assignment probably until the fall, so he asked me to check into some rumors he has heard."

"Rumors about what?" Conor asked.

"Diamonds."

"Diamonds!" Pike repeated.

Beau nodded. "Two men named Phil Arnold and John Slack have been hinting that they've discovered a diamond field, perhaps as big as the find in South Africa."

"Where?" Conor's blue eyes were alight with interest.

"That's just it. They won't say where. There's speculation

that it's in Arizona Territory, or Colorado Territory." Beau paused. "Or Wyoming Territory."

Conor and Pike looked at each other. "Close to here?" Conor queried.

Beau shrugged. "Could be. Arnold has been spending a lot of time in Laramie City."

"So ya were doin' some checkin' around last spring, lookin' for this diamond field." Pike toyed with the carving knife.

Beau nodded. "I didn't learn much. But I do know that Arnold has a lot of people interested in investing in his company. Charles Tiffany himself, of the New York jewelry house that bears his name, has examined some of the stones from this field and has proclaimed them to be quite valuable. General McClellan is also involved."

"*The* General McClellan?" asked Conor.

"The same. It's a good bet Richard Petrie is one of those interested investors."

Pike expelled his breath in a long stream. "If Petrie thinks those diamond fields are around here, it would explain why he's so damn desperate—beg pardon, Alina—ta buy up the valley."

Beau nodded grimly. "That is exactly my thought."

"Does your friend think the fields could be here?" Conor leaned forward.

"No." Beau shook his head. "That's why he asked me to look into it. Clarence has already surveyed this area. He swears there are no diamond fields. He'll look mighty foolish if it turns out he's wrong. That's why he wants to come back as soon as he can, and conduct a formal investigation."

Pike looked at Beau accusingly. "Ya coulda told us sooner."

"Clarence asked me not to mention it to anyone, Pike. I hope he understands why I decided to tell you now." He squeezed Alina's hand again. "I don't want any secrets between me and my wife."

"It's just as well ya told her," Pike commented as he stood

again to finish carving the chicken. "She was afraid ya was seein' Madeline Petrie when ya was gone all those days."

"She told me that," Beau said with a smile. "Did you tell her at the time how groundless those fears were?"

"Tried ta."

Alina decided to change the subject. "There's one other thing."

"Go ahead, Cousin." Conor took a sip of wine.

"Pike, we assume and hope that you will continue to make your home here."

"I'd like ta, Alina, if ya think ya can stand me."

"Don't be silly. It would break my heart if you left. Conor, we want to extend the same invitation to you. I don't know what your plans are, but you will always be welcome to live here. We think that, together, we can build this ranch into something real nice."

Conor smiled. "So you will stay here." He nodded in approval. "Somehow I couldn't see Beau feeling too comfortable with Chicago society."

Alina noticed that Conor did not comment on her invitation. "Beau would be fine in Chicago," she said. "It's me who doesn't want that life any more. This is where I want to be."

"We also hope to someday add children to this family." Beau winked at his blushing wife.

Pike raised his eyebrows. "This cabin's gonna get mighty crowded."

"Exactly," Beau agreed. "We plan on either enlarging this place, or building a new, bigger house. Any ideas you have will be welcome."

Conor raised his glass. "To the future."

"To the future," Alina repeated. She touched her glass to Beau's. The warmth she found in his gaze caused her heart to thump. She read the promise of love and of unspoken pleasures in those eyes. A thrill of anticipation ran through her.

* * *

The morning of the Fourth dawned clear and sunny. Pike pronounced that, according to his leg, the day would stay that way. Shortly after noon, he and Conor saddled their horses and Beau brought the buggy up to the house. He loaded the supper baskets in the box behind the seat, then guided Alina up to her place and handed her rifle to her.

"I'm glad you're wearing my favorite dress," he said for her ears only. With a shy smile, Alina self-consciously smoothed the skirt of the burgundy calico dress. She was not yet used to the love and passion that showed freely on her husband's handsome face when he looked at her. Beau climbed in next to her and they set off, with Sundance running ahead.

Two vacant city blocks on the outskirts of town not far from the Satin Slipper had been turned into fairgrounds for the Fourth of July celebration. Booths were set up along the streets, with vendors selling everything from lemonade and beer to sandwiches and pickles to small American flags. The centers of each block were filled with families who had staked their claims on a space large enough for a blanket. Some had erected tarps over their spot in order to create a little shade on the treeless land.

A large area at the end of one block had been left clear for games and contests. The excited shouts and shrieks of children involved in foot races and tug-o-wars filled the air. An enormous tent had been set up at the end of the other block. The sides were rolled up, and from within came the sounds of various musical instruments being tuned.

Alina and Beau strolled arm in arm along a row of booths, with Conor, Pike, and Sundance following.

"Alina! Beau! Over here!" Katie stood in front of a booth several feet away from them and waved. She was easy to spot in the crowd, for she was wearing an outlandish dress made of red, white, and blue silk. A length of bunting was draped over one shoulder and across her generous bosom, the ends tied in a big bow at her hip. Tiny American flags waved from the hat that rested on her burnished curls. Katie threw her arms around Alina when they drew near.

"Good to see ya, girl! Gents, how the hell are ya?" Katie beamed at the men, who had all removed their hats. "We got cold beer here at our booth. The first one's on me."

"Thank ya, Miss Kate." Pike clapped his hat back on his head and moved over to the booth. "I'll take ya up on that."

Katie held Alina at arm's length. "Just look at ya," she marveled. "What a pretty outfit. Ya look lovely, girl." She tilted her head and scrutinized Alina. "No, more than lovely. Ya look different, almost radiant. What's going on?"

Pike turned from the booth counter and wiped foam off his upper lip. "She's in love, that's what's goin' on. Don't Beau look radiant, too? They been all mushy-eyed over each other for days now."

Katie looked from a blushing Alina to a smiling Beau. "What's this old coot trying to tell me, Beau Parker?"

"Alina and I are married, Katie, really married, here." Beau placed his hand over his heart.

"Ya mean ya're gonna stay on, Alina?" Katie cried.

Alina nodded. "This is my home now, here with my husband." She looked at Beau, her eyes soft with love.

"See what I mean?" Pike exhorted, pointing a finger at Alina. "That's how they been a'lookin' at each other, just like that. Ask Conor if I ain't right."

Katie threw one arm around Beau and the other around Alina. "I'm just so happy for the two of ya I could cry." She squeezed Alina extra hard. "Didn't I tell ya he was a fine man?"

"You did, Katie," Alina agreed with a laugh. "Over and over and over, until I told you not to mention his name again."

Beau raised his eyebrows questioningly.

"After you came calling at the Slipper on New Year's Day, Beau," Alina explained. "Katie didn't miss a chance to tell me how wonderful she thought you were."

"And you didn't believe her?" Beau demanded, a twinkle in his eye.

Alina shrugged. "I do now," she said with a sweet smile.

"That'll do." Beau placed a tender kiss on her lips.

"They been doin' a lot of that, too," Pike complained.

Katie laughed boisterously. "Of course they have. And well they should." She moved from the happy couple to grab a beer from the counter of her booth and handed the mug to Conor. As she glanced over his shoulder, her eyes suddenly narrowed. "Now what's this?" she muttered. All eyes turned to see Madeline Petrie approaching on the arm of an elegantly dressed Donovan Randall. Beau pulled Alina protectively against his side. Sundance sat at her feet and growled a warning.

"My, my, look what we have here," Madeline tittered, spinning her dainty parasol. Her striking military-style gown sported a huge bustle and a small train that dragged in the dust. She eyed Alina's simple calico dress and straw hat with disdain, then caught Katie's forbidding glare.

"Conor O'Rourke," Donovan sneered. "What hole did they finally find you in?"

"Nice to see you again, too, Donovan." Conor leaned against the booth counter. His tone was lazy, but his eyes flashed a warning that Donovan did not miss.

"So this is Randall." Pike looked Donovan up and down in a manner that clearly stated he was not impressed.

Donovan flushed. He turned his haughty, burning gaze to Alina. "It would appear that you are doing quite nicely as a cowboy's wife, Alina dear. Your outfit is very . . . quaint. Obviously you belong here."

"Indeed I do, Donovan." Alina raised her chin with pride. "Somehow, though, I cannot think you do."

"God, no!" Donovan laughed, a harsh sound. "I'm just here for a short visit." He patted Madeline's hand where it rested on his arm. "This lovely lady and I have become close friends."

"A match made in heaven, I'm sure," Alina said, her tone sweet, and met Madeline's hateful look fearlessly.

"Come along, Donovan." Madeline pulled at his sleeve. "Let's leave these people to their . . . beer."

Donovan led her away. Alina looked up at Beau. "Well, I wondered how I'd feel when I saw Donovan again." She willed her stomach to calm down.

"How do you feel?" Beau asked.

"Unsettled." Her troubled gaze followed the finely dressed couple. At that moment, Madeline turned and looked back over her shoulder. Alina caught her breath at the evil hatred she read on the blond woman's face. She had felt that malevolence before. The memory of the night riders flashed to her mind, of the last rider to leave, the one who had stared at them as he slowly rode out of the yard. A warning rushed though her.

"What is it?" Beau followed Alina's gaze and saw Madeline and Donovan disappear into the crowd.

"They're up to something, Beau. I can feel it." Alina turned back to her friends. Her eyes met Conor's. "We must all be very careful," she said quietly.

"And we will, Alina, honey." Katie's cheerful tone broke the somber mood. "But this is a day for fun, and I know that as soon as Richard Petrie gets through with his boring political speech, they're fixing to have the shooting contest. That's something I don't want to miss."

Alina smiled, determined to hide her feelings of dread. But she was distracted all throughout the long afternoon. They found the Freemans and spread their blankets next to that family. Alina won the women's division of the shooting contest with ease. Katie urged her to challenge the winner of the men's contest, but she refused. Her concentration was not what she needed it to be in order to win against real competition. She could not shake the powerful feeling of foreboding.

She kept up the cheerful front through dinner, and through the fireworks, and as they waved good night when the Freemans set off for home with a wagon full of sleepy children. Later, when she and Beau were dancing, he rubbed her back comfortingly.

"What is it, honey?" he asked softly. "You've not been yourself all day, ever since the meeting with Madeline and Donovan."

Alina sighed. "I'm sorry, Beau. I've tried to hide it, but something is wrong. I don't know what. This is more than discomfort over meeting two people I don't care for."

"Do you think it is one of your warnings?"

Alina nodded, her brow lined with worry. "But I don't know about what, or concerning who."

"Would you feel better if we went home?"

"Do you mind?" She looked up at him hopefully.

"When I know that our bed is waiting for us?" Beau's eyes were warm and loving.

Alina laughed. "Beau Parker, you are insatiable."

"When it comes to you, I most definitely am," he assured her, and whirled her off the dance platform.

Conor and Pike had no objection to leaving, and they were soon on their way. An exhausted Sundance rode in the buggy with Beau and Alina, while Pike and Conor rode ahead, each with a lantern in hand to aid the weak light of the quarter moon.

"I hope everything is all right at home," Alina said absentmindedly. Beau did not comment. His mouth was set in a tight line as he encouraged the horse to move as quickly as was safe.

The little party reached the cutoff that led to the Freeman and Parker ranches without incident. When they topped a rise from which they could see the Freeman homestead in daylight, Alina gasped. She could see the homestead now, for it was lit up by the flames that consumed the barn. Several men on horseback were highlighted by the fire.

"Damn!" Beau flicked the reins and urged the horse to a run. He turned the animal into the road that led to their neighbors' home. Conor and Pike raced ahead of them, then suddenly pulled to a halt. A small figure ran toward them.

Beau stopped the buggy and jumped to the ground. A frantic Tanya hurtled herself into his outstretched arms. Alina climbed down and knelt beside them.

"Mr. Parker!" Tanya cried. Her eyes were wide with fright and terror; tears tracked down her cheeks. Her breath came in gasps. "They said . . . they will . . . kill . . . Papa! They put a . . . rope around . . . his neck!" The little girl sobbed against Beau's shirt. "Mama sent . . . me for you!"

Beau briefly met Alina's eyes over Tanya's head, then scooped the girl up in his arms and carried her to the buggy. He grabbed the harness and led the horse off the road and behind a gathering of scrub oak. "Alina, stay with her."

Alina picked up her skirts and followed him. "But I'm the best shot with a rifle," she said stubbornly. She tossed her hat into the buggy and pulled Betsy from the floor, then calmly faced him. "And if we are too late, Cynthia will need me." She took a box of shells from one of the supper baskets and filled the side pocket of her skirt.

Beau nodded reluctantly. "Sit tight in this wagon, honey," he instructed Tanya. "I'm counting on you to keep Sundance safe until we come back for you. Don't let him go, or those bad men might shoot him. Can you do that for me?"

Tanya sniffled and nodded. She wrapped her arms around the dog's neck. "Save my papa," she whispered pleadingly.

"I'll try, honey." Beau placed a gentle hand on the child's shoulder, then pulled his pistol from the holster. He took Alina's hand and led her back to where Conor and Pike waited.

"Kill the lamps," Beau ordered. "Alina and I will work our way over the rise and get in range. Don't shoot until you hear from us. Pike, you ride around the house and cover us from there. Conor, get as close as you can, but stay on the far side of the road and try to cut off their escape. I want these bastards. Now let's go, and pray we're not too late!"

The lamps were extinguished and the shadows of four people, two on horseback, faded into the night.

Beau led Alina down the road until the light from the fire threatened to expose them. He pulled her off to the left and down to the ground. They inched forward on their bellies, then came to a stop. Beau strained to make out the situation in the dancing light. Alina stared in horrified shock.

The barn was entirely engulfed, the flames shooting toward the moon. A rope had been thrown over the crossbar that rose over the opened corral gate. David was seated on a horse under the crossbar, one end of the rope encircling his neck. His hands were tied behind him, and he sagged forward in the saddle, as if he were unconscious. A man standing on the ground held the horse's bridle. A cloth covered the lower half of his face.

A scream split the night. Beau's searching eyes fell on a struggle by the water trough. A large man held Cynthia in his arms, and she struggled to escape him. The man viciously backhanded her across the face. She was thrown to the ground by the force of the blow; the man fell on top of her. Three other riders milled about the yard on nervous mounts.

"We've got to get closer," Beau whispered. Alina blinked and shook her head. Her shock faded as a raging anger flooded her veins with an intensity unlike anything she had ever known. She followed her husband, her rifle grasped firmly in her hand, her jaw clenched in grim determination.

They made their way to the relative cover of David's buckboard. The new cow, wandering in confused freedom near the wagon, started and trotted off. Beau and Alina froze. One of the horsemen turned sharp eyes to examine the area, then apparently decided nothing was there but the cow.

"Let's get on with it!" the horseman shouted.

The man who held Cynthia to the ground dragged her to a kneeling position and grabbed her chin, cruelly forcing her to watch what they did to her husband.

"It's over forty yards, Alina," Beau warned in a whisper. "You have to hit the rope."

"I will," she said with quiet certainty. She rose to her feet behind the wagon, resting Betsy's barrel on the top of the wagon side. Beau stood up next to her to cover her. She sighted down the barrel; the rope was clearly outlined against the flames. Alina closed her eyes. She reached deep into her heart and a strange power filled her. Her eyes opened and she sighted again. Beau held his breath.

One of the riders lifted his hand. The man holding the bridle of the horse on which David sat pulled his pistol from his holster. He aimed it into the night sky.

The rider dropped his arm. Alina squeezed the trigger. The man holding the horse released the bridle and jumped back as he fired his pistol. The horse bolted forward across the yard with David still on its back. The length of severed rope swung from the crossbar.

"What the hell!" one of the riders shouted.

Beau opened fire and dropped the man on foot. Alina swung her rifle to the man who held Cynthia. He looked around, startled, holding Cynthia against his chest. Alina took aim and squeezed the trigger again. The man's hat flew off and he fell back with a shriek of agony, clutching the side of his head with one hand. Cynthia twisted from his grip and crawled out of his reach, then got to her feet and ran after the frightened horse that carried her husband's limp form.

"Let's get out of here!" shouted the rider who seemed to be in command. He turned his horse to the road and spurred it. A shot came from the direction in which he was headed and the man fell from the saddle. His horse continued on down the road, hooves pounding in the night. Alina saw Pike come from behind the Freeman house on foot. She turned her aim to the man she had wounded and was startled to see that he was gone. The two remaining riders rode across the pasture. Beau crossed the yard at a run and took aim at the fleeing horsemen. He fired and noted with satisfaction that one of the riders slumped in the saddle. Beau emptied his pistol, but they disappeared over a hill. He turned back to the scene in the yard.

Conor raced his horse past Beau and dropped from the

saddle as Cynthia and Pike lowered David's body to the ground. Alina and Beau joined them.

Conor whipped a knife from his boot. "That was a hell of a shot, Cousin. Well done," he said while he sawed desperately at the thick rope around David's neck. The last strands parted and he turned to the bonds at David's wrists, finally freeing him. They gently rolled the injured man onto his back.

Cynthia cradled her husband's head in her lap. David's breath rasped through swollen and bloody lips. One eye was puffed and bruised; blood ran from a cut on his forehead. Cynthia smoothed his cheek, tears sliding down her face. "Check on my babies," she pleaded. "They're in the house."

Conor stood. "I'll get Tanya and the buggy." He took off up the road at a run. Beau raced to the house, followed closely by Alina. He grabbed a lighted lamp from the kitchen table as Alina leaned her rifle against the wall by the door.

"David! Lincoln!" he called. "It's Beau Parker. Where are you?" A muffled sound came from the back room. Beau led the way past the curtained entrance to the bedroom, holding the lamp high. David Junior peeked over the top of the mattress. Alina moved around the bed and saw David Junior, Lincoln, and Margarite crowded into the corner, holding tightly to each other, their eyes wide with fright and shock. Margarite whimpered.

"It's all over," Alina said soothingly. She crouched down and held out her arms. "You can come out now."

Lincoln crawled to her and wrapped his arms tightly around her neck. Tears welled in his big eyes. Alina straightened and held the boy to her. "It's all right, honey," she murmured. "Everything is all right now."

Beau set the lamp on the dresser, then stepped around Alina and picked up Margarite. He held his free hand out to David Junior. "You did a good job of protecting your brother and sister, son," he said as the boy slipped his hand into Beau's. "I'm real proud of you." He led the boy to the kitchen. Alina followed with Lincoln in her arms.

"Where's Papa and Mama and Tanya?" David Junior asked in a small, scared voice.

"They're outside. You stay here with Mrs. Parker and I'll go get them." His eyes met Alina's and she nodded. She set Lincoln down on a chair and took Margarite from Beau. He went back outside.

As Cynthia watched anxiously, Beau and Conor carried David into the house and settled him on the bed. They left and joined Pike in the yard.

Cynthia stood at the table in shocked silence. Her face was stark white, her eyes huge and haunted. Her hair had fallen down her back, the neckline of her dress was torn, one cheek was scraped and bleeding, and blood trickled from the corner of her mouth. Alina motioned for David Junior and Tanya to sit down and gave Margarite to Tanya. She went to Cynthia's side and wrapped her arms around her friend's thin shoulders and held her close. Cynthia began to cry. For a minute, the only sound in the kitchen was that of quiet sobbing.

"What's wrong with Mama?" Lincoln asked worriedly.

Cynthia straightened and brushed the tears from her cheeks. She looked down at her son with a weak smile. "Mama's going to be fine."

"But your mouth is bleeding," Tanya anxiously pointed out.

"It's nothing serious. Now I have to tend to your papa. Alina, will you get the fire up and put some water on to boil?"

"Of course." She glanced at the children. Four pairs of fearful eyes were on their mother. Alina pushed Cynthia toward the bedroom. "Go take care of your man. We'll handle things out here."

Cynthia flashed her a grateful smile and disappeared behind the curtain.

"David Junior, please get me some wood. Tanya, wash your sister's face and get her ready for bed. Lincoln, do you know where your mama keeps her clean rags?" The little boy nodded. "Please get me some." The children scurried to do her bidding.

The men returned to the house a half an hour later to find the children in bed and the women keeping vigil at David's bedside. Cynthia had washed her face and put on a fresh dress. Her long hair was pulled back and tied at her neck. The scrape on her cheek had begun to turn purple.

"How is he?" Beau asked quietly.

"He's breathing easier, but he hasn't awakened." Cynthia laid a cool rag on her husband's dark forehead.

Conor came forward. "May I look at him?"

"Do ya know about doctorin'?" Pike asked.

Alina moved out of Conor's way as he approached the bed. He took his hat off and handed it to her. "A little. My mother was a healer." He examined David quickly, running his hands over the man's head and body. "He has a nasty bump on the side of his head here. That's why he's still unconscious. If he doesn't wake up by morning, we'll have to get a doctor out here."

"They beat him before they put him on the horse." Cynthia's voice was dull. "He was knocked into the corral post."

"We killed two of them, Cynthia, but neither was known to us," said Beau. "Did you recognize anyone?"

Cynthia shook her head, not taking her eyes from David's face. "Their faces were covered. But I think the one who had me was Log Carter."

"Are you sure?"

"No," she said sadly.

"It would fit, though," Pike interjected, his rage barely controlled. He gestured toward Cynthia's bruised face. "The bastard, beg pardon, ladies, likes ta beat up on women."

"Well, two of them are dead, and I wounded one," Beau said.

"I'm sure I hit the one that had Cynthia, Beau, but he disappeared," Alina added.

Cynthia nodded in agreement. "He was hit."

"Well, we've done what we can for tonight. The barn is a total loss, but it won't spread to any of the other buildings. Were any animals in there?" Beau twisted his hat in his hands. Soot smudged one of his cheeks.

"The new cow was."

"The cow is safe. She's tied to the fence by the water trough. One of us will take the dead into town tomorrow and make a report to Sheriff Boswell."

"I'll go," Conor offered. "If you don't mind, Cynthia, I'll stay here tonight, in case you need anything. In fact, I'll plan on staying for a few days. You'll be needing some help."

"Thank you," she whispered.

Alina gave her a quick hug. "I'll come by tomorrow to help with the children and the house." Cynthia nodded, her expression wooden. Not knowing what else to say, Alina glanced helplessly at Beau and left the room. Beau and Pike followed her. The ride home was a quiet one.

Chapter Eighteen

The incident at the Freeman ranch caused an uproar in the Laramie Valley. A hastily convened town meeting turned into a shouting match, with some calling for the resignation of the sheriff. Others suggested that Richard Petrie be hanged, or at least burned out.

Petrie was interrogated, and he vehemently denied any knowledge of the burnings and the attempted lynching; he had a solid alibi for the time of each incident. The two dead men had not worked for him, and there was no evidence to contradict his word. No charges were brought against him.

A great number of people showed up for the barn-raising at the Freeman ranch the last week in July, including many who had previously ostracized the family. Alina had asked Bert Johnson about it while they were setting up the tables. Bert had explained that while many folks felt it wasn't right to marry between races, they also felt no one should have to suffer being terrorized in his own home.

Richard Petrie himself had come with several of his hands, including Ross Latham, and had insisted on helping. A subdued Madeline had spent most of the day sitting in her buggy. There was no sign of Log Carter. The new barn had gone up in a day.

An uneasy peace settled over the valley.

One night a few weeks later, Alina stretched between the

cool sheets, delighting in the feel of the soft cotton against her naked body.

"You look like a contented cat," Beau teased from the end of the bed. He hung his shirt on a hook and opened his pants.

"I'm not completely contented yet, husband," Alina cooed, her voice silky with suggestion. "But I do like sleeping naked." She boldly perused Beau's now nude form. "And I like it when you sleep naked."

"And you call me insatiable," he retorted as he took up his hairbrush.

"It's your own fault, Beau Parker. You are simply too magnificent a lover." She sat up against the headboard. The sheet fell down to her waist.

Beau glanced over his shoulder. Alina stared at him, her beautiful eyes shining with love and desire. The hardened tips of her lovely breasts peeked impudently from the curtain of her hair. He felt the familiar tightening in his loins. It seemed he could not get enough of her. Beau faced himself in the mirror as he returned the brush to its place on the dresser. He was a lucky man. The warmth and passion Alina gave him delighted and awed him. He was filled with a rush of love for his young wife. He turned to the bed, fully intent upon proving that love.

Alina scooted over as she pulled the sheet back. "Cynthia is coming tomorrow to show me how to put up those plums we bought last week," she commented. "When I mentioned that you're going to knock out the back wall in Pike's room, she said she would ask David to come with her and help out." Beau laid next to her and took her into his arms. She reveled in the feel of his hard body pressed against hers, of the soft hair of his chest brushing against her breasts.

"We could use the help, but is he up to it?" Beau caressed her back.

She nodded. "Cynthia said he's still sore and a little stiff, but he's much better."

Beau kissed the tip of her nose. "I'm glad to hear that. I

meant to ask you at dinner if you had a nice visit with Cynthia, but I forgot."

Alina brushed a lock of hair off his forehead. "I'm not surprised you forgot. You've been working so hard lately, Beau, trying to keep up with the ranch, and the plans for the house, and that diamond situation. Have you figured out what General McClellan is doing in town?"

Beau shook his head. "He's been meeting with Phil Arnold, though, and I think both of them met with Petrie. There's a rumor that McClellan will act as trustee for the Diamond Company. I sure wish Clarence King could get here."

"No wonder you've had a lot on your mind." Alina smiled and kissed him quickly. "But no more talk of business. Do you remember that marvelous jelly Cynthia brought us last spring?"

Beau nodded.

"She said there's a lot of chokecherry bushes growing along the creek banks, but they won't be ripe for another few weeks. She's going to teach me to make that, too." Alina wrapped one leg over Beau's and slid her foot up and down his calf.

Beau chuckled at her enthusiasm. "You like cooking, don't you?" he marveled. His hand traveled down over the silken curve of her hip.

"I do," Alina admitted. "It's hard work, but I get such a satisfying feeling from it. Maybe it's something primeval, like contributing to the hunt. Does that sound strange?"

Beau nuzzled her hair. "No. I get the same feeling when I finish a piece of furniture, or chop a pile of wood. Like you, I never had to contribute to the immediate survival and comfort of our family until I came out here. It's a good feeling."

Alina's eyes turned sultry. "So is kissing you." She moved her slightly opened lips to his, the tip of her tongue darting to touch him. Beau moaned and opened his mouth for her, one hand wrapping in her scented hair. With a thrill of womanly power, Alina felt his manhood stir to life against her leg. She slipped her hand down between their bodies to stroke his growing length.

Beau caught his breath and rolled her on her back, positioning himself between her thighs. "You have started something now, woman," he warned. His lips moved to her ear, his teeth gently nibbling. He worked his way down her neck and finally fastened his mouth on one tight nipple. Alina shivered with pleasure and opened herself to him. She sighed as Beau eased himself into the haven of her body, and she held him close, joining him on his journey to ecstasy.

"I can't believe he did this!" Richard Petrie slammed the newspaper down on his desk and jumped up from his chair.

Ross Latham stood back, his hat in his hands. "I thought you'd want to know right away."

Madeline hurried into the room, her skirts rustling. "What is it, Father?" she asked worriedly. "I could hear you all the way upstairs."

"That damn Phil Arnold spoke to a reporter from the *Daily Independent.*" Petrie waved at the folded paper and moved from behind the desk to glare out the window.

Madeline snatched up the paper. Her eyes scanned the pages until she found the headlines. "The Great Diamond Fields of America," she read aloud. Her hand fell to her side, clutching the paper, her concerned gaze on her father.

"Damn the man!" Petrie pounded his fist into his other palm. "He promised me more time! I needed more time to persuade these fools to sell to me! Now it's too late."

Madeline glanced at Latham, who shrugged impassively.

"Father, what will you do?" Madeline's fist closed tighter and tighter on the newspaper, crunching it.

"I don't know! If that damn Beau Parker had sold to me after his brother died, I would've had an easier time getting the others to sell! They look up to him for some reason. I wanted to own this whole valley so that no matter where the elds are, I would control access to them. But I still don't now where they are!"

"If the fields are in Colorado or Arizona, like the paper ays they could be, owning this valley won't be of much elp," Latham pointed out.

"I don't believe the fields are that far away," Petrie spat. Remember that I've been there. Oh, we wandered around r four days, and Arnold made us wear those damn blind-lds, but we could not have gone as far south as Arizona. If e fields are in Colorado Territory, they aren't far from the order." His piercing gaze fell on Ross. "Didn't you say IcClellan's private car was attached to the westbound that ft last night?"

Ross nodded. "And Arnold left this morning, but he eaded south to Pueblo. Why would they go in two different irections?"

"To confuse us, to buy time. Who knows?"

"What will you do, Father?" Madeline asked again, her ace pale. She dropped the crumpled paper to the floor.

"I don't know, but I'll damn sure think of something." etrie turned back to the window, his brow wrinkled. "I've ivested fifty thousand dollars in that damned Diamond ompany, and I intend to see a good return on my money. rnold and McClellan had better not be planning to cut me r anyone else out. No one had better cross Richard Petrie."

Madeline stared at her father's back for a moment. So eau Parker had crossed her father, she thought, a fierce etermination evident in the set of her jaw. She turned and ft the room.

Beau whistled loudly and slapped his looped rope against is thigh. The stubborn cow running in front of him grudg-ngly joined the small group of cattle. He waved to Conor, ho was riding the opposite flank of the herd. "That's the nly one in this ravine," he called as he tied his rope to the addle.

Conor lifted a hand in acknowledgment and pulled his horse to a halt. He took his hat off and wiped his forehead as the herd passed him, then replaced his hat and rode to join Beau. "They sure are ornery about going where we want them to."

Beau nodded in agreement. He took a swallow from his canteen and wiped the excess water from his mustache with the back of a gloved hand, then handed the canteen to Conor. He squinted against the glare of the sun. A trail of dust rose in the distance. Beau pulled his field glasses from his saddlebag.

"We've got company," he murmured as he focused the glasses. "Lone rider." Conor put the lid on the canteen and hung it from his saddle horn. His hand moved to rest nonchalantly on the butt of his pistol as his eyes riveted on the approaching horseman.

"Looks like Latham." Beau returned the field glasses to the bag. He crossed his arms over the saddle horn and waited.

Ross Latham kept his horse at an easy lope until he was close, then pulled the animal to a stop. "Parker, O'Rourke."

"What are you doing way out here?" Beau asked.

"Heading to Cheyenne. I saw you from the Pass Road."

"You could have taken the train to Cheyenne," Conor commented.

Latham smiled and patted his horse's neck. "Could have, but I don't care much for trains."

"Why did you want to see me, Latham?" Beau demanded. "Did Petrie send you with another offer for my land? Since the diamond story broke, he's been upping his offers to everyone. If that's why you're here, you're wasting your time."

"I don't work for Petrie any longer."

Beau's eyes narrowed. "Since when?" He took in the bulging roll tied to the back of Latham's saddle and the full saddlebags.

"Since this morning. I was told to do something that didn't sit right with me, so I quit." Latham shrugged.

"I am curious about where you draw the line, Latham. Log beating up a Chinese boy didn't bother you, but you wouldn't let him hurt my wife. How do you feel about kittens?"

An ironic smile twisted Latham's mouth. "I knew that was foolish."

"What about lynching David Freeman?" Conor demanded.

Latham shook his head. "I had nothing to do with that. I was at the Satin Slipper with Delilah that night. Don't know who did it. But I don't know that I would have stopped it if I had been there. If a man can't defend himself," he looked meaningfully at Beau, "or his family, he deserves to die."

Beau stared at him. "What are you trying to say?"

Latham shrugged again. "Nothing. Just that I know the story of another man who didn't defend himself. But it happened a long time ago."

Beau's eyes narrowed as his hand dropped to his gun handle. "It's difficult to defend yourself against a bullet in the back." His voice was low and dangerous. "Did you kill my brother?"

Latham shook his head. "No, Parker, I didn't. But that's not important, not any more." He shifted his weight in his saddle and took up the slack in the reins. "What is important is that you get back to your lovely little wife, *right now.*"

Beau's heart slammed against his ribs. He met Conor's eyes, then forced his horse along side Latham's. "What are you talking about?" he ground out.

"Your wife's a good woman, worthy to stand beside a man. Someone wants to hurt her, and she doesn't deserve it." His voice took on an urgency. "Get home to her, man!"

Beau needed no further encouragement. He kicked the bay to a gallop.

Conor kept an impatient Charlie from following Bay and stared at Latham. "What's your game?" he demanded.

Ross adjusted his hat against the glare of the sun. "Damned if I know. I just don't want to see that woman hurt."

"Thank you for that." Conor allowed his horse to run.

"I did not kill Ambrose Parker!" Latham shouted. Conor raised a hand in acknowledgment.

Latham watched the two riders disappear from view, then turned his horse's head to the south. "Maybe we'll skip Cheyenne and just head for Denver," he muttered.

Alina set the last of the filled jelly jars on the table to cool and wiped her damp forehead with a corner of her apron. Even though she knew there were twelve jars, she counted them again with a sense of satisfaction. Those jars would be hoarded; it was far more work to make chokecherry jelly than anything else she had attempted so far.

"Well, that's done," she remarked to Sundance, who lay on the hearth rug with his head resting on his front paws. She turned back to the sink full of dirty dishes, trying to ignore the uneasy feeling in the pit of her stomach. The feeling had been growing all afternoon. If it was a warning, again, she did not know who it was for. She hoped Conor and Beau returned from the pasture soon.

She glanced out the window above the sink. She had not heard Pike's hammer for some time now. Perhaps he was already finished with the metal bar he was forging to use as a branding iron. They had finally decided on the design for a brand the night before. Alina was curious to see if Pike really could force the metal into the image of a rose. She poured hot water into the washbasin. She would check on Pike as soon as the dishes were clean. If she hurried, she'd have time for a bath before dinner.

A few minutes later, heavy footsteps reverberated on the porch. It was not the sound of Pike's unusual gait, and Alina had not heard Beau and Conor return. Sundance growled, low in his throat. A warning screamed in her head. Her heart thumped in her chest as the latch lifted. She glanced over her shoulder at the rifles above the fireplace just as the door was pushed open with enough force to slam it against the wall. Alina turned to face Log Carter.

"Well, if it ain't Mrs. Nosy Britches," he sneered. Alina reached for a towel, wondering desperately what she could use for a weapon.

"You are not welcome here," she stated, her voice harsh.

"Not welcome?" Carter's ugly face twisted in a hate-filled snarl. His bulbous nose was still bent from the breaking Beau had given it in the fistfight. A dirty bandana under his hat covered his right ear.

Sundance growled again as he rose and came over to stand by his mistress, his ears flattened against his head.

"I suggest you leave immediately, Mr. Carter. Pike is in the barn, and my husband and my cousin are expected at any minute." Alina stared at him fearlessly. "I'm certain that you don't want to meet my husband again."

Carter stepped toward her. "Yeah, that one-legged old geezer is in the barn, all right." Alina's stomach knotted in fear. What had Carter done to Pike? "And you're wrong about me not wantin' to meet up with yer man. I got a score to settle with Beau Parker. He broke my nose and shot off my ear."

"So it *was* you that night. If I hadn't been so concerned about hitting Cynthia, I would have put that bullet between your eyes and done the whole world a favor."

Carter's eyes narrowed in suspicion. "Are you tellin' me that you're the one what took my ear?"

Alina's mouth curved into a grim smile. "I'll do more than that if you don't leave my house this minute." Sundance growled more ferociously.

Carter whipped his gun from the holster and pointed it at Sundance. "And I'll kill yer dog if you don't lock him up."

Alina blinked, her throat dry with fear. She backed

around the stove to the bedroom door. "Come, Sundance," she urged. The dog reluctantly obeyed, glancing back at Carter. Alina pulled the door closed. She stepped closer to the stove. Sundance whined and scratched at the door. Suddenly, with two hands, Alina grabbed the empty cast iron skillet that sat on the stove. She whirled and threw it with all her strength.

Carter bellowed in pain as the skillet bounced off the side of his head. He staggered against the counter. Alina darted toward the fireplace. Carter shook his head and closed the distance between them in two quick strides. He caught her just as she reached for her rifle. "You bitch," he grunted as he wrestled her to the door. "We'll just go visit yer old friend in the barn." Sundance howled.

Carter dragged Alina across the yard; she could not break away from his grasp. He pulled the barn door open and forced her inside, pushing her to the ground.

Her eyes adjusted to the late afternoon light in the dim building. A skinny young man with bad skin leaned carelessly against the side of a stall. Another man, this one stocky and not so young, came from the shadows by the back door. A horse nickered. Alina's frantic gaze fell on a still form in the center of the aisle between the stalls.

"My God!" she cried. "Pike!" She lifted her skirts and got to her feet, then ran to her friend, dropping to her knees beside him. Pike was lying on his stomach, his head turned to one side. He moaned but did not move. What little Alina could see of his face was bruised and bloody. His breathing was raspy and shallow.

"What're we gonna do now, Carter?" whined the youth at the stall. "I thought we was just supposed ta fire the barn."

"Wilbur's right, Carter. Let's do it and ride." The stocky man came forward. "We wasted enough time with the old man. I've never met Parker, but I've heard enough about him to know that I don't want to meet him. Let's get out of here." He stepped around Alina and Pike and moved toward the door.

"First I've got a score to settle with this bitch. The boss won't care what I do to her." Carter dragged Alina to her feet and over to the ladder to the hay loft. "Climb," he ordered, his foul breath washing over her face.

A wave of nausea rolled through Alina's stomach. "No." She faced him unflinchingly.

"What're you gonna do, Carter?" Wilbur asked. "If you're gonna have her, I'll have her, too." He licked his lips as his cruel eyes raked Alina's slender form. "We're in this together."

"If there's anythin' left when I'm done, you can have it." Carter pushed at Alina. "I told you to get up the ladder."

"There'll be no rape," the older man said from the door, his voice harsh. "We're to fire the barn, and that is what we'll do."

Without warning, Carter pulled his pistol, spun on his heel, and fired. Alina watched with horror as her defender clutched at the wound in his chest and slumped to the ground. "I'm goddam sick of folks tellin' me what to do." Carter turned back to Alina and cocked the gun again. "If you don't get up that ladder, I'll put the next one in the old man's head."

Alina reluctantly gathered her skirts in one hand. Wilbur moved under the ladder and watched as she climbed, reaching out with a dirty hand to caress her exposed calf. She kicked at him and almost lost her balance.

"Leave her be," warned Carter as he started up after Alina. "You'll have yer chance."

Alina topped the ladder and stepped onto the hay-strewn shelf. Her eyes frantically searched for any kind of weapon. Had Beau left the pitchfork up here? She could not see it. Her eyes closed. *Please, Beau, come!* Her mind reached out to him.

Carter grunted behind her as he pulled himself up the last rung of the ladder. Alina turned to face him and backed away.

He returned his pistol to the holster, then took his hat off and threw it to the ground below. The side of his face where the skillet had hit was red and swollen.

Wilbur started up the ladder. "Can I watch?" he pleaded.

Carter didn't answer him, nor did he take his eyes off Alina. "Get out of those clothes," he ordered, a wicked leer on his face. He rubbed his crotch with obscene abandon.

Out of the corner of her eye, Alina saw Wilbur's head pop up over the edge of the loft. "No," she said, her voice ringing with determination. "I'll not help you do this. I'll fight you until the breath is gone from my body."

"Suits me fine." Carter lurched for her. Alina ducked away from him, but there was nowhere to go.

Carter grabbed for her again and caught her arm. He jerked her to him. "We'll finish everything now," he promised. One huge hand grasped the collar of her blouse and with a swift motion, tore the garment to the waist. Alina bit her lip to keep from screaming. She'd die before she'd let this man see her fear. She lashed out with her nails and raked his face as her foot flew out, connecting with his shin.

Wilbur laughed. "Do you need some help, Carter?"

"Goddam it!" Carter swore. He backhanded Alina across the face and knocked her against the wall. She moaned and slipped to the floor. Carter turned and kicked Wilbur in the head. "And you shut yer mouth!" The young man's hat flew to the ground below as he sagged against the ladder.

Alina's head spun and she tasted blood. She felt Carter standing over her. She scrambled to her feet and pushed her hair out of her eyes.

"Beau will kill you," she promised breathlessly, her tone heavy with loathing. Her breasts heaved through the tattered remnants of her blouse, protected only by the thin material of her camisole.

Carter spat. "No, missy, I'll kill him. Then the two of you'll always be together." His hand bit painfully into her shoulder and he jerked her into a cruel embrace. He fell forward, carrying her with him onto a pile of hay, and landed heavily on top of her. He pulled viciously at her hair, holding her head in place. He lowered his mouth to the soft skin of her breast and bit her. Alina could not stop herself from crying out. Carter fumbled with her skirt, trying to raise it above her knees. She struggled against him; one hand searched desperately for his pistol.

Her hand found the butt of his gun. She forced the hammer back and tried to pull the weapon far enough from the holster so that she could reach the trigger. The holster was not tied at Carter's thigh; the leather sheath shifted up between them. The gun slipped out further. She felt his hand groping between her legs. Alina twisted to Carter's side and forced her wrist to bend enough to get her finger in the trigger.

"Hold still, damn you!" Carter looked at her set face. He fell silent; his glazed eyes registered a dawning confusion. "What the hell are you doing?" he shouted, his voice tight with sudden fear. He lifted off her and reached for his gun. Alina closed her eyes and squeezed the trigger. The gunshot echoed through the barn.

"She shot me!" Carter screamed. He fell back on her, grabbing his thigh. Alina struggled to get out from under him, but she could not escape. His free hand found her throat. "You bitch!" he rasped. "You'll die now, and that's for sure!"

"No!" Wilbur croaked from his position on the ladder. "You said I could have her!"

Carter tightened his hold on Alina's throat. She clawed at his hand, desperate for air. Wilbur threw himself on top of them, trying to force Carter aside. He pried the larger man's hand from Alina's neck. She pulled herself from under the struggling men and crawled toward the ladder, dragging blessed air into her burning lungs. Wilbur grabbed at her ankle. She rolled and kicked at him with her free foot, forcing him to release her.

"Goddam!" he cried. "She's a wildcat!"

Alina struggled to her feet and reached the top of the

ladder. She heard the sound of a gun being cocked. She whirled.

Carter held his gun out in a shaking hand. Her calm, determined eyes met his enraged ones.

"No!" cried Wilbur as Carter squeezed the trigger. Alina felt something burn into her side. Without a sound, she fell back out of the loft to the ground below. There was a snapping sound. She lay still.

Wilbur crawled to the edge and peered over. Alina lay on the ground, one arm flung out. Her skirt was up around her knees; her head tilted to one side. Blood spread over her side.

"You killed her, Carter," the youth said mournfully. "You killed her before I had her."

"Get me down that damned ladder or I'll kill you, too," Carter rasped.

Wilbur helped him struggle down the ladder. "Get the horses," Carter ordered. Wilbur snatched his hat from the ground and ran to obey. The sound of frenzied barking came from the cabin.

Carter stumbled over to lift a lantern from its hook on the wall and sank to a sitting position with a groan. Blood ran down his leg from the bullet wound. He tore the filthy bandana from his head and tied the material around his thigh. He leaned back against the wall. Sweat rolled off his face as he pulled a match from his vest pocket and lit it with a flick of his thumbnail. He touched the flame to the wick.

Wilbur came to the door of the barn leading three horses.

"Throw this into the loft and get me on my horse," Carter commanded. Wilbur took the lantern and flung it up into the hay. The fire fed greedily on the dry grasses as it raced along the length of the loft. The horse in the stall whinnied nervously and stomped its foot.

Wilbur draped Log's arm around his shoulders and helped him up. As they worked their way past Alina's motionless body, Carter struck out brutally with a booted foot, striking her bloody side. Wilbur pushed the big man up into his saddle and led the animals away from the barn door. He closed the door and barred it, then leapt into the saddle. "What about ol' Harry's horse?" he asked over the growing roar of the flames.

"Leave it," Carter gasped. The two horsemen headed toward the bridge.

Beau and Conor urged their tiring mounts across the last stretch of pasture and over the fence to the road that led to the homestead. As they rounded the stand of pines, they saw two men on horseback cross the bridge and come toward them at a run. One of the men fired. Conor's pistol appeared in his hand; a flame seemed to jump from the barrel. The rider who had fired fell from his saddle; his horse shied and trotted off toward the trees.

The other rider was a big man. "Log Carter," Beau said to himself with grim satisfaction. Carter fired his pistol twice in rapid succession. The shots were wild.

Beau looped the reins loosely around the saddle horn and slipped his rifle from its case with practiced ease. Carter shot again and missed again. Beau attuned himself to the rhythm of Bay's gallop, then took careful aim. He fired once, then once more. The big man fell to the ground. His horse continued on down the road and gradually slowed to a walk.

Beau was out of the saddle before Bay came to a complete stop. He stood over the fallen man, his rifle ready.

Carter was on his back, his breath wheezing through the holes in his chest. The sun dipped behind the mountains, casting the three men into shadow.

"She said . . . ya'd kill me," Carter said hoarsely. He coughed. Blood trickled from the corner of his mouth. A smirk twisted his ugly features. "But I kilt her first, Parker."

The blood drained from Beau's face. He vaulted back into the saddle and raced toward the homestead, Conor right behind him. They pounded across the bridge and into the yard.

Frantic barking sounded from the cabin; the terrified scream of a horse came from the barn.

"Alina!" Beau cried. He flew from his saddle up the steps and into the cabin. "Alina!" He opened the door to his bedroom, fearful of what he might find. Sundance tore out of the room, then through the front door and across the yard to the barn. Beau followed him.

Conor was at the barn door. He heaved the bar out of the brackets, then helped Beau pull the massive door open. Smoke billowed out. The roof was in flames and in danger of collapsing at any moment. Both men pulled their neckerchiefs over their noses and ventured into the barn. Beau's desperate gaze fell on Alina's still body. With a cry of despair, he fell on one knee beside her and took her up into his arms. He ran back outside with her and laid her gently on the ground by the water trough. He jerked the cloth from his face. "Alina." His voice was an agonized whisper. He laid a finger on her bruised throat. His shoulders sagged in relief when he found a weak pulse.

"Beau!" Conor's cry came from within the barn. Beau tore his eyes from his wife's battered face and ran back to the barn. Conor was just inside the door, dragging Pike. Beau grabbed one of Pike's arms and they pulled him across the yard and laid him next to Alina.

"She's alive," Beau assured Conor in response to that man's anguished look. Sundance whined and licked Alina's face, then Pike's. He laid down between them and rested his head on Pike's chest. Pike moaned, but his eyes did not open.

Conor whipped his vest off. "There's another man in there, just to the right of the door!" he shouted as he ran back toward the barn. "I'm going after the horse!" Beau followed him.

Beau found the man slumped on the ground. He grabbed the man's hands and pulled him out the door, but he knew the man was dead. He looked up to see Conor disappear into the smoke. Beau pulled the dead man a short distance away, then ran back to the barn. "Conor!" He could not see through the smoke. The ceiling shifted ominously. "Conor!"

Conor opened the stall door. "Come on, Lucy!" The terrified horse reared. Conor threw his vest over the animal's eyes and grabbed the halter. A flaming section of the hay loft fell, blocking their escape through the front door. Conor turned his watering eyes to the barred back door; it was their only hope.

He urged the horse to follow him. He forced the bar from the brackets with one hand and shoved the door open, then whipped his vest from Lucy's head as the mare thundered past him. Conor raced after the horse. Several yards from the barn he fell on his face, breathing deeply of the sweet evening air.

"Conor!" Beau's frantic voice reached him. Conor stumbled to his feet and ran around the side of the barn. He noticed that the chickens had fled their coop.

Beau's soot-darkened face lit up with relief when he saw Conor, then he dropped his eyes to Alina. He moaned in agonized fury at the thought of Carter touching her, hurting her. He sank to the ground beside her and gathered her in his arms, awkwardly pulling the sides of the torn blouse over her exposed camisole.

The sound of approaching hoofbeats reached their ears a moment before David Freeman raced into the yard and jumped from his horse. David looked helplessly at Beau and Alina, then motioned to Conor. The flames licked along the edge of the wagon shelter. David and Conor pulled the buggy to safety, then the wagon, with the help of David's horse.

Conor fell to his knees at Pike's feet and sat back on his heels. David stood behind him. Beau tenderly brushed the fine hair back from Alina's bruised forehead with a shaking hand as he unconsciously rocked her limp form. He glanced at Pike's still body, then stared at his burning barn with glazed eyes, the firelight dancing on his stunned and haunted features.

Chapter Nineteen

"Where is the doctor, for God's sake?" Beau raised despairing eyes to Cynthia. He sat on a chair next to his bed.

"I'm sure he'll be here soon." She glanced at Conor, who stood by the bedroom door. "I'll check on Pike," she said softly.

Beau inched the chair closer to the bed. With Cynthia's help, he had removed Alina's clothes. He had sponged her body and wrapped a bandage around her ribs. The bedclothes covered her up to her collarbone, with one arm lying on the covers. Beau tenderly took her hand in his. He caressed the soft skin while he looked over her bruised face. The lamplight showed every detail.

The ugly purpling marred the right side of her forehead and curled around one eye. One side of her mouth was swollen, and another bruise spread its color along her jaw. Her long lashes rested on cheeks that were deathly pale. Her breathing was shallow and faint. He glanced at Conor, then his eyes widened with hope at the sound of an approaching horse.

Conor ran to open the door. Sam Trudeau stood on the porch, his eyes narrowed as he stared at the smoking remains of the barn.

"Sam." Conor was disappointed. "We were expecting the doctor."

Sam entered the cabin. "Doc's on his way. Howdy, Mrs. Freeman." He took off his hat and nodded at Cynthia.

"Hello, Deputy."

"Where's the doctor, Sam?" Beau's strained voice came from the bedroom.

"He's not far behind me, Beau." Sam crossed the room and stood at the foot of Pike's bed. "He's in his buggy, so it'll take a little longer for him to get here."

"We moved Pike's bed out here, where we can keep an eye on him," Cynthia explained needlessly. "My young'uns are asleep in the back bedroom." She gestured toward the closed door to Pike's room. "Did you see David?"

Sam nodded. "That's how I knew to come. David's horse was a bit winded, so he's taking the return trip slower." Sam's eyes fell on Pike's face, his mouth tightening in a grim line. "Is he bad hurt?"

Cynthia nodded, her eyes filling with tears. "They both are," she whispered. "Neither one has awakened."

Sam shook his head and stepped into the doorway to Beau's bedroom. His eyes widened at the sight of Alina's face.

"I'm glad you killed the bastards, Beau." Sam's voice shook with anger. "What kind of a man could do that to a woman?" He twisted his hat in his hands. "I found Log Carter out there on the road, just like David said I would. I don't know the young fool that was with him. I'll borrow your wagon and haul them into town in the morning." He looked at his silent friend. "Can you tell me what happened?"

Beau shrugged and brushed one hand over his bloodshot eyes. "Latham came out to the pasture where Conor and I were working the herd. He warned us to get home."

"*Latham* warned you?"

"Yeah, surprised the hell out of me, too. Said he had quit Petrie, and that he didn't want anything to happen to Alina. We stopped Carter and the kid from leaving, then found Alina and Pike locked in the barn, half dead, the barn on ire. Another man was there, too. One of them, I think, but he'd been shot dead. He's laid out by the woodpile. None of us knew him."

Cynthia slipped around Sam and handed him a steaming cup of coffee, which he accepted with a nod of thanks. She offered another cup to Beau, but he refused it with a shake of his head. She gave him a worried look, then left the room as quietly as she had entered.

"I want Petrie, Sam." Beau's voice was cold and hard.

"I know. So do I. The sheriff is in Cheyenne until next week, so I'll be handling the case for now. I'll talk to Petrie in the morning. You can come with me."

"It'll depend on Alina. I may not want to leave her." The ound of an approaching buggy reached their ears. Beau's houlders slumped with relief.

Doctor Benjamin Adams bustled in from the porch, with David right behind him. The doctor was a kindly man with a bushy white mustache, wire-rimmed spectacles, and a businesslike air.

"Let me see both patients, then I'll decide who needs ending first." He set his bag and hat on the kitchen table and took off his coat. His sharp eyes fell on Cynthia.

"Hello, Mrs. Freeman. I'll bet you have plenty of hot water ready for me, don't you?"

Cynthia smiled weakly. "Yes, Doctor, I do."

The doctor washed his hands, then moved to Pike's side. After a quick examination, he washed his hands again. "Who saw to him initially?" the doctor asked.

"I did." Conor spoke from where he leaned against the wall by the front door.

The doctor nodded in approval. "Good job, son." He went into the bedroom. Beau stood and pulled the chair out of the way. The doctor listened to Alina's heart and checked her pulse, then looked in one eye.

"A bullet creased her side, and I think her right leg is broken," Beau said.

Dr. Adams nodded. "I'll treat her first. Mrs. Freeman,

please bring my bag, and I will need your assistance," he called.

Cynthia left David's side, grabbed the bag from the table, and hurried into the bedroom.

"I'll help," Beau protested.

"No, young man, you won't. You will have a stiff drink and keep an eye on Mr. Pike. If his breathing changes or stops, call me. Now go." Beau reluctantly left the room.

A half an hour later the bedroom door opened. "Please come here, Mr. Parker," the doctor requested. Beau quickly crossed the room and moved to the side of the bed.

"Your wife is badly injured," the doctor began gently. "Her right leg is indeed broken, just above the ankle. Although the break isn't bad, it will take about six weeks for the bone to mend. A bullet creased her ribs, but it's not serious. There are bruises on her legs and arms, indeed, all over her body. This one," he pulled the sheet down to expose the top swell of Alina's right breast, "was caused by a bite. She was not violated, although I think that was someone's intention. Someone also tried to strangle her, which accounts for the bruises on her throat. But the most serious injury is to her head."

The doctor pointed to the bruise on Alina's forehead. "She was struck with something, or fell some distance. She has a concussion, and perhaps other internal injuries."

Beau's jaw clenched. It was as if he could feel each of Alina's injuries in his own body as the doctor described them. "Will she live?" he asked quietly.

"I think so." Dr. Adams worked a finger behind one of his lenses and rubbed his eye. "I've done all I know to do for now. I must see to Mr. Pike."

"Dying was too easy for Carter," Beau muttered as he resumed his seat at Alina's side. "Damn the man to hell!"

"I'm sure that's where he is," Conor said from the door. Helpless rage flashed in his blue eyes.

The doctor stitched a long gash in Pike's scalp and checked the bandage Conor had wrapped around his ribs.

After dressing the rest of the many bruises and cuts that covered Pike's body, he repacked his medical bag, his old shoulders rounded with fatigue and dejection.

"Don't be alarmed if both of them cough a lot during the next few days. I'm sure there was some smoke inhalation, but because they were on the ground, it isn't as bad as it could have been." He buckled the leather bag. "I suggest you pray for your friends," he said somberly as he put his hat on. "I'll be back tomorrow afternoon."

"Thank you, Doctor." Conor escorted the gentleman to his buggy. "Can we settle up with you then?"

"Of course, young man. Goodnight." The doctor shook the reins against his horse's back and the buggy rolled away.

David stepped out onto the porch. "If there's nothing else I can do, I'll take the young'uns home."

"No, no, go on home." Conor clapped David on the shoulder. "We can't thank you enough for your help. I've been meaning to ask: how did you know to come?"

"We heard gunshots coming from the road, so I hightailed it up here. When Cynthia saw the smoke from the fire, she packed up the children and followed."

"Thank you for going for the doc." Conor held out his hand.

"You're surely welcome." David grasped Conor's hand. His white teeth flashed in a tired smile.

Conor and Sam carried sleepy children to the Freeman's wagon. When the children were settled on quilts and David's horse was tied to the back of the wagon, Cynthia turned to Conor.

"You're sure there's nothing more I can do tonight?" She laid a gentle hand on his arm.

Conor shook his head and patted her hand. "Just pray."

Cynthia squeezed his arm. "I will. I'll come in the morning."

"Thank you." Conor waved as the wagon pulled away. He raised his weary eyes to the star-studded heavens and said a prayer himself before he followed Sam back inside.

* * *

Beau leaned forward in his chair, his head resting next to Alina's thigh. His hand covered her small one. Through the night he dozed fitfully, coming fully awake every now and then to stare hopefully at her face, to ensure that her breasts still rose and fell with her breathing. He would stroke her hand and her brow, whispering words of love and encouragement to her, sometimes begging her to wake up. He tried to ignore the tearing guilt that clawed at his heart. *I didn't protect her. I didn't keep her safe. I promised her I would and I didn't.*

The early morning light was stealing in around the curtains when he felt her hand move. He was instantly awake. Alina moaned.

Beau rubbed her hand. "I'm here, honey," he murmured. "Alina, I'm here."

Alina's brow wrinkled. Her head rolled to one side as her eyes fluttered open. Her fingers tightened on his. "Beau." Her voice was a raspy whisper. Her free hand moved to her throat, and she grimaced in pain.

"Ah, honey, I'm so glad to see you awake." Beau brought her hand to his lips.

"Water, please," Alina croaked. She coughed weakly.

"I have some right here." Beau jumped up from the chair. He stuck his head out the bedroom door. "She's awake!" he whispered jubilantly, his eye on Pike's sleeping form. Conor and Sam crowded to the doorway. Beau filled a mug from a small pitcher on the dresser. He sat on the edge of the bed and slipped an arm under her shoulders as he guided the mug to her swollen lips. She drank eagerly, until the mug was almost empty, then she fell back against his arm.

Beau set the mug on the table and settled her on the pillows, but he did not move from her side. He brushed fine curls away from her forehead.

"They hurt Pike," she rasped, her eyes clouded with worry.

"I know, honey. He's all right. The doctor bandaged him

up and he'll be clumping around here before you know it, telling us all what to do."

Alina's eyes closed and her lips curved at the ends. She moaned again, softly. Her head tossed restlessly on the pillow and finally her eyes opened, a wild look in their blue depths. "It was Log Carter, Beau." She clutched at his arm. "You have to get him."

"Shh, shh," Beau soothed. "We got him, Alina, Conor and I. He's dead. He can't hurt you, or anyone else, ever again."

Alina's frantic eyes met his, then softened and closed. She relaxed against the pillows. "I hit him with the frying pan. And shot him with his own gun."

Beau smiled and shook his head in wonder. "I'm sure you did." He trailed gentle fingers over her brow. "How did your head get hurt, Alina? Do you remember?"

She wrinkled her forehead in concentration. "I don't know," she whispered. "He hit me. And he shot me, Beau. I fell from the loft. I don't remember anything after that." She looked at him. "He was going to have me, Beau." Her eyes filled with tears. "But I wouldn't let him." She shook her head. "I wouldn't let him. Only you can have me."

Beau gently gathered her into his arms. "Shh, honey," he crooned. He stroked her hair. "I should have been there." The words came out in an agonized whisper. His tormented eyes met Conor's.

"But you came. You're here now." Alina's eyes fluttered closed. "I'm so tired." Her voice faded.

"Then sleep, my love." Beau laid her back on the pillows and pulled the blankets over her shoulders.

"Be sure someone waters my rosebush, Beau," she whispered.

Beau nodded and placed a soft kiss on her cheek. The mention of the rosebush brought a fresh wave of pain to his already burdened heart. He stared down at her for a long time, then quietly left the room, pulling the door closed behind him.

He ran a hand over his whisker-roughened chin as he stood by the stove.

"How is she?" Pike's old voice came weakly from the bed. Beau moved to his side.

"She's injured, Pike, but she's alive. She just woke up."

The older man's eyes teared. "I'm damned sorry, Beau. They ambushed me when I went inta the barn. Had no idea they was there."

Beau sat down on a chair that had been pulled next to the bed. "Don't blame yourself, old friend. They did quite a job on you, too. Alina will get better, which is what you need to do."

Pike grabbed Beau's hand and clung to it. "I got ta know, Beau. Did the bastards rape her?" He coughed.

"No, Pike, they didn't," Beau assured him.

Pike's eyes closed with relief.

"Alina shot Log with his own gun," Beau added.

A smile curved Pike's battered mouth. "That don't surprise me. Did she kill him?"

"I did."

Pike nodded in satisfaction. "Good." His grip on Beau's hand tightened. He opened his eyes and fixed his intense gaze on Beau. "Ya know I'd die for her, don't ya?"

"I know. Please don't blame yourself. Just rest now. We'll see what we can find for breakfast." Beau stood and moved to the stove.

"Guess I'll have ta trust your cookin'. Smells like ya're burnin' somethin' already." Pike's voice was weary.

"They fired the barn, Pike, with you and Alina inside. It was a close call." Conor spoke from the table.

"Damn!" Pike's startled eyes flew to Conor. "Lucy was in there."

"I got her out. The barn is gone, though."

"Damn," Pike repeated. "Guess we'll have ta have another barn-raisin'. Well, howdy, Sam. Didn't see ya standing there."

"Good to see you, Pike. I'm glad you're still with us." Sam

stepped out on the porch at the sound of an approaching horse. "You're up early, Mrs. Freeman," he called as Cynthia pulled her horse to a stop. She rode astride, her skirt covering the horse's flanks.

"I thought you could use some breakfast." Sam helped her to the ground. "If you'll hand me that sack that's tied there behind the saddle, I'll get to cooking." Cynthia smoothed her skirt as she spoke. "Are they awake?"

Sam nodded. "I think Mrs. Parker is sleeping again, but Pike's talking up a storm." He handed her the sack.

"That's a good sign," Cynthia said with a smile as she stepped through the door. "Good morning, gentlemen." She placed her bundle on the counter and took her gloves off.

"Thank you for coming, Cynthia." Beau's voice was strained. He turned to Sam. "Since Alina is no longer unconscious and Cynthia is here, I'd like to go with you to Petrie's."

"You bet," responded Sam. "Conor, what about you?"

"I'll stay here and keep an eye on things."

Sam nodded and reached for his hat. "Let's go."

"You'll go right after you eat," Cynthia firmly interjected. "And I'll have no argument. I know you and Conor had no supper, Beau. By the time you get the wagon hitched up, I'll have something ready."

"Yes, ma'am," Sam said with a laugh. "She's right, Beau. Let's see to the wagon."

"I'll help," Conor offered. The three men left the cabin.

"I'm telling you, I had nothing to do with it!" Richard Petrie shouted as he rose from his chair and leaned his weight on hands that were braced on his desk. "I don't wage battle on women and one-legged old men!"

"Well, Log Carter did, and he was working for you," Sam snapped.

"I haven't seen Carter since the Fourth of July." Petrie moved around his desk. "I suspect he had something to do with that incident at the Freeman ranch, but if he did, it wasn't by my order, and I've not seen him since."

"Why do you suspect he was involved?" Sam asked.

"Because he disappeared." Petrie leaned back against the front of his desk and crossed his arms over his chest. "As I've told you each time you've questioned me, Deputy, I'm not behind these acts of terrorism. I know everything points to me, but I swear I know nothing about them." One forefinger stabbed the air in Sam's direction. "And even if you don't believe me, which I suspect is the case, you have no proof."

"How did Ross Latham know to warn me?" Beau demanded.

Petrie shrugged. "Damned if I know. He collected his pay yesterday and rode out."

Sam turned his hat in his hands. "I want to talk to your men."

"I will instruct them to cooperate fully," Petrie said as he straightened.

Beau stepped over in front of Richard Petrie. "If this leads back to you, Petrie, I'll kill you."

Petrie flushed. "Don't threaten me, Parker."

"It's no threat. It's a promise." He stormed from the room, passing a startled Madeline in the hallway. She backed against the wall and watched Beau and the deputy leave, her eyes wide and worried, her hand at her throat.

Dr. Adams closed his bag. "They are both much improved," he said with satisfaction. "Mrs. Parker is young and healthy, and Mr. Pike there is just plain stubborn." He gestured toward Pike, who was wide awake and propped up on numerous pillows, some with lace decorations. Katie Davenport was seated on the chair by his head. "Barring any unforeseen complications, they both should pull through," the doctor continued. "I'll stop by again tomorrow, just to be on the safe side."

"Thank you for coming, Doctor." A grim-faced Beau

stood in the doorway of his bedroom. "I appreciate it more than you know."

"Thanks for the ride out, Doc," Katie called.

Dr. Adams waved and stepped out onto the porch. No one spoke until the doctor's buggy pulled away.

"I guess I'll get on home, too," said Cynthia as she untied the apron at her waist. "I'm sure David's had his hands full with those children all day."

"I'll saddle your horse," Conor offered, and headed out the door.

Cynthia walked over to gaze affectionately down at Pike. "You certainly look comfortable," she teased.

Pike rolled his eyes. "I told ya these frilly pillows would be bad for my image, Kate," he complained. "And they smell all sweet, too."

"I knew ya'll didn't have enough bedding for a hospital, Pike. I'da brought more if Doc's buggy had been bigger."

"Are ya sure Alina has enough?" Pike asked. "Ya could give her some of these here."

"Alina has plenty," Katie said firmly as she stood up. She smoothed the skirt of her surprisingly simple dress. "Why don't ya show me what ya made up for supper, Cynthia? It smells so good. It sure was nice of ya to come and help out like this, when ya got a passel of young'uns at home." The two women moved over to the counter.

"I was glad to do it. Alina was such a help to me when we had our troubles last month." Cynthia glanced worriedly at Pike. "I hope this is the end of these problems, with Carter dead."

Katie nodded in grim agreement. "I hope so, too. Well, it looks like ya made a stew. I can't hardly mess that up, now can I?" Her self-deprecating laughter filled the room.

"I'll say goodbye to Alina," Cynthia said as she ducked around Beau. She approached the bed and sat gingerly on the edge. Alina's eyes drifted opened. Cynthia bit her lip and tried to keep the outrage and concern she felt at the sight of her friend's face from showing on her own features. She took Alina's hand in hers.

"I'm going home now," Cynthia said softly. "Katie is here, and she's going to stay for a few days to help out. I'll come by every day, also. We don't want you worrying about anything except getting better."

Alina managed a weak smile. "Thank you," she whispered. She squeezed Cynthia's hand. "I treasure your friendship."

Cynthia blinked suddenly teary eyes. "And I yours." She leaned forward and kissed Alina's forehead. "You rest and heal, and I'll see you tomorrow."

Alina nodded wearily and closed her eyes. Cynthia tiptoed from the room. She pinched Pike's toe as she passed the foot of his bed. "Katie better not tell me that you didn't eat when I get here tomorrow," she warned.

"No, ma'am." Pike turned his head to face Conor, who had just stepped back into the cabin. "I think there's too many women here, a'tellin' us what ta do."

"They are bossy," Conor agreed with a grin.

"Thanks for your help, Cynthia," Beau said brusquely. He backed into the bedroom and closed the door.

Cynthia's brow furrowed with worry.

"Don't pay him no mind," Katie soothed as she draped an arm around Cynthia's shoulders. The two women walked out onto the porch. "He just needs some time. It's hard on a man when his loved ones are attacked and he can't stop it."

"I know. David was real upset for a time after what happened to us, too. I've just never seen Beau like this." She hugged Katie and pulled on her riding gloves. "I'm real glad you'll be here."

Katie nodded. "This'll work out just fine. Conor gave me his bed and stretched a tarp over the opening where part of that one wall is still tore down. We'll make do, especially if ya come over and give a hand with the cooking. That's one thing I'm not too good at."

Cynthia stepped from the porch into the stirrup and

swung gracefully into the saddle. "I'll see you tomorrow." The horse trotted away. Katie waved after her, then went back inside.

"Lord Almighty, that dog is on the bed again," she said, her hands on her hips.

"And that's where he'll stay, woman." Pike shifted his leg so that Sundance had more room. The dog rested his head on Pike's calf.

Katie threw her hands up. "I'm not gonna argue with ya." Her eyes fell on Conor. He was slumped in a chair at the table.

"Conor O'Rourke, you look done in." Katie pointed toward her bedroom. "Get on in there and rest up before supper. Go on, now. There ain't nothing that needs doing right now, and besides, we gotta keep it quiet around here so these ailing folks can rest."

Conor gave in. "Yes, ma'am." He stood up.

"There'll be some bathing later on, too," Katie said as she settled herself at Pike's side. "Everybody smells like smoke."

Beau came from the bedroom, Alina's bowl in one hand, and quietly closed the door. He looked down at Pike. "Did you eat?"

"Don't ya think Kate would be right here, stuffin' that stew down my throat, if I hadn't?" Pike's voice sounded tired, and his eyes were half closed. He coughed.

"You sound like your old self, Pike." Beau set the bowl next to the sink. "I'm glad for that."

"Come on over and sit, Beau. The stewpot's here on the table and it's still warm." Katie motioned to him. Beau obeyed her and sank wearily into his chair.

"How is she?" asked Conor.

Beau rested his elbows on the table and leaned his face into his hands. He rubbed his eyes. "She ate some and is sleeping again. She doesn't complain, but I think she's in a lot of pain." Beau sat back in his chair, his hands clenched into fists. "I want to kill Carter over and over. One death wasn't enough for him." His tone was vicious, his twisted, outraged features almost unrecognizable.

Conor glanced at Katie, his concern evident. "You need some rest, Beau," he said cautiously. "You didn't really sleep last night." Beau did not respond.

Katie set a full bowl in front of him. "Ya eat every bit of that stew, Beau Parker, because ya're not getting up from the table 'til it's gone." Katie's tone was light, but she was worried, too. "After supper, it's into the tub with ya. Conor's already had his bath, and together he and I got Pike cleaned up." She eyed his stubble-covered chin. "Ya need a shave, too."

"I appreciate your concern, Katie, but don't mother me," Beau said flatly as he picked up the spoon.

"Well, someone has to, because ya aren't taking care of yourself." Katie handed him a piece of bread.

Beau's lips tightened, but he didn't say anything. He accepted the bread with a nod of thanks.

"Some of the boys want to come out in a few days and start clearing the mess of the barn, but they figured to wait a bit, so Alina and Pike can build their strength in quiet." Katie scraped the side of her bowl with her spoon.

"That's nice of them," Conor commented as he leaned back against the windowsill. He ran a hand over his wet hair. "We do need to get that burned wood out of here. The smell won't go away until we do."

Katie turned to Beau and was satisfied to see him eating. "Ya'll have lots of help with the barn-raising. It'll probably go up in one day, like the Freeman's did."

"I don't want Petrie helping," Conor said warningly.

"Petrie and his men are not to set foot on my land," Beau growled. He did not look up from his bowl.

"We'll keep them away," Conor promised. He raised his eyebrows at Katie. She shrugged and stood up. She carried her bowl to the sink and returned with the coffeepot.

Beau pushed his half-empty bowl away and sagged back

in the chair. Katie filled his cup and took his bowl with no comment. She cleared the table except for the cups and returned to her seat, a new brandy bottle in hand. She poured a generous amount in each cup. For a few minutes no one spoke; the only sounds were those of Pike's soft snoring and the ticking of the clock.

"As soon as Alina can travel, I'm taking her to Chicago." Beau spoke suddenly, harshly.

Conor and Katie looked at him in amazement. "What?" "Why?" They spoke at the same time.

"I have to go on to Washington, and she'll be safer there."

"But the Randalls are there," Conor protested.

"Then I'll hire the entire Pinkerton force to stand guard outside her aunt's house!" Beau slapped the table with an open palm. "Perhaps they can do a better job of protecting her than I've done."

Conor and Katie were stunned into silence. Beau pushed his chair back and rose, then stomped out the door, slamming it behind him. Pike stirred, but did not awaken.

"Conor, he's not taking this well." Katie shook her head. "I'm real worried about him."

Conor nodded. "I feel bad about this whole mess, too, Katie, and guilty, real guilty. I keep thinking we should have been here. But we weren't, and there's nothing to be done about it now. At least Alina and Pike are alive."

"Can ya tell Beau that?"

Conor twisted to look out the window, his brow furrowed. He could make out Beau's dispirited form by the corral fence. "I can try, but I have a feeling he's not in the mood to listen."

Chapter Twenty

Conor talked to Beau, as did Pike and David, but he would not be swayed. As soon as Alina could travel, he took her to Chicago. He stayed with her for several days, then left for the East Coast. He did not say when he would return.

One morning a month later, Alina sat in a chair, a blanket over her knees, and stared out the bedroom window with unseeing eyes. The first leaves were turning a soft gold; one broke free of its branch and fluttered against the glass on its way to the ground far below. Her fingers tightened on the crumpled page she held in her lap.

A knock came at the door.

"Come in," Alina called softly. Elizabeth bustled into the room, a cheerful smile on her lined face.

"Hello, my dear." Elizabeth kissed Alina's cheek and perched on the edge of the massive four-poster bed. She looked at her great-niece, noting with concern the sadness in Alina's blue eyes. The traces of the bruises that had remained when Beau had brought her here were now gone, but she was still pale and weak. Her leg had mended nicely; the doctor had removed the splint the day before. Alina's spirit, however, had not mended.

"What did Beau say in his letter?" Elizabeth asked.

"Not much." Alina held the paper out. "He is still in Virginia with his family." Her voice was dull.

Elizabeth took the letter and perused the few short lines. "There's no indication of when he expects to return."

"Or if he expects to return." Alina's soft voice shook and tears welled in her eyes.

"Now, what is this nonsense? Of course he'll be back." Elizabeth crossed her arms over her chest, worry and exasperation about her great-niece's emotional state warring within her.

"He's changed, Elizabeth. I don't know that he will come for me." Alina pointed with a trembling finger to the paper in Elizabeth's hand. "There are no words of love, no terms of endearment in that letter. It could have been written to a business associate. I don't understand what has happened."

Elizabeth stood up and set the letter on the bed. "Beau seems deeply troubled right now, but he'll work through it. Of one thing I am very certain, though, Alina." She paused until her great-niece looked at her. "That man loves you with all his heart. I knew it when I visited you last May, and I know it from how he cared for you here the short time before he left. He'll be back." Elizabeth settled her hands on her hips and continued. "But I am very concerned about you. You've moped around since you arrived, and I'll have no more of it. You must rise above this melancholy, Alina. You must make yourself well."

Alina raised startled eyes to her great-aunt's face. She opened her mouth to protest.

Elizabeth held up her hand. "No arguments, my girl. I know you've been through a terrible ordeal, and I know you love Beau, and that his actions are confusing and painful to you. But you survived, and you will continue to survive, no matter what Beau does or does not do." Elizabeth pointed toward the dressing table. "Take a hard look at yourself, Alina. See how sick and sad you have become. It is your life, girl. Only you can decide how happy or unhappy you will be."

The old woman steeled herself against her beloved niece's tear-filled eyes and trembling lips. "Now it is time for your walk," she said briskly. "You must strengthen that leg. Your father will be here next week, and I'm sure you'll want to dance with him at the reception I am planning. I will send Chambers to you." Elizabeth's skirts rustled as she crossed the room. "Pull yourself together, girl," she urged kindly. "Find your old fire." She closed the door.

Alina brushed at the tears that clung to her lashes. Her eyes fell on Beau's letter; the piece of paper looked small against the expanse of the crewelwork bedcover. She absent-mindedly twisted the wedding band on her finger. She ached with longing for him, for her life with him in Wyoming. Never had she known such painful and gut-wrenching loneliness. She felt new and intense sympathy and understanding for the pain her father must have felt at the death of her mother.

Alina sighed. She did not share Elizabeth's faith that Beau would return, but her great-aunt was right in telling her to shake the sadness that had gripped her since the day Beau had taken her from the ranch. She threw the blanket from her knees and rose, then limped over to the dressing table. She sank onto the stool and stared at her reflection in the mirror. What she saw shocked her.

Her skin was pale, with the exception of the gray circles under her sad and weary eyes. Her hair was dull and limp, and her dress hung on her too-thin frame. Alina raised a shaking hand to touch her cheek. "My God," she whispered sorrowfully. "What has happened to me?"

She reached for the brush and vigorously ran it through her hair, then captured the long tresses in a ribbon at the base of her neck. She pinched her cheeks and scrutinized the result. The bright splotches of red looked unnatural. Alina sighed again. It had taken weeks to come to this condition; it would take longer than a few minutes to recover.

"But recover I shall," she told herself aloud, through gritted teeth, as she stared into her own eyes. "This will not defeat me." She stood and whirled to face the bed. "And you will not defeat me, either, Beau Parker." She limped to the bed and snatched up the letter, crushing it in her hand. She crossed to the fireplace and threw it on the flames. "First I will see to healing myself, then I will see to my troubled marriage."

A knock came at the door. "Come in, Chambers," Alina called as she reached into a drawer for her shawl. She greeted the old butler with a full smile. "Are you ready to assist a wobbly woman on a turn around the grounds?"

"Oh, yes, Miss Alina, with pleasure." Chambers' face wrinkled into a grin. "You seem to be feeling better this morning, if I may say so. I'm glad to see it."

Alina took his offered arm. "Yes, I am feeling better." They moved out into the hall and toward the stairs. "I've been meaning to ask you how you and Effie have been, and if you have enjoyed working for Aunt Elizabeth."

"Yes, Miss . . ." The sound of their voices faded as they descended the stairs.

A week later, Alina was again at her dressing table. She was pleased with the difference the past several days had wrought in her appearance. She was still too pale and thin, but the gray discoloration was gone from underneath her eyes, and her hair was more lustrous and full.

She twisted her locks into a simple knot at the base of her neck and secured it with pins. That was one difference she had noticed since her return from Wyoming Territory, she reflected. She no longer needed a maid to dress her and arrange her hair. Indeed, Alina had no patience for it any longer, certainly not for everyday living.

She patted her hair and a memory flashed to her mind, of Beau's long fingers pulling the pins from her knot of hair, of him burying his face in the black curling tresses, of those fingers running through the strands and laying them out across the pillow. Her eyes closed as a wave of loneliness and homesickness washed over her, so intense that her stomach knotted. She braced her elbows on the table and rested her face in her hands. Dear Lord, how she missed him!

Alina's painful reverie was interrupted by an impatient

knocking at her door. She raised her head and dabbed at her eyes as she called, "Come in."

Maggie burst into the room, her young face aglow with excitement. "Oh, Miss, you must come down at once. Hurry!" The maid grabbed Alina's arm and hurried her to the door.

"Maggie, for heaven's sake, what is it?" Alina laughingly demanded.

"It's your papa, Miss Alina! Captain Gallagher is home at last!" Alina's eyes widened with surprise and joy. Maggie's white cap waved on her dark hair as the girl nodded her head. "It's true! He's in the parlor!"

Alina picked up her skirts and fairly flew down the hall.

"Be careful of your ankle on the stairs, Miss!" Maggie called after her. Alina grabbed the railing and heeded Maggie's warning. She paused at the bottom of the stairs. Chambers stood at the open door to the parlor, a huge grin on his face. She heard her father's deep voice. Alina closed her eyes in a moment of thanksgiving, then hurried to stand beside Chambers.

Elizabeth sat on a chair, and another woman with black hair whom Alina did not know sat on the sofa, an infant in her arms. Neil Gallagher stood before the fireplace. His fine suit fit a man that did not seem as tall as Alina had remembered him, nor as stocky. His graying hair still had traces of red, and his hazel eyes still sparkled with humor and life. Those eyes lit up when they fell on Alina.

"There's my bonny girl," he said softly as he held out his arms. Nearly blinded with tears, Alina ran across the parlor and threw herself into her father's arms. "Oh, Papa," she whispered. They held each other tightly for a long time, then Neil set her back from him and looked at her carefully. "You're a woman grown, daughter, and lovely besides, like your dear mother was." He tilted her chin with one hand, concern narrowing his eyes. "You look pale. Have you been ill?"

Alina dropped her eyes. "Yes, Papa, but I'm better now. 'll tell you about it later."

"I also understand that you have married. Where is your usband? I want to meet him."

Alina glanced at her great-aunt before she answered. "My usband is not here. He had business in Washington, then vent to Virginia to visit his family. I'm not sure when he will eturn. But I want to hear about your adventures over the ast year."

Neil's sharp eyes did not miss the look between Alina and lizabeth. "We'll talk later, daughter, about your husband nd your illness. But before I tell you my story, there is omeone I want you to meet." He turned Alina to face the voman on the sofa. He stepped to the woman's side as she tood, and took the child from her arms. It struck Alina that er father was nervous.

"Alina, I would like to introduce you to my new wife. Lan, his is my daughter. And this is Kevin, our son, and your rother." He shifted the sleeping child on his arm and vaited.

Alina's eyes widened and her jaw dropped. Her father had narried? She had a new brother? She saw anxiety and hope n the lovely dark eyes of the new Mrs. Gallagher, and ealized that all were waiting for her reaction. She smiled nd moved to stand in front of the small, very pretty woman.

"Welcome to our family, ma'am," she said sincerely, and eld out her hands. Lan shyly accepted Alina's hands and miled.

"Lan means 'orchid' in English, and I think she's as pretty s a flower." He smiled lovingly at his wife, then looked at lina. "Would you like to hold your brother?" At her eager od, he carefully placed the baby in her waiting arms. Alina radled the tiny bundle against her body and looked into the lankets. Her new brother had a sweet face and black hair. Her eyes filled with tears. Joseph and Sean were gone, but ow here was Kevin. She loved him instantly.

"He's beautiful," she whispered in awe. "How old is he?"

"He'll be six weeks tomorrow," Lan said softly. Her voic had a distinct, interesting accent.

Alina looked at her in amazement. "He was born at sea?

"That he was," her father boomed. "He'll grow to be seafaring man for sure."

"Neil, I think it's about time you told us exactly wher you've been this last year, and what has happened to you.' Elizabeth spoke from her chair. "You said in the first cabl that you had been injured. Obviously, you weren't too in jured." She arched a meaningful eyebrow at the babe i Alina's arms.

Lan blushed as Neil laughed out loud. "You never wer one to mince words, Elizabeth," he commented.

"Chambers, will you please bring tea for all of us?" Eliza beth asked, as everyone settled into their seats. "Lan, m dear, feel free to remove your hat and gloves. You are wit family now."

Lan smiled gratefully and pulled a hatpin from her ha then removed it. She laid the hat on the table, where it wa soon joined by her gloves. "I am not yet very well acquainte with western fashions. I am afraid I find these clothes heav and somewhat cumbersome."

"I'm sure Alina and I agree with you, my dear." Elizabet glanced at her great-niece.

Alina sat in a chair, still holding her sleeping brother. Sh looked up. "Forgive me," she said with a smile. "My brothe has completely captivated me. Yes, fashion can be a cru master. I learned to dress much more comfortably in Wyo ming."

"Well, I've told her she doesn't have to wear this Ameri can get-up to please me." Neil sat next to his wife on the sof and took her hand in his. He placed a gentle kiss on the bac of her hand. Alina felt a pang of nostalgia and strangeness t see her father treating Lan as he had treated her mother lon ago, the same way Beau treated her.

"Tell us your story, Papa," Alina encouraged.

Neil settled against the back of the sofa. "Well, as yo

know, the *Brianna* ran aground in a typhoon off the coast of China last September. I was on deck, trying to get to the wheel, when I was washed overboard." His voice sobered. "What a terrible night! I was sure the ship would break apart and go down, and I thought she had, until I received Percival's cable in July. You can't imagine the elation I felt to learn the *Brianna* and most of my crew had survived. When I went into the sea, I thought I was dead for sure." He squeezed Lan's hand. "I woke up with a very bad headache, in the home of a French missionary. It turned out he had pulled me from the surf that terrible night, and had taken me into his home to care for me."

"But why did it take you so long to get to Hong Kong, to get word to us?" Elizabeth asked.

Neil shrugged. "The *Brianna* had been blown off course. I was washed ashore in a country called Vietnam, which is far to the west and south of Hong Kong. Also, I was lost in September. When I awakened, it was November. I had been unconscious for the entire two months."

"You were in a *coma?*" Alina worriedly asked.

Neil nodded. "Father Pierre and Lan nursed me all that time, not knowing who I was, or if I was a pirate, or a convict, or a ship's captain." He smiled lovingly at his wife. "Even once I was awake, it took a long time to recover. I had to learn to walk again. Lan never once lost patience with me, not through my darkest days. And there were dark days, daughter, let me tell you." He waved a hand. "There was no way to communicate from the village."

"Tell me of this country, this Vietnam," interjected Elizabeth. "I've never heard of it."

" 'Tis an independent empire," Neil said. "I didn't know much about it myself, until I made my way to Hong Kong, and the American Consulate there. Vietnam enjoys diplomatic relations with many countries—Japan, Britain, France, and our own United States, to name a few. However, I believe the French have an eye toward colonization.

The Vietnamese are resisting the idea, but they will allow th
missionaries in."

"Forgive my curiosity, Lan, but how is it you speak suc
excellent English if Father Pierre was French?" Elizabet
asked.

Lan smiled. "I do not mind your question, ma'am. I spea
English because Father Pierre is fluent in English, as well a
in French, Chinese, and Vietnamese. I was orphaned at a
early age and raised at the home Father built in the village
He was educated at Cambridge. He is very generous, an
shared his extensive education."

"Is Vietnam part of China?" Alina asked.

Lan shook her head. "No. In fact, the Chinese are usuall
considered our enemies. They have invaded us many time
through the centuries."

"Was it difficult to leave your home?" Alina asked softly

Lan glanced at her husband. "In some ways. I get home
sick every now and then, for my land and for my language
but my life is with my husband and my son now, and I an
happy to be here."

Chambers came in with a tray laden with a silver teapo
and several cups. He set the tray in front of Elizabeth on
low table. "Would you like me to pour, madam?" he asked

"Thank you, Chambers. That would be lovely."

"I will fill in the details of my adventure later," Neil said
"Now, I am most anxious to learn what has been going o
in my absence. I especially wish to learn why I cannot retur
to my own home."

Beau read Alina's wire again: *"Dear Husband: Father ha
returned. Please come as soon as you can. Your Loving Wife."* H
stared out of the carriage window with unseeing eyes. It ha
been well over a month since he'd left her here in Chicag
She had written him a few informal letters, acting as
nothing was amiss between them. Was she still his "lovin
wife," even after his desertion of her? He sighed and put th

piece of paper in his coat pocket. He would soon find out, for the carriage was pulling up in front of Elizabeth Hammond's mansion.

Chambers opened the massive front door. "Mr. Parker," he said, a welcoming smile on his weathered features. "How good to see you, sir."

"Thank you, Chambers," Beau responded as he stepped into the grand foyer.

"I shall see that your things are taken to your room, sir. I believe Mrs. Parker has gone for a walk along the shore. I shall send someone for her straightaway."

"A moment, if you please, Chambers." Neil Gallagher came from the parlor. "I would enjoy the opportunity to speak privately with my son-in-law, if you don't mind, Mr. Parker. Let's leave Alina to enjoy her walk."

Beau eyed the older man with curiosity. Neil Gallagher was not a tall man, but he was powerfully built. He little resembled his daughter, although Beau recognized the same spirit that Alina exhibited. He held out his hand. "Captain Gallagher, I presume. Beauregard Parker, at your service, sir."

Neil clasped Beau's hand in a firm grip. "Good to meet you, Parker. I've heard a lot about you."

"And I about you, sir. I'm relieved you have returned in good health. Alina always knew you were alive."

The two men moved into the parlor. Neil closed the doors behind them. "So she told me. Would you care for some brandy?"

"Yes, thank you. I came directly here from the train station. It has been a long day."

Neil handed Beau a crystal snifter and pointed him to the sofa. Beau sank down on the cushions with a sigh and took a sip of the liquor. The fiery potion burned a welcome path to his stomach. "That hits the spot," he murmured.

"It does indeed," Neil agreed from his chair. His sharp gaze raked over Beau. "First of all, I want to thank you for coming to the aid of my daughter. She told me how you rescued her from the Randalls, and that you were a perfect gentleman for the many months it took you both to develop an affection for each other. I shudder to think what would have befallen her had you not been there."

Beau shifted uncomfortably. "No thanks are necessary, sir. Alina is a remarkable woman. It is I who am fortunate."

"Still, please accept my sincere thanks."

Beau lifted his glass. "You are welcome, Captain Gallagher."

Neil raised his glass in response and both men drank. The room was silent for a moment, then Neil spoke in a brisk tone. "I don't believe in beating around the bush, Mr. Parker. Exactly what are your intentions toward my daughter?"

Beau sat up straight. "Sir?"

"You heard me."

"Captain Gallagher, I am married to your daughter."

"I'm aware of that, man. Is it your intention to remain married to her?"

Beau leaned forward and set the snifter on the table. He raised his eyes to meet those of the older man. "Are you suggesting that there will be a problem should I remain married to your daughter, Captain Gallagher?"

"There will be if you don't love her, Parker. She feels that you abandoned her. Is she wrong?"

Beau stood up and ran his hands through his hair. "I left because I had business in Washington. She was too ill to travel so far with me. I had to leave her here."

"Why did you take so long to return?"

"I went to see my family. I had not been home in a year."

"What was the real reason, Mr. Parker?"

Beau whirled and faced the Captain. His jaw clenched, then his shoulders sagged. "The real reason is that I'm not worthy of her, Captain Gallagher," he said quietly.

Neil's eyebrows drew together in puzzlement. "Not worthy of her? Why do you say that?"

"I didn't protect her, sir. Surely she has told you what

happened, how she came to be injured." Beau resumed his seat on the sofa, bleak despair in his eyes.

Neil nodded. "Yes, she told me. She seems to think that you saved her life."

"She should never have been hurt. That man should never have touched her. I promised her I would protect her, and I did not keep my word." To Beau's surprise, Neil laughed.

"Good God, man, do you think you can protect her from life?" At Beau's bewildered look, Neil continued. "I don't mean to make light of your feelings, son. It's just that we can't protect our loved ones from life. I could not keep my son from dying at Gettysburg, nor could I keep my other son from drowning. Does that make me a bad father?" He held out his hands and shrugged. "I could not keep my beloved wife from drifting away into death after Joseph died. Does that make me a bad husband? I did all I could. You did all you could. Your wife is alive and healed, and she loves you."

Beau looked at the man, hope in the depths of his eyes.

"Don't let your grief and guilt destroy a beautiful relationship, as my first wife did. Brianna never recovered from our son's death. A tragedy will either strengthen a marriage or break it. For Alina's sake, and your own, you must put this behind you." He paused. "Do you want my daughter as your wife?"

"Yes, sir, I do."

"Then I suggest you go find her and tell her that. She's walking along the shore, which she does every day to strengthen her leg. Chambers can direct you."

Beau stood up. "How is Alina, Captain?"

Neil took a sip of brandy before he answered. "She's fine, except for the fact that her heart is wounded, and she misses you like the dickens. You'd better mend her heart, Parker, or you'll answer to me."

"Yes, sir," Beau said with a smile as he walked toward the door. He paused with his hand on the latch. "Thank you," he said softly.

"You're welcome, son. Take care of my daughter."

"I will." Beau was gone.

Neil emptied his snifter. "You'll do, Mr. Parker," he murmured with a satisfied smile. "You'll do."

Beau found Alina on a small point a half mile from the house. A cool fall wind blew off the lake and tugged at her cape. She moved slowly, looking out at the water.

"Alina!" Beau called. She paused, then turned to face him. A happy smile curved her lips. He was struck anew by her beauty. How could he have considered letting her go? He approached and stood before her. He wanted desperately to take her into his arms, but he was not sure of her reaction.

"You look better," he said lamely.

Alina nodded. "I am."

"How's the leg?"

"Fine. Getting stronger every day. How are you, Beau?" Her blue eyes searched his face. A stray black curl waved against her cheek.

"I'm fine, too. I came as soon as I could."

"You got here very quickly. Thank you for coming." They lapsed into an awkward silence. Finally Alina spoke again. "Would you like to walk with me?"

Beau nodded. "I would, very much." He offered her his arm. She took it and they walked for a while in silence.

"Why did you leave, Beau?" Alina's question was sudden, her tone quiet and nonaccusing.

Beau stopped. He stared out over the water, idly caressing her hand where it laid on his arm. "When I held your unconscious body in my arms the night of the fire, I thought you were going to die. You have no idea what that did to me, Alina."

"No, I don't," she gently scolded, "because you did not tell me."

Beau sighed. "Maybe I did not emerge from the war as unscathed as I thought." He paused and glanced at her, then returned his gaze to the water. "There was too much death, and it was all so senseless. At Cold Harbor, I held my dearest childhood friend in my arms as he died, after he stepped between me and the saber that gave me my scar." His hand absentmindedly moved to his side. "War has a way of putting things in perspective, Alina; when I came home, I could not take the difficulties of life seriously. It was as if I had lost my capacity to feel. But when Ambrose died, the pain was reborn. I buried my murdered brother, whose killer I have not found. When I found you and Pike that night, it was like something inside me snapped. I couldn't bear to lose any more loved ones. I should have been there that day, Alina. I should have protected you. It tore me apart to see you in our bed, broken and bruised, in such terrible pain. It was as if my own heart was being ripped from my body."

Alina reached for his hand and gripped it with both of her own. "Did leaving help?"

"No." A sardonic smile twisted Beau's lips. "I never stopped thinking of you."

"Nor I of you."

Beau covered her hands with his free one and looked into her eyes. "I want to be your husband, Alina. Will you have me?"

"You are all I want, Beau Parker." Her eyes were shining with love. A smile played around her lips. "But if you ever leave me again, I swear, I'll come after you with my rifle."

"And shoot me?"

"No. I'll force you home. Madeline Petrie is not the only one who always gets what she wants." Beau raised his eyebrows in confusion. "She told me that once," Alina explained with a grin. "She was talking about you."

Beau slipped his arms around Alina. "I didn't realize I was such hot property. Maybe I shouldn't have made it so easy for you," he teased.

"Conceited oaf," Alina whispered as his lips descended upon hers. She melted against him, her arms clinging to him.

"God, woman, I've missed you." Beau nuzzled her neck, delighted to smell roses.

"That big bed has seemed so empty, Beau," Alina said breathlessly. Beau's mouth claimed hers again, lovingly insistent. When it seemed she could no longer breathe, his lips released her. He held her tightly against him, one hand cradling her head, his fingers buried in her hair.

"I will never run away from you again," Beau promised.

"I know," Alina whispered. They turned and began the walk back to the house, each with an arm around the other.

The next afternoon, Beau loudly rapped the knocker on the impressive door. "Mr. and Mrs. Beauregard Parker to see Mrs. Randall and her son," he informed the haughty butler.

The man sniffed. "I shall see if madam is receiving. You may wait in the parlor." He closed the door behind them and waved toward the open parlor doors as he walked leisurely to the staircase. As soon as he was out of sight, Beau opened the front door again, allowing Neil to enter.

"I'll wait in my study," Neil said quietly as the three advanced into the foyer.

"You won't recognize the room," Alina warned in a whisper. The sound of a closing door reached their ears. Neil held a finger to his lips and slipped into his old study, almost completely closing the door. Alina and Beau crossed to the parlor.

Alina was sitting composed in a chair by the fireplace, Beau standing at her side, when Cordelia swept into the room, followed closely by Donovan.

Cordelia stopped in front of the sofa and sank onto it. "I must admit that I'm surprised, Alina." Her glittering eyes roamed over the couple before her. "What is the meaning of this visit?"

"We are here to ask you to voluntarily relinquish your control of my father's estate and return that control to the proper persons." Alina spoke in a firm, clear tone. Cordelia looked at her in amazement, then burst into laughter.

"Proper persons meaning yourselves?" Donovan demanded.

Alina raised an eyebrow. "Certainly it is more appropriate that we handle my father's estate, as I am his heir."

Cordelia shook her head in mock regret. "How sad that you and your cowboy lover have grown weary of life in the Territory." Her gaze hardened. "You had your chance, Alina. Had you married Donovan, you would have been living in luxury all this time."

"It's not too late," Donovan interjected. "End your farce of a marriage and come back here."

Now Alina laughed. "And live in fear of my physical well-being, if not my life? I think not. Never would I allow you to touch me, Donovan. And, I assure you, my marriage is no farce."

Donovan stiffened. He glared at Alina, then at her husband. Beau met Donovan's hateful look with a challenge evident in his flashing brown eyes. His hand moved to lie protectively on Alina's shoulder. Donovan looked away.

Cordelia rose. "I won't allow you to insult my son in my house. There is no point in continuing this ridiculous conversation. I want you both to leave."

"This is your last chance to rectify your crimes against my family without facing dire consequences, Cordelia," Alina warned.

Cordelia's eyes narrowed as her thin lips curved into a mocking smile. "Or you will do what, Alina? Take me to court? Go ahead. I have the funds to engage in a court battle. I might rather enjoy it, in fact." She looked with derision at Beau. "Somehow I doubt your . . . cowboy . . . has the money, though."

"I have the money," Beau assured her. "But my money won't be necessary. We will not be the ones who take you to court."

"Then who?" Cordelia demanded. "Has Alina found some fool to champion her cause?"

"I am hardly a fool, Cordelia Randall." Neil Gallagher's quiet voice came from the door.

Cordelia blanched and whirled to face him. "My God," she whispered. Even Donovan was shaken.

"Whatever is the matter, dear? You look as if you've seen a ghost." Neil's voice was deceptively solicitous. "Surely Alina told you I was alive. Aren't you pleased to see me?" He advanced into the room.

"Mother only did what she felt was best for Alina," Donovan blurted out.

"Indeed." Neil's eyes hardened as his penetrating gaze pierced Cordelia. "Indeed."

Cordelia swallowed. "Since you have returned safely, Neil, the judge's decree is no longer in effect." Her voice cracked.

"So my house is once again mine?"

Cordelia nodded.

Neil looked around the opulent room with distaste. "I do not like what you've done to my house, Cordelia, nor do I like what you've done to my daughter. I believe Alina warned you that you would rue the day you crossed me. Be assured that you will." Neil walked to the door. "You and Donovan will leave this house immediately. You may take with you one change of clothing, nothing more."

"But where will we go?" Cordelia cried. "How will we live?"

Neil paused at the door. "No doubt you have some of my money squirreled away in some account in your name. Live on that while you can, before my solicitor locates it and lays claim to it."

"How can you be so heartless?" Donovan shouted.

Neil whirled and advanced on the young man. "Heartless? I? Don't speak to me of heartless, Donovan Randall! Count yourself lucky that I don't give you the beating you so richly deserve!" Donovan retreated, his eyes wide with fear. Neil continued, his voice thundering around the room. "How dare you and your mother take my house, my estate, my daughter's inheritance? How dare you drive her from her home with threats of bodily harm and rape? How dare you, man? Get from my sight, you despicable brute!"

Donovan bolted from the room. Cordelia followed more slowly.

"Mr. Percival is waiting outside, Cordelia. Before you leave, he will give you a notice of the charges I am bringing against you for fraud, embezzlement, and breach of faith."

Cordelia stopped and looked at Neil, horrorsticken. "Neil, you can't. I beg you. I'll be ruined."

"Alina offered you a chance to redeem yourself, madam. You refused her. The matter will now be righted in court."

Cordelia's shoulders sagged; the resolution on Neil's face was easy to read. She left the room without another word.

"I'll get Percival," Neil stated, and disappeared into the foyer. Beau took Alina's elbow as she rose.

"So this was your home," he commented as he looked around the room.

"It wasn't decorated like this when I lived here," Alina said with a laugh. "My parents had better taste." Beau draped an arm across her shoulders and they walked toward the door leading to the hall. "It's strange," she mused.

"What is?"

"I thought I'd feel more victorious when this day came. I don't really. I just feel relieved that it's over."

"Me, too, although I would feel better if I had been able to teach Donovan a lesson myself." Beau raised a clenched fist.

"You're a bloodthirsty man, Beau Parker," Alina teased.

"I am when it comes to people who try to hurt you," Beau agreed. He looked up as Seamus Percival and Neil Gallagher came through the front door. "Welcome back to your home, Captain," he said as he held out his hand.

Neil shook it vigorously. "Thanks for your help, son. Why don't you take Alina back to Elizabeth's? You two don't need to be here for the fireworks, unless you'd like to stay."

Alina shook her head. "I'd rather go, Papa." She kissed

her father's cheek. "I'm glad this day has finally come. I always knew it would."

"Aye, daughter, it's long overdue. You run along with your man. Seamus and I will be home for dinner, and we'll plan our strategy for court."

Alina nodded and Beau guided her down the steps to the waiting carriage.

Later that night, Beau stripped off his pants and slid under the blankets to join his wife in the big bed. "It sounds like your father has things well in hand." He gathered her into his arms. "It feels so good to hold you, wife," he murmured, as he nuzzled her hair.

Alina pressed her naked body against him. "I don't think there will be much of a court battle, not with my testimony and Mr. Percival's." She shivered as Beau nibbled at her ear. "What are your plans when the trial is over?"

Beau's lips stilled. He shifted his head on the pillow and stroked her hair. "I've been thinking about that. Do you miss your home here?"

"No, not any longer. I don't miss my life here at all. I miss our home, yours and mine, and I miss Conor, and Pike, and Cynthia, and Katie. I miss our life in Wyoming." She looked at him. "Did you find that you missed Virginia when you went home?"

"No. I don't belong there anymore, nor do I belong in Washington. Caldwell, my younger brother, he belongs there. I told him the place is his." He hesitated. "You didn't want to live in Virginia, did you?"

Alina laughed. "No, darling. I want to live in Wyoming. I want to build a life and a home with you, and I want to fill our home with children."

A wild happiness sang through Beau's veins. He covered Alina's shapely legs with one of his and snuggled closer. "We'll have to get to work, then, if we're going to fill the house with children." He nipped at Alina's neck until she squealed with breathless laughter. The feel of his teeth on her skin sent tremors racing through her body. She wrapped her arms around him as he shifted his weight to cover her.

"You'd better make love to me right now, Beau Parker." She ground her hips against his in the age-old dance of mating.

"Yes, ma'am," Beau whispered, and gladly obeyed her.

Chapter Twenty-one

Alina pressed her face to the window as the train slowed to a stop. "I can see Conor!" she cried. Beau smiled at his excited wife and stood. Alina turned her shining eyes up to him. "It's good to be home," she said softly.

Beau nodded in agreement. He took her hand, then led the way along the narrow aisle and steadied her as she stepped down to the platform. She threw herself into Conor's waiting arms.

Conor lifted her off her feet and swung her around in a circle. "It's good to see you, Cousin!" A happy grin covered his handsome face. "You look much better than the last time I saw you." Conor held out a hand to Beau. "Welcome home, Beau. You look better too."

"I am," he replied with a smile as he took Conor's hand. "It looks like you brought a welcoming party with you." He gestured toward a small group of people waiting by the depot. Alina turned and saw Katie, Emerald, and Cynthia. She left Conor's arm and hurried to her friends, where she was enveloped in a series of joyful hugs.

The men waited for the baggage. "Where is Pike?" Beau asked.

"He stayed at the ranch. There were some things he wanted to fix up for Alina. I should tell you that we've made substantial changes to the house, Beau. I took you at your word and made use of the funds you left, and I was careful to keep an accounting of everything. I think you'll be pleased."

"I'm sure I will be." Beau glanced back at the excited group of women. Conor followed his gaze.

"It's good to see her happy," Conor commented softly. "It's good to see you happy, too, Beau. We were worried about you."

"I'm fine now," Beau assured him.

After dropping Katie and Emerald at the Satin Slipper, Conor directed the horses toward the Cheyenne Pass Road. He glanced over his shoulder. "Are you two comfortable back there?" Most of the wagon was piled high with trunks and boxes.

"We are, Conor. Don't worry about us," Alina answered from her seat on a box. Cynthia nodded in agreement.

"Then tell me about Uncle Neil."

"He's fine, Conor. He seems happier than I think he's been since Mama died. Lan has really been good for him, and you should see him with Kevin." Alina laughed. "Papa said that no man should have children until he is over forty, because he's too busy working and trying to establish himself to really enjoy his children." She poked playfully at Beau's back. "You're only thirty, honey. We have to wait ten years."

Beau looked at her over his shoulder, his eyes smoldering with a sensuous fire. "I don't think so," he said dryly.

Conor saw the look and laughed. "I'm not sure he'll wait until tonight, Cousin, let alone ten years."

Alina blushed. "Never you mind, Conor O'Rourke."

The smile did not leave Conor's face. "We'll change the subject. Are Neil and his new family settled in his house?"

"No," Alina answered. "I forgot I didn't write to you about that. Cordelia had redecorated the house. It was truly awful, Conor, so overbearing and gaudy. Papa didn't like it at all, and he'd have had to redo the entire interior, so he decided to sell it. He and Lan will live with Elizabeth."

Conor nodded his approval. "Good. I'm glad Elizabeth

won't be alone. She's a feisty old gal, but she's getting on in years. It'll be good for her to have family around her. Does she get on with Lan?"

"Perfectly. And she adores Kevin."

"Did you get to see the *Brianna?*"

"My father's ship," Alina explained to Cynthia.

"We did." Beau answered Conor's question. "What a beautiful ship! I didn't know she was a clipper until we got to the dock. Neil did a wonderful job of refurbishing her. He's thinking about putting in a steam engine, but I know he doesn't really want to. He loves to sail her. He took us out on Lake Michigan for a day, and I can understand why he wouldn't want to add the steam. She is a graceful, quiet lady."

"I think he should leave the *Brianna* just as she is," Alina added. "He has plenty of other steamships."

Conor nodded his agreement. "What's happening with the Randalls? I assume the trial is over."

"The case never went to trial," Beau explained. "Cordelia agreed to plead guilty."

"Did she go to jail?" asked Cynthia.

Alina shook her head. "No. The judge fined her and put her on probation. The other judge, the one who conspired with her and signed the original trustee order, resigned. I almost felt sorry for her. She's a broken woman. She's technically a criminal, and she's been ruined in the eyes of society. All those high-and-mighty friends who were so important to her won't even speak to her now."

"You're amazing, Alina," said Cynthia with an admiring smile. "After all that woman has done to you, and intended to do, you can still feel sympathy for her."

"Well, it's only a little sympathy," Alina admitted.

"And what of Donovan?" demanded Conor. "He's the one I'd have liked to get my hands on."

"You and me both." Beau adjusted his hat against the sun. "No charges were brought against him."

"What?"

Beau shrugged. "He had no real part in the trustee arrangement. The only thing he did was threaten Alina, and there's no law against that."

"What about conspiracy?"

"It would have been hard to prove. The judge warned Donovan to stay away from Alina, but that was about all he could do."

"That doesn't seem right," Conor muttered. "What will the Randalls do now?"

"I don't know. They'll probably leave Chicago. Alina was right . . . they are ruined there."

Conor guided the horses onto the road that led to the Freeman ranch.

"Thanks for letting me ride along with you, Conor," Cynthia said. "I just couldn't wait to see Alina."

"I was glad for the company. Besides, Alina probably would've had my head had I not brought you." He winked over his shoulder at his cousin. The wagon pulled into the yard and excited children seemed to come from all directions. David emerged from the barn with a huge grin on his dark face.

After joyous greetings and promises to visit soon, Alina settled herself on the seat between Beau and Conor for the final leg of the trip home. She waved as the wagon climbed the small hill back to the road, then faced forward. "I'm so anxious to see Pike and Sundance and Lucy and Bay," she said happily.

"Conor said they made some changes to the house."

"I'm sure it's beautiful," Alina murmured.

Beau watched her radiant face with pleasure. He caught her hand and brought it to his lips for a quick kiss. Alina smiled and squeezed his fingers.

They rounded the stand of pines and the homestead came into view. Both Beau and Alina caught their breath in amazement. The original cabin was still there, but a two-story addition had been added to the end of the structure where Pike's and Conor's room had been. The walls of the new barn were still pale and clean, and another building wa under construction across from the main house. Sundanc raced toward them, barking ecstatically, his tail waggin furiously. Two men emerged from the partial structure, an there was no mistaking Pike on the front porch. The wago clattered across the bridge and came to a stop in front of th house.

Conor jumped from the seat and lifted Alina to the porch She faced Pike in silence for a moment. Pike looked back a her with suspiciously watery, love-filled eyes.

"Oh, Pike," she whispered, and threw her arms aroun him.

"Hello, Alina," he replied in a soft voice. "Welcom home." They held each other tightly for a long moment then Alina wiped her eyes as she bent to greet Sundanc while Pike held his hand out to Beau. "Good ta see ya Beau."

"You, too, Pike." Beau grabbed Pike's hand. "You loo good; how are you feeling?"

"No, Beau, Alina's the one what looks good. Not me, o you neither, for that matter. And I'm feelin' just fine. It'l take more'n the likes of Log Carter ta do in Sebastian Ama deus Pike." Pike looked up suddenly and saw the two me standing off to the side. "Damn," he muttered, "beg pardon Alina." He pointed a finger at the men. "The two of ya jus better forget the first part of my name, if ya know what' good for ya," he called.

Pike turned to Beau and waved back toward the smilin men. "Do ya remember the Rafferty brothers? Michae there played his harmonica at the McAllister barn-raisin' and they both helped with David's barn, and ours. The othe one's Ian."

Beau nodded. "I remember."

"They been helpin' out with the house and with the cattle Over yonder we're puttin' up the bunkhouse Conor wrote t ya about. I reckon the Raffertys would like ta stay on, if it' all right with ya."

"We'll need the help if we're going to turn this ranch into a profitmaking operation." He turned to Alina. "How do you feel about feeding a few extra mouths?"

"It's fine with me, if they're willing to risk my cooking," she answered with a smile. "But we'll need a bigger table."

"We already took care of that." Pike motioned to the brothers. "Come on up here and say hello ta the Parkers."

Michael and Ian swept their hats from their heads and shyly approached, shaking Beau's hand and bowing to Alina. They looked like twins, although it was obvious that Michael was older. They were both lean and of average height, with thick, unruly dark hair and laughing eyes.

"Welcome home, ma'am, sir." Michael's voice was heavily accented with an Irish brogue. "We hope ye like the changes to the house."

"I would like to see these changes." Alina's eyes sparkled with anticipation.

"Well, come on, then." Pike opened the door and stood back. Alina stepped through and gasped. Beau stood at her side. The kitchen was expanded to include what had been the back porch, and the door to Beau and Alina's bedroom was gone, as was the top half of the wall that had divided the bedroom and the living area.

"We turned your old bedroom into the dining room, and lowered the wall to waist level so it'll be warmer in there. We added a bathing room at the back of the kitchen; it'll have a water heater and a small stove by winter," Conor explained.

Alina strolled around the room, her expression one of delighted wonder.

"We'll need ta get more furniture, of course," added Pike. "Things look kinda empty now."

"It looks so much bigger," Alina marveled.

"Where's our bedroom?" asked Beau.

"Upstairs," answered Conor. "There's two bedrooms on the ground floor in the new addition, and two upstairs. Pike and I have the downstairs rooms, and you two have one upstairs, then there's a room for when the children come."

At the mention of children, a delicate blush painted Alina's cheeks with a becoming shade of pink. She looked at her cousin with shining eyes. "Thank you. It is just lovely." She kissed his cheek, then turned to Pike. "Thank you."

"Don't go gettin' all mushy on me, woman," Pike warned.

Alina smiled. "Thank you, Michael, Ian." She nodded at each brother in turn. They stood at the door, pieces of baggage in their hands.

"Well, let's get the trunks in and get settled," Beau suggested. "We brought a lot of things from Chicago. Alina's father was very generous."

"Your family sent a lot with you, too, Beau. Wait until you see it all, Pike. China, glassware, linens, books. This place will be beautiful."

"Sounds awful fancy ta me," Pike said suspiciously. "I ain't gonna drink my coffee outta no china cup."

"You won't have to," she promised with a laugh as she pulled off her gloves.

Late that night, Beau slipped under the blankets and took Alina in his arms. "Welcome to our new bedroom, wife," he murmured. He planted a light kiss on her lips.

She nestled her head into the hollow of his shoulder. "It is a lovely bedroom," she said as she eyed the smooth expanse of the ceiling. She breathed deeply of the fresh wood smell. "I expected an open ceiling, like in the original cabin. Who knew how to square it off?"

"Michael was a carpenter's apprentice in Ireland."

"But I thought he came out here working for the railroad."

Beau shrugged. "You do what you have to do, I guess, to make a living."

"Did you notice how excited he got when he learned that you can teach him to engrave and carve wood like our headboard?"

Beau nodded. "He's a good man, a hard worker, and eager to learn. Ian is cut from the same cloth. Pike and

Conor made good choices when they hired them. That reminds me of something—Pike asked Conor if he should move to the bunkhouse when it's completed."

"What?" Alina raised her head for a moment to look at him. "Pike is not moving to the bunkhouse, Beau. He's family."

"I agree. There's something I'd like to do, and I want to know how you feel about it."

She swirled a finger through the soft hair that covered Beau's chest. "What is it?"

"I want to offer Pike an equal partnership in the ranch. Conor, too, if he's interested. A man needs to have something to call his own. Maybe Pike won't feel strange about living in the house if he's part owner."

"Beau, what a wonderful idea! It's perfect!" She pressed a kiss to his chest. "And thank you for including Conor. I don't know what he will do. He's never actually said he's going to stay. There's a restlessness in him, Beau. I hate the thought of him leaving, but I don't think he's ready to settle down."

He stroked Alina's hair. "I don't think so, either, but I want to make the offer, and let him know that it's an open one. If he's not ready now, perhaps someday he will be."

Alina shifted her position so that the top of her body was angled over Beau's chest. She deliberately pressed her naked breasts to him as she maneuvered one slender leg over his legs. "Enough talking," she whispered. She kissed his lips lightly. Beau closed his eyes and sighed with pleasure as his wife wiggled against him again.

"But I haven't told you everything yet," he protested against her lips.

"Then you'd better talk fast, Beau Parker, because I'm an impatient woman." Alina's voice was sultry and full of promise. Her lips moved to his neck. Her roving hands preceded her mouth in its downward exploration of his long, lean body.

Beau struggled to remember what he needed to tell her.

His hands dropped to caress her back as she kissed his shoulder. "There was a letter from Clarence King in that stack of mail. He has finished his survey and will . . . be here sometime in the next few weeks. I . . . may have to . . . leave for a few days to help him settle the issue of . . . the diamond field." He caught his breath when Alina nibbled along his ribs.

"You'd better not be gone long," she warned. Her tongue trailed across Beau's abdomen. His hands tangled in her hair; his fingers tightened convulsively on the silken strands when her mouth moved lower.

"No, ma'am," he whispered hoarsely. A tremor raced through him. "Alina!"

A week later, Alina came out onto the porch, a bedroll in her hands. Beau was adjusting the cinch on Bay. She wordlessly handed him the roll.

"I don't know how long we'll be gone," Beau said as he tied the roll behind the saddle. "Thanks to the information some of the witnesses have given him, Clarence has an idea of where to look for this diamond field. We'll take the train west, probably all the way to Rock Springs. Clarence wants to concentrate his search in the Uintah Mountains. We'll be gone a week, maybe longer."

Alina pulled her shawl more tightly around her shoulders and crossed her arms over her chest. "It's only October, Beau, but you know winter can come early. Please be careful." She hesitated, chewing on her lip. "Are you sure you don't want Conor to go with you?"

Beau joined her on the porch and rested his hands on her hips. "With the three men Clarence has picked, we'll be fine." He kissed the tip of her nose. "Do you have a bad feeling about this trip?"

Alina hooked her hands behind his back and thought for a minute. "No." She shook her head. "No, I don't." A smile lit up her face. "You'll be fine. But you'd best remember that I warned you about being gone too long."

Beau's lips curved under his full mustache. "I certainly do remember that warning, and with great pleasure, madam." His eyes gleamed as Alina's cheeks turned suspiciously pink. "How long is too long?"

"One hour." Alina leaned back against his arms and smoothed his vest lapel. "Listen to me," she sighed. "I sound like a nagging wife. I know you have to do this, Beau, and it will take as long as it will take. But I'll miss you terribly."

"And I you, darling. My thin blanket on the cold ground and the thought of you alone in our bed will be a fitting punishment for leaving you, even for this little while."

"You deserve it," Alina pouted.

"Heartless woman," Beau said with a laugh. "Now give me a good, wifely kiss and let me be on my way, or night will fall and I'll still be standing here with you in my arms."

Their parting kiss was deep, but more loving than passionate. Beau patted her bottom with affection, then climbed into the saddle. "I'm to meet Clarence and his party at the hotel, then we'll catch the westbound. If anyone goes to town in the next few days, check the wire office; I'll try to keep in touch." He touched his heels to Bay's sides. Alina hugged herself and watched him until he was out of sight.

The late October wind blew off the distant mountains in increasingly colder gusts. Beau pulled the collar of his duster up around his neck and burrowed his chin into its warmth. He hoped it didn't snow. It would be impossible to track the path to the diamond fields if it did. He nudged Bay into a lope and came up beside Clarence King.

"If those cottonwoods ahead indicate water," Beau pointed, "I think we should rest the horses and get our bearings."

Clarence nodded in agreement. "These gullies and ravines twist around themselves. I don't even know for sure what direction we're heading now, with the sun behind those clouds. Do you think it'll snow?"

Beau eyed the sky. "It's hard to say. It could blow over."

"Let's hope it does."

The two riders rounded a large rock formation and found that the cottonwoods hugged the banks of a narrow creek. Beau slipped from the saddle and led Bay to the water. His eyes fell on the remains of a campfire close to the trunk of one of the trees. He looped the reins over the saddle horn and bent to examine the charred wood and ashes. One by one, his companions joined him.

"Well, someone's been here," Beau commented. "I'd say this fire is old, though, at least a month."

"I'll check our position, then we'll spread out and explore the area." Clarence pulled a roll of maps from a specially designed leather tube that he carried on his back. Beau stood over the group as Clarence spread the maps on the ground. The one he wanted was on top. It did not take him long to determine their position. He sat back on his heels as the maps slowly rerolled themselves.

"It's impossible to know whose fire that was, but comb this area. Look for anything out of the ordinary. I don't care if it's an old bean can. Anything."

The men moved away, with the exception of Beau. Clarence tightened the roll of maps and slid them into the tube. He slipped the leather strap over his head as he got to his feet.

"Beau, it's got to be around here somewhere." He pounded a fist into his palm. "I know it."

Beau nodded in understanding. He looked at Clarence. His friend was a short man, not much over five feet, but of muscular build. Dark blond hair showed under his hat, and a full, neatly trimmed blond beard covered the lower half of his face.

"Do you think Arnold and Slack salted the field?"

Clarence slapped his glove against his thigh. "They *had* to have salted it. I certainly hope they did, or I'm going to look nighty foolish. I surveyed this entire area a year ago and ound no evidence of precious stones of any kind. I just don't hink I could have missed something so important, Beau. If he Arnold claim is true, my professional reputation is jeopardized, if not my career."

"Mr. King!" One of the men, an elderly German prospecor, ran toward them, waving a piece of paper. "Look vat I ound! It vas folded up and impaled on a stick by the vater!" He handed the paper to Clarence.

Clarence quickly scanned the sheet. His face lit up with excitement. "It's a water claim, signed by Henry Janin!"

"You sound as if you know him," commented Beau.

"He's a mining engineer of some renown." Clarence stuffed the claim slip in his pocket. "He's also a stockholder n the Diamond Company. He was allowed to trade his professional expertise for shares, and Arnold brought him to he fields on at least one occasion. I've seen a copy of his eport. He claims it to be a very rich field. This is what we needed, gentlemen! We'll spread out in a circle. There *must* be tracks!"

The men ran to their mounts and set off on a diligent search. A half an hour later Beau found the tracks of a party of riders, about one hundred yards from the site of the campfire. He whistled and the others joined him. The trail ed them on a winding journey that eventually climbed to the op of a sandstone mesa. The five men sat their horses side by side and stared in awed silence.

The ground in front of them fairly sparkled as determined ays of the sun forced their way though the clouds and kissed he gems that seemed to cover the earth.

"My God," Clarence whispered.

" 'Iss like finding the treasure of pirates," the old German said breathlessly.

Beau felt an excited shiver run down his spine. It was ndeed like finding treasure. "Let's check this out."

Clarence nodded and urged his horse forward. The men

spread out and stepped down from their saddles. Each man soon had a handful of stones. They met again.

"This doesn't make sense." Clarence shook his head. "These are not all diamonds. I have a sapphire here, and a ruby, and Beau, that dark stone you have is an emerald, if I'm not mistaken."

Beau held the indicated stone up and examined it.

"This field has to be salted," Clarence said with conviction. "Nature doesn't put these jewels together in one place like this."

"Look at this, Mr. King." The old German held up a shiny stone. "Nature cut this vun for us!" He cackled with glee.

Clarence snatched the stone from the man's hand. "Well done, Mr. Dietrich! You've earned your pay on this trip." He held up the stone and laughed. "This is the proof we needed, gentlemen! Cut diamonds, indeed!" He turned to his saddlebag and pulled out a folded cloth bag. He dropped his stones, except for the cut diamond, into the bag and held it open. The other men emptied their hands. "We'll conduct a thorough search of this area. Retrieve every stone you find as well as anything else you think may be used as evidence." The men spread out again.

Beau clapped Clarence on the shoulder. "Good job, man."

A happy grin wreathed Clarence's face. "I just *knew* there was no field, Beau. I could not have missed such a find."

"Who gets the stones?"

Clarence shrugged. "I would guess they're the property of the Diamond Company. I can't wait to see the look on Phil Arnold's face when I confront him with this." He kissed the cut stone and slipped it into his shirt pocket.

"I can't wait to see the look on Richard Petrie's face when we tell him," said Beau, his voice soft and grim.

* * *

"We found the diamond field, Mr. Petrie." Clarence King dropped the cut diamond on Richard Petrie's desk. "It was salted. This whole thing was a hoax from the very beginning." King's words sounded unnaturally loud in the quiet office.

Richard Petrie stared at the stone, his face ashen. "I don't understand." His words came out in a rough whisper.

"It's all been for nothing, Petrie." Beau spoke harshly from his place by the door. Madeline whirled in her chair to glare at him, then turned back to her father.

"Where is Arnold?" demanded Clarence.

Petrie picked up the stone. His fingers tightened around it. "Gone. Arnold is gone."

"Gone where?"

Petrie slowly shook his head. "I don't know. He was becoming a problem, so we bought him out. Slack, too."

"When? For how much?" Beau asked.

"A week ago. Five hundred thousand to Arnold, one hundred thousand to Slack." Petrie dropped the stone and leaned back in his chair, running a hand over his brow.

"Oh, Father," Madeline whispered, her hand at her throat.

Clarence glanced at Beau, then reached for the stone. "I'll prepare a formal report and send it to the board of directors of the Diamond Company. We recovered many stones at the sight; they'll help alleviate part of the loss, but they aren't worth anywhere near six hundred thousand dollars." He walked toward the door. "I'll be at the Laramie Hotel until tomorrow if you have any questions, Mr. Petrie."

Beau followed him out. Somehow this triumph felt hollow. Petrie had suffered great financial loss, and his reputation in the community had been severely damaged, but Beau felt no sense of real satisfaction. Perhaps the fact that the question of Ambrose's murder had not been answered was what was troubling him, he reflected as he stepped out onto Petrie's porch. He was convinced that Ross Latham knew who the murderer was, but that man had disappeared after he had warned Beau of the danger threatening Alina. A smile came to Beau's lips at the thought of Alina. How he had missed her! Perhaps, for her sake, he should face the possibility that his brother's murderer might never be caught. Beau hated the idea of giving up, but perhaps it was time to leave the past behind. He put his hat on his head and stepped off the porch.

"If you're hungry, I'm buying," Clarence invited. "I think they're still serving breakfast at the hotel."

"I'll take you up on that, but then I've got to get home. I've been away from my wife for too long. These last ten days have felt like ten years."

"You sound like a newlywed, Beau," Clarence laughed. "She must be quite a woman."

"She is, Clarence, she is." The two men walked their mounts away from the Petrie house. "Come out to the ranch for supper tonight and see for yourself."

"I think I'll do just that," Clarence answered with a grin.

Meanwhile, Madeline stared at her father with fear-filled eyes. Never had she seen him like this, so quiet, so . . . defeated.

"Father?" she whispered.

"Go away, girl," he snapped. He suddenly jumped up from his seat and strode over to the long window that looked out over the yard. He braced his hands on the middle window frame and leaned his weight on his arms. His head fell forward in despair.

Madeline swept from her chair. "Father, we'll find Arnold and Slack and get your money back." She approached him, then retreated a step when he turned on her.

"It isn't just the money, Madeline! Don't you see? Parker was right. It's all been for nothing! All of my plans, my dreams, *everything*, is gone! My reputation is destroyed!" He pounded his fist into his other hand. "It's bad enough that I'm blamed for the fires and the attacks, but I also encouraged some very important people to invest in that damned diamond company. I am ruined!"

"But you didn't have anything to do with the fires, Father, nd no one can prove that you did. It was Log."

Her father placed his hands on his hips. Madeline flinched t the withering, scornful look he gave her. "And Log vorked for me, Madeline. He was a brute and a fool. You now as well as I do that Log Carter wasn't smart enough ɔ plan those attacks. Whoever was behind him was very, ery clever."

"Maybe it was Ross Latham."

"Maybe it was, but we'll never know, will we? The man as disappeared." Petrie waved both of his arms at her. "Just o. Get out of here. I don't want to talk to you."

"But, Father, please let me help!" Madeline pleaded.

"Get out!" he roared.

Madeline stiffened. She backed toward the door, then vhirled and ran into the foyer and up the stairs to her room. he threw herself across the bed and pounded her fists on the nattress as she screamed again and again into the pillows. Vhen the storm had passed, Madeline sat up and listlessly ushed at her disheveled hair. She was quiet for a long time. Gradually a rage grew in her; it started as a flicker, and built ɔ an inferno. She lifted her head. A slow, wicked smile urved her lips as the fire inside reached her eyes. Those esponsible for her father's pain would pay, as they always id. She would need help, and she knew where to get it. Oh, es, they would pay. She jumped off the bed and ran to her vriting desk.

Chapter Twenty-two

"Hold on tight while Lucy takes us up this hill, Tanya," Alina instructed. "It's very steep." The child obedientl wrapped her arms around Alina's waist. The stalwart mar scrambled up the rocky incline and heaved herself onto th level hilltop. Alina patted the animal's damp neck. "Goo girl."

"Where is the trestle?" Tanya asked.

Alina pointed. "I think we'll be able to see it from ove there." She angled the horse toward a lone pine a shor distance away. When they reached the tree, Alina pulled o the reins. Lucy stopped and tossed her head with a gentl nicker. Alina lifted her right leg over the saddle horn and sli to the ground, then helped Tanya down. Tanya took he hand and they walked to the edge of the hilltop.

It was a beautiful November day, perfect for showing o the magnificent vista spread out before them. Alina caugh her breath at the sight of rolling hills covered with pine tree intermingled with stretches of open prairie. Far to the sout and west the snow-capped Rocky Mountains marched on i timeless majesty. A cool wind blew her skirt against her legs Except for the sound of the wind in the trees that covered th hillside below them, it was absolutely quiet.

"I see the trestle!" Tanya pointed to the bridge that wa visible in the distance.

"So there it is," Alina agreed with a smile. "How did you spot it so quickly?"

"I followed the railroad tracks with my eyes. Do you think a train will come?"

"I hope so. The engineer always blows his whistle before he crosses the trestle, and we'll be able to hear it up here."

"Oh, I hope a train comes, too." Tanya squeezed Alina's hand. "I'm so glad you and Mr. Parker came home. I missed you."

Alina dropped to her knees and hugged the child. "I'm glad we came home, too. Let's sit here for a while. Lucy can rest, and we'll see if a train comes."

Tanya sat down and wrapped her skirt around her legs. Alina settled to the ground and took off her broad-brimmed felt hat. The wind ruffled the fine curls around her face. She breathed deeply of the crisp, clean air as her eyes wandered contentedly over the land. This was a good place to live and raise children, she thought. Her hand went to her flat belly. Her monthly time had not come since they had returned from Chicago. A soft smile touched her lips. Perhaps Beau's child already grew within her.

A sudden chill ran down her back. Alina frowned and looked around. The sun still shone; the wind had not picked up. Tanya seemed not to have noticed anything. Alina concentrated with all of her senses. The familiar feeling of uneasiness crept over her.

"Tanya, we have to go." Alina rose and clapped her hat back on, then tightened the string under her chin.

"But we haven't seen the train," Tanya protested as Alina pulled her to her feet.

"I know, honey. We'll have to save that for another time." Alina swung up into the saddle. She adjusted the skirts of her wool dress around her knees and slipped her left foot from the stirrup, then held down a hand for Tanya. "Take my hand and put your foot in the stirrup, just like we did at your house. That's right. Now you jump and I'll pull." Tanya flew up to her seat behind Alina.

Alina positioned her booted feet in the stirrups and turned Lucy's head in the direction from which they had come. "Hold on, Tanya. We're going to go very fast." She urged Lucy to a lope across the hilltop, then slowed her to a walk as they descended the hillside. Alina breathed a sigh of relief when they safely reached the bottom. The ride from here to the Freeman ranch was an easy one. She searched the terrain. Only the tree branches and tall stems of dead grasses moved, obeying the gentle command of the wind. She nudged Lucy on.

"Is something wrong, Mrs. Parker?" Tanya's voice sounded small and nervous.

"I don't know, honey. I just have a feeling we should get home as quickly as we can. But let's both be brave and try not to worry, all right?" She felt Tanya nod against her back. "That's my girl."

Alina slipped her rifle from its case and held it loosely in her right hand. She leaned forward over the saddle horn and urged Lucy to a run.

Conor held his horse to a trot as he came across the bridge into the yard. He pulled up in front of the house and jumped to the porch. "Alina!" he shouted as he burst into the main room. "Alina!" He ran to the foot of the stairs.

"Ya don't need ta be yellin', Conor, 'cause she can't hear ya, 'cause she ain't here." Pike clumped through the back door with an armload of wood.

"Where is she?"

Pike dropped the wood next to the stove. "She said somethin' about goin' for a ride. Beau'll know for sure."

"Where is he?" Conor was back at the door.

Pike shrugged. "Damned if I know. Say, there ain't nothin' wrong, is there?"

Conor didn't hear Pike's question as he was already outside. He spied Ian on the roof of the finished bunkhouse, wrestling with the stabilizers for the tin stove chimney. "Where's Beau?" he shouted.

"In the barn, I think!"

Conor waved his thanks and ran toward the barn. Beau emerged from the building, wiping his hands on a piece of old blanket.

"Looking for me?"

"Is Alina back from her ride?"

Beau shook his head. "Not yet. Should she be?"

"The Randalls are here."

"What?"

Conor pushed his hat back on his head and placed his hands on his hips. "Ran into Sam at the post office. He said the Randalls arrived the day before yesterday. When he asked what they were doing back in town, they told him Madeline Petrie had invited them for a visit. He had no grounds to kick them onto the next train out of town." Conor adjusted his hat. "Petrie closed up his house in town and has retreated to the ranch. I assume that's where they all are."

Beau whirled and strode back into the barn. Conor followed. "I'll feel a whole lot better if one of us is with Alina at all times, at least until the Randalls are gone," Beau said as he moved to the stall that held Bay. He threw the rag down and grabbed the bridle hanging on a nail by the stall gate.

Conor nodded his agreement. "Do you know which way she was headed?"

"She said something about an overlook where you can see the Dale Creek trestle. She was going to take Tanya with her."

"I know where that is. Pike and I found it when we rode the fence last summer."

Beau's stomach tightened. *When you left so that Alina and I could be alone.* He slipped the bridle over Bay's head and led the animal from the stall. "We'll check with the Freemans first. If we're lucky, she's got Tanya back home already and is drinking tea and gabbing with Cynthia."

"I'll let Pike know what's going on. Meet me at the porch."

Beau nodded as he threw the saddle blanket over Bay's back. "Get my hat!" he called. Conor waved in acknowledgment. Beau prayed that they worried for no reason.

Alina slowed Lucy to a walk. The little mare's sides were heaving.

"Can't we keep running?" Tanya asked.

Alina shook her head. "Lucy can't. We have to walk her for a little while, just until she catches her breath. Then we'll run again. We aren't that far from your place, Tanya. We'll be all right."

They walked a short distance. Alina's eyes darted all around, searching for anything out of the ordinary. She could feel that whatever or whoever threatened them was very close. Lucy nickered as they rounded the base of a small hill.

Alina was not surprised to see a man standing on the trail in front of them, nor was she surprised at his identity. The man stood in an arrogant pose, his weight leaned into one hip. He held his mount's reins in one hand and his rifle in the other, the barrel resting back on his shoulder. Alina pulled Lucy to a stop a short distance from the man and waited for him to speak.

"Well, well, well. Look who we have here." Donovan Randall's lip twisted in a sneer.

Alina met his insulting gaze with cool dignity. Her chin lifted. "Let us pass, Donovan."

"I've come a long way to talk to you, Alina, and talk we will. Get off the horse."

"I'm not alone, Donovan," she warned. "I am also not unarmed." She shifted the rifle, but did not raise it.

Lucy sidestepped nervously and Donovan was able to see

Tanya. In one quick motion he maneuvered his rifle into firing position. "Too bad about the kid, Alina." He shook his head. "Get off the horse or I'll kill her."

Alina analyzed her situation with calm detachment. She was a marksman, but not necessarily a fast one. She could not shoot Donovan before he shot at them. If she tried to run, Tanya's back would be Donovan's target. There was no choice but to obey him.

"I'm going to put the rifle in the case, then I'll get down. Don't shoot, Donovan." She slid the rifle into the leather case, then lifted her left leg over the saddle horn and slipped to the ground. She turned her back to Donovan. "Scoot into the saddle, Tanya," she whispered as she looped the reins over the saddle horn. "You must do exactly as I say. When I tell you to ride, hold on tight and ride as fast as you can. Tell your papa what's happened. You know the way from here." She pushed her hat off her head so that it hung down her back.

"But what about you?" Tanya's eyes were wide with fear. She took up the reins. Her thin legs dangled high above the stirrups.

"Quit talking, Alina, and get over here!"

"I'll be fine," Alina whispered to Tanya. "Be brave and do as I say. My life may depend on it." She turned and faced the man. "Let her go, Donovan." She walked toward him, her hands held out at her sides. "She's only a child."

"She's old enough to talk, so she's coming with us." Donovan strode forward and grabbed Alina's arm in a cruel grip. He jerked her back toward his horse. "Get up there."

Alina put a foot in the stirrup and glanced over her shoulder. Donovan was looking back at Tanya. He raised the rifle. Alina grabbed the saddle horn and lifted her weight onto the leg in the stirrup, then threw herself backward with all the force she could muster. She slammed into Donovan and knocked him to the ground. His rifle discharged into the earth in front of Lucy. The startled horse reared. Tanya screamed.

"Ride, Tanya!" Alina cried. She rolled off Donovan and struggled to reach his rifle as Tanya raced past them, clinging to Lucy's neck.

With a vicious curse, Donovan pulled Alina toward him. He rose to his knees and struck her across the face. When she fell back, he grabbed the gun. He stood and shot after the disappearing horse.

"No!" Alina struggled to her knees and wrapped her arms around his legs, throwing him off balance. "For God's sake, Donovan! She's a child!"

"God damn it!" Donovan kicked at her and hit her arm with the butt of the rifle. Alina cried out and released him. She sank back into a sitting position and massaged her right forearm. The sound of Lucy's hoofbeats faded away.

Donovan turned to her, his face mottled with fury. He dragged her to her feet. "Get on the horse."

Alina staggered, suddenly dizzy. She grabbed at the saddle horn and pulled herself into the saddle. She slumped forward.

"Get your feet out of the stirrups," Donovan growled. Alina obeyed him. He climbed up behind her and roughly pulled her against him. His arm deliberately brushed against her breast. "We'll just have us a cozy little ride, won't we, Mrs. Parker?"

Alina jabbed him with her elbow. Donovan slammed his rifle into its case, then grabbed her chin in a brutal grip with one hand, while the other traveled up her thigh under her skirt. "Don't fight me," he warned, "or I'll begin your long overdue lessons in submission right here, right now." He released her chin and sadistically pinched the tender flesh of her thigh until Alina bit her lip to keep from crying out. Donovan moved his hand from under her skirt to her waist again and directed the horse off the trail and into the trees.

When Beau and Conor arrived at the Freemans and learned that Alina and Tanya had not yet returned, a pressing sense of dread overcame both of them. They did not waste any time starting out, heading toward the bluff as fast as they safely could over the rough ground.

Beau searched the trail ahead of them with desperate eyes. He slowed Bay to a walk. Conor pulled up along side him.

"How much further is it to the overlook?"

"I'd guess two miles." Suddenly Conor held up his hand. "Did you hear that?"

"Sounded like a gunshot to me," Beau said. His lips pressed in a grim line. They urged their mounts to a trot.

After a few minutes, Beau stopped. "Listen. Someone's coming." He motioned with his head. He and Conor moved into the trees on opposite sides of the trail and pulled their pistols. A moment later a wild-eyed Lucy raced into view. Beau saw Tanya clinging to the saddle. He slammed his gun back into the holster and moved Bay out into the trail. Lucy shied with a piercing squeal and slowed to a trot. Conor grabbed the reins while Beau guided his horse next to Lucy and lifted the terrified child from the saddle. Tanya wrapped her arms around his neck in a deathlike grip.

"Where's Alina, honey?" Beau asked gently.

Tanya sobbed against his collar. "Back . . . there, with that . . . awful man!"

"Shh, shh." Beau held her close. "Do you know the man?"

Tanya shook her head.

"Did Alina know him?"

Tanya nodded.

"Did she call him Donovan?"

Another nod.

"Did he say where he was taking her?"

Another shake. "He was going . . . to shoot me!" Tanya wailed.

Beau's jaw clenched. He looked over Tanya's head at Conor.

"I saw Petrie with his herd south of the Pass Road a few hours ago," said Conor. "Do you think he's part of this?"

"What do you think?" Beau snapped. "We can't have Tanya along with us. Take her home, then go back to where you saw Petrie, and if he's still there, get him to his ranch house. I'll follow Donovan, and I'll bet we meet at Petrie's."

Conor tied Lucy's reins around his saddle horn and held his arms out for Tanya. He settled the girl in front of him and wrapped one arm securely around her. "Watch your back, Beau."

Beau touched the brim of his hat in a gesture of farewell and was gone.

Donovan shoved Alina through the door with such force that she almost fell. She caught herself and straightened. She was in a hallway that ran the length of a large, elegantly decorated log house.

Her captor slammed the front door and took her arm once again. He pulled her down the hall to a room on the left and pushed her into what proved to be a parlor. Cordelia looked up from her chair with a startled expression on her pale face. Madeline stood with her back to the room, staring into the flames in the fireplace.

"I found her." Donovan's voice held a victorious note that sent a shiver down Alina's spine.

Cordelia rose from her chair. "What is the meaning of this, Donovan?"

"Oh, come, Mother. You said you wanted revenge," Donovan said with impatience. "Well, so do I. And so does Madeline. Now we'll have it." He stomped to a side table and poured a generous amount of brandy into a glass.

Cordelia's worried gaze moved from her son to Madeline. "What do you intend to do with her?"

"Exact revenge." Madeline spoke quietly, but her words carried throughout the room. She slowly turned to face Alina. Her lips curved in a triumphant smile that did not reach her burning eyes. "At last I will have my revenge."

Alina straightened her shoulders and stared fearlessly into Madeline's eyes. "Beau will come."

Madeline nodded. "I hope he does."

"Uh, he may come sooner than we expected." Donovan spoke from the side table. He took a quick drink from his glass.

"What do you mean?" Cordelia snapped.

"One of those half-colored brats was with her." He gestured toward Alina with his glass. "The kid got away."

"That is unfortunate," Madeline said in a soft tone. "We will have to move much more quickly then." She eyed Alina with distaste. Even with dirt on her face and her hair tangled around her shoulders, the bitch managed to look beautiful. Madeline fought the urge to scratch the defiant look from Alina's face. She took comfort from the fact that Alina wouldn't look so beautiful and defiant when she was dead.

"Everything is your fault, you know," Madeline began conversationally. "If you had only done as Cordelia wished, none of this would have happened. You never would have come here, and Beau would have married me, and my father would have had the timber on the Parker land."

Madeline wandered about the room, her skirts swaying behind her. "You have been a problem since you arrived here in Wyoming Territory, Mrs. Parker." She laughed, a tittering sound with a hysterical edge to it. "But I'll see that you aren't a problem much longer, just like you won't be Mrs. Parker much longer." Donovan moved away from her as she approached the side table. She opened the small drawer below the marble top. A moment later she turned with a Colt revolver in her hand.

"Put the gun away, Madeline," Cordelia ordered.

"Mother, she just wants to be sure Alina doesn't try anything. Will you relax?" Donovan took another swallow of brandy.

"She intends to kill her, you idiot! She has wanted to kill her all along! She told us that herself in Chicago!"

Donovan, suddenly alarmed, set the glass down.

Madeline advanced on Alina, seemingly oblivious to the Randalls' conversation. "What did he ever see in you?" Madeline sounded truly puzzled as she waved the gun to indicate Alina's simple plaid skirt and dark blue jacket. "He could have had me, and instead he chose you. I promised he would regret the day he married you, and so he will."

"Madeline, the idea was to give her to me," Donovan interjected. He walked toward Alina. "You said I could have her."

Madeline stiffened and turned slightly to face him. "But what of me, Donovan?" Her eyes were narrowed, her voice dangerously sweet. "I thought you wanted me. Surely you were not lying all those times you took me to your bed."

Cordelia stared aghast at her son.

Too late Donovan realized his mistake. "Uh, no, of course I wasn't lying. Let me have her first, then we can, uh, kill her." He stepped back.

Madeline shook her head. "Poor Donovan. You're obsessed with her, too. Well, I can fix that." She raised the gun and fired twice, striking Donovan in the chest with both shots. His eyes widened in stunned disbelief, then he staggered backward and fell to the floor.

Cordelia screamed, a horrible, agonized sound, and rushed to her son's side. She fell to her knees and cradled Donovan's head on her lap. Alina knelt at his other side. She tore her riding gloves from her hands and pressed them to the wounds in Donovan's chest in a vain attempt to stem the flow of blood. Madeline stood at Donovan's feet, her face devoid of all expression.

Donovan grasped Alina's hand and held it tightly as he lifted his gaze to his mother. "That judge . . . was right, Mama," he rasped. "Alina would . . . have been a handful." Blood streamed from the corner of his mouth. His grip on Alina's hand loosened and his breathing stopped.

Alina eased her hand from his and closed his lids.

"No!" Cordelia wailed. She held Donovan's head to her

breast and rocked back and forth. "No, no, no." Her voice dropped to a moan. Suddenly her head jerked up.

"Murderer!" she screamed at Madeline. "Murdering bitch!"

Madeline pursed her lips, then raised the gun and fired again. Cordelia slumped backward. Blood ran down the side of her head and over the collar of her silk dress.

Alina raised horrified eyes to Madeline, fully expecting to find the gun trained on her.

Instead, Madeline motioned with the weapon. "Get up. Get over by the fireplace."

Alina cautiously obeyed, never taking her eyes from Madeline. "How are you going to explain the bodies of your guests?"

Madeline daintily shrugged her shoulders. "You killed them."

Alina blinked in surprise.

"You had a motive . . . revenge!" Madeline laughed again, the same hysterical sound. "And your skill with a gun is well known. I came home, found my guests murdered, and was forced to kill you in self-defense. It's so simple."

Alina backed up against the mantel. Her eyes darted about, searching desperately for anything that could be used as a weapon. "Do you hope to regain Beau's affections if I am out of the way?"

Madeline's lips tightened. "That bastard," she spat. "He had his chance. He'll die, like his brother before him."

Alina gasped. *"You* killed Ambrose?" she asked, incredulous.

Madeline shrugged. "I had to. He spurned me. We were lovers, and then he backed out of our engagement. He said the only reason I wanted to marry him was so that my father could have access to his timber."

"Wasn't that true?"

"Of course it was true! I would never have thrown myself away on a worthless cowboy, except for my father." Madeline's eyes clouded with confusion. Her voice fell to a whisper. "I would do anything for my father."

Alina inched closer to a small table that held a collection of china figurines. A movement at the door caught her eye. Beau held a finger to his lips. She forced her attention back to Madeline.

"Everything was arranged." Madeline's voice was stronger now. "Then Ambrose ruined it. So he had to pay."

"Like I'll have to pay?" Beau demanded from the door. Alina snatched up the nearest figurine and raised her arm to throw it. Madeline squeezed the trigger and a bullet struck the mantel not two inches from Alina's chest. She froze.

"The next one kills her, Beau." Madeline's voice was cold and determined. She motioned with the gun; Alina set the figurine on the mantel shelf.

Beau edged into the room, his hands out at his sides. "Don't shoot, Madeline. Let's talk."

"You had your chance to talk a year ago," Madeline snapped. "I even gave you a chance to redeem yourself last spring. I was willing to forgive you everything. You should have gotten rid of her then." She kept the gun on Alina and motioned with her free hand without looking at him. "Come closer, so I can see you."

Beau cautiously moved further into the room. He stood behind one of the matching sofas that faced each other in front of the fireplace.

"Now I have to change my story," Madeline complained. Her brow furrowed in concentration. "It's too bad, but you'll have to die, too, Beau." She shook her head regretfully. "I've always wanted you. I wanted to know if you are as good a lover as your brother was. But you fought me, too. And you fought my father. That is the real reason you must die. You hurt my father. The stupid peasants in this valley would not have defied my father if you hadn't set the example. Then your friend, that geologist, he ruined the Diamond Company."

"You can't blame Beau for that!" Alina protested. "He didn't salt the area, or take your father's money."

"But he helped expose the hoax before my father had time to figure out what he would do."

"Madeline, put the gun down and let's discuss what we can do to help your father." Beau moved closer to the fireplace.

Madeline paused for a minute. "You want to help my father?" A puzzled expression covered her face. She was silent for a moment. "I'm tired of talking," she said suddenly. "Say goodbye to your wife, Beau." She took aim at Alina.

"No!" Beau shouted as he ran toward Alina, knowing as he did that he could not reach her in time.

Madeline shifted her arm and fired.

The bullet slammed into Beau's shoulder. He staggered and knocked into the table of figurines. Alina instinctively reached for him.

"Oh, God, Beau!" she cried.

"I'm all right," he said roughly. "Just stay there." Blood welled from the wound and soaked his shirt.

"What in the hell is going on here?" Richard Petrie's voice thundered from the door. Conor stood beside him. Both men had their guns drawn.

"Father!" Madeline glanced over her shoulder, then looked back to Beau and Alina. Her left hand joined her right on the pistol grip. "I have to kill them, Father."

Petrie and Conor advanced into the room. Conor moved quickly to the Randalls. He checked Donovan, then pressed two fingers to Cordelia's throat. He tore his neckerchief from his neck and pressed the cloth to her head. "Donovan is dead, but Cordelia is still alive," he said quietly. "The bullet only creased her scalp."

"Madeline, put the gun down," Petrie ordered.

Madeline shook her head.

Petrie glanced at Beau.

"Madeline shot the Randalls, Petrie. She also killed Ambrose."

"I had to!" screamed Madeline. "Ambrose wouldn't do what you wanted him to!"

Petrie turned horrified eyes to his daughter. "You killed Ambrose Parker?" he whispered.

"I had to," she repeated. "Surely you can see that, Father." The gun shook in her hands.

"You were behind the fires? You told Carter what to do?"

"Carter was no good," Madeline spat. "If he had done his job, she would be dead." She indicated Alina. "I should have taken care of her myself."

Petrie looked at Beau. "I swear, Parker, I had no idea. I had nothing to do with it." There was no mistaking the revulsion in his voice.

Madeline blinked. "But, Father, I did it all for you," she whispered. "I even rode with them sometimes."

"You burned people's homes and barns! You terrorized and assaulted and murdered people and you have the nerve to tell me you did it for me?" Petrie's outraged words seemed to reverberate off the ceiling.

Madeline's lower lip trembled. "But I thought you'd be pleased, Father. You wanted their land."

"My own daughter. My God, I raised a murderer."

Madeline straightened. She blinked the tears from her eyes. Savage resolve filled her face.

"Madeline, put the gun down."

"I can't, Father. Not until they're dead." She pulled the hammer back. "Especially now."

"You can't kill both of us, Madeline. You only have one bullet left." Beau held a hand to his shoulder.

Madeline paused in confusion. "Then I'll kill her. She's the one to blame for all of this."

"No, Madeline!" Petrie shouted.

Beau threw himself in front of Alina as Madeline squeezed the trigger. The bullet struck the mantel, for at the same instant that Madeline fired, Richard Petrie raised his gun and shot his only child in the head.

Epilogue

A soft, early-morning breeze whispered through the boughs of the pines and ruffled the young leaves that had sprung from the branches of Alina's rosebush. Spring had come again to the Laramie Valley.

Alina stood on the porch, her arms crossed over her rounded stomach. She drank in the beauty of the valley spread before her and tried to ignore a gnawing sense of sadness.

Voices came to her from the direction of the barn. She turned and saw a group of men emerge from the building, one of them leading a horse. As she watched, Conor shook hands with Michael and Ian Rafferty; she could not hear their words. The brothers stood back as Beau, Conor, and Pike approached the house. Conor held Charlie's reins in one hand.

Alina forced a smile to her lips and went to meet the men.

"I ain't one for long goodbyes, Conor." Pike held out his hand. "Ya just take care of yourself, and know that ya always have a place here."

Conor took Pike's outstretched hand in a warm grip. "Thank you, Pike. You take care, too, and watch over that dog." He nodded at Sundance, who sat at Pike's side. "I'll expect to see him when I come back."

Pike nodded, then climbed the steps to the porch. "Watch your back, son, and come home ta us," he gruffly said over his shoulder. "Come on, dog. I saved ya a biscuit." He disappeared into the cabin.

Conor turned to Beau. "Thank you for everything." They shook hands.

"Thank you, Conor. Like Pike said, you have a home here. Equal partnership in the ranch is yours whenever you want it."

Conor nodded. "I can't quite see myself as a respectable landowner, but who knows? Maybe some day. I appreciate the offer. I'm also real happy you married up with my cousin. You're good for her."

"As she is for me, Conor. I'll take care of her."

"I know you will." Conor looked at Alina as he blindly handed the reins to Beau and took off his hat. "Motherhood agrees with you," he said with a smile.

Alina's return smile was tremulous as she held out her arms. "I'll miss you, Conor."

Conor held her tightly. "And I you, Cousin. Be happy and may God grant you a safe delivery. I'll come for a visi before the year is out."

"I hope you find whatever it is you are looking for."

"So do I," Conor whispered. His arms tightened around her before he released her. He placed his hat on his head and accepted the reins from Beau, then vaulted effortlessly into the saddle.

"If you go through Colorado Territory, look up my friend Susannah if you get a chance," Alina suggested as Beau moved to her side and draped his arm around her shoulders. She leaned into him. "The last letter I received from her at Christmas said she and her father left Charleston and were thinking of settling in the mountains west of Denver, near a little town called Georgetown. His name is Thomas Duncan."

Conor touched his hat. "I'll do it." His eyes softened with affection as he gazed at the couple before him. "You two have something rare. Treasure it, and each other." He raised a gloved hand in farewell and touched his heels to Charlie's sides.

"Goodbye!" Alina cried. "Go with God!" She waved frantically and blinked against the tears that filled her eyes.

Beau held her close. "He'll come back," he assured her.

"I know." She sniffed against his shirt. "But I'll miss him, Beau. I love him like a brother."

They turned toward the house, each with an arm around the other. "Conor is right, you know," Beau said as they topped the steps to the porch. "Motherhood does agree with you. I swear, you get more beautiful every day, Alina Parker." He stood back and looked at her, the warmth and depth of his love shining from his eyes.

"If I'm beautiful, it's your love and your child that makes me that way," Alina responded with a smile. She pressed a quick kiss to Beau's lips and turned within the circle of his arms so that her back was to him and his arms rested on her stomach. He caressed her belly with one hand.

"I love it here, Beau." Alina looked over the expanse of their land. "And I love you, more than I can say."

Beau pressed his face to her scented hair and sighed in perfect contentment.

Dear Reader:

I hope you enjoyed reading *The Irish Rose*, and that it carried you back to another time and place. I write historical romance for two reasons: first, because I believe in the power of love, and second, to indulge my fascination for history. It gives me the opportunity to live in another time through my words. I enjoy weaving historical fact into stories of romance and love. For instance, the Great Diamond Hoax in *The Irish Rose* really happened, much as I depicted it. Clarence King really was a geologist, and he went on to organize the United States Geological Survey.

My next novel, *The Mountain Rose*, will be an August 1994 release. It is the story of Conor O'Rourke, a drifter who is perhaps too good with a gun (you met Conor in *The Irish Rose*), and Susannah Duncan, a spirited young woman who came from the East with her aging father to build a new life in the mountains of Colorado Territory. Conor and Susannah join forces against a ruthless mining baron who is determined to have both the Duncan land and Susannah.

It is my sincere wish that you find entertainment and escape in my novels, and that the triumph of love brings gladness and hope to your heart. You may write to me at P.O. Box 461212, Aurora, Colorado 80046. A self-addressed stamped envelope would be appreciated.

With warm regards,

Jessica Wulf

About the Author

Jessica Wulf is a native of North Dakota and has spent most of her life in Colorado, where she now lives with her husband and two dogs. She has a B.A. in history, as well as a passion and fascination for it, and often feels that she was born in the wrong century. *The Irish Rose* is her first novel.

IT'S NEVER TOO LATE
TO FALL IN LOVE!

MAYBE LATER, LOVE (3903, $4.50/$5.50)
by Claire Bocardo
Dorrie Greene was astonished! After thirty-five years of being "George Greene's lovely wife" she was now a whole new person. She could take things at her own pace, and she could choose the man she wanted. Life and love were better than ever!

MRS. PERFECT (3789, $4.50/$5.50)
by Peggy Roberts
Devastated by the loss of her husband and son, Ginny Logan worked longer and longer hours at her job in an ad agency. Just when she had decided she could live without love, a warm, wonderful man noticed her and brought love back into her life.

OUT OF THE BLUE (3798, $4.50/$5.50)
by Garda Parker
Recently widowed, besieged by debt, and stuck in a dead-end job, Majesty Wilde was taking life one day at a time. Then fate stepped in, and the opportunity to restore a small hotel seemed like a dream come true . . . especially when a rugged pilot offered to help!

THE TIME OF HER LIFE (3739, $4.50/$5.50)
by Marjorie Eatock
Evelyn Cass's old friends whispered about her behind her back. They felt sorry for poor Evelyn—alone at fifty-five, having to sell her house, and go to work! Funny how she was looking ten years younger and for the first time in years, Evelyn was having the time of her life!

TOMORROW'S PROMISE (3894, $4.50/$5.50)
by Clara Wimberly
It takes a lot of courage for a woman to leave a thirty-three year marriage. But when Margaret Avery's aged father died and left her a small house in Florida, she knew that the moment had come. The change was far more difficult than she had anticipated. Then things started looking up. Happiness had been there all the time, just waiting for her.

Available wherever paperbacks are sold, or order direct from the Publisher. Send cover price plus 50¢ per copy for mailing and handling to Zebra Books, Dept. 4445, 475 Park Avenue South, New York, N.Y. 10016. Residents of New York and Tennessee must include sales tax. DO NOT SEND CASH. For a free Zebra/Pinnacle catalog please write to the above address.